MARK LAWSON

THE DEATHS

D0754961

PICADOR

First published 2013 by Picador
an imprint of Pan Macmillan, a division of Macmillan Publishers Limited
Pan Macmillan, 20 New Wharf Road, London N1 9RR
Basingstoke and Oxford
Associated companies throughout the world
www.panmacmillan.com

ISBN 978-1-4472-3568-2 HB
ISBN 978-1-4472-4529-2 TPB

1 3 5 7 9 8 6 4 2

A CIP catalogue record for this book is available from the British Library.

Printed and bound by CPI Group (UK) Ltd, Croydon, CR0 4YY

Visit **www.picador.com** to read more about all our books
and to buy them. You will also find features, author interviews and
news of any author events, and you can sign up for e-newsletters
so that you're always first to hear about our new releases.

In memory of

FRANCIS LAWSON
(1930–2010)

and

SAM GRIFFITHS
(1992–2009)

When that hour comes — when they realize they can't do without me any longer — when they come upstairs to me in this room and go down on their knees and beg me to take up the reins at the bank again — the new bank — which they founded and can't manage — here I will stand and receive them.

Henrik Ibsen, *John Gabriel Borkman*
(version by David Eldridge)

> In my last will I have not much to give;
> A many hungry guests have fed upon me;
> . . .
> I pray thee look thou giv'st my little boy
> Some syrup for his cold, and let the girl
> Say her prayers, ere she sleep.
>
> John Webster, *The Duchess of Malfi*

I wonder if that's why we sleep at night, because the darkness still . . . frightens us? They say we sleep to let the demons out — to let the mind go raving mad, our dreams and nightmares all our logic gone awry, the dark side of our reason. And when the daylight comes again . . . comes order with it.

Edward Albee, *A Delicate Balance*

> Tell me again
> When the victims are singing
> And Laws of Remorse are restored . . .
>
> Leonard Cohen, 'Amen'

ONE

THE COFFEE GUY

The deaths are discovered because of the country's sudden obsession with perfect coffee.

After three years of studying History and Politics, Jason hadn't expected to be driving a van, but it was one of only two interviews he got (the other fast food) from 200 applications. And it can be argued that delivering expensive caffeinated drinks is vaguely relevant to his studies: at what point, in its politics and history, did England become Italy and why wasn't he told?

Because he's young-looking, customers often assume he's on a gap year and he doesn't correct them. The company, run from a trading estate off a junction low on the M40, is called CappuccinGo. The fun of the pun, Jason worries, results in missed web sales from customers uncertain of the spelling. He delivers capsules, advertised as compressing the essence of the finest Italian and Brazilian beans, to members of Club CappuccinGo, who possess a black-and-chrome machine that crushes the colour-coded bullets with water, convincing the drinkers that their English homes are actually Florentine restaurants.

When the government declared Britain bankrupt, Jason feared for his job; in a recession, posh hot drinks seemed an obvious candidate to be judged a luxury. But his clientele stubbornly refuse to condemn their taste-buds to the jar or even – Jason can remember his parents' excitement about these – that previous post-dinner status symbol, the cafetière.

He relishes the empty motorways this morning, an advantage of working Saturdays, if you get ahead of the football traffic (although most matches at the moment are frozen off), and as long as it isn't half term, which seems almost a religious holiday now, at least among people like this.

Jason checks on the dashboard clock that he's ahead of target time. It is part of the firm's smart marketing to inject a sense of emergency into every purchase. Calls to the Hotcoffee-line promise delivery within twenty-four hours, with Christmas Day the only date on which club members are left thirsty or to slum it. The consignments are rushed around the country in zipped bags, as if they are drugs or transplant organs. At some drops, he will be handed a pouch of spent pellets for recycling; a service the business offers to convince club members that their pretension is ecologically sound.

The lapel badge and his contract identify him as a 'coffee courier'. He is just happy that the title is not cutely Italianized – *couria* – with its dreadful echo for his employment generation of *barista*, another manifestation of the nation's late-found coffee mania.

Numerous drivers are off – this new 'killer bug', in many cases, is the rumour at the depot – and Jason has worked eight days on the spin, but is happy to take this weekend early shift as well because, since Dad lost his job, his folks have talked about having to charge him rent.

Although his patch forms a wide loop round London, the areas and even the addresses are repetitive. In seven months, he has not yet made a delivery to a house that shares a wall with another. CappuccinGo's natural territory is the sweeping green stretches between London and Brum, where bankers, lawyers, surgeons and CEOs live in what used to be farmhouses, bakehouses, schoolhouses or post offices, from which they drive a dozen motorway junctions or ride a high-speed train for thirty minutes to the capital to work.

Middlebury, where houses seem to have a minimum of six bedrooms and at least two cars, is scattered among fields and hills that give the lie to the radio-phone-in moan that Britain is crowded. Every home is almost a village of its own.

He has four regular clients round here, but this morning it's only the one: a last-minute dinner-party panic, probably. These minted women all look pretty much the same to him, but he thinks this is the fit, flirty one, which would be sweet, although he doesn't really believe the banter in the drivers' room about the customers who don't just want their coffee hot and wet. There's a glammy nanny here as well, although Jason mainly seems to hit her mornings off. That sort of tail is untouchable for him, anyway.

Having almost skinned the side last time, he takes the turn through the lower gate carefully. Looking up the hill, he again thinks that he should have gone into crime rather than driving. His folks talk about him getting his own place one day – and mentioned helping with a deposit, at least when Dad was working – but the idea seems increasingly like fiction.

What did you have to do to get a house like this? A winding, white-gravel drive, screened on both sides by trees, leads to a honey-coloured stone house, two-storeyed and three-sectioned, with substantial wings flanking a central block. Some of the window spaces have been bricked up, a relic of the period in English history when access to daylight was taxed.

These guys have a cylindrical post-box, American-style, at the bottom of the long approach, but, because they are either caffeine addicts or crazy entertainers, their CappuccinGo boxes are always too big to fit. The section of his chit headed 'Delivery Instructions' tells him to take the package up to the house and, if Mrs Snooty-Booty is out, leave it inside the green-doored barn, first on the right in the courtyard. But they won't be out on a Saturday morning which, if his mum and dad are any guide, is when old people do sex.

Opposite the post-box at the entrance to the property is a shield-shaped sign speared into the ground, advertising the name and number of the company that runs the security systems: Rutherford Secure. Matchingly branded metal boxes flash from beneath the eaves of the main building. Robbers are obviously supposed to see the first logo and abandon the blag.

Glancing sideways, Jason checks that his lanyard is on the passenger seat. A few weeks previously, the company's couriers were given new, more impressive identity necklaces. Apparently, some of his colleagues had been turned away by club-members convinced they were a front for something else. With the have-nots increasing in number, the haves are panicking.

It is one of the dogs he sees first. Turning the final curve, the house now in full view to the left, he spots the woolly shape on the verge and suddenly, stupidly understands why this delivery feels different: there has been no little yapper screeching warnings from the house, enjoying his game of comically improbable guard dog. Normally, you can hear barking from the bottom of the hill.

In this job, road-kill becomes as familiar as traffic lights. He gets out of the van and approaches the shape, which looks like a rug left on the grass after an abandoned picnic. The dog's body has lain there long enough to be frosted. An ice-streaked tennis ball lies just beside it. Although British Summer Time begins next month, the mornings, after a stubbornly unfinishing winter, are still raw.

He gently lifts the head, but it falls back, the weight and torpor confirming his stomach-pinching suspicion. Unlike many of his mates, Jason is not obsessed with the forensic shows, watching them only when he is in and there is nothing else on, but he is enough of a sofa pathologist to identify a bullet wound to the head; a single hit, he guesses. The back of the skull. They have Labradors at home, but he is vague about dogs: a westie, is this?

The smack of sadness surprises him. He almost wants to stroke the coat, uselessly thick, white with interlocking whorls of black and ginger. He is imagining it being one of his mum and dad's dogs. That must be how grief works until you have losses of your own.

So he is slow to see the implications of the killed animal.

Catching up, confused, and frightened for himself, he looks towards the buildings for an explanation or reaction of some kind.

Apart from the nearby neighing – no, almost roaring – of a horse, everything is silent, not only here but across the whitened fields and hills around. From this house can be seen three others that are almost identical, presumably the result of a landowner or architect's pattern two centuries or so ago. They form a wide square, each positioned on a high rise, facing towards each other, like some massive amp system made of stone. The residents are all his clients now, which is no surprise because they seem to have the same kind of stuff. He hopes he never has to pick out the wives, cars, dogs or children in an . . . identity parade. The realization that he may be in a crime scene finally strikes.

He fingers the phone in his pocket, a surrogate gun. Then, out of instinct, or perhaps some buried memory of how a hero behaved in a thriller he watched, he locks the vehicle with a squeeze of the key ring and walks the last part of the drive. In a garden at the side of the house, a rugby ball, a goal-keeper's glove and a basketball are frozen in the grass, like an advert for a Nordic sports channel.

As he walks closer, there's a dark mound beside a flower-bed. He's trying to work out which piece of sports equipment this might be, when he sees that it's the family's other dog, a Labrador, flat and still against the strip-mown lawn, the morning sun catching its black pelt and, like a torch, picking out the ragged red circumference of the bullet hole in the back of the scalp.

All his previous deliveries here have been weekdays, timed for 9.30 a.m., when, the delivery notes told him, the school run was finished and there would always be someone in. He has never seen the husband: probably killing himself to pay for all of this. So he has no idea how the house should be on Saturday morning. He wants to believe that they are sleeping in after a late night with lots of his coffee, and will wake up to discover

5

that burglars have shot their dogs. But don't you have dogs to stop that happening?

Television has made everyone a semi-detective and he notices that there are three cars – a 4x4, a saloon and a soft-top – on the expanse of gravel beyond the courtyard. Surely even people as fuck-off rich as this wouldn't have four cars, would they? Stepping closer, CSI Jason observes that the windscreens all have the sugar-scattered cake-top look of overnight chill. They have not been driven this morning.

He thinks of banging on the door, but he is an under-employed graduate, a coffee guy, not a cop. Changing his phone contract a month ago, he vaguely read that 999 calls were free. But, until now, this inducement has been irrelevant to him as a consumer.

TWO

MEMBERSHIP QUESTIONS

The coffee they serve is horrible – over-stewed and with a strange whiff of piss off it – but Simon drinks it because, on such a short journey, it is the only real perk of First Class. Without his 'complimentary refreshment' – even on these super-fast new trains, the language is redolent of the Orient Express – the cost of the tickets on his Visa statements each month would feel even more like theft.

Simon is happy to travel scum class when he's on his own and even sometimes deliberately aims for the 6.25, knowing the others favour the .38. But today the .25 is delayed to 6.44 by signalling problems at Crewe and so Jonny Crossan finds him on the platform.

'Good man, yourself.'

Jonny's standard greeting at the moment involves, for some reason, a hideous attempt at an Irish accent, although Simon is from Northern England, which led his friend for many years to hail him with 'Ow do?'

'Jonny,' he replies.

This is the almost daily station-ritual between them, accompanied by a mutual head-jab.

'So, what's this, Lonsdale? Have they Daleked that it's in reverse formation this morning?'

Simon knows exactly what Jonny is getting at but says: 'What?'

'You're standing down the pleb end, chummy.'

'What? Oh, yeah. Bit of a fight with the alarm clock this morning: not quite in gear.'

'The prosecution accepts this submission. If one had spent the night in bed with Mrs Lonsdale, one would not have slept much either.'

Jonny's coveting of his friends' wives is such a part of his repertoire that Simon merely rolls his eyes and follows him to the Gold Zone, where they are surprised to find Max Dunster. Max doesn't often travel with them because his factory is a ten-minute drive – five at the speeds he likes to go – from Middlebury.

'Your Highness!' Jonny Crossan booms up at Max. 'What matters in the capital?'

Max is standing with his mock-military stiffness at the place on the platform where the First Class carriage closest to the buffet car is most likely to open its doors. It is the mark of alpha commuters to know the stopping spots, although there are mornings when they have to keep their nerve when a sizeable queue forms beside an unexpected section of the yellow safety line and the fear sets in that they have missed an announcement that others heard. But, generally, barring a late switch of train-stock, their positions will be vindicated.

'I've a meeting at the bank,' Max tells Jonny, who asks: 'Oh, dear. Smacked-botty time?'

'On the contrary. I wouldn't be surprised if the buggers want to borrow money from *me*.'

Jonny looks around the platform, his head swivelling as ostentatiously as a presidential bodyguard, then declares: 'Missing member of the Monday Club alert! Where's Tom Rutherford? Has he texted excuses to anyone? Certainly not to me.'

Simon and Max shake their heads. Max's careful anticipation of the length and formation of a Virgin Pendolino pulling in at platform 4 puts them on the train first and, though the red-eye from Manchester can be crowded, they nab an empty four with a table. Simon, who is prone to claustrophobia in trains, planes and theatres, stands back to let Jonny take the window.

Max, because of his height, also likes an aisle and so they leave the other window seat empty.

'Room for a small one?' asks a voice from beside and above.

'Speak for yourself, cock,' says Jonny. They all look up to see a squat, stocky guy who is not a regular member of the travelling squad, but an occasional sit-in if the seats fall that way. Simon can never remember his name: Nicky something? Max stands, as usual cracking his head on the luggage rack, to let past the mystery voyager, whose shape gives him no plausible claim to leg-room.

'Shouldn't you lot be travelling in the chav carriages to show us all you're sorry?' Jonny teases the new arrival, who good-naturedly parries: 'Yeah, yeah. Could we have a Be Nice To Bankers Day? I'd be surprised if any of you lot are going to be *Guardian* Person of the Year.' Sardonic vibrato on both *Guardian* and *Person*. Then, holding out a hand to Max: 'Nicky Mortimer. I think we've occasionally met here on the dawn treader.'

'Max Dunster,' comes the confirmation. *Nicky Mortimer,* Simon thinks. Copy that for future reference. Silent, he imagines himself as a camera, cutting between the speakers.

Jonny: 'Max is going for a spank from the bank. Don't know if it's yours?'

Nicky: 'Oh. Who are you with?'

Max: 'Well, in this instance, Cooper Macauley.'

Nicky: 'Classy. Want to split a taxi to Belgravia?'

Max: 'Oh, er, yeah, sure. You're in Belgravia as well?'

Nicky: 'HQ is.'

Max: 'Who are you? As a bank I mean?'

Nicky: 'Well, more corporate finance, really. Robbins Schuster Geneva.'

Max: 'Right. Nice.'

Jonny: 'Is it just me or has this train *stopped*?'

Like lab rats, the commuters have learned to distinguish the meanings of different sensations. A repeating screech is the result of someone pressing the disabled help button in the loo, usually an able-bodied person trying to flush the bog or dry their hands; a single ping followed by static indicates an announcement from the artist formerly known as the guard, now the train manager.

Who says: 'As you've probably noticed, ladies and gentlemen, we're currently held by a red signal. And I regret to say that we could be here for quite some time.' From along the carriage, the sigh of meetings, deals and earnings stalled. 'The reason, I'm afraid, is a person under a train at Watford Junction.' Another low moan of disapproval at the thoughtlessness of the corpse. 'I'll keep you updated when I have any further information. In the meantime, thank you for your patience and cooperation. The buffet is open in carriage G and a complimentary beverage and hot-and-cold-breakfast sandwich service will be coming through First Class.'

'I've got a case conference at eight,' complains Jonny.

'I am right, aren't I,' Simon asks, 'that they used to say "an incident" or a "fatal incident"? I think "person under a train" is quite recent, isn't it?'

'Very much so,' Max agrees, only half-lowering his *Financial Times*. 'I assume it's to stop people abusing train staff in the way that those posters at stations ask us not to.'

'I'll tell you why it is,' Jonny joins in. 'One is supposed to feel sympathy for the fucker who jumped under the train. Which, as you can probably guess, one doesn't. It's absolutely their *yuman right*" – the words satirically inflected – 'to do themselves in, but I propose this: they stick to pills and whisky, we get to London in the advertised thirty minutes.'

'Am I right in thinking you're a barrister by trade?' asks honorary club-member Nicky . . . (shit, he's forgotten his surname again – early mornng or something worse?), in the tone of probing an improbability.

'He is,' Simon smilingly confirms. 'I always say, if I ever kill anyone, I wouldn't ask Jonny to defend me and pray he wouldn't be prosecuting. Actually, I met a British Transport Policeman at a dinner party . . .'

'Exciting social life you have, Si.' Max from behind the paper. 'Thank the Crucified Christ you didn't ask us to that one.'

'No, seriously . . .' Simon blames *Top Gear* for the fact that so many British men now regard conversation as violently belittling banter. 'What he said was really interesting . . .'

Max makes snoring noises from behind his pale-pink barrier. Jonny says: 'I'll be the judge of that, Lonsdale.'

Simon continues: 'According to him, Monday morning and Friday evening are the hot-spots for railway suicides. They're the rush hours that cause maximum disruption. I suppose because people have more to get in for or more to get home for. So it's a sort of last swipe at the world you hate.'

Nicky Who, a far better audience for Simon's story than his usual co-commuters, nods: 'So you can bugger up thousands of people for a couple of hours. I wonder if that's true across the world or if it's a British thing.'

'I'm only interested in the ones on this line,' Jonny says, with that little flicker of camp he has when rattled.

'The Virgin suicides!' declares Max.

Simon is surprised and impressed by the reference: 'I didn't know you read books.'

'What's that?' Max lowers the paper. 'I didn't know it *was* a book.'

'I wonder, though. Do you think it *is* that?' this Nicky asks.

'Do we think what is what?' barks Jonny.

'That people jump under trains on Monday mornings and Friday nights to inconvenience other people? What if that's when someone feels most vulnerable? Another Monday morning without a job; another weekend to be spent alone . . .'

'Interesting,' says Simon, who thinks it is. But Jonny mocks: 'Thought you were a banker, not a social worker!'

The tannoy peal again, then the train manager crackling: 'Ladies and gentlemen, I've just been informed that we can expect a delay of at least another hour, while the body is removed from the track.'

'The body!' Max says. 'What is this? Snuff Rail?'

Mentally rewriting schedules, most passengers groan, then, as they alert their workplaces, the carriage fills with finger-tapping and ear-splitting voices, amplified by mobile over-projection and hands-free headsets.

Once more, the tocsin and the boxy sound: 'Ladies and gentlemen, train manager again.' The callers pause for more information to relay. 'Okay, we've had a message from Control. We're going to be pulled backwards to Leighton Buzzard and then come into London on the slow track. We'd hope to give you a revised arrival estimate in the station . . .'

His apologies for any inconvenience caused are drowned out by passengers bellowing revised arrangements into phones.

'They'll probably charge us extra for the backwards leg,' the guest member predicts.

It is at this point that Simon realizes he has a second-class ticket. Surely, though, there will be no inspections on a train that is travelling late and in the wrong direction.

Max has scrunched his newspaper under the seat and opened up his MacBook Pro on the table. The latest model, of course; he goes through laptops as others change socks. Its lightweight frame looks fragile under his huge hands. Jonny is pulling the ribbons off a legal brief, until Max says: 'Oh, Jonny. Message from the Management. A feasibility study has been done on Marrakesh.'

Spinning on the shiny table-top, the computer reveals a screen scattered with rectangular images of blue skies, pink sunsets and red-bricked palaces.

'Bit steam-age that, isn't it, Max?' Jonny teases. 'I expected you to have an iPad Retina wotsit.'

'Oh, I have. Shipped one in straight from the States. Just, boringly, the figures for today are on this and I haven't zapped them over. According to blogs, and people who've been, the smart move is to stay in what they call a *riad*.'

'That's exactly what *we* did,' says Nicky is-it-Morton? but is ignored as Max continues: 'What used to be top wallahs' villas turned into small private hotels. Pop out Friday lunchtime – three hours down the same time-zone, so no lag – stay in one of these and come back Sunday.'

Jonny nods vertically, chin up and down very straight, like a boxer being knocked about: 'Looks just the ticket for Libby. Shop until she drops in the souk and so on, while we chaps seek out the belly-dancers. Are there *lap*-belly-dancers, do you reckon? Libs has got a thing about bringing carpets back. I said we've already got them wall-to-wall, darling, and we've only got two feet each, but you know.'

Simon tries to look uninterested, skimming through his roll of newspapers, but that old word 'clubbable' was made for Max: 'Hey, Simon, why don't you and Tasha come along? The Rutherfords are already signed up. It's the last but one weekend before Christmas.'

'For some reason, those dates ring a bell,' says Simon, although they don't, adding, 'I'll talk to Tash tonight,' although he won't.

'Come on, Simon,' Jonny yells at him. 'You – and especially Mrs Lonsdale – must be there. It's a state visit of The Eight.'

The sensation of being pulled backwards, even slowly, is disconcerting, like the reverse leg on a theme-park dipper that sets you up for the dizzying drop.

'Tickets and passes from Milton Keynes, please,' comes the voice from behind them. Like all those who speak for a living, the train manager has a variety of tones: clear but contrite for the delay announcements, courteous but firm for what is now called 'revenue protection', previously the inspection of tickets.

Jonny and Nicky flash their First Class season tickets quickly and coolly from their wallets, as if they are police IDs. These are received with gentle gratitude, as is Max's machine ticket, although it is scribbled on to prevent him re-using it fraudulently. Simon is already muttering 'I, er, need to . . .', hoping for deafness or discretion from his friends, when the ticket guy says: 'You'll need to upgrade this, sir?'

'Er, yes. I realize. How much is it?'

Jonny and Max stare with icy surprise at the imposter. Simon has a sense of how South Africa and Berlin must have been in their decades of division.

'The difference is sixteen pounds, sir. How will you be paying?'

He reaches for the credit card first but it has been used already once at the ticket machines that morning, and payment for a second journey so quickly is the sort of 'irregular spending pattern' that might trigger a stop on payments. If his card is rejected in front of Max and Jonny, and even the relatively disinterested Nicky Mortimer, Simon will need to become the line's second suicide before breakfast. He is not, though, completely sure how solvent the debit account is.

He risks it. The gap as it bleeps through the reader feels like waiting for the opening of the result envelope on a TV talent show.

'That's fine, sir. Here's your new ticket and receipt.'

With the revenue-protection officer gone, the pack-leaders yap at him.

'A steerage stowaway!' hoots Jonny. 'Explain yourself, Lonsdale!'

'I'm not angry, Si, just disappointed,' adds Max, mock-headmasterly.

'I was getting the earlier one, but it was delayed. I knew you guys wouldn't be around, so what was the point of being here? To be honest, I only travel First for the company, not the coffee.'

'I'll grant you it's not Club CappuccinGo,' says Jonny. *Please*, Simon prays silently, *don't start up about the fucking Rajasthani macchiato you've got on trial.*

'Work hard, play hard, travel fast but soft,' says Max. He has a way of speaking like a sports coach or motivational guru.

'I do keep thinking it's a ludicrous expense,' says, yes, got it again, Nicky *Mortimer*. 'On a run as short as this, what are you really getting for your buck?'

The others look at him as if he is a foreigner who doesn't speak the language.

'Bugger this for *un jeu de soldats*,' announces Jonny. 'I'm going for a Smedgewick, if I can work the damn doors.'

Simon stands to let him clamber out.

'What's a Smedgewick?' asks Mortimer. 'Some sort of sandwich?'

'Good Lord, I hope not!' guffaws Max. 'It's what Crossan calls a number two. He's one of those chaps that has his own words for things. A tip from me: if you happen to know someone called Dobson, don't ever tell Jonny you've shaken his hand.'

After travelling several miles backwards, they are shunted, spilling the disgusting free drinks across the table, across to the slow track for another assault on London. If the person under the earlier train chose their time of death in order to bugger up the lives of those who survived, the strategy has been impressively effective. Simon texts the office that he will definitely miss his nine and will let them know about the ten.

*

There was an article in the *Telegraph* about one of the smarter supermarket branches somewhere banning shoppers from entering the store in their pyjamas. Apparently some people – from an estate, you'd guess – were coming to the shop direct from bed or, more likely, staying in their sleepwear all day, trackies and hoodies a 24-hour outfit now. Even the nuns at school were rumoured to change into a different shapeless garment at night.

So Tasha's just a little worried about going into her shop in her gym stuff. Even though she's wearing a smock dress and cardigan over her shorts and t-shirt, she has got her trainers on (too much hassle to be changing in and out of heels at the club, although some of the other girls do) and, while they're clean and white and Nike, they are still just, as they used to say at school, pumps.

Actually, the more she thinks about it, how are estate trolls who spend all day in their pjs able to afford to go to a shop with a dress code, anyway? Benefits, it will be. Shocking when you think that even she, when Simon has been giving her an especially hard time about the finances, sometimes has to do the weekly shop in Tesco for a while instead, which just isn't the same, although, oddly enough, it's the only one of the super-markets to have baguette-holders on the trolleys as standard.

From the long shining line under the porch beside the cash-points, she takes a trolley. Unlike the other food shops, hers doesn't chain them together or require a pound coin as deposit. It's a sign that the shop trusts its patrons and the community, although you do sometimes see one abandoned on the grass beside the bypass, ridden as a pikey-bike through the night.

The guilt tin at the door today is holidays for disabled children. Officially, Tasha's deal with God is that she donates for diseases she might otherwise get and becoming a disabled child is one of the few medical plotlines definitely closed off to her. *You could still end up with a paraplegic kid, though, with Josh and Henry playing rugby, and Polly driving now.* She drops in a pound coin, and then a second because one of the alternative lives she has been most grateful to avoid is as the mother of a son or daughter with something wrong. God forgive her, but she flinches when she sees some mum wheeling along a great lolling teenage lump. How do they keep up those brave smiles?

'Bless you,' says the collector. Tasha wonders if she has a crippled child herself.

The double entry doors slide apart. Tasha stops at the Shop-and-Scan stand and swipes the joint-account debit card smoothly down the black plastic slot on the right. After a few times now, she's got the angle of entry and the speed just right – the newbies stand there frustratedly putting the card back in again and again, like those elderly American tourists you see looking baffled outside hotel rooms with plastic keys – and, at the first time of asking, the screen in the middle scrolls out the greeting GOOD MORNING, MRS NATASHA LONSDALE and one of the hand-sets at the bottom of the rack starts to flash and vibrate. It always reminds her of the moment in a sci-fi film when the astronauts board the spaceship.

She frees the price-reader and pushes it into the custom-made soft grey plastic slot they've just added to the front of the trolleys, then places in its base the three green branded canvas bags given to her when she subscribed, patting them open ready to receive the goods. Standing in his gleamingly clean apron in company colours, in the middle of his island empire to the right of the newspaper rack, the meeter-and-greeter beamingly lives up to his job description or, anyway, the one she has given him.

'Good morning. Mrs Lonsdale, is it?'

The shopper as celebrity. 'Er, yes.'

'You've used Shop-and-Scan before?'

Though he will know this from the bespoke bags in her trolley.

'Absolutely.'

'Excellent. Any problems, though, don't hesitate to ask me. Enjoy your shopping.'

What genius this is to make a mum on a food run feel like the Duchess of Whatever in Fortnum's in the forties. The floor-walker is the elder brother of a boy in Josh's Sunday-morning rugby team. Tasha knows the family slightly from fund-raising race nights and barbecues. The name badge pinned to his apron says Andrew, although he's always Andy at the rugby club: such touches make the shop feel like the BBC of food retailers.

With Shop-and-Scan, the awful chore of the big weekly grub run is suddenly exciting. Feeling like her boys with those endless PlayStation games, she zaps each bottle or packet (or the printed label at the self-weigh fruit-and-vegetable section), expertly placing the green laser line in the dead centre of the bar-code and then clicking ADD. Sometimes an item – this morning, the Colgate Total Toothpaste and the couscous – surprises you and the hand-set plays a little tune, like the right-answer jingle in a TV quiz show. 3-FOR-2 OFFER, reads a box that appears on the scanner's screen, blocking out the rolling summary of her purchases.

She always feels slightly mugged by this – knowing that it's no more than a posh version of the spivs on Oxford Street with one eye on the cops – but Tash submits to the machine's greediness because, in a recession, it's seems wrong to miss a bargain, although she can hear Simon's voice saying: 'But they made you spend more than you meant to, which must be a pretty eccentric way of saving money.'

In the Health-and-Wellbeing aisle, Tasha takes a packet of Super-Plus (her periods, though less regular, are getting heavier, a warning of the menopause, she supposes) and a box of Regular for Polly. Then she adds a pack of Durex Pleasure Me. Ridiculously, she still has to resist the urge to look guiltily round, a throwback to when she first bought contraceptives as a teenager in her home town, terrified that the priest or teachers or a family friend would see her.

Tampons and condoms: an example of contradictory shopping, like food and loo roll. No, actually, those are complimentary. Even so, she always tends to stand the toilet tissue – two sixteen-roll packs, how full of the stuff a big family is – separately in the trolley outside the bags, disliking the reminder of how all this meat, fruit, bread and vegetables will end. The sanitary products click on to the list under their brand names, but the contraceptives are recorded as Chemist Goods, a residue presumably of the religious opposition to selling them, although more likely, now, intended to allow teenagers (or adulterers?) to buy them without the evidence showing on a crumpled receipt.

She used to rely on Simon to get them, until, a couple of years ago, he started to use not having any in the bedside drawer as an excuse for not doing it. Not that providing her own supply guarantees a shagging these days.

There's a South African Chenin Blanc at half price, so she takes six bottles. Flinching slightly at the final total, Tasha wheels her trolley to Andrew's private Shop-and-Scan island, enjoying the superiority over the lines of shoppers waiting to have their items scanned in the old way, and then laboriously pack them. She relishes the sense of being trusted to tot up her own bill, like honesty bars in smart hotels.

Although you couldn't call it a queue, it's mildly annoying that, just as Tasha's eyes meet Andrew's welcoming smile (he's working here on a gap year, she thinks, but it wouldn't be very surprising, as he was Head Boy at Eastbury Manor, if they put him on the management fast-track), another self-billing customer emerges from the bottom of the Refrigerated-Items aisle and cuts in front of her towards the desk.

'Find everything you were looking for today?' Andrew asks the pushy woman. 'And everything scanned okay?'

'I think so. It's really convenient.'

But suddenly there's a sound Tasha hasn't heard before in the shop: a jumble of rough percussion, not unlike the alarm call on her BlackBerry, and indeed a couple of people nearby scramble for their phones. The noise is coming, though, from the woman in front's scanner, which is also flashing red, rather than the cool green of the bargain alert.

'Oh my God!' she gasps. 'What's it doing?'

'Nothing to worry about, madam,' soothes Andrew. 'You've been randomly selected for a verification scan by hand. We're looking out for teething troubles during the trial period.'

The cutter-in blushes like she's been caught with a trolley full of vibrators and Vaseline. 'Really? But why me?'

The voice of someone experienced in answering back to officialdom: middle-class, definitely.

'As I say, madam, it's purely random.'

He brandishes his own scanner in the sensitively competent manner of a radiographer. 'If I could just start unpacking your bags, madam.'

This early in his retail career, there's already a hint of 'modom', like Captain Peacock in *Are You Being Served?*

The blushing queue-jumper turns her trolley towards the fresh-produce section.

'Look, do you know what?' she tells Andrew. 'I think I've just forgotten some stuff.'

19

Blimey O'Reilly, a shoplifter! A high-tech, keeping-quiet-about-one-of-the-bottles-from-the-honesty-bar type shoplifter, but a thief nonetheless. It would be so easy: just 'forget' to scan a few items, either not realizing that a checking system exists or gambling that it won't be you.

Tasha raises an eyebrow but Andrew is too corporately responsible to reciprocate, busying himself with tapping on a keypad. Is he summoning a store detective to apprehend the blushing culprit as she hastily scans the stolen food and drink? Or will the woman simply be barred from self-pricing ever again?

Tasha centres her green line on the barcode at the exit station that declares her shopping finished. The total (she calculates how long until Simon's payday) ghosts up on the screen and she swipes her card to settle the bill.

GOODBYE, MRS NATASHA LONSDALE. WE HOPE TO SEE YOU AGAIN SOON.

She likes the fact that the screen greeting even includes the vocative comma, just as the quick-service tills here are marked FIVE ITEMS OR FEWER, rather than LESS, as some of the less-classy supermarkets have.

Wheeling her trolley towards the car, she feels honoured and privileged to have the trust of the shop. But Tasha just hopes, startled by the echo of teachers' words from long ago, that one wrong-doer doesn't spoil the system for everyone.

*

Marry a chef and you get the scoop on new recipes. And, if your spouse is a concert promoter, there is surely a supply of complimentary tickets. But living with a doctor is what it must be like if your partner's a prozzie: they came in from work determined not to do more of it at home.

If Tom had turned up at the surgery of Dr Emily Rutherford as a slightly overweight, asthmatic man of fifty-one complaining of a wheeze in his breathing and aching in his arms and legs, there would be tests and ECGs and, which is really the point, a flu jab as a precaution.

But turn to the very same Dr Rutherford at 6.45 a.m., with the alarm squealing like the life-support machine of a flat-lining patient, and report the identical symptoms and you get this brisk examination: 'Any central chest pain or discomfort?'

'Er, no. But I don't think I'm having a heart attack. I think I'm going down with this new flu.'

'If you had flu, you wouldn't be able to get out of bed.'

'Well, I don't know if you've noticed, but I haven't.'

'Rubbish. You went for a wee twenty minutes ago. And don't start up about your prostate. Once in the night is fine at your age. Look, if there were a fifty-pound note on the lawn outside, would you be able to go and get it?'

They have been married so long that he remembers when Emily's test involved a five-pound note.

'With the amount they pay GPs now, I wouldn't have to.'

She elbows him in the ribs with affectionate violence.

'I do have a very slight, burning isn't quite the word, sensation, here, in the, is this the gullet?' he persists.

'How much did you drink last night?'

'Two medium-sized glasses of red.'

'Tom, there's no point lying to the doctor about how much you drank when you were drinking it with the doctor. You had two-thirds of the bottle at least. I saw you tip half of my glass into yours when I was at the Aga. And, when I was taking the dogs out, you took another sneaky splash into your study.'

'When I woke up in the night I was wheezing.'

'Let me listen.'

She leans across him in the dark. Both of them are holding their breath from sensitivity to morning halitosis.

'Give me your hand,' she says.

'Em, I'm not well enough to do anything like *that*.'

'Ha ha. Remind me not to break a rib laughing.'

Her fingers brushing the tips of his in turn, her ear against

his chest; a parody of romantic intimacy. One reason, presumably, that doctors are not supposed to treat their own families.

'The finger thing's to check my circulation?'

'Do I tell you how to be a security consultant?'

He anticipates the diagnosis because he has heard it so often before: 'You'll live.'

'You always do that. When did I ever suggest I was dying? I'm worried I'm going down with something.'

'It's probably acid reflux. Make an appointment with Surinder.'

'Em, if you just gave me a flu jab, I'd stop worrying about it.'

'I've told you I can't.'

'Why?'

'Because you're not in an at-risk group.'

'Nor were some of the people who've died in this epidemic.'

'It's not an epidemic and there are always anomalies.'

'The relatives accept that, do they? I'm so sorry, Mrs Widow, I'm afraid they were an anomaly. How do I know I won't be one?'

'It's statistically very unlikely. You're more at risk going to London this morning.'

'I'm not going. I'll work from home.'

'Up to you. But I wouldn't sign you off.'

'Em, isn't there something you can give me?'

'Oh, alright, yes, I suppose there is.'

Her rapid back-down surprises him. 'Seriously?'

'Yes. An Oscar. For this extraordinary portrayal of someone who's got something wrong with them.'

The alarm trills its five-minute reminder. Tom lies and imagines the day ahead. He can deal with the intruder reviews for the department store and the art gallery on his laptop and prepare for the presentation to the university just as well at home as in the office.

Without the irritations of colleagues, he can have those done by noon and, after lunch (sushi from Waitrose?), while watching the week before last's *Mad Men* on Sky+, he could crack on with his history of the village. With all the weekend chauffeuring (Felix's volunteering at the hospice, Phoebe's cross-country, Henry's U-14 county running and rugby), it has been three weeks since he wrote a word.

He left off in the middle of the section about the Middlebury church and graveyard. Even thinking the word, he shivers involuntarily. He has reached an age when, driving past a cemetery, it is impossible not to imagine the procession you will one day lead.

Time. That is why he can't face London today. When you are young, old people warn you of the awful speed at which life passes, but you don't believe them until the day when you feel a desperate need to grab the hands of the clock and force them backwards, like Richard Hannay at the end of *The Thirty-Nine Steps*.

His father, a civil servant, used to talk of a system by which, twice a year, an employee could ring up and say that they were not coming in. Although, realistically, the organization must have been vastly over-staffed to make this benefit work, these sudden leave days were presumably intended as a protection against exhaustion and depression. Human beings are not built for treadmills. Duvet days, people had started to call them, once the quick-make bed had come to busy Britain.

While Emily showers, he listens to the news in the dark. The number of New Variant SARS cases has risen again; an MP is calling for a mass-vaccination programme. When the water stops running in the bathroom, he starts to cough loudly.

*

Their Monday-morning Pilates, Libby often tells the others, makes no sense. They exercise for an hour and then eat pastries: a perfectly self-cancelling arrangement, like an umbrella with a hole in it. Jenno Dunster, a yo-yo dieter who never quite shifted the baby fat the last time and so maybe they need to be careful with the weight references, always reddens and says that she hardly ever eats afterwards, anyway. 'I never really feel hungry after Pilates,' is her line, although she always seems to have room for a forkful of what other people order.

But, while Libby won't be complaining if she loses a few pounds before Marrakesh, her trips to Middlebury Spa are more about friendship than fitness. She would never want to be busy like the blokes are – never seeing their homes in daylight or their children in any light for much of the year – but she likes the idea of a full though varied diary: that she and the other three are fitting in the gym between work (Emily, Tasha), shuttling kids around the county (*toutes les femmes*) and presiding as a justice of the peace (herself) or volunteering at the CAB: Jenno.

Libby tries, across the week, to get a balance between things she ought to do – presiding on the bench, fetching Deirdre Leeson's shopping, chairing the Parish Council – and the stuff she likes to do: shopping, walking the dogs, tennis, getting The Eight together for a meal on a Friday or Saturday, or sometimes one night at someone's and the other at someone else's. Pilates – like the school-run and sex with Jonny (joking, joking) – occupies a middle-ground, containing stuff that is obligatory but can also be enjoyable, especially if you include the gabbing together after the exercise. The Pilates she is talking about, not the sex!

Of course, when you look at it coldly, what we call love and friendship is just a matter of who you happen to meet. She and Jonny were quite a chance couple – when you think of all that had followed from meeting in that bar in Hong Kong – but most of the people she knows had hooked up through college (Tom and Emily) or work: Max and Jenno. She isn't sure about Simon and Tasha. Even so, there is a difference between the friends you make at school – where it tends to be types and shared interests – and the ones you add later, which is just geography. If they lived in another village – if they hadn't bought the house in Middlebury from Jonny's dad – she wouldn't know any of these people.

She goes and squeezes a ball between her thighs with these three ladies every week because they live in the four big houses on the hills and all have kids at Westbury Park. A friendship of convenience, you could probably say, and it is Pippa and Pongo from Tudor Hall she'd want to speak at her memorial service, but she is really quite fond of this lot, particularly Emily and Jenno. Tasha can be tricky because the Lonsdales are a little, how shall she put it?, lighter in the pocket than the others. Tasha always says they couldn't have afforded a private prepper, which is why her three went to the church school in the village until eleven, which, frankly, must have put them at a disadvantage, but it is all a question of priorities.

Tasha is also given to moaning that they do the same thing every Monday and should try to be a bit more spontaneous one week but, in Libby's opinion, one of the best things about Middlebury Spa is that you know exactly where you are. In her view, change is generally a mistake, although, when she mentioned that at one of the dinner parties, Simon Lonsdale went all *J'accuse* on her and said, in that way he sometimes has, as if he is being really reasonable when actually he is being mean: 'Nothing should have changed? Child chimneysweeps? Slavery? Women voting? Well, actually, in some cases, the latter . . .' Tasha and Emily had to tell him to stop being like that.

It's a funny thing about men and women, at least in their circles, and certainly among The Eight, that, if you showed most people photos, they'd say that the man was lucky to have landed the woman. Not the other way round. Jonny is handsome obviously and Max keeps himself trim, but the only way poor Simon Lonsdale would end up in an art gallery would be if Damien Hirst starts pickling human heads.

Her hubby's view is that the men look older because they are worn out paying for the women to look younger. The blokes accept the march of death, he says, while the women coat their hair in creosote, as he calls it. Emily, who has this whole glad-to-be-grey flapdoodle, says there are studies suggesting that hair dye might cause brain tumours, but Libby joked that she would rather die young and raven-locked and the other girls agreed with her.

She, Tasha, Jenno and Emily arrive pretty much together, as normal. They are able to get their cars next to each other, which isn't always possible because lazy parkers who bulge over into the next bay don't always leave enough space for a Disco. It's silly, but she likes it when they all park in a line. It's one of those little signs, like ambers or greens all the way on the school run, that everything is going to be okay, although she certainly won't be telling Tasha's Simon her traffic-light theory of life.

They show their Gold Member cards to the check-in Pole, as normal. Nobody is quite sure why the spa seems to recruit only from Krakow, but presumably one is let in and then fixes jobs for the others. Which sounds racist, but isn't, just an observation.

Agnes, if that is the one this one is, puts the plastic cards with those hideous against-the-wall Polaroids of them through the scanner (the girls still tease Libby for having her pass picture reshot) and hands them back, with the mechanical manners they have – 'Thank you, Mrs Crossan, Mrs Dunster, Dr Rutherford' – but then gives a little 'oh' sound, like secretaries do when the office groper gets them at the photocopier in old films, and sing-songs: 'Oh, Mrs Lonsdale, there seems to be a membership question.'

'Oh, really?'

Tasha is instantly teenage beetroot, which makes you feel sorry for her, even if it is completely impossible not to feel a little bit of relief mixed with glee at someone else being in trouble. *Schaden*-whattie. Jonny always says that it isn't surprising, given the history, that only the Krauts have a word for enjoying other people's suffering.

'Yes. I am not so very sure what the problem is, Mrs Lonsdale. I go ask manager.'

'It will be fine, Tasha. There was a problem with mine once,' Emily says, which almost certainly isn't true, but, if Em found herself sitting next to an amputee, she'd tuck a leg up underneath her bum in sympathy.

'I think the shiny bit sometimes gets worn off, from rubbing too much,' adds Jenno.

Libby can't resist the, as it were, opening: 'But enough about your private life, Jen!'

Which means that even Tasha is laughing when Miss Warsaw 1994 comes back and says: 'Yes, Mrs Lonsdale, what has happened is that the payment has not been processed for the latest membership.'

Ooh-er. Poor Tash. Rather lock yourself out of the house naked than that. This is a weird one; she must tell Jonny over dinner.

'This happens, variously, with the bank,' Agnes-is-it goes on. 'You have perhaps a new card. You call them, can you?'

'Now?' Tash looks at her watch to emphasize the inconvenience.

'Oh, no, not necessarily, Mrs Lonsdale.'

'Sure, I'll text my husband as soon as we're done here. So you can let me in today?'

'I'm sorry? Oh, no, today I charge you the session rate. But, I'm thinking, need only be off-peak rate as is not Gold Membership time.'

You can actually see Tash going twangy-buttocked when she hands over the card for the day pass. If that bounces, then, as Jonny says, it's Hello Harry Carey. But the machine purrs like a happy pussy (no pun intended), although the poor woman is already sweating up like she's done an hour on the mats.

'I'll kill that bloody husband of mine. He'll have forgotten to renew it, knowing him,' Tash moans, as they choose lockers – unlike the car park, they take four spaced well out, a girl wants some elbow room with a towel – and get into their gym-jams, although Tash, as usual, has her work-out kit on under her clothes. She is always saving time, although it is never entirely clear what she does with it.

'Is yours Joint Gold?' Jenno asks her.

'What? I think so. Simon does it all. Supposed to, anyway. He's the money man.'

Libby sees the opportunity to spill her top goss.

'Ladies, that reminds me,' she drops in. 'The Osbornes have invited J and I to lunch at Dorneywood.'

'Oh, I hate you!' blurts Jenno, pleasingly. But, wouldn't you just guess? Tasha pretends to misunderstand: 'What? Ozzy and Sharon? Wow?'

Tasha can be very Welsh sometimes.

'No, Natasha,' Libby rubs it in. 'George and Frances, at the Chancellor of the Exchequer's weekend residence.'

'Does Jonny know them?' You can always rely on Emily for a sensible question.

'Circles within circles. George just overlapped in the House with Jonny's Pa. He was his pee-pee-something, I think.'

Even though they are late because of the border arrest, Tasha insists, before they go into the exercise room, on texting her wretched husband, speaking out the message as she jab-types it, as if to underline his male-autism disorder: 'Have you done gym membership?'

'No x at the end, I take it?' Emily wonders. Tasha growls.

The pay girl seems to work herself harder than usual during the session: probably all that adrenaline of embarrassment or perhaps because she has stumped up extra for this one herself, the way that Jonny always says you can spot someone on a plane who can't really afford First Class because they grab every snack and glass of bubbly and are watching movies even after the landing announcement, trying to get the value from it.

Afterwards, when they are waiting for the cakes that Jenno Dunster claims she is too taut and endorphined to eat, Tasha Lonsdale suddenly says: 'Hey, I went to the supermarket before I came here . . .'

'The glamour of it!' Libby wryly replies to her.

'Behave!' says Tasha. 'What I was going to say is, have you tried Shop-and-Scan yet? It's fantastic . . .'

She listens mainly on mute while Mrs Lonsdale bangs on about some honesty system and how she caught some biddy in the act of shoplifting. But it doesn't mean much to Libby, who hasn't actually been inside a food shop for three years.

As soon as she can, she cuts in with: 'But it's still shopping, which you actually physically have to go and do. We swear by the Ocado vans . . .'

'So do we! I do the whole big weekly shop online now,' echoes Jenno, which takes some of the gloss off it, but you can still see Tasha realizing that being your own Check-out Betty isn't necessarily the social revolution she thinks it is.

'Oh, dear!' says Emily. 'I hope they're not trying to phase out the tills. A lot of the ladies on them are patients and the money they get makes such a difference.'

Which is Saint Em all over. Although now she suddenly says: 'Do you think Laura's a lesbian?'

'You mean Trainer Laura?' Libby checks. A nodded yes.

'Why? Have you caught her peering up your lycra?'

'She's certainly a Nazi,' Jenno complains, tenderly flexing her thigh.

'No. Just she doesn't seem to know much about middle-age marriage. Every week, during the Magic Circles, *literally* every week, she says 'your husbands will thank me for your pelvic floors, ladies.' I don't think Tom would notice if mine was gift-wrapped in a presentation box and handed to him.'

'Speak for yourself!' Libby tells her. 'Jonny's still like a teenage Etonian. I wake up both weekend mornings to find the old telescope prodding into my back. Sometimes weekdays as well, although he has to go so early, poor poppet.'

'Get her!' says Emily. Tasha and Jenno busy themselves with cake; the same slice because Jenno, as normal, hasn't ordered any. Libby wonders, trying not to feel smug, if things are entirely right between Emily and Tom in that department, but is distracted by the text alert on her iPhone:

Bloody Virgins. Just got to London. Jumper at Watford Junction. Luckily judge delayed start. jxx

'Poor love,' she tells the others. 'Somebody topped himself under Jonny's train. Threw the Old Bailey into total chaos.'

'Does he know it was a man?'

Sometimes Emily can go all *Newsnight* on you.

'What are you on about, Ems?'

'I was just interested. People often assume it's men but women kill themselves as well.'

Jenno frowns. 'Is that based on your patients?'

'Well, obviously. *Generally*, I mean. I'm not talking specifics.'

Emily is super squeaky about patient confidentiality, which drives Libby mad sometimes. It is such exquisite torture to have a friend who knows which of the husbands are on Viagra, and whose kid has absolutely the wrong blood-group to really be the dad's, and yet she never lets on. When the news was texted around about Bill Adamson's lymphoma coming back, and Libby brought it up after Pilates, Dr Em sat there completely shtum, which is like having Colin Firth to dinner (Oh my God! he might be at Dorneywood, it's unlikely to be just the four of them) and him pretending he doesn't know who Mr Darcy is. Emily is actually Tasha's own GP, which Libby couldn't cope with. She goes private in London for muff stuff and lumps, and Dr Rafi in Eastbury for sore throats and sick kids. How can you have a good gossip after Pilates with someone who knows you came in worried once that your hubby had given you the clap after a tribunal in Hong Kong? It turned out to be something called honeymoon cystitis, which apparently happens if you go at it like the clappers after a gap, but that isn't the point.

Jenno puts a pantomime worried face on: 'Max is up in town today. Wonder if he was on that train?'

'Simon went even earlier than normal,' Tasha says. 'So probably missed it.'

'I'm sure they'd have told you if there was a problem,' Libby tells them, basking in the glory of having a fully texting husband.

By ritual, after Pilates, they are in the Poolview lounge, standing out, in their civilian post-exercise clothes, from the fat trailer-trash ladies on their Pamper Days, which always sound to her as if they put you in nappies, although the costume you actually get is a white fluffy monogrammed towelling robe. Jonny, when they, as it were, come together, always calls them Essex Gangster Molls and claims actually to have recognized a couple of the women from the public gallery at tax-fraud trials.

Sipping with twisted lips, Emily complains: 'If this is skinny cappuccino, I'm Kylie Minogue.'

'I have raised it,' Libby tells her. 'The members' committee is aware. I'm trying to persuade them to link up with Club CappuccinGo, if they do franchises, or at least get one of the machines.'

'Oh, yes!' whoops Emily, in one of those moments when you see the little girl at Christmas someone used to be. 'I meant to tell you! Tom and I have finally signed up. We got the first consignment on Friday.'

'The Three-Continent Taster Starter Pack?'

'What? I think so.'

'Did the luscious Justin bring it?'

'Jen, he's called Jason.'

'Who cares what his name is?' Libby cuts in. 'He can lick my froth off anytime!'

'Urrgh!' groans Tasha. 'Mental-image delete!'

'Even with Jonny's telescope in your back every morning?' asks Emily.

'I think with Simon,' Tasha says. 'It's more like a key-ring.'

Tasha definitely has this bitter Welsh streak sometimes, which isn't just about money. To shift the mood, Libby joke-toasts Emily with her spa-logo cup, saying: 'Excellent, we're all members of the coffee club now.'

'I hope there's not an induction ritual,' Emily frets. 'Like at school.'

'Well, they do take off your arm and your leg,' Libby warns her. Pause for effect. 'Though only through Visa card.'

Everyone laughs.

'You know what, though?' Libby says. 'Jonny and I are already getting a bit bored with Club CappuccinGo. We're desperate to try that coffee that's shat out by those catlike things that are fed beans by Tibetan monks. Civets, is it? You can order it from Fortnum's, apparently.'

'Seriously?' queries Tasha. 'You're drinking dissolved animal droppings?'

'I think so. But don't pull that face. Caviar is fish menstruation.'

'Not exactly,' says sensible Emily.

They do the children for ten minutes.

'Did I tell you that Tilly has made County Under-17 at 100 and 200?' Libby asks. 'Although she still won't thank me for persuading her to drop the middle distances. I've always known she was a sprinter, just like I was. And Plum has got Under-15 trials next Tuesday. Oh, and Emily, did I tell you, we've fixed up to look round Valecroft next week?'

'Oh, really?' Jenno is the one she'd expected to pick up on that. 'Are you thinking of taking him away?'

'We've talked about it. Westbury Park has a lovely atmosphere but we're not sure they're pushing Lucas enough.'

'Oh. Well he is only eight, Libs,' Jenno comes back. 'Jamie was away with the fairies half the time when he was at the prepper, but since he got into the seniors they've bucked him up. Rosie's always been focused right through, but girls are so different. They do everything quicker.'

'Except coming!' jokes Libby. Tasha rolls her eyes and the other two don't seem to understand.

'I'm a great believer in horses for courses,' says Tasha. 'I think Polly would have knuckled down anywhere. But the discipline of WP has brought the best out of Josh and Henry . . .'

Everyone agrees that they are all lucky to have a mix of boys and girls. Those families where it is all one or the other must get a bit samey.

This is a ball Libby should run with: 'I pinch myself sometimes for having two of each. Jonny always says, if it had been four girls, we wouldn't have got in the bathroom for eighteen years. Four boys, and there's no one to look after you in old age. I know there are lots of theories about vinegar douches –

ew! – and so on, but this was just how they, as it were, came out. What I was saying about Lucas and WP is that he's a brilliant kid, in his way, but he's not another Hugo, certainly not in Maths. Hugo's got his Cambridge—'

But she never gets to do Hugo and uni because Tasha, wouldn't you know it?, cuts in and, after that, it's *lah lah lah* on everybody else's lot. Libby listens on skip, mainly. Tasha and Simon's Polly has decided on biochemistry and really liked Leeds when she looked round. Emily says it is top of her Felix's list for medicine as well, and they joke a bit about a possible romance. Tasha says she's worried that Josh is getting too close to this girl at school, Jessica, and is it time to say something? Emily says that they slipped a box of Durex into Phoebe's knicker drawer when she was fifteen or so and she'd stormed downstairs, in a right bate, saying they had filthy minds and were treating her like some crack whore from Northbury estate, so you couldn't win. They trade news of riding rosettes for Rosie, Tilly, Phoebe and Plum, although, as Libby points out, it seems pretty devalued these days. Pretty much everybody gets a ribbon as long as horse and rider come back with six legs between them.

'I'd better run,' says Jenno. 'It's a volunteer afternoon. And it's not going to be much fun with all the deaths.'

Oh my God, what have I missed? Had there been a massacre in Middlebury?

'The deaths?' she echoes.

'What? I . . . no, *debts*, I said.'

Tasha Lonsdale laughs and says something like 'clart-lugs' or some such regional vulgarity.

'It didn't sound like debts,' Libby objects, hitting the 't' and silent 'b' crisply. 'It's your slovenly pronunciation, Jenno. You've started talking this sort of mockney, darling.'

'No, I haven't. 'Aven't. I really don't know what you're on about sometimes, Libs.'

'Not so fast, Mrs Dunster,' Libby says in her Los Angeles cop voice. 'We haven't fixed anything for Friday or Saturday.'

On Friday, the Dunsters are seeing other (unspecified) friends in Chipping Norton, so they settle on Saturday for the next gathering of The Eight, Libby hostessing. Jenno leaves to work among the poor.

'Now, Tasha,' Libby changes the subject. 'I need to talk to you about an urgent charitable mission to help the economy of Africa . . .'

*

Most mornings, straight off the train, whether he's walking to the courts or the set, Jonny buys something at the fruit stall on the Euston Road. The first time he saw it, years before, he was puzzled by this confusion of country and town, the petrol fumes from the grid-locked road somehow diluted by the sweet bouquet of oranges (always the strongest tang), apples, plums and strawberries, set out like over-sized gems on trays lined with blue tissue paper. Under the grey winter sky and light, the harvest gleams like coloured light bulbs. Glossy clementines, with their leaves intact, look as bright as the traffic lights beyond.

'What will it be today, young man?' asks the junior of the two proprietors, Mediterranean Londoners, looking like father and son, of whom Jonny thinks as Geezer 1 and Geezer 2.

Only the younger man is here today, standing in a wooden hut with a hinged flap at the top, like a Punch and Judy box, above an angled fold-out shelf crammed with the boxes of produce. Alongside the fruits pictured in a child's alphabet book, there are sometimes more exotic offerings: papery-skinned Chinese pears, knobbly lychees.

A trembling at his breast and then the winter fiddling of answering a phone call with gloved hands.

'Good morning, Mr Crossan,' resounds the booming old-London voice of his clerk, a terrible loss to televised Dickens.

'Victor?'

'Sir, the excellent Miss Hannah Dunn at Burlingham Masham Fitch wishes to retain our services in the matter of an emergency anonymized injunction application.'

'Do we know the client?'

'Er, yes, sir . . . one Sir Adrian King-Jones.'

The identification byte on Jonny's mental hard-drive whirrs. 'The banker?'

'Indeed, I believe so. Opposing the publication by a news-paper of the details of a relationship.'

'He's the boss of a chum, as it happens. But I can't believe that debars me. Who's the duty beak?'

'Er, Skinner, I believe.'

'Ah! Onward, Christian judges! Not who you want on a leg-over app. It's not a CFA, is it?'

'Miss Dunn is very familiar with our views on conditional fees, sir.' Against the worrying trend towards no-win-no-fee agreements, Jonny holds to the old religion of no-fee-no-chance. 'The arrangements are entirely satisfactory.'

'Okay, we're on.'

'Court 13, 2 p.m. She'll send the bundle round to chambers.'

Since his twenties, when he began to earn regularly, Jonny has imagined his income as an inflatable cushion – something like a bouncy castle, green in colour – holding him above the ground and keeping him from hurt. School fees, Cotswolds cottages, new cars, safaris or skiing holidays flatten the billowing pillow, until a run of decent briefs re-inflates it. The rush of alpha males gagging newspapers has left him feeling that he is bouncing skyscraper-high. Jonny has fast become acknowledged as the master of convincing judges of the privacy of sinning.

He dizzyingly thinks that he is easily rich enough to buy the fruit stall and relocate it in his garden, where Geezer 1 and Geezer 2 could be exclusively employed providing smoothies and fruit salads for him and Libby and the squids. But Jonny begins with a more modest investment. His mouth feeling, for some reason, dry, he points to the juiciest-looking fruit.

'Some clems? Good choice, young man.' Have any customers, he wonders, ever been criticized for their selections, or addressed as elderly? 'A pound okay?'

They got over the jokey confusion between weight and price

long ago. Geezer 2 tips the glowing globes on to the scales and squints until the pound line settles. Jonny should doubtless make a citizen's arrest under metric law, but the stubborn continuation of imperial measures is one of the pleasures of this farmland mirage in the stinking middle of the city.

The clementines are handed to him in a brown paper bag, twisted at the corners like the hankie-sunhat of a factory worker at the seaside.

'Have a good day, young man.'

'And you,' Jonny generously tells his future employee.

Crossing opposite the big new hospital, he splits the saggy skin of one fruit, so richly orange that it is nearly tinged with red. Flinching as the juice stings a hang-nail, he pops the whole oval in his mouth, crushing the segments between teeth and tongue and sensually sluicing the juices towards his throat: citruslingus.

As the thirst subsides, he feels confident, wanted, rich. Striding ahead, he symbolically overtakes two chaps in anoraks with rucksacks, dawdling towards whatever jobs they have.

*

The advantage of getting a train back at lunchtime is that First Class is often almost empty, the smart compartments' main business coming around the two seven o'clocks. So Max, going home, gets a level of comfort and service more common on planes than trains. One scarlet-coated Virgin gives him his complimentary evening paper – less of a perk now that they hand them out for free to every Londoner – while another dispenses snacks (he hopes that no Italian tourist will ever sample what they call ciabatta) and a third, although she might on reflection be the paper girl coming round again, pours the wine.

Clumsily. She can't open the screw-top bottle and has to get the other one to help, not that she seems much more up for it. It's like watching a pair of pterodactyls trying to feed a parking meter. Who had said that about something once? Simon Lonsdale. You worry about what he might say when you are out of the room, but it is bloody funny to be in it with him.

'Sorry it's taking so long, sir. We're as bad as each other.'

Max tries to flash them the smile he has in the best family photographs. 'Really, no problem. No. That's absolutely fine. Don't worry. I can wait.'

At least, alone at a tabled four, he gets the first glass from a bottle of perfectly drinkable Merlot. Although Saffer wines don't really ring his bell and this one might have benefited from breathing.

Only one other bloke in the whole of Coach D. In jeans and an American athletics-club shirt, he doesn't obviously have the look of a First Class passenger. Sometimes Standard rabble gamble on there being no inspection, scuttling back to the cheap seats if they hear the shout for tickets and passes. The Stumble of Shame. Crossan occasionally challenges them, like some barrister's equivalent of a citizen's arrest, but Jonny is bonkers like that and, anyway, has had to back down in the past. The IT sector has broken the dress-code: tycoons and interns wear the same uniform now.

His iPhone rattles on the table. This is technically a Quiet Zone but only a total bozo would object to tremble.

Rosie: *Daddy, i've found one!!!!!!!! Xxxxx.*

The emoticon of the smiley winking yellow face – only the young really know how to use them – plus a URL to web-pages full of pages of grinning horses, one of them highlighted by his daughter as ideal. He reads the *Standard* – heavy December snowfall forecast, alert over killer bug, the UK's terrorism alert level raised to imminent – then retrieves the *FT* from his brief-case and tries to concentrate on the columns of figures, but finds himself staring out of the window. This distraction from work is a flashback to exams at school, although not the red-breasted woman hovering to refill his glass of Merlot. He should say no but, fuck it, he's fitter and thinner now than twenty years ago. He will burn it off later, with Barry.

Flipping open his laptop with an efficient flourish, he fleetingly sees himself from outside, as you sometimes do: the successful businessman with no minute to waste. The other bloke is on the opposite side of the opposite table, so won't be able to see his screen. Good. He opens the folder and goes to work.

Deeney has one more game of his three-match ban to serve after the red card at Plymouth, so Max is short of options for the cup replay at Watford. There's Zola, his record signing, but he hasn't scored in four and is averaging 6.22 performance rating, which doesn't go near to justifying his fee.

He clicks up the position stats on Harrison, his mercurial play-maker. The much-travelled attacking midfielder is categorized 'adequate' as a forward. Holding a slug of the cherryish wine on his tongue while he thinks, Max decides to go 4–4–1–1, with Harrison in the hole off Zola and the young lad Carter on the bench as an impact sub if they're trailing in the later stages.

Watford are up and at them from the whistle and hit the bar from a free kick in the seventh minute. Max notices that the fitness level of Burton, the left centre-back, has dropped to 54 per cent and is thinking of bringing him off as a precaution, when the red cross injury icon flashes up on the screen and he has to replace him.

It's even-stevens at the break and the lads' energy levels are all good, so he decides not to change anything. On sixty-seven minutes, Jacobs skins their left-back and crosses. Zola heads it down for Harrison to drive past the despairing Hornets' stopper.

Sharing the moment with the fans in the away end to his left, Max punches the air and cannot be certain that he doesn't shout aloud as well. The IT guy looks up, surprised, from the thin slice of aluminium he's tapping.

So 0–1 up away, with twenty-three plus maybe three or four on the fourth official's board to go. It's looking good but, with only three of the ninety minutes left, Harris, the substitute centreback, brings down Sordell in the area and, although it's thankfully only a yellow not a red, so he won't face going into extra with just ten, the big striker coolly converts the penalty himself to bring the home side level.

'Fuck!' Max fails to stop himself saying audibly, and his pulse and guts react as if he has had actual bad news.

'Uh-oh! Are the markets jumpy?' asks the other First Class passenger. 'I'm offline at the moment. Otherwise I don't get anything done.'

'What? Oh, no. Just emails. You know, bollocks from the office.'

'Now there's a growth industry. What line are you in?'

Max covers the pause with a swirl of Merlot. 'The luxury gift sector.'

'Uh, *right*. Well, I'll not disturb you anymore.'

They're already at Leighton Buzzard when it goes to penalties. The helplessness is hardest. In the Subbuteo he played as a boy, the match was in your own hands, well, fingers. But these games are like watching an airport departure board, the outcome driven by software.

The first three for each side are converted, but then Mackay blasts over the bar for them and, though Smith nets the next, so do Akinfenwa and Carter (talk about nerve for a 16-year-old on his debut!) for us and we're through to the next round.

Jenno says he is addicted to the game and always makes the saddo face when he double-tasks with it while they watch the 10 o'clock news. But it's his relaxation. As he gets older, he can see football-simulation games gradually replacing drinking and sex.

Max's banging on the table prompts his fellow traveller to say: 'Some good news, then? Give me the name and I might invest.'

'What? Oh, we're not listed. It's a family business.'

As Max stands up to obey the instruction to make sure he has all his belongings with him on leaving the train, the chatterbox in the t-shirt says: 'Cheers. Good to meet you.'

Does this kind of thing go on back in Standard? He doubts it. The point is that they are The Few.

*

The Michaelmas term meeting of the Hardship Committee has been a total nightmare to arrange. Libby had to cascade at least four round-robin emails before they settled on a date. Jack Bracken was in Singapore on business on the two dates that Fi Irving-Law and Claire Upton could do and, just when she thought she had the ducks in a row, it turned out the Uptons were planning a sneaky weekend in Mauritius, taking Oscar and Honey out of school on a Thursday and Friday, which they didn't really want to flag up to Dr Welling, whose three days at a Heads' conference in Wiltshire didn't help the logistics either, and Libby isn't the type to dob them in.

But here they all are at last, over coffee from a jar and bourbon biscuits, sitting on the hard sofas in the head's office. There's a sense of urgency because Jack Bracken's driver is outside, waiting to whisk him straight to Heathrow after the meeting. He's off to Denver for a sales conference but says he is quietly hopeful of some quality time on the slopes. When Libby sympathizes about jet lag, he says he hasn't even recognized the concept since he started restricting himself to isotonic drinks and protein on the westward legs, carbohydrate and ionized water when going east. Declining tea and biccies, he produces from his briefcase a plastic bottle of Evian in a chill-sleeve.

'Over to you, Libby,' says Welling, after the usual flapdoodle about how grateful he and the school are for the time, discretion and money they put into dealing with these delicate matters.

'Thank you, Headteacher,' Libby begins. 'And to all of the committee for being here. This time, it sometimes felt as if one was organizing a small war!' When the laughter has subsided, she continues: 'Let's begin – as usual – with the financial position. Our contingency fund has taken a hit on the stock market like everyone else . . .'

'Tell me about it,' grimaces Jack Bracken.

'Jeremy says he's never known the City this jittery,' adds Fi Irving-Law.

'*But*,' Libby cuts in firmly, 'sensible investment means that we should certainly be able to make disbursements at the level of recent terms, and even beyond that, if required.'

Using words like *disbursements* and balancing her reading glasses halfway up her nose in a manner she began as a magistrate, Libby feels transformed, judicial. She smiles at Dr Welling over her spectacles. 'At which point, Tom, perhaps you should tell us if default rates remain fairly constant?'

The head makes a suction noise with his lips like one of those grey rubber wine-stoppers popping out. 'Would that I could, Libby. Would that I could. Many, many heads were saying at conference last week that they've never known times like these. The bursar has shown me some of the settlements we get. A single envelope containing several cheques from different people – grandparents, godparents, presumably – and even amounts made out to other people and counter-signed to the school account. In fact, Mr Mobbs tells me that two bills were paid – in an absolute first – entirely in cash. He didn't want to ask too many questions . . .'

'If they brought in tax relief on school fees,' Jack Bracken says, 'there'd be less temptation to keep things off the books.'

Dr Welling makes his snogging noise again. 'I hear what you're saying, Jack. But fat chance of that, with politicians nibbling away at the charitable status of schools like ours.'

In the seven general elections of her enfranchised life, Libby has voted Conservative and, having lived for two decades in a constituency where Colonel or Scruff could get elected if they had a blue rosette pinned to their collars, can never quite believe that the governments resulting from these polls have been three Tory and three Labour and now this Frankenstein's monster botch-together with the Liberals. But, secretly, she feels uneasy when people like Jack Bracken or Dr Welling (or Max Dunster)

41

suggest that the system is unfair to people like them. She has never dared ask how a fee-paying school qualifies as a charity.

'You're pulling a face, Libby,' says the head, although she hasn't realized that she is. 'But I made a speech at conference on this very topic. The popular idea that we educate the offspring of a super-rich elite is increasingly comical. I've got more students on fee-deferral and phased payments than I think I've ever had before, frankly, although – hopefully – most of those will never reach this committee. The families will make sacrifices and cobble something together, as so many do. And what are these hardship grants, if not charity?'

Libby can hear Jonny saying, as he often does, that if you haven't got the money for the fees, you shouldn't be sending your children to the school. But Libby, who has always assumed that she would be among the first to be shot in a workers' revolt, takes a more tolerant view.

'Tom,' she says, 'perhaps you should open the file?'

The names surprise her, as they usually do. Families (the Brocklehursts, the Fenton-Chambers), who seemed wealthy and secure, even enviably so, are seeking hardship grants of up to 100 per cent of the fees. Some of the reasons are timeless – a parent's sudden death or serious illness or the division of resources through divorce – but mainly the pleas result from bankruptcy or a slump in business.

As they consider the applications, Libby's panel adopt their characteristic positions. Jack Bracken snappily analyses the cause of shortfall – 'Another fool seduced by the dotcom mirage', 'perfectly workable idea but two years late to market' – while Claire Upton seems shocked at the possibility of anything ever going wrong ('Wasn't he up for an Oscar not that long ago?') and Fi Irving-Law is keen to make the payouts dependent on educational performance: 'Doesn't Jolyon Brocklehurst have a history of being disruptive? India and Finn have certainly given me that impression.'

At the end of ninety minutes, they have made eight disbursements from a total of twelve applications. Although Jack argued that the Macnees were simply punching above their social weight – the cash-flow statement required in support of each claim reveals that the fees were always more than 40 per cent of their disposable income – Dr Welling persuaded the committee to take them, as they were just the kind of deserving cases who might be useful with the charity commissioners.

The funds are available to meet all of the dozen claims but Libby's view, which Fi and Jack endorse, is that the process will be weakened if every applicant is satisfied: the best education must remain a privilege rather than a right. As a result, Jolyon Brocklehurst, Callum Robinson and Holly and Giles Parker-Stiles will be asked to leave Westbury Park unless the outstanding fees are paid or the head feels able to agree a further deferral.

With Jack glancing pointedly out of the window at the gravel where his chauffeur waits, Libby stresses the need to tap their backers for another round of donations. The Eight will again be asked to dig deep, or more likely The Six, as the Lonsdales are so stingy. (A simple fact, nothing to do with Simon being Jewish at all, any more than Tasha being Welsh.)

'I think it's high time my good friend Max Dunster made another contribution to our coffers,' Libby says.

Kissing himself on the lips again, Welling says: 'Well, whoever, wherever. As always, the school is enormously grateful to the committee and its donors.'

Jack Bracken stands. 'A humbling experience, as ever. But I have to – as it were – fly.'

He sends a text and, almost at once, they hear a car engine starting up outside.

*

Eventually, concerned about arriving late, she opts for a black cashmere sweater with stone-washed jeans. She puts on – then takes off – her tenth-anniversary brooch from Max. Checking herself in the walk-in wardrobe's mirror, it strikes Jenno that she only needs a black woollen hat to look like a burglar. She next reflects that this might be an appropriate garb for many of her clients, then mentally slaps her wrist for such an awful thought.

It's always a challenge, choosing outfits for CAB afternoons. Pearls would always be obscured by your lanyard. And you don't want to look too much like a consultant paediatrician or a magistrate (which, again, some customers might – *stop it, Jenno!*). Words frequently repeated on the training course were 'approachable' and 'sympathetic'. For this reason, Jenno drives there in the shopping Beetle, still with a scratch on the passenger side, from when Max scraped the Crossans' gate, because she's self-conscious about parking the four-wheel or the sportster outside the branch.

She also registered as 'Jenny', which she accepts nowhere else, not just because her pet-name sounds posh, but because she dreads beginning every consultation with an explanation or correction. Conscious that some colleagues view her as a rich man's do-gooding wife, she is terrified of being taken as a visiting dignitary. Coming into the staff room unexpectedly to get a throat lozenge from her bag – volunteers, early on, make their throats raw with all the talking – she is sure she heard the words 'Lady Muck' hanging in the air.

Another aspect of her class camouflage is drinking without a flinch the filthy Nescafé the volunteers club together to keep beside the kettle. She is staunchly sipping at it now, as her first customers of the day are shown over. They are a morbidly obese bloke and a fat or pregnant woman, who, walking side by side like a bride and bridegroom, fill most of the wide aisles between the desks, designed for the significant percentage of inquirers who use mobility scooters.

The man holds like a shield the laminated number-card that marked their position in the queue. The woman is pushing a buggy, through the dripping rain-hood of which can be seen a chubby child, stoppered with a dummy. Despite her precautionary wardrobe, Jenno still feels overdressed, as they unzip glistening rainproofs to reveal a pink fleece for her and trackie bottoms and an over-stretched red football shirt (Manchester? Arsenal?) for him. She should feel lucky. Apparently, last week, Sue Booth had a couple in onesies under quilted coats. Her clients shake themselves like dogs and water pours on to the floor.

'The rain is one thing we can't help you with,' Jenno smiles.

'Scuse me? No, you're all right,' says the female of the species.

On the training course, she inwardly yawned at the suggestion that the climate could be a perfect ice-breaker but, in her two years at the bureau, has come to the conclusion that the weather is the one thing the English have in common.

'I'm Jenny,' says Jenno. 'What should I call you?'

The woman points at herself – 'Mandy' – and then jerks a thumb at the man: 'Danny'.

In most of the couples she has dealt with, it is the woman who takes the lead, both in speaking and deciding to seek advice. Jenno was originally tempted to see this as evidence of female superiority, although experience suggests a more pragmatic explanation; the mother, in so many of the family units they see, is the only one with a link to all the other members.

'And who's that hiding away in there?' Jenno asks, pointing at the plastic shroud. Although she hates it when the girls tease her about it, she is conscious of taking down her accent, like Tony Blair.

'That's Gavin,' says the family spokeswoman.

'Good as gold, isn't he?' Jenno says. 'Now, what did you want to talk to us about?'

'Like the Gas put us on to yer? And the bank obviously,' says Mandy. 'They say yer can help with paying and that?'

In the branch's most recent audit, 60 per cent of inquiries involved debt and benefits, up by a fifth on the previous year.

'You have a problem with debts?' Jenno checks.

'With . . . ? Yeah.'

Danny aggressively nods assent.

'Mandy,' Jenno asks. 'Have you received any final demands or court orders?'

A fine spray of rainwater hits the desk as the woman rummages at the rear of the stroller. In various stages, she pulls out pieces of paper that have come out of windowed envelopes as obviously as birds burst out of shells. Jenno spreads the letters across the desk, creating symmetrical lines of red print and perforated tear-sheets that remain untorn. Gas, Electricity and broadband, she rapidly establishes, have been unpaid for months and are threatened with disconnection. A bank account has been frozen for longer than the bills have been ignored. It is a depressingly familiar pattern; the only upside she can see is that they might be too dodgy to have put much on plastic.

'Do you have any credit cards?' she asks, realizing she is making the shape of a rectangle with her fingers. With so much of what she says meeting blankness, she often finds herself trying such mimes.

'We don't have none now,' Mandy says. 'But we have one of them loans, obviously.'

Obviously. Oh, dear. *With whom* . . . 'Who is the loan with?'

Another sheaf of papers from behind the child. Jenno is surprised by neither the name of the online loan-shark nor the extortionate APR. She rubs her hands together, feeling the dried residue of the antiviral foam she applies in the branch bathroom before sessions.

'Okay. Mandy and . . .' Without losing the eye-line, she manages a blurred check of the man's name on her notepad. 'Danny. The first thing we need to do is to draw up a budget sheet . . .' She brings an empty template up on her screen. 'That's just a list of what you've got coming in and going out, so we can see where we are. I'm afraid the first part is a bit boring . . .'

Fust. Bih. She must sound like a bad audition for *East-Enders*. She takes the names – Turville for him, Walters for her – and address: the estate she expected.

'And is it just the three of you living there?'

'No. I've got three . . . from before. So has he, but they live with the mums. Well, obviously one's in care. Gavin's arse . . .'

What? Oh, *ours*. 'And your other three, Mandy, are they at home?'

'No.'

The inevitable pattern, again. 'Ah, I see. Are they in care?'

'Where?'

'What are the arrangements for the other children?'

'Well, they're at school.'

'At least we hope they are.' Danny speaks for the first time, revealing jagged teeth with gaps between. He's ogling Jenno's boobs, in a way she's not used to men doing so openly. 'Her Kevin could be anywhere.'

'Oi, not funny, fella,' Mandy rebukes him.

Jenno can feel her face aflame with the shame of having fallen into two of the traps – assumption and judgement – against which her training and appraisals regularly warn.

'I'm sorry. I got hold of the wrong end of . . .'

'Easily done, darling,' leers Danny.

'So there are six of you living at this address?'

'Yeah. Yeah, definitely,' says Mandy. 'And obviously I've another on the way.'

Jenno often thinks that they should hand out condoms as well as advice. She runs through the incomings – housing benefit, child benefit, heating grant, jobseeker's allowance – and the outgoings: utilities, food, clothes, car loan, Sky-broadband sub, entertainment and, it turns out, from another roll of threatening letters pulled from the buggy, four unsecured loans from web lenders. At a rough estimate, the couple are down by several hundred pounds a week, a debt always accelerating with the menacingly leveraged interest. However, she notes, there are three or more children under nineteen living on benefits, which qualifies the household for the tap bonanza.

'Okay,' she says. 'Well, the first good news is that we can get your water costs capped.'

She enjoys revealing these jackpots hidden within the state's provision for its weakest subjects, although Mandy and especially Danny look less gratified than she had hoped.

'Okay,' she says. 'What we need to do now . . .'

Mandy's midriff starts singing 'Chasing Pavements'. Eventually, she locates the sound in the folds of nylon and pulls out an iPhone. Squinting at the ID on screen, she silences the ring-tone and says: 'Sorry, doll. I'll have to call you back . . .' A gruff guffaw. 'I fucking wish . . .'

The contracts for the phones, Jenno guesses, are either included under Entertainment or, more likely, not mentioned at all.

'Okay,' she says. 'We need to work out a schedule of payments you can afford – especially for the loans and the gas and electricity bills. Most companies are actually pretty reasonable if you can pay a little a bit now and show willing . . .' Although, as she says this, she suspects that the only real solution for the pair on the other side of the desk is to start fraudulently claiming benefits in the names of several dead relatives and a few invented identities as well, if indeed they haven't already. 'But first we need to see if we can get your out-goings down a little bit as well. I'm going to put two columns on this sheet of paper – luxuries and necessities . . .'

'Can't we just have our money?'

Although not quite a shout, Danny's tone is loud enough for other advisors and customers to look in their direction. Jenno takes note of the position of the branch supervisor. She has not yet had a violent client herself, but there are stories. Karen Bartlett once got to her BMW convertible to find a guy she had just lectured on extravagance standing beside it, which is one reason Jenno always drives the Beetle here. Although, in all honesty, her biggest problem so far has been male clients giving her the eye; she's young enough to be the daughter of most of the other volunteers, which is understandable, as most people only have time to put something back in retirement.

'I'm sorry, Danny?'

'I don't fucking get this, *Jenny*.' He speaks her name like he's saying the c-word. 'What I thought was you'd give us our grant today, like. We've gotta get back for the bairns.'

Maybe *Our Grant* would be a good name for their next *bairn*.

'Oh, no, no, no,' says Jenno, starting a laugh that she tries to swallow and hating how posh she sounds. *I'm afraid that's not quite*. No. 'We don't give out loans. That's not what we are. We help you to . . .' – *maximize*, no – '. . . make sure you're getting all the money you're entitled to and sort out a payment plan for people you owe money to.'

'Told you this was a fucking waste of space, Mand,' spits Danny, then turns to face Jenno. 'Bet you could give us what we need, *Jenny*, if yer just sold that fucking rock on yer finger . . .'

She instinctively cups her right hand over her engagement ring, the one piece of jewellery it had never occurred to her to remove before coming here. She resists the sting of tears physically, like trying to keep down a hiccup. What shocks her is the unfairness of it all.

*

The price paid for taking the earlier, empty train is the heavier traffic heading from the station. On the ramp to the dual carriageway, he's cut up by a black Beamer X5 and, first chance he gets, does a fuck-you overtake, with his fist hitting the horn and a finger jabbing at the driver who turns out to be a great slab of a man with a shaven pate, mercifully a white guy but, for a while, it looks like he might give chase. Max only relaxes when three successive glances in the rear-view mirror show no trace of the SUV. His pulse is almost normal when he reaches Dunster Manor.

The torturer is waiting in reception, flexing his knees and buttocks as he sits. In the way that the eyes of a bodyguard permanently swerve, Barry's muscles always seem to be twitching.

'Evening, boss,' the thug greets Max.

'Barry.'

'Am I going to cause you pain tonight, boss.'

'Oh, good.'

How stereotypical that conversation sounds: brutal South African, wimpy English.

'Good evening, Mr Dunster.'

Max turns to the desk. The new girl. Having already switched from his driving to his work glasses, he has to lean and peer to just about make out her name badge.

'Becky. Hi.'

He is about to tell her that she should call him Max and can come to him with any settling-in issues, when he is interrupted by Steve Pearson appearing through the swing doors from Production, overcoat collar up and the fur-trapper's hat he bought on that sales trip to Canada pulled down almost to his nose against the predicted snow.

They do the name-swap and then Steve asks him: 'Was it okay?'

'What?'

'London. The appointment.'

'Oh, yeah. I'm afraid the doctors had rather bad news . . .'

'Shit. Really? Max . . .'

'For you lot. You're stuck with me in charge until I'm ninety, apparently. I, no pun intended, *maxed* every test.'

'Excellent news, MD. And nine tomorrow is okay for our routine?'

'Absolutely. Written on my heart.'

'I've run the figures for the next twelve months.'

'Good. Can you mail them to me and I'll have a look tonight?'

He changes in the private bathroom that his father installed. You'd struggle to get that sort of corporate indulgence past an FD now, even during boom years. In this bust, they are lucky Steve still authorizes urinals.

Max enjoys the ritual of robing: like a soldier, astronaut or pope. The swooshes on the beanie, sweatshirt, trackies, socks and trainers form a line of ticks down his body, resembling a check-list on a foreman's clipboard. There is a physical pleasure in swapping the stiff, shaped fabrics of business suit and shirt for the wafting softness of running kit.

In reception, the hyperactive Barry is now jogging on the spot, chatting to Becky the receptionist. Max wonders if the trainer has hit on her. Chat-ups must be easier if you have the body as a professional topic.

'You know what, boss, I'm disappointed in you!' Barry shouts. 'Only fucking wimps run in trousers. Never mind how many fucking minus degrees it is, my knees feel the breeze. Forgive the curse-words, Becky. It's the only language these people understand.'

Barry's tactic is that Max should never be able to guess what the hour will contain. ('If our bodies know what's coming, they put their feet up. We gotta take them by surprise.') The warm-up, though, is mandatory: step-ups on the stone bench at the entrance to the Business Park; crunches and twists on the grass beside it, regardless of how hard or cold the ground is.

'Boss, did I hear you telling your colleague you'd seen a doctor today?'

'What?' Max asks upwards from between his feet, straightening to add: 'Oh, yes. Medical in London. My so-called Key Man insurance policy.'

'Okay, long as it was that. Just bad for business if one customer drives past and sees me kneeling giving CPR to another.'

Barry hands him a twin of the hi-vis jacket he is wearing himself: he insists on this for winter sessions.

'Little risk of that, Barry, from what they say. Touch . . . *stone*. In fact, I guess I have you to thank for my scores in the tests.'

'Flattery won't let you off the pain, lard boy. Come on, let's run.'

Very occasionally, Jenno has come along for a double session – Barry offered a twofer but Max insisted on paying double – and was shocked by the savage way they were addressed. Personal trainers are civilian sergeant majors, she said. But it's worse than the army. In the fitness business, social hierarchies are completely overturned. In how many other professions do employees get to shriek belittling insults at their employers?

'Come on, you fucking city large-arse. Let's get some of that fat-cat fat off you,' Barry spits as they begin a sprint–jog–walk sequence, the increasingly irregular transitions signalled by blasts from a whistle on a black-and-yellow string around his tormentor's neck. Dragon breath spouts from their mouths as they set off in the freezing air. Intermittently, they pass what seems to be a street-fight but turns out to be another CEO and his trainer kickboxing.

'Mrs Dunster might like love-handles, but not love-*banisters*!' Barry barks.

During the early sessions, Max had vomited in the later stages of the circuits, as the gaps between the sprints decreased. Barry had stood grinning beside him, like a sadistic parent, until the last sour strings dribbled out. Now, it never got worse for Max than becoming slightly wheezy or spaced.

The first painful, then pleasurable sensation of running in sub-zero temperatures: the freeze in your feet and cheeks slowly thawed by the glow flowing through your blood, like the children centrally heated by their breakfast cereal in those TV commercials of long ago.

During one of the gentler stretches, Barry asks, as Max tries to match his rolling, almost balletic rhythm: 'Business good?'

'Well, as the prime minister keeps insisting, we're all in this together. But we seem to be ahead of the curve in our sector.'

'*Right?*' Barry has a default tone of belligerent scepticism, for which, alone, Max would never have employed him in any capacity except exerciser. 'I thought new technology would be the problem for your guys.'

'Well, sure. But we diversified.'

'*Right?* To stay ahead? You know what: that's a motto I approve of.'

Blowing his whistle, the South African sadist races off

towards the darkened rises of Westbury Park, shouting over his shoulder: 'Come on, Lord Fucking Snooty. Let's burn off all that claret and cigars.'

Sometimes he wonders if Barry is an anarchist who has found a more enjoyable form of anti-capitalist protest than smashing in the windows of American coffee chains in Oxford Street.

*

Natasha gets into bed with Simon determined to raise it. Libby Crossan would turn that into some kind of innuendo but, personally, Tasha finds double entendres a bit school-age.

She had planned to ask at supper but the conversation was frosty because she'd started by saying: 'Oh, did you get my text about the spa? It was really embarrassing at the front desk—'

'Yeah, yeah,' he cut her off. 'It was a cock-up with the standing order. This month's didn't go through, for some reason. But it's sorted.'

'This *month's*? I thought we paid annually?'

'What? I don't think so. We have so many of them, it's hard to know. Anyway, I've done it.'

So bed is her next opportunity. As usual, he is turned on his side, facing the window, his back to her side of the bed, moving the book closer and then further away again because he has started to find that his close sight is getting better. He went to the optician and come back saying that apparently such improvement is one of the few consolations of middle age.

'What are you reading?'

He just holds the cover up over his shoulder, which she always hates. As if he actually can't bear to talk to her. It is called: *Why Work Doesn't Happen At Work.*

'What's it about?'

'There are quite hefty clues in the title.'

Jesus Christ! She tries to keep it going but there are times you just weep.

'Oh, well, if you're going to be like that.'

She reaches for her Hilary Mantel and her reading glasses.

The wind outside shrieks with a horror-film intensity. It is one of the problems of living in such a remote house.

Simon surprises her with a semi-friendly concession: 'No, you're right. Titles tell you nothing now. In a bookshop the other day, I picked up something called *The World Will End In 2022*, assuming it was by one of those American futurologists. And it was a French novel. But *Why Work Doesn't Happen At Work* actually does, in that dreadful expression, do what it says on the tin. It's sort of what used to be called a time-and-motion study. They looked at all these offices and proved that the employees spent all their time in endless tedious meetings on subjects where the decision is taken before or afterwards by someone else. And, when they're not in meetings, they're up-dating their Facebook pages. It's all made worse by open-plan, which was introduced to save money but just turns workplaces into cafes.'

'Isn't that what they've done at Samson Brothers?'

'That's why I'm reading it.'

Then, wonder of wonders, he actually starts a conversation: 'Has Libby said anything about Jonny being a bit odd?'

'What? Only that he won't leave her alone with what she calls his telescope.'

'Mmm? *Oh*. I'm assuming that he hasn't taken up astronomy?'

It is a reminder of how they used to talk to each other. She fell for him originally because he made her laugh. Now she realizes that's like buying a car because it's really shiny.

'Not exactly.'

Simon has always been one of those human radiators, toasty when everyone else is shaking with the cold. She mentioned it once to Emily, who did that quick little frown and said, 'Has he had his blood pressure checked recently?', which is one of the problems of having a doctor as a friend, but, when she casually passed it on to Simon, he just said: 'I'm fine. I've told you before. My family all die in old folks' homes, smelling of soup stains and poo, worried about their savings running out.'

She presses her feet against his calves, through the pyjamas, which seems fair to her, but he protests, 'Christ! Your feet are freezing', and shakes her back to her own arctic wastes.

'What did you mean about Jonny acting odd?' she asks, her swift correction to 'oddly' infuriatingly overlapping with his.

'Just at Euston. When the train got in, finally got in . . .'

'Oh, was yours bad as well? Libby got a message from . . .'

'Yeah. We were on the same one.'

'Why didn't you tell me?'

'What's the point? It's a popular suicide route. If I told you them all you'd be: *enough with the jumpers!*'

Although Simon isn't technically Jewish, because his mother wasn't, he has certain phrases and mannerisms picked up from his dad.

'*Jonny*,' she prompts him.

'No, I'm Simon. You're getting mixed up. Is it him your shagging?'

'Very funny!'

She kicks him for emphasis. How dare he when he hasn't touched her for eighteen months at least?

'Ouch! Get your bloody toenails cut! Oh, I see, you meant: *about* Jonny. Should have said. I may have warned you before about clarity of language. Stop kicking me! No, it's just that, when we got through the ticket barriers, he suddenly went all twitchy and went off across the concourse to the taxi steps, looking around from side to side all the time, like we were at Helmand Central and there were snipers in the coffee outlets.'

'Maybe he had the wrong ticket.'

'Hardly. It started after the barriers and, anyway, you know Jonny. He'd pay them *more* for the trains if they'd let him.'

'I don't know, then. Weird.'

They read their books for a while, until she senses him go inert, then snap alert again and do the clumsy juggle with the book that is the curse of the before-sleep reader. On a bad night, one of them will come-to at 1 a.m. and find that they have both zonked out with the lights on, their hardbacks spatchcocked on the floor or two thirds down the duvet.

Now or never. Her feet feeling warmer, she risks resting them against his legs again. And, though he doesn't wriggle a welcome like in the past, he doesn't repulse her again.

'Si?'

'Mmm?'

'The other six are going to Morocco, third week of December, for the weekend . . .'

'The other three what?'

Oh, he's going to play it that way.

'Crossans, Rutherfords, Dunsters.'

She does the surnames sing-song and fast: a running joke among the couples, based on the roll-call in *Trumpton*.

'They're going to Marrakesh. Bit of sun in this bloody endless winter, and Christmas shopping in the markets.'

'As you do. New York is so last millennium. Actually, I think Jonny might have said something on the train.'

'And what do you think?'

'I think, not for the first time, that these people don't seem to understand that they're living in a bankrupt country in which those of us who have got jobs, just about, should feel bloody lucky to have them and not go Christmas shopping in Africa.'

That bit in the middle frightens her into letting the holiday go for the moment: 'Just about got a job? Are you worried again?'

'I'm always worried. Darling . . .' When they started, 'darling' meant he was being nice to her; now it means nasty. 'I'm Director of Public Relations for a bank. I don't know if you've noticed what the state of the public's relationship with banks is at the moment but it's just possible that someone might make the connection.'

'Oh, but none of that's your fault, Si.'

'What happened to Bill Adamson wasn't his fault. He was a teetotal non-smoking marathon runner, as we all endlessly said at that awful do afterwards. Unemployment and cancer don't always seem to bother about fault.'

Is he trying to tell her something?

'Do you think you're ill?'

'No. I'm fine, all things considered.'

Even she flinches at the breathy, Marilynesque voice she hears coming out of her mouth, but all is fair in war and marriage: 'Three days in the sunshine would cheer you up. *Without the kids.*'

An old code? Will it work now? Apparently not: 'Jesus, Tash.' He turns to face her, but not in a good way. 'Read my lips. Jonny Crossan pulls down millions a year for persuading judges that roads should be built through the bits of the countryside he doesn't live in. Emily and Tom, between them, earn at least double what the two of us do. I can't personally quite see how Max and Jenno live like that on the proceeds from a company making things people don't use any more, but they seem to. We can afford to play some home matches with them but we're not in their league for away fixtures.'

He turns away from her and back to *Why Work Doesn't Happen At Work.* After struggling with his pyjama bottoms and wrist-wriggling through what surely can't be arthritis yet at her age, her hand finds and fondles his willy. Oh dear. Poor cold dead worm again.

'No!' he tells her, edging away. 'It should be because you want *it*, or even me. Not because you want *something.*'

They separate. She sulks with her novel for a while, then turns back because she wouldn't be able to sleep with so much unfinished business. But Simon is already snoring, or pretending to, and she sees no benefit in proving which it is. She turns off the light but leaves his book across him where it is.

*

Emily never expected, at fifty-three, to be sleeping on a lumpy put-up, like when she was a junior doctor. In truth, she never expected to do nights again. But, once Tony Blair, whatever you think of him otherwise, started paying doctors properly in exchange for one or two concessions, such as semi-privatizing out-of-hours, she was on a camp bed twice a week, covering emergencies across the borders of three counties.

Odd how the names of politicians survive them in the professions they affect; some of the older teachers at the village school still refer to in-job training as Baker days. And she will always think of her Mondays and Thursdays in the basement of a hospital in Aylesbury as Blair nights.

She hasn't had to bother about the concrete mattress tonight, dealing with a constant string of calls since she clocked on at seven. She's had to leave base twice: a gastric bleed in a palliative patient and a question-mark pneumonia on the twelfth floor of a tower block, where she felt apprehensive in the piss-stinking stairwells and lifts, even though the Night Doc driver comes in with her on such vulnerable visits.

Everything else she has dealt with on the phone, including a student convinced that he was bleeding to death from a foreskin torn during sex; she eventually convinced him that the frenulum sometimes splits during vigorous intercourse but will almost always heal through its own means and so there was no need to despatch an ambulance.

But most of the time, as on most Blair nights, she's an alternative Samaritan, talking to people whose symptoms – racing pulses, struggles to catch breath, agonizing pains in head or abdomen – are rapidly revealed, through the ease and even eagerness with which they are able speak to her, as psychological not medical. Lonely through bereavement, redundancy or failed relationships, probably seen off as rapidly as possible by their own harassed GPs, they place on speed-dial a number where, in the long and empty hours of dark, they are guaranteed at least a hearing of a few minutes. And sometimes, if there is no other call waiting in the queue, Emily, disliking the common view that such patients are timewasters, will give them more minutes of sympathetic attention than is diagnostically necessary.

1.10 a.m. The house, when she gets home at dawn, will have that heart-lifting warmth that comes from four people peacefully sleeping. Duty rather than financial need (she has been so lucky with her pension) keep her doing nights and she wonders once again if she should stop soon. In two years, Henry will be the only one at home; in five years, it will just be her and Tom.

The scarlet tremor of an incoming call, considered significant enough by the triage nurse on switchboard to be put through to her. Emily freezes *Desperate Housewives* on her laptop.

'Hello,' she says. 'Night Doc. How can I help you?'

'Oh. Er, I've just woken up with a pounding headache and trembling all over.'

'Oh, poor you. Well, first, could you just tell me your age and whether you're being treated for anything at the moment?'

'I'm forty-seven and I've been seeing my doctor about, er, depression.'

Emily relaxes: almost certainly a Lonely Moanly call, in which the only pressure is to rule out likely suicide. Normally, she would check what prescription the patient is on, but, in this case, there is no need. As must happen frequently to local priests in the confessional, she retrospectively recognized the voice.

'This is Emily Rutherford,' she says gently. 'Is that Becca?'

A pause. 'I'm sorry, Doctor.'

She has been treating Becca Adamson for anxiety and sleeplessness in the four months since her husband's death.

'Nothing to be sorry about, Becca. Nights are tough. We've talked about it. Now, what I need to know at this stage is do you have any symptom you haven't had before?'

'Oh. Gosh. No, I don't think so.'

'Are you taking the tablets I gave you?'

'Mmm. But they don't seem to be working . . .'

'Becca, we've discussed this. Grief will never be an on–off switch. Look, I think you need to make an appointment to see me again. For tonight, the breathing exercises, camomile tea, everything we talked about . . .'

'Thank you, Doctor.'

'But you can call again if you need to.'

'Thank you, Doctor.'

For what? During that call, the mother of a four-month-old child has phoned in: the baby is feverish, listless, diarrhoeic. Triage has marked it for a ring-back but Emily puts the post-code into *Where To?* and tells the driver they will house-visit. She considers it her strength as a doctor – Tom, her children and her colleagues as her weakness – that she has a morbid fear of missing the fatal case.

*

Who are all these drivers at this time? In the stillness of the middle of the night, when the wind is blowing in a certain way, the cars on the road at the bottom of the fields sometimes sound as noisy as a racing track. And Jonny can make this compar-ison, with Silverstone just across the county line. On Grand Prix day, sitting in the garden is like being in the engine room of a ship, the gear changes sounding almost in your ear. And, for two hours before and after, the helicopters filling the air. Every year, someone makes the joke about it being like *Apocalypse Now*. Usually Simon Lonsdale, who may even have coined it back in the last millennium.

He can't sleep. Again. Tom Rutherford is writing that pamphlet on the village, which they'll all have to pretend to have read sometime, and Jonny could slip him a few paragraphs on Middlebury at 1.30 a.m. Tonight, he doesn't even need to cup his hand over the touch-screen alarm clock to check. This volume of cars – about one every ten or fifteen minutes – means somewhere around half one. From 4.30 a.m., certainly from 5, it's a constant stream: the influx Londoners heading back to the place where they refuse to live but have to work to earn the amount of money they need to fund their country living.

Here comes another one, taking the Eastbury crossroads turn

too fast. Once, two years ago, the Crossan household woke to the squeal and bang of a car smashing into Farmer Mosey's wall, and then sirens. If it happened again, these days, he'd already be awake. Perhaps it's something left hanging in the county air from the Grand Prix, some sort of spiritual exhaust fumes, that makes the midnight drivers gun it round the corners.

Who are they all? Emily Rutherford, possibly, returning from a patient, if this is one of the nights she does, no longer obligatory but paid separately for her trouble; doctors have got it made in this country.

Not dinner parties, surely, on a Monday night, even in Middlebury. Not even the Dunsters, who would barely eat elevenses without having at least a couple of other couples round, entertain at the beginning of the week.

He's aware of a quivering in the top left-hand corner of his abdomen. Is that liver? Or pancreas, which is an even worse one to get, often already incurable when diagnosed. No, as he starts to think about it, the trembling in his belly starts to feel like a gushing. Internal bleeding? Surely then he'd feel faint, which he doesn't. Wired, if anything, as if he's drunk too much coffee, which he hasn't, because of having so much trouble sleeping. Could it be his kidneys? The adrenal glands: do they actually gush in this way, like a sort of internal pissing? Or, wait, does the feeling actually resemble a second, echoing heartbeat? He has read in the health pages of the *Telegraph* that this can be an early warning sign of cardiac issues.

But his heart rate, when he takes it, in the way that Dr Em showed him once, two fingers pressed against his wrist, just under the translucent protuberance of his pulse, is firm and almost perfectly in rhythm with his watch. An athlete, although he isn't one, would be pleased with 60 bpm.

Beside him, one foot against his leg, as she prefers, Libby sleeps easily and deeply, as she always seems to. No matter what you do about your five a day and giving up booze for Lent and having the full English only when staying in hotels, there is luck in the body you got. They're like cars, even two of the same marque. Some shake and stop and splutter; others purr along and fire up each morning without protest. Libs seems to have an effortless regularity in everything: Smedgewicks, Ladies Days, Tremblers, Bedfordshire.

Although he doesn't really need to pee, he goes to the loo for something to do. He doesn't switch on the bathroom light because he has read of surveys suggesting that failing to spend enough time in total darkness can increase the risk of malignancies. Flight attendants, whose circadian rhythms go out of sync on night flights, were said to have a higher incidence of breast tumours. He isn't at much risk of a tit tumour – although there was an article the other day about that policeman who had to have a mastectomy – but it's silly to take pointless risks.

But the harsh security lights on the courtyard outside mean that he can see himself in the bathroom mirror, as he washes his hands after a desultory dribble that makes him panic about his prostate as well.

Unlike many men, Jonny almost welcomes the whitening of his hair as he nears the end of his fifth decade, because he has grown up and then lived with the casual hostility dispensed to gingers. Libby spends more time and money each month trying to keep her hair the colour it was; he's happy with the tinting of decrepitude.

A bit more fluff on the hairline, a bit less flesh on the chin-line would be nice, but he doesn't hate what he sees. The storm-cloud pouches under both eyes are the most striking sign of decline, and another night like this won't help them.

Back in bed, savouring the stored warmth after the chill of the house between the central heating's timed ignitions, he is startled by a sudden pardon. So many bits of him are giving notice of their impending retirement but his Walter still seems fifteen.

He presses himself against Libby's back. Her nightie has ridden up and he is able to wedge himself there. Soon, she half-wakes.

'Oh!' she slurrily inquires, 'what are you doing to me, Jonny Crossan?'

'I can't sleep, again.'

'Poor you. You feel quite wide awake.'

His pressure against her cleft receives some moistening welcome. Good girl. Always up for it. Like a man with mammaries.

'I was actually asleep, Johnny. But would it help you sleep?'

'I think it might.'

'Go on. But can you be quick and use a thingy?'

If he is ever struck blind, the one area in which he won't need RNIB retraining will be dressing up Walter. Even on a moonless winter night, he easily locates and opens the boiled sweet tin on the bedside table – between the last two Sharpe books, paperback and hardback – and lifts out a spongy square. His fingers find the little guide nick and rip down the side. Libby turns on her back.

Five minutes later, she's asleep again but he feels no closer to oblivion. He removes the viscous balloon, and pushes it under the bed, reminding himself to tissue and bin it in the morning (Libby thinks they lost a cleaning lady once when he forgot); later *this* morning, in less than four hours, when he gets up for the train.

He has a good job, tons of money and even regular sex, when he suspects some of the other men he knows were reduced to relying on a Dobson in the shower long ago. He has nothing to be worried about.

But nothing is what he's concerned about. Precisely that. He has admitted it to himself. Lying in the dark, as cars mysteriously cross the darkened village, what Jonny Crossan thinks about is death.

THREE

THE DREAM HOUSE

It has long been a consolation to Kate Duncan that none of the murder scenes in her career has involved more than one body. She has colleagues who have worked family slayings, terrorist atrocities, school shootings. Yet even the worst serial killer on her CV despatched one at a time.

Lorenzo, though, meeting her at the door of the house, confirms what the sketchy details on the call-out suggested.

'Be prepared, it's a spree.'

'Yeah, Rob, they warned me.'

At first, she fears that the screened areas beside the drive and in the courtyard – a precaution against opportunistic press photographers, who will already be enthusiastically roaring north – are for the kids. Then she remembers the dogs. If the presumed TOD is even ballpark, the bodies of the children will be in the house. They would have been asleep. *I want to die in my own bed,* you hear people say.

Delaying the moment of knowing and seeing, she makes an exaggerated inspection of the external area. The gravel beyond looks like a showroom forecourt, and in a way it is, although what's being advertised is that this is a place where cars are bought rather than sold. And, though smart, they are used: thick spatters of mud on the chassis, rugby-club stickers on the back windows.

'Three vehicles here,' she says. 'Was that – it seems weird to say *all* – they had?'

'No. DVLA records show a fourth . . .'

'Are we . . . ?'

'On it.'

As she looks at the sign to the stables and paddock, Lorenzo says: 'At the moment, if we had to guess at the order, I'd say: the dogs, the three kids, then the wife.'

'Yeah. And there'll be people in this country who'll think the really awful bit is the ones with four legs.'

'Yeah. Left alone the horses for some reason.'

'They'd be the hardest to do, wouldn't they? The family were asleep, the dogs are smaller than . . .'

She stops to avoid saying 'him', snared in her own murder-room rules.

'Not much use as guard dogs, if you can shoot them in the back of the head,' Lorenzo rumbles, then corrects himself before she can. 'Oh, that's the thing, isn't it? They must have been shot by . . .'

'Someone they trusted, certainly,' she cuts in to prevent a premature assumption as to the killer's identity, a long-held precaution confirmed in her by past humiliations.

Kate takes in the beautiful solidity of the house and the hills around, such peace and emptiness always magical to an urbanite.

'What they call a dream house,' she says.

'Yeah. They didn't deserve this, though.'

'I wasn't suggesting they . . .' But there will be those who think the deaths of the wealthy matter less: *it only shows that money doesn't . . .* , as if anyone had ever really thought it does. 'Although the thing about being out here is that no one would hear screams.'

'Yeah, guv, we're going to be stiffed on witnesses. Although it doesn't look like we're going to need them.'

'Why not?'

'Well, you assume . . .'

'Day one, rule one, detective school: don't . . .'

'Listen. Two family dogs shot without protest. You ever had

one? They bark if a bird flies past. Then the family, hardly stirring in their beds. This was someone who didn't count as a stranger.'

'Stranger's a strange word. I know the way it looks. But the way it looks can be dangerous. Make a list of all the people who could get into your house without setting off the dogs. It would be longer than you'd think. These . . .' – she nearly says *sort of* – '. . . people have cleaners, nannies, gardeners, just for a start.'

'I suppose. No. Okay.'

'In fact, where *is* the nanny? Despite all the evidence to the contrary, people are basically trusting. The number of victims we get who shell out for invisible sensor-pads on the path and then give a spare key to a poverty-stricken . . .' – she nearly says *immigrant* – '. . . cleaner they've hardly met. At the moment, we have four murders and a shooter still on the loose. We urgently need to locate the owner of this property. Where are we on that?'

His shoulders tensing, which is how his stubbornness shows, Lorenzo gestures to the line of vehicles. 'The textbooks say we'll find *him* in the other car somewhere in the . . . are they called *grounds*?'

'And I say we'll wait until we do. And, Rob, I want a lockdown on the names until we've cleaned up NOK. This time, I don't want tributes on Twitter before someone's mother knows they're dead. So, A, B, C, D in the house and we're looking for E . . .'

Fearing the revelations to come upstairs, she looks around again. On the drop-down steps of one of the squad vans sits a slim young black man in a thermal jacket with a company logo stitched into the breast. Between his gloved hands, smoke rises from one of the Styrofoam cups the scene-sealers offer witnesses for shock.

'He's the one who . . . ?'

'Nined it in? Yeah, guv. He's the coffee guy.'

'What?'

'Even Starbucks isn't enough round here, apparently. Their elevenses come from London in a van.'

'Really? Thank God I stopped worrying about what the Joneses have long ago. If that's his business, the spew we brew must be a shock to him. He any use beyond . . . ?'

'Nah. Straightforward groan-and-phone. Says he does all four of these big houses. According to the local force, they were all as thick as thieves.'

'I assume that's a figure of speech rather than a character assessment?'

'Guv? Oh, yeah. The house phones and the mobiles are going off like 7/7. Same few numbers showing on ID. It's getting out.'

Kate starts putting on the overshoes that will allow her to attend the death-scenes inside the house.

'Over there,' Lorenzo says. 'Someone coming up the hill.'

'Fuck, not the hacks already.'

His younger eyes see further than hers. 'Don't think they use bikes these days.'

She joins his gaze down the icy incline. A cyclist, gender disguised by woolly hat and scarf but likely to be female from the rainbow stripes of the warm clothing, pedals up the track, until stopped by one of the native plods who have set up a cordon just before the turn where the tarpaulin covers the first dog. The cyclist – yes, now clearly a young woman – dismounts, makes protestations of horror you don't need to be a lip-reader to decipher and, wheeling the bike, begins to follow the officer towards the house.

Lorenzo's handset crackles. He listens and passes on: 'She's the live-in nanny. Says she wasn't here last night.'

'That's interesting.'

They meet her at the wagon-stop of vans, where the delivery driver still cradles his complimentary soother. Settled on another set of steps, holding a consoling cup of her own, the au pair looks up at them with a challenging blankness that is partly generational but also bewilderment at the changed circumstances of her workplace.

'What happened?' she asks. 'Is everyone okay?'

An Aussie or a Kiwi, from the interrogative accent and the almost white-blonde sculpted cut above the puppy-fatted face, pinked from cycling and fear.

'We're still trying to work it out,' Kate tells her. 'But you won't be able to go in at the moment. How long have you worked here?'

'Oh, five months, I think. Since September.'

Sip-timber. New Zealand, then.

'Why weren't you here last night?'

'Me and my friend, she nannies at one of the other houses round here, we went to London?'

'Okay. And why last night?'

'That was the night the tickets were for? *Dirty Dancing*?'

'Why did you decide to go last night? You weren't working?'

'Well, no, it was that . . .' The girl looks in the direction of the house and then snaps her head back, as if the building has caught her staring. 'The tickets were for last night.'

'Ah. And you stayed in London?'

'I slept over at hers. *Theirs*. We didn't get back until, like, one, on the last train, and they could let her have a car last night?'

Lorenzo gestures to the gleaming fleet on the gravel. 'They couldn't spare you one of these?'

'What? Look, I haven't *done* anything.'

A liquid sniff predicts tears: a teenager, 11,000 miles from home, cycling into an episode of television. Kate softens her voice: 'This isn't *questioning* or anything, not like you think. I'm sure you're not involved. But we need to know as much as we can about what's been going on here. I mean, the houses are pretty close. Cycling distance. Couldn't your friend have dropped you back here last night? Wouldn't they – the family – have needed you this morning?'

'Right. I did say that. I usually do the rugby run on Saturday, while she rides? But he was worried about the dogs?'

'Mmmm?'

'The little one especially, they go ballistic if they hear a car. Wake everybody up. He said they wouldn't need me. Let everyone get a good night's . . .' – the tears torrential now – '*sleep.*'

FOUR

HOW MUCH IS TOO MUCH?

They've arranged to meet at Paddington, between the Heathrow Express ticket machines and the croissant shop, but Simon and Tasha still haven't shown with six minutes to go on the countdown screen. Jenno's worried that Si has thrown another wobbly over going, because he's been so tight about the whole thing. But she texts Tasha *wear u X* and gets one straight back: *At the airport. S got times wrong X.* If there was a smiley face with rolling eyes, she'd send one back. Men claim women are scatty but, in their gang, it is the girls who keep the show on the road. That isn't feminism, just common sense.

Max has got the tickets and dishes them out. Emily glances at Tom and says, 'Oh, is it really worth going First Class for such a short journey?' But Jenno is glad because it feels, this Friday lunchtime, as if everyone is leaving freezing Britain. Standing all the way, ricocheting between those wardrobe-sized suitcases everyone seems to have now, would take the edge off the adventure for her.

Jonny, being Jonny, says: 'Oh, come on, Em, don't you get enough stinking working-class arses at work? This is our well-earned break, not a liberal guilt trip.'

Tom brings out his wallet and asks, 'What do we owe you?', but Max says they can sort it all out later. They'll be paying for various different things in Marrakesh and can divvy up on Sunday night.

She knows that Max, bless him, will never settle up. He's

just being sensitive to being wealthier than the rest. Like when, on the way to the Gents in a restaurant, he quietly pays for the wine at the desk so that it doesn't show on the bill that they bring. It's one of the things she loves about him.

The departure blast sounds and the late passengers do their sprint and tummy-tuck as the doors slide in towards them. Isn't it strange how much of a victory or defeat it feels to just catch or just miss a train? Presumably because so many people have too much to do, their plans shattered by a single delay.

'Right-oh. This is where we suddenly remember everything we forgot to do and bring!' says Libby.

Which begins a blizzard of texting, frustrated by intermittent dips and tunnels. As if to reduce the rudeness of conducting silent conversations with their fingers instead of speaking, every-one summarizes aloud the messages they are sending. Jenno tells Jamie not to leave his rugby kit rotting in his sports bag all weekend, but to put it in the utility-room basket, and then texts Rosie to remind her not to get the bus on Friday evening because Squeezy's mummy is picking them up and giving them tea. Emily reminds Felix that he has a driving lesson booked for Sunday and flags up to Phoebe that she needs to give Buster his eye drops, although she might have to get Felix or Henry to help hold him down if he tries to bite. Libby texts Tilly that Lucas can only have an omelette if he absolutely refuses to eat the lasagne she's left Abby to warm up for them and to remember that the blacksmith is coming to Glory on Saturday p.m.

As they usually do on trains and planes, the couples have divided by sex rather than partners. Libby would get some joke from that. Please God there won't be too much stuff in Marrakesh about how she and Jonny are working through the Kama Sutra.

They swap horse stories for a while, contrasting local vets and smiths.

'Have you noticed?' Libby asks. 'When they have their

hooves trimmed? Colonel and Scruff go after the clippings like they're canine crisps or something. What's that all about?'

'Like bones, I suppose. Something hard to chew on?' says Jenno, then sees the joke Libby is going to make and warns: 'Libs, no!'

'I wasn't going to say anything,' she lies.

Across the aisle, in their four-seat, the boys are quiet. Although a lot of that Venus and Mars malarkey is aimed at credulous Americans who think that you can run a marriage from a manual, there's definitely something in the fact that women talk to each other but men don't.

Tom is starting the latest Le Carré, which he just got at Smith's at the station, despite Emily scolding him that he had dozens of unread books at home he could have packed. Jonny, furrowing his brow and sucking a pen top, as if he's being filmed for a documentary about crosswords, is halfway through the *Telegraph* cryptic. 'It's a hard one this morning!' he says, which brings the inevitable giggle from Libby. And her Max is tapping on his laptop, the screen turned towards him, which means it must be confidential work figures. Occasionally, he frowns and sighs, although at other times he clenches his fist and smiles.

He's such a competitor, probably because of all those years of proving to his father that he was worthy of the company, although she wouldn't say that any more because he is touchy on the subject, even though the fifth Maxwell Dunster is now dead. Max still has to win at everything, which makes him a good businessman, although it also means that, when Jamie was little, she had to remind him to let his son win at football in the bottom field. From the number of times, even now, Jamie stamps in, crying, she is not sure that the advice has been taken.

Poor Max. He works too hard. She hopes he will be able to switch off this weekend.

Then Libby suddenly yelps that she also needs to remind Abby that the coffee guy is coming on Saturday morning, which introduces the topic of whether Jason from CappuccinGo might shag one of the nannies and leads to the more general subject of domestic help.

So, for the rest of the journey, they argue about the relative merits of au pairs and nannies, live-in and daily, agency-supplied or teenage daughters of friends on gap years. They discuss the village legends of the help running off with husbands and the stroppy Bosnians who insist on putting red wine in the fridge and instantly commandeer a Range Rover for going off to shag the boys from the local comp and then have to be begged to get out of bed next morning and do any work at all. They all agree that they prefer the Antipodeans because your children will grow up speaking recognizable English, give or take a couple of vowel sounds.

'You know the Commons?' says Libby. 'The inaptly named Commons, as Jonny always calls them. Their Josh is in Tilly, Phoebe and Tasha's year at Westbury Park? Reportedly, they had to pay for years of elocution lessons because their son, at ten, sounded exactly like a Kurdistani gangster.'

As they stop at Heathrow, and the doors release hundreds of people who will wake up in a different country tomorrow morning, Jenno has a quick rush of wonderment at the world they inhabit. Within their adult lives, this journey, from London to Heathrow, would have taken an hour by Underground or motorway, instead of these fifteen whizzy minutes. And they would need to have found a phone box, and jabbed useless coins in a blocked-up slot, to send these urgent instructions to their children.

Emily's BlackBerry rattles. Looking at it, she says: 'It's Tash. They're at the Costa closest to Gates 40–42.'

'Em,' says Libby. 'I keep telling you to get an iPhone. Look, have a go on mine.'

*

Fucking couples. Fucking happy couples. Fucking happy fucking couples. Increasingly, even when she's with Simon, especially when she's with Simon, Tasha feels like the only person eating alone in a restaurant on February the 14th. A difficulty widows have – she has read in books and articles – has hit her while still married. Everyone else looks so happy, casting shadows over your own state.

Well, to be fair, not everyone. This coffee shop in the departure lounge clearly has its share of unhappy marrieds: wearily disagreeing over what they want to eat and drink, whether they should go to the departure gate yet and why their partner didn't order that snack or coffee in the first place rather than eating most of theirs. The older ones look thankful for the erratic bladders that spasmodically permit them to escape the relationship.

But the problem with airports is that they contain a disproportionate number of people who are not only comfortable in each other's company but are looking forward to even more time together. She recognizes the vibes between the toned, tanned pairs around them, their legs interwined under the table as their hands cat's-cradle on top. If their eyes had subtitles, they would say: *the minute we get to the hotel.* She feels the pang of a forgotten language, like the Spanish she crammed for an exam almost thirty years ago but which survives now only in a few shaky phrases.

'Which ones have you finished with?' she asks.

Without looking up, her husband flicks a finger at the smaller of the two hillocks of newsprint in front of him. Simon says that he has to get through ten a day because of his job – these days, more than ever, banks need to judge the public mood – but she seriously wonders if it simply reduces the need to speak to her, their lives a permanent silent breakfast time, like the husbands and wives in pocket cartoons, a broadsheet dividing their table as neatly as the toast-rack. He says he's too old to get used to reading them on-line.

On his used pile are the *FT*, *Guardian* and *Sun*. The tabloid, its title chiming with their goal this weekend on the edge of Christmas, suits her mood of pre-vacation sluttishness. She is trying to decide if her easy recognition of reality TV stars is a character weakness or a strength, when Jonny Crossan's voice roars across the concourse.

'We're just deciding on a forfeit for the Lonsdales! Failed to show for the first rendezvous!'

Simon stands, smiling, shaking his head at his own idiocy: 'Sorry, Jonny, completely my fault. Thought we were meeting here. I really should listen to Tash.'

'Well, we're just jolly glad she persuaded you to come.'

'It was always tempting, Libs. And now that it's snowing here . . .'

Small-talk, but bigger than anything she ever gets from him. *This.* This is what makes her want to scream. He's a completely different person now that the other couples have arrived: wry, self-deprecating, friendly. Or is this normal? Is everyone pretending all the time?

They stand for the greetings. Natasha receives double cheek kisses from Jonny (who's sweating badly for some reason), Tom and Max, and returns them, plus air hugs, to Libby, Emily and Jenno.

There's a sudden flash-cramp in her stomach and she's about to calculate her dates when she realizes her body is anticipating what will happen at check-in.

Which it does. The Dunsters, Rutherfords and Crossans head for the empty desks at the end of the section, where staff with nothing to do except smile invitingly wait in front of lengths of blue carpet cordoned off by golden rope. Her husband is turning towards the terminal's revolving doors, the only point at which it is currently possible to join the huge, resentful queue in which he believes they belong.

The passengers who have arrived by road carry melting white flecks on their shoulders, hats or hair. She hopes that the weather, the morning's icy drizzle now thickening into bird-poo bursts of snow, won't cause delays.

'No, no, Lonsdales,' Jonny loudly scolds. 'We always turn left when we get on.'

'Well, *right*, as it's an Airbus A330-300,' corrects Tom Rutherford, who has a Big Chief I-Spy side. 'On this bird, there's nothing left of the aft doors except galley and heads. And pilots, of course. But we turn right into Business . . .'

'Seriously?' Simon has his TV interviewer face on. 'It never occurred to me. We're travelling Economy. On account of the economy. Maybe send us down a canapé in a napkin or . . .'

'Si?' He will assume Tasha's dirty phone-call voice is calculated, but it happens naturally when she's on the wrong side of him, though she wishes it didn't. 'I'm afraid I put us in with the others.'

'Did I tell you, the first time I flew Virgin Atlantic . . .' Jonny begins, but Max finishes: 'You were surprised to find the other passengers weren't in Middle and Working. That's your airport joke, Jonny.'

Libby tries to help her: 'Simon, with this lot, it's not *business* business. Not like First. They call it Scum Plus or something. It just gives you a few extra inches to play with, as the Cardinal said to the altar boy. And priority baggage, which means we might be able to whizz into town before dinner.'

Simon falls into line, his social face more or less returning, but he keeps far enough back from the others to ask quietly: 'How much did this cost us?'

She is shocked at how unexpected it feels to have him whispering in her ear.

'It was . . .' – she is schooled enough to remove the word *only* – 'a couple of hundred more. As Libby says, it's not like long-haul . . .'

'Which account did you use?'

'Er, Joint Flex, I think.' Her voice is back to normal, her last remark not a phrase that can be Marilyned. 'Look, Si, I just thought it was easier. Can you imagine Max and Jonny carrying on?'

'Yeah. Tash, we can't afford to go mad this weekend.'

'No. But let's just have a good time and relax. You've . . .'

76

'Don't tell me I deserve it because I've been working so hard.'

They know each other too well.

*

Max has always remembered a phrase, one of those famous sayings that Dunster's print at the bottom of diaries: *Who has but once dined his friends has tasted what it is to be Caesar.* He hadn't got it at first – who talked these days about *dining* their friends? – but if the chap had written *entertained* he would have understood it immediately.

Waiting for their flight to be called, he feels – no, *Caesarean* can't be the word, surely – Caeseresque, imperial, lavish. If this were a photograph in *Forbes* magazine, the caption would read: 'UK luxury gifts tycoon Max Dunster, fifty-six, at the end of another exhausting but successful week, relaxes with close friends in the Champagne Seafood Bar at London Heathrow's Terminal 3, ahead of a pre-Christmas . . .' – no, the yanks would say holiday – '. . . pre-holiday shopping trip to Marrakesh.'

The waitress – student-type, cute, he'd bet heavily on a thong and a landing strip under that skirt that must be worth its cost in extra tips – hands him a big, shiny menu and is about to pass them around, still serving the ladies first, which must be a blow to Germaine Greer, but Max says: 'Actually, I can order for us. Okay, team?'

Bloody Simon and Dr Emily give him a bit of a look but he carries on: 'Can you do the Lobster Platter Feast for eight . . . ?'

'Eight? Sure.'

'Great. And, you know what, we'll have a couple of the Salmon Trio Blinis while we're waiting for that. And is the Krug cold?'

'The . . . er . . . sir?'

'The Krug. At the bottom of where it says Champagne?'

'I can check.'

'Only if it's from the fridge. Don't use one of those bloody blood pressure things. If you haven't got the Krug chilled, come back to me and I'll rethink.'

When the pert serving wench has gone, Tasha Lonsdale says: 'What, Max, are we having a blow-out *now*? I thought Libby had booked some sort of fifteen-course restaurant for tonight?'

'The only course on the menu for Mrs Crossan is inter-course,' says Jonny and everyone groans. And, actually, although that comment is so very him, there's something not quite pukka about Crossan, just like he has been on the trains recently, slightly sweaty and his eyes darting around as if looking for someone, or more, in fact, as if someone is looking for him.

Max is clocking Jonny when Simon's voice turns him to the other side of the table: 'I'm not sure how hungry I am either right now, Maxie. We just halved an almond croissant.'

'And what would your sadist trainer say?' adds Tom Ruther-ford. 'I'm amazed he lets you eat lunch at all, let alone lobsters.'

'I'll run it off tomorrow morning,' he tells them.

Libby does her open-mouth thing: 'You're even going to go jogging in Morocco?'

'Why not? Running is a perfect way to see a country. Anyway, look, this is my treat. Tuck in and don't worry about the calories or the cost.'

'It was nothing to do with the money,' insists chippy Simon, who isn't strictly a four-by-two because his mother wasn't, but who's obviously got it in the blood.

There's a definite odour between the Lonsdales because of Tasha upgrading the tickets. Max would have offered to refund them the difference himself but her husband, as he's just shown yet again, can be such a moody bugger.

The girl comes back with two promisingly frosted bottles, but also two silver buckets of ice, so he lays a hand on the champagne to check she's not trying to fool him with lukewarm Krug.

Wiping his chilled palm on the white tablecloth, he tells her: 'That's great.'

'You're sure you want two of them?' she asks.

Is she worried that they are alcoholics or that they might default on the bill?

'My dear girl, would I have ordered them if I didn't?' he asks as sweetly as he can.

'Uh, okay. I'll get the glasses.'

While she's gone, Jenno does that frown of hers: 'You were a bit tough on her, darling. That could be Rosie in a couple of years and you wouldn't want—'

'I simply never understand,' he cuts across, 'why they ask you if you really want to buy what you've said you want to buy. The only possibilities are that you're too thick to understand what you're choosing or you don't have the money to pay for it. And no to both, frankly.'

'I'm just saying . .'

The three most lethal words in the English language. He's on the verge of doing a speech about where Dunster Manor would be if they kept pressing the customers on whether they really want the stuff, but the girl comes back, a tinkling juggler. If she drops them, there'll be a cheer, like in the school ref.

The girl pops the cork, quite efficiently, without too much cum around the rim, but when she starts to pour there's no tilt at all and so he says, as friendly as he can, to stop his wife going off on one again: 'Don't worry, love, I'll do it.'

'Oh my God!' says Tasha. 'I don't think she is your love, Max, especially now,' but then Mrs Lonsdale has always been a bit of a feminazi.

He fills eight flutes of fizz without a spill. Always a relief, because two grandparents died of Parkinson's. *With* Parkinson's, they say now.

'Toast!' he proposes, and he's going to specify 'Marrakesh' as the subject, but everyone goes off at different times like that year the National kept false-starting and had to be abandoned.

Tom: 'Cheers!'

Emily and Jenno: 'Holidays!'

Libby: 'Us!'

Tasha: 'Fun!' (Simon just smiles and lifts his glass.)

Jonny: 'Sun and sex!'

To which Jonny then adds, 'Which reminds me!', and stands up, just as their sulky server is putting the platters of blinis on the table.

'Where are you going, hun?' Libby asks him and he replies: 'Chemist goods.'

'Oh!' she squeals, and Max decodes their joke, from his history with haemorrhoids (brief) and contraception (longer).

'Poor you, Jonny!' he quips. 'Have you got arse grapes?'

'What, old boy?'

'What on earth are you on about, Max Dunster?' Tasha Lonsdale adds.

'Oh, I get it!' says Emily, with a doctor's secret smile, and then there's a lot of 'go on!' and 'you tell them!' but he decides not to explain. Even with people who have known each other for years, and are non-religious (except for Tasha) godparents to each other's kids, there are so many areas where you have to be careful with each other. Like the time in Alpe d'Huez when Libby was trilling on about how brilliant big families were and Tasha Lonsdale was suddenly like Gazza at Italia'90 because she'd bled one out that week, but no one knew. He really doesn't want to introduce bottom problems as a lunch-party subject.

Definitely something up with JC: look at how he almost runs across the departure lounge, like the airport they're in is in Beirut or somewhere hairy.

Tasha's knockers vibrate gently, pleasantly. He tries not to look as if he's looking. She finds and answers her mobile inside her jacket: 'Hello? . . . Mum? . . . what? . . . oh, on the left-hand side of the larder, second or third shelf from the top, under the tinned tomatoes, I think . . . no, just having some lunch before . . . really? . . . no, it's showing as on-time . . . tell Henry to ring me if he's iffy at bedtime . . . yeah, we will, lots of love.'

Returning her iPhone to its customized leather pouch, she

says: 'Heavy snow there, apparently. Westbury Park have cancelled the Friday-night clubs and are putting them on the buses at four.'

'Christ!' says Libby. 'I hope bloody Abby actually reads the text from the school office. I sometimes think she just vegges out in front of box sets of *Neighbours* if I'm not standing over her with one of Jonny's hunting guns.'

'*You* text her,' says Jenno, sensible and practical as ever, so Libby does.

'Is your mum looking after the kids?' Emily asks Tasha.

'Yes. And my dad. By which I mean she'll be looking after him as well, in our house. We're still rather between au pairs.'

They're already attacking the lobsters with hammers, and skewering juicy, orange-veined white flesh from the far corners of claws – eating as autopsy – when Jonny comes back, with a Boots bag he hands sideways to Libby, who puts it in her massive hold-all. After a spell when they kept their gubbins in bags the size of wallets, the girls are suddenly lugging round big, *baggy* (pun intended) things the size of plumbers' tool-kits.

Although Jenno uses a diaphragm, Max knows enough, from the spell during the breakdown of his first marriage, when he was dating chlamydia-conscious younger colleagues, to recognize, through the undiplomatically semitransparent bag, a box of condoms. It looks like the largest assortment, containing eighteen sheaths.

'Crikey! We should call you Rubber Jonny!' he mutters under his breath to JC, who gives him a big wink.

Trainspotter Tom Rutherford, who's gone to watch the planes taking off and landing, comes back to say their flight has been called for boarding.

When the bill comes, there's a bit of ritual getting out of wallets and insisting on splitting it, although note how our half-Hebrew friend, Simon, busies himself with the mints on the little silver tray they use to bring the damage.

But he insists, 'When Max Dunster says *my treat*, that's what he means.'

He briefly wonders about putting it on the Dunster Manor card, but Steve Pearson will give him more grief about blurring personal and business expenditure, so he smashes it with his private platinum. He sticks two twenties on the silver tray, so that the girl won't remember him as a dick.

*

An odd one on the walkway. While they're waiting in the suctioned tunnel to board the plane – an A330-300 is better accessed with steps from the ground, in Tom's opinion, because, as he explains to the others, it allows the use of aft and front doors, maximizing passenger flow-through – there's a cry from behind of: 'Ha! *Planes* and trains, if not yet automobiles!'

Half-getting the film reference, it takes Tom a moment to realize it's Nicky Thing, *Mortimer*, from their morning Pendolinos. It's always a bit weird, seeing someone out of context, like that shock in childhood of spotting a teacher at the shops.

And Mortimer, it now turns out, has an African wife, which Tom knows shouldn't throw him, but does, because, even nowadays, you still expect, as it were, matched pairs among their sort of people.

There's a quick round of introductions to the ladies (although it turns out they're patients of Emily's, information, of course, volunteered by the Mortimers, not his wife) but this Nicky, who moved three places forward when he saw them, squeezing down the side, is English enough to go back to his original position in the queue, which means Libby can safely say: 'I wouldn't push him off a lilo. You know him from the train, you say?'

'We often see him on the 38,' says Jonny. 'He's a sort of Fifth Beatle.'

'If we're the Fab Four,' Simon responds. 'Which of the girls is Yoko Ono?'

*

As Tom Rutherford more than once predicted over the lobsters, Business (or Superior Traveller, as this airline calls it, with a canny eye on the sort of people who weekend in Africa) on these jets is six abreast: two-two-two, separated by aisles.

So they divide neatly in the usual configurations. Across row C, Emily sits with Tasha, Libby with Jenno, and Max and Jonny pair up. In the middle seats of the otherwise empty Row D, behind Libby and Jenno, Simon, ending up alongside Tom, is suddenly struck that they have divided not just by gender but by couple. Each man is paired with the husband of the woman his wife is alongside. This relationship intrigues him: as if their socializing is guided by invisible grids.

Certainly, these arrangements work out best for their little community. Libby and Jenno often seem locked in an ostentation competition, desperate to adopt the hair-cut, four-wheel drive or coffee-maker that the other has, a game which makes his Tasha, for reasons of both temperament and budget, resentful, naturally pairing her with Emily, who, perhaps because of spending half the time with her hands up the cracks of the chavs from the Northbury tower-blocks, has a saintly way of getting on with anyone. And Max is a tribute act to Jonny, anyway, so they're a natural duet, while Tom, though he can be a bit dull, is less waistcoat-and-topper than the other two.

The child of Lancashire parents who were both the first in their families to reach university, Simon can never quite switch off his class radar. In public situations, he frequently cringes as his friends trill on about Plum something and Bramble that and Juno whatever, the names bizarrely interchangeable: which outsider could honestly distinguish between dogs, horses and children? Frequently, he wants to mouth apologies to fellow diners or passengers who, eavesdropping, are clearly fantasizing about the deaths of these pseudo-aristocratic monsters in some post-revolutionary terror.

A few of the others have a roster running for the window seats – those who don't get one going out will be compensated coming home – but Simon is happy with his middle aisle.

Though not a nervous flyer, he prefers to ignore the fragile cushion of clouds outside. Even from the centre of the cabin, he can see the snow hitting and sticking to the port-hole windows, but the plane leaves on time.

Just before they close the doors, there's a splashing and crackling on the jet's roof and wings. Jonny jumps like he's sat on a pineapple and turns and asks Tom: 'What the fuck's that? Is the fuel leaking?'

Tom explains that planes are sprayed with de-icer before flying in freezing conditions and Jonny settles, although he's opened up a tease-hole for Max: 'Never had you as a nervous flyer, Crossan. Well, make sure the sick hits the waxed bag, not me, do you hear?'

Once the plane levels and the little seat-belt picture blinks and pings off, Simon stretches for his laptop and asks Tom: 'You're not bothered if I do a bit of tapping?'

'No. Not at all. I think I'll do the same. I've brought my little history along.'

*

The stewardesses are calling it Prosecco, though Jenno would be interested to see the bottle. It has the hard, gassy taste of supermarket Cava, but she doesn't make a scene, just in case it's the altitude. Max has said that you might as well serve Fanta on an aeroplane because wine wasn't meant to be drunk in the sky.

'We've always known Scruff was bright,' Libby is saying. 'But, even so, the other day, he just amazed me with his vocabulary. What we do in our family is spell it out: W-A-L-K. So Colonel and Scruff don't go completely bonkers if nobody's up for taking them. But, now Scruff, bless him, actually recognizes the letters. What was that someone said about the B of the Bang? When we get to the W of Walk, he's at the door looking like Jonny on a promise. I sometimes think I'm denying a blind person the most marvellous guide dog. So we've had to start saying it in French: *marche*. Luckily, Plum's doing Spanish, so we've got the next one lined up – *paseo* – for when Scruff gets the hang of the frog one . . .'

God forgive her, but Jenno tunes out of the next bit – something about Hugo's interviews for uni – and is enjoying the little tickle of the fake champagne bubbles bursting against the top of her mouth when she realizes the conversation has stopped. She always feels obliged to fill the silence: 'Have you seen how many bank holidays there are at Christmas this year? There's nothing worse than Christmas and New Year falling at weekends . . .'

'I absolutely agree,' says Libby. 'For some reason, I feel uneasy when the shops are shut. Even knowing there's a 24-hour M&S Simply Food at the petrol station helps me. Just if one is suddenly completely out of crème fraiche or something.'

'Discussing Schopenhauer?' butts in Simon Lonsdale from behind. 'Ah, no, shopping hours!'

Sometimes, when they're all together, it worries Jenno that they're simply talking nonsense to fill time, like some sort of sponsored yap. But, now, she has something she is burning to say. Conscious that Simon Lonsdale is listening, she whispers: 'Libs, do you think that Yoko joke was aimed at me?'

'The whatto, honey?'

'The Beatles thing and Simon saying one of the wives must be Yoko? That would have to be me . . ,'

'Really? Are you a tone-deaf Jap conceptual—?'

'Ssssh, Libs. They may be some on the plane . . .'

'Unlikely. Oh, the Jap bit. Do you believe sleeping in late will achieve world peace, Jen?'

'The point is, I'm the only second wife here. Wasn't he, in his Simonish way, saying that I've broken up the group?'

Although she sometimes feels smug about being younger than the others, Jenno also worries that she doesn't really fit. Starting primary school when the others were at university, she spoils the symmetry of their set. It doesn't help that she only has two children to the three or four of the others. Probably only she remembers the babies she lost.

'Oh, darling,' Libby reassures her. 'Simon's just a bit chippy. It's a Northern thing, I always think. But we hardly even remember the first Mrs Max. Hilary or whoever. They weren't together long. To be perfectly honest, she was a bit uptight. You've been the making of him. Cheers!'

Libby wafts her glass hopefully at the stewardess.

*

Sleeping with his mouth hanging open, Jonny oozes drool onto the fat knot of his Garrick Club tie. With the seat reclined, he has the small man's luck of being able to lie almost horizontally. Garlicky gusts of breath – or at least Max hopes they come from the lungs – occasionally float through the chill recycled airline air.

Max is doubly happy for his neighbour's coma, both because Jonny looks so knackered these days and because it means he can attend to his work without interruption or suspicion.

Flipping open his MacBook Pro at 33,000 feet, he again has the sensation of being filmed for a documentary about his business success. *While colleagues catch up on sleep, Dunster uses the time constructively . . .*

He clicks the Management icon and opens the email folder.

A voice from behind: 'Gates, Branson, Buffet – when you read their books, they always have regrets about the time they can't get back. I haven't read Sugar's . . .'

Turning to see Nicky Mortimer, stopping on the way to the bogs, Max makes a quizzical face.

'Seeing you hunched over that laptop, give yourself a break.' Mortimer has lowered his voice from respect for the flat-out passenger. 'Take a tip from your resting friend – Jonny, is it? – we all need downtime. Monifa made me switch off my crackberry as soon as we got in the taxi. I'm allowed to check for messages once each night before dinner.'

'Yeah? Jen and I have philosophical disputes about whether the plane counts as the holiday.'

In conversation with strangers, he always calls his wife Jen rather than Jenno, the latter necessitating a long conversation about why she styles herself so differently from other Jennifers.

With Mortimer finally out of the way behind the white plastic door, Max feels safe to left-click the first message.

The board is very unhappy with your performance and demands an urgent meeting.

*

Although the flight attendants keep hovering with bottles, Emily has one glass of fizz and then sticks to water. Her professional knowledge of in-flight dehydration plays a part in this decision, but there is another medical imperative as well. Several times in her career, she has answered the nervous-sounding announcement for a doctor on board – one birth, one death, two emergency diversions to the nearest airport – and so, on planes, she always feels curiously on-duty.

She explains this to Natasha, who has taken her sobriety as a moral example.

'No, no, not at all, Tash. You get stuck in. It's just that, if I had to go into action, the implications of being tiddly don't bear thinking about.'

Feeling freed from disapproval, Tasha drinks deeply from her bubbling plastic beaker, and asks: 'You know when they ask for a doctor . . . ?'

'Mmmm?'

'Is there, like, a badge you have to show?'

'Oh. No, well, we have an NHS card. And, actually, the PCT sent out a sort of shield you can stick on your windscreen at an accident. But the local police tend to know you and, on planes and in the theatre that once, I've never been asked for one . . .'

'Really? So anyone could pretend to be a doctor . . . ?'

'In theory, yes, I suppose so. It does happen: there was a case in the Tube bombings, I think. Why? Are you worried I'm an imposter?'

'What? *No.* I just always wonder what it must be like to

87

know stuff . . .' Tasha's speech is already slushy, from the flight attendants' frequent refills. 'To actually be qualified to do something . . .'

'Don't be silly, Tasha, you run a very successful catering company.'

'Do I? People seem to have stopped eating . . .'

'I don't think so. You should see some of our patients. You know Surinder?'

'Is that Dr Rafi in Eastbury?'

'Mmm. He says he wants to have a weigh-bridge at the entrance to his Medical Centre. Above a certain BMI, you drop into a moat.'

'There you are. You've got all that jargon: BMI. Toasted pine-nuts just isn't the same. There isn't a National Quiche Service. I don't get a badge to put on my car. I wish I had a proper job!'

Something in the tone, even allowing for the contribution of the two thirds of a bottle she must have put away, twitches the tuning fork Emily can never quite still: 'Tasha?'

'Yesh?'

'If you were properly depressed, you'd come and see me, wouldn't you?'

'What? Oh, no, I'm fine. Oh, Em . . .' Her arm is rubbed by Tasha, in that way she has, always the most tactile of the four of them. 'It must be awful knowing so much about what goes wrong with people . . .'

'If this is the one again about which of the men in the village are on Viagra, you know I'm not allowed to tell you . . .' She's already gone further than she should. 'Which isn't to say that any necessarily are.'

'I think Simon could do with a packet.'

Emily lets it go, as the standard banter of a long marriage. It is always difficult when her friends do this. When does ordinary girl-talk disguise a cry for help? Sometimes, at dinner or the cinema, she notices someone rubbing a blemish on their face or arms so pointedly that she conducts a quick skin-cancer clinic for them, then and there. But Simon is a blank to her medically; in twelve years, she has never seen him professionally, which isn't unusual for middle-aged men. Emily still secretly believes she could have saved Bill Adamson, if he hadn't spent six months ignoring that lump when he was shaving. Jonny and Libby are on Surinder's list, which they say is to avoid social embarrassment, but probably means they go private. Same with Max, who intermittently mentions appointments in London, but never reveals the details.

'It must be such a, no pun intended, pain,' Tasha continues, 'being able to see what everyone's got . . .'

'Oh, no. We switch off. One of my professors was very good on that. Actually gave a lecture on when to stop being a doctor. If you think someone's having a heart attack, say something. But, he said, for your friends, it shouldn't be like smoking dope with a chief constable in the room . . .'

This liberates Tasha to take another big slurp, some of which sprays out as she goes on: 'And knowing everything that's going wrong with yourself? That must be odd. I mean, we civilians think: I've got a throbbing ache above my left kidney . . .'

Emily can't stop herself asking: 'Have you?'

'No. It's an example. What I mean is that most of us won't even know it's the kidney. But you'll know the Latin for what you've got and how bad it is . . .'

'Well, you say that. Actually, the research shows that doctors present very late. Later even than middle-aged men, who are otherwise the worst. The theory is that they worry about seem-ing weak in the eyes of their patients or other doctors. There's actually a hush-hush surgery in London, only for GPs, with a back entrance so they won't be seen going in. No, you see, what I think is that an ordinary patient, they get a pain or a lump, they immediately assume it's cancer, which is why they eventually come to see you. And, usually, you tell them it's one of a hun-dred other things. But a doctor already knows the other hundred things it could be, so it's easy to put off seeing someone.'

Tasha's eyes are set at polite, so she stops. For all the talk about being able to close the surgery door firmly behind her, Emily often sees in conversations the possibility of consultations: 'Reassure me: Simon checks his testicles and everything . . .'

'He seems to find it quite hard to leave them alone sometimes.'

'Tasha!'

Discussions on aeroplanes, unlike those on phones or in the street, lack easy opportunities to say: 'I must get on.' Emily, feeling like the swot she has so often in her life been called, opens her *Rough Guide* to Marrakesh, checking the index for the Covered Souk she saw in the film on the Discovery Channel.

Libby, a little squiffily, is pressing buttons on her iPhone.

'You won't get reception up here, will you?' Emily asks across the aisle.

'No. It's just so I have my Tweets ready to go when we land.'

*

The board has not sacked Max, but warns him that the supporters expect promotion this season. So, although his natural instinct is to attack, with wing-backs and wingers both overlapping, he switches to 4–5–1 away at Macclesfield and manages to bring in on loan from Perth Glory a central defensive midfielder called Ellory Rudkin (he's playing the 2018 season now, so the players are mainly made up) with stats of 19 for tackling, and 20 for heading and fitness.

After four minutes, Zola heads in a free kick from Harris. But, five minutes into the second period, the debutant Rudkin is given a straight red for a two-footed lunge on one of the Silkmen's midfielders. Then the home team's sub scores with a twenty-five-yarder, two minutes into stoppage time.

'Fuck fucking Macclesfield!' he complains, louder than he intended, just as Jonny wakes up, saying, with a gunge-tongued after-sleep slur: 'No, no! *Marrakesh*, I told the pilot. Don't they have satnav? What is it, Dunster? Have you been let down on an order from the stinking North?'

'Something like that,' Max replies, clipping the laptop shut –

what sensual beauty Apple stuff has, technology as sex – before his travelling companion sees it.

*

The scents of flowers and vegetation, pungent enough to overcome the kerosene stench belching across the runways from their cooling jet, make Simon glad that he took his antihistamine pill with the last glass of wine on the flight. A white canopy juts above the entrance to the terminal, but there are so many fugitives from the British winter that its shade isn't even enough to cover all those who had paid for the privilege of leaving first, past the resentful inspection of the passengers in the cheaper seats, whose exit was blocked by the stewardesses, sorry flight attendants, standing there like London Fashion Week's idea of riot cops. He wanted to mouth: it wasn't my idea.

It's mainly couples in the passport queue. Just in front, Nicky Mortimer and his wife stand hand in hand, an affectation which, in the middle-aged, seems to him as uncomfortable as your parents kissing. The Eight, though, remain in their buddy pairs from the plane. Desperate for something to say to Tom, Simon looks around.

A single, sleepy-looking soldier stands guard on the tarmac, so youthful and slight that the automatic weapon at his hip looks too big for him, like a boy carrying his dad's cricket bat.

'Safe sort of place, Tom?' he asks.

Jonny, overhearing and turning round, answers first: 'I checked the FO advice site. It's fine.'

But security consultants, like plumbers and dentists, always have to question the decisions of others in the profession, and Tom says: 'Monarchy with a secular semi-democracy, so it's an obvious target for AQ to try to radicalize. But it's in the interests of the government to keep it safe for tourists. Though that was true in Egypt and Bali as well, of course, and . . .'

'Thanks, Rutherford,' Jonny booms, characteristically monopolizing a conversation that wasn't even his. 'Trust you to be the bloody albatross on the boat.'

His bald patch already feeling like a burger on a barbecue, Simon pats the hot tonsure with Factor 50+ from the tube in his pocket. He should have packed his hat in his hand luggage.

The girls' BlackBerries and iPhones, finding and joining the local network, start bleeping. Escape and isolation, the original aims of travel, have been killed by their generation's desperation for connection.

'Oooh, Libs,' exclaims Jenno. 'It's from you to say you've arrived.'

Almost simultaneously, Tash and Emily click and scroll as well, and near-harmonize: 'Got it!'

'Why are you looking at me like that, Simon?' Libby challenges him.

'What? I, er, just can't quite see why you're texting the others to say you're here? I mean, surely even the more inattentive of them would know that?'

'But I didn't text them. I Tweeted I was here and they follow me. Duh!'

Libby is one of those people who seize on popular speech mannerisms but then continue to use them after the herd has moved on to another word; only recently has his sustained sarcastic assault stopped her adding an ironic 'not!' to positive statements.

'How many followers do you have?' Simon asks her; a question once restricted to political and religious leaders but now democratized by technology.

'You know what? It's going jolly well.'

Even as she speaks to him, Libby is tapping at the small keyboard and, before they have all shuffled closer to admission to the country, the other three women are summoned to their phones again.

'You're right. The palm trees are amazing,' his Tasha says.

Simon leans across and lifts the rectangle from hands which move too late to stop him.

@libbycrossan. Anything worse than waiting in airport line? Only time I'll be an immigrant lol

'I agree the trees are nice but what's so funny about them?' he asks.

'Bit of a *duh* day you're having, Si. Who said they were funny?'

'Lol means laugh out loud.'

'No way, Jose. It means lots of love.'

'Much as it pains me to say this, I fear the Simonator may be right,' Jonny advises his wife. 'Remember in the papers—'

But he is interrupted. There's a bit of pantomime 'oh no – yes it does – doesn't' before Libby declares: 'You know what? We don't care what it means to other people. This is what it means to us.'

Soon, ceiling and desk fans in the security hutch flutter the pages of their passports as two immaculately uniformed soldiers briefly consider then accede to Her Britannic Majesty's Secretary of State's request that they may pass freely without let or hindrance (bored at airports, Simon always enjoys the ancient diplomatic language in his hand) and be afforded such assistance and protection as may be necessary in Morocco.

*

They need two taxis – both bright white Mercs – which drive in convoy to the city. Tom is in the lead vehicle, with Max, who's claimed the front seat because of his height, which leaves Tom wedged against the door in the back, straining to stop his thighs touching Jenno Dunster, who has volunteered for the middle, claiming she's smaller than Emily, which, even allowing for spousal loyalty, he'd like to see tested in a court of law.

The roads remind him of India, resembling a moped race into which vying lines of cars and animals have strayed after taking a wrong turn. In size and sheen, though definitely not speed, their transport has the feel of a presidential motorcade.

'That smell?' Max asks the car at large. 'I mean, behind the bike fart. Camel shit?'

'Yes. Probably quite a lot of donkey dung as well,' Tom tells him. 'For all the cars there are, the *cart* holds its own here.'

Soon they see the red curve of the city wall and drive through a gate into narrow streets which slow the procession of wheels and hooves to a crawl.

Emily, with that head-girl earnestness he has always loved in her, reads aloud from one of the three guidebooks in her bag: 'Many of the houses are built from bricks of local mud mixed with straw. The thick walls absorb heat to keep the rooms cool in summer and warm in winter . . .'

The words start to blur and soon it's like the radio being on in another room, but he feels a pleasure at being here with her. They are lucky to be able to fly to the sun on a winter's day and he thinks it is important to acknowledge that fortune.

He tries to speak this idea out loud but it comes out more vicarish than he intended, and, though Emily supports him ('Really lucky, yes!'), Max is typically dismissive of what he would see as liberal soppiness: 'Not as if it's a handout from anyone. We work bloody hard for it.'

Max likes to tell people that he can't believe Tom was ever really in the army; must have been drummed out for reading the *Guardian*.

Through the tinted window, the exotic – intricately carved arches and canopied balconies – alternates with the international Esperanto of red-and-white no-entry signs and the logos of mobile-phone companies.

The streets become quieter, which must mean more expensive, and, when their cars come to a stop, there are no other vehicles in view.

The *riad* holds no surprises after his virtual tour online, although the simple studded wooden entrance from the street – presumably an attempt to disguise the site from beggars, burglars and terrorists – belies the luxury inside.

A small swimming pool is set into the shining tiled floor of a large central courtyard, overlooked on all four sides by three balconied levels supported by pillars. The regularly spaced aged-oak doors, he guesses, are the bedrooms.

A young black boy, in white linen tunic and tasselled fez,

bows deeply in greeting and suggests through semaphore that they should follow him past the pool. Tom senses Emily's unease at this display of subservience: in Bangkok, once, she boycotted the hotel restaurant because the staff served the courses while more or less prostrate on the floor.

Through an arch, on which Max inevitably smacks his scalp, they reach a room of bamboo-frame chairs and sofas, with over-stuffed cushions in dazzling fabrics, where their guide points to the furniture and has left the room almost as soon as they sit down. There aren't quite enough seats – most of the business will be couples, he suspects, rather than parties of eight – and so Libby sits on Jonny's knee.

'Ooh-er,' she says, 'where's he gone? Is this where they sell us into the white slave trade?'

'The tiles in the lobby?' wonders Jenno. 'Do you think they'd sell them in the souk? They're exactly what I wanted for our pool house but couldn't find anywhere at home.'

A different African – of such height that he has to stoop into the room to avoid Max's fate – comes in. On a Manila folder, from which edges of pink paper peep, he balances four old-fashioned hotel keys, the big shiny kind that open secret doors in children's stories, attached to wooden cylinders that could be pepper-pots. The young boy follows, carrying a tray of steaming thimble glasses of mint tea. Everyone glances discreetly at Emily for dysentery advice. She feels the heat of the glass between finger and thumb, nods and takes a sip.

'A refreshing drink to welcome you please to Marrakesh and our traditional *riad* at your disposal,' explains their host.

None of the surnames – Dunster, Crossan, Rutherford, Lonsdale – falls easily on the local ear but, after a certain amount of confusion, they are eventually directed to their quarters.

Max stands and, curved against the low ceiling, looks at his watch. Instinctively, like a gang in a heist film, they all mimic his action.

'It's just after five local time, Our host has made a booking at a restaurant for 8.30 . . .'

'Very good place,' the hotel owner asserts. 'The best.'

'So if we can meet down here at eight. Free time until then, I guess . . .'

'I know what Mrs Crossan and I will be doing,' Jonny announces.

'I'm sure that won't take you three hours,' Simon replies, that needle between them always there.

In one of those many middle-aged moments that would astonish his adolescent self, Tom wonders if he can be bothered to have sex this weekend.

*

Men, Jenno thinks, are simple creatures. She doesn't mean that in a particularly patronizing way, just that they are less complicated machines than women. She sees it in their kids. Even allowing for the fact that Rosie, at fourteen, is limbering up for spots and stroppiness, and Jamie, at eleven, still has enough of the sweetness and missing teeth for her to go on pretending he's her little boy, their attitudes to life are completely different.

Their daughter's homework is completed immaculately and on time and shown to them for approval; their son's rushed off between games of football on television or in the garden and never discussed with his parents until he has to admit that the failure to complete an assignment is the cause of a Saturday-morning detention. Jamie needs to be forced to wash his hair once a week, and sometimes merely pretends he has; Rosie's en suite shower-room is lined with bottles of shampoos, conditioner and body-rinse, used in a complex daily and weekly sequence. Their firstborn has flirted with her father and other men since she was four (if Jenno ever says no to Rosie having anything, she just goes and blags it from her dad), while her brother is still at the stage of thinking girls are silly and smelly, although, as Maxie says, in a couple of years, he'd die for a smile from one of them.

Is this social or parental conditioning or simply that oestrogen and testosterone are such different drugs to be under?

Anyway, Jenno's theory is that most of the problems between men and women are caused by sexual tension. The right to make love with each other is what makes you a couple and so, if you don't, you aren't. Yucky though it is to think it, she always feels Mummy and Daddy still have that twinkle. And Max doesn't talk much about his first marriage, but she'd bet all their offshore investments on the fact that he and Hilary had stopped doing it.

Men expect sex regularly and particularly if they haven't seen you for a while – when the kids were younger and Max came back from a business trip, she'd just lock the bedroom or sometimes the bathroom door and get it over with – or if they find themselves alone with you in a hotel room and the children far away.

She's enough of a feminist to know that this approach can be seen as giving in to terrorism but it's not as if she's lying back and thinking of England. She likes sex and she likes sex with Max. It's uncomplicated.

So, in room 12 of the *riad* in Marrakesh, Jenno kisses her husband as soon as they have dropped their bags on the rack. Their lips meet so strongly that it almost stings.

'Wow. What's that for?'

'Who says there has to be a for?'

*

Even though they're only here for two nights, Emily can't abide living out of a suitcase or, more accurately, holdall. Room 18, in the corner of the second floor, has a nicely sized wardrobe and she quickly stacks or hangs the clothes that she has chosen to cover the various possible types of weather – although her guidebooks agree that December promises highs of 19, which is 66 in old money, and lows of 7, or 45 as they were taught in her day – and the mixture of daytime sightseeing and evening restaurants which, knowing Max, won't be come-as-you-are.

Despite having wrapped it in tissue paper and a plastic holder from the dry cleaners, her red cotton Whistles dress has a bag-crease just below the waist, so she hangs it in the bath-room, where the steam from their showers should help: a trick her mother told her at least thirty years before, one of the little bits of wisdom that outlive us. One day soon she will hand it down to Phoebe.

With an efficiency that pleases her, Emily, when she carries in the dress, thinks to bring her toilet bag, so she can lay out her brush, toothpaste, floss and moisturizer. There are double side-by-side sinks, as in most upmarket bathrooms these days, each with its own cabinet, which would hold her mini-medi-kit, but probably best to keep that out. She's brought adrenaline in case of allergic reactions and broad-spectrum antibiotics. One of them is bound to get the squits. She wonders if Jonny hasn't got a bug already, he was so pale and sweaty on the plane, although he seemed to perk up once they were here.

Tom is sitting at the table in their room, having pushed aside the cellophane-wrapped complimentary fruit bowl to clear space for his laptop.

'Do you want to unpack your stuff?' she asks him.

'What? You know I don't do those sorts of questions.'

Years ago, when they were past love's young blush, Tom had begun to bridle at that turn of phrase from her: he complained that '*do you want to?*' meant '*I want you to but you probably don't.*'

'Okay. Do you want *me* to unpack your stuff?'

'Better. Well, okay, if you really want to?'

She fits his slacks and shirts and jackets into the gaps she's left for him in the cupboards and drawers, then places her hairbrush and the paperback she's brought – *Mister Pip*, for this month's book club – on the table at the right side of the bed, which will be, by three decades' understanding, hers. Then she lies down.

Her sigh of relaxation – an audible *oooomph*, another help-less inheritance from our parents as we get older, it seems – makes Tom turn round.

'Are you doing your Middlebury?' she asks.

'Yep.'

Men and their conversation.

'Which bit?'

'Close to home. Literally. The four houses. I can't decide whether to write about us.'

'*Us?*'

'The people who live in them now. I thought I might do it by professions: from farmers and estate staff to . . . whatever. I keep meaning to walk round the churchyard . . .'

'Lot of my patients there. Say hello for me. Why?'

'Find out how many of the earlier tenants of the houses are buried there. I keep wondering.'

A silence. He adjusts his spectacles and stares at his hand-written notes: theatrically, in the way of those who know they're being watched.

'What am I reading?' she says.

'What?'

'*What am I reading?*'

'Oh, I see. I thought we'd had an Alzheimer's moment there. What are you reading, darling?'

This bickering, forcing talk out of him, is basically tender, she thinks. Not like the strain there sometimes is between, say, Simon and Natasha, when you just know it will be shouting or silence when they get home. God forgive her, but she often half-waits for Tasha to turn up at the surgery with a fifteenth-round eye, saying the car door caught her.

Emily tells him about the novel and, though she knows he couldn't have passed even one of these easy GCSEs they have now, he makes a good show of listening. Then Tom, at the desk, writes; she, on the bed, reads.

*

Whether through computerized lottery or human design (some Moroccan concept of privacy), the couples have been placed at the four corners of the second storey, with whole corridors between them. Tasha is pleased because there's no risk of hearing Libby hollering, like that time in Alpe d'Huez. 'The Hallescrewedya Chorus,' they all called it.

As soon as they're in the room, Tasha has a shower. She always feels stale and sticky after flights, and is disappointed to find that Superior Traveller makes no difference to this. As she begins to run the water, Simon walks in and, as if they are foreigners reliant on sign language, points towards the porcelain. She leaves the bathroom. He reaches back to close the door.

She hears him trying to do a poo that seems to be mainly wind and is worried by how disgusted she feels. When you start seeing someone's body as charnel rather than carnal, then love has gone. Tash had known it was over with Alastair – her longest-running bloke before Simon – when she suddenly noticed one evening the loud and spitty way he chewed his food.

Her husband comes back. Since they took occupation of room 22, they have not spoken a word to each other, which is depressingly normal. His only conversation with her is in front of others. Returning to the bathroom, she braces herself for a smell, fearing she will retch if there is, but is hit by nothing stronger than the bowl of potpourri between the basins.

Soaping herself under the impeccably hot and strong water (the main point of hotels is a power of shower impossible at home), Tash finalizes her plan. Since she was twelve – so thirty-six years ago, making her four times her age then, how terrifying these sums become – she has devotedly read the problem pages in newspapers and magazines.

At the beginning, she always consulted the horoscopes as well, secretly believing for some years that they were God's way of speaking to her, but that addiction lapsed after settling with Simon, when it became inconvenient to be told that you would be meeting the love of your life around the 16th of the month, even though the cannier magazines expanded their market by offering alternative predictions for readers in relationships and for those who weren't.

Even as an engaged and then married woman, however, she

has continued to check the confessions, especially those so intimate or painful that they have to be kept anonymous ('name
and address withheld'), to which a professional counsellor
('Zelda reads all your letters but regrets that she cannot reply
to unpublished correspondence personally') or female journalist
with a kind face and wise style replies.

I'm having an affair with my boss at work. I'm having
sexual feelings for my cousin. I don't think I love my husband
any more. My dad comes into my room when mum is on night
shifts. My husband and I no longer have sex. He's a good man
and father but I've never felt anything in bed with him. My
boyfriend keeps pressuring me for oral sex but I don't know
what to do. I don't think my husband loves me any more. I was
paying a bill on our computer when I discovered my husband
had been looking at porn sites.

*My husband and I no longer have sex. I don't think I love
my husband any more.* To the latter dilemma, one of the
emotional specialists recently offered advice that Tasha found
fascinating. Many human problems, the relationship maven
stated, are based in the mind, but the mind can be trained.
An actor or sports performer who becomes too frightened
to function can be taught, through behavioural therapy and
'visualization', to see the stage or the pitch as a place of victory
and fulfilment. In the same way, the agony aunt argues, it's
possible to think your way back into love with someone. Just
remember the feelings you used to have and tell yourself that
you still have them. Experiments have shown, the sage claims,
that people who imagine themselves exercising can lose weight.
It's easy to think that the mind controls us, but we control the
mind.

Tasha can see that this is just a twist on positive thinking
but, as she soaps and washes the parts that her husband hasn't
touched for (let's see, Alpe d'Huez would probably have been
the last time) at least a year and a half, it seems as good an
option as any other. Even during the silent horror movie of the
last year, she has been determined to keep her marriage going

until Polly, Josh and Henry are well out of the nest and, if truth is told, until her mother is dead: she can't bear the thought of admitting defeat to her.

So, when she leaves the bathroom, she will be, in her mind, on her honeymoon. She thinks of walking out naked, which has reliably kick-started him in the past, but the humiliation would be too great if the tactic failed. So she will enter in her fluffy white bathrobe. She will seduce him and shag him. The un-opened box of Pleasure Me is in the bedside drawer at home but she's forty-eight, for Christ's sake.

When she makes her dramatic entrance, Simon doesn't even look up. As usual, he's hunched over, fingers sliding, technology making everyone a pianist these days. But this one twisted over to hide what he's playing. He's even sitting at the edge of the table, rather than in the middle, where the chair was, with the screen turned away from the room.

A suspicion, stupidly slow, dislodges the positive thoughts in her mind: *I discovered my husband had been looking at porn sites.*

*

No sooner are they through the door than Jonny grabs for her bag and gets out the big box of thingies, which he stands on the bedside table like a skyscraper. He seemed a bit quiet, for him, at the airport and on the flight and she worried that it was going to be one of those holidays when he's so zonked from a trial that he spends the whole time sleeping it off, but he seems perky enough now, standing with his legs wide, so she can see the front of his trousers bulging, and his arms stretched out.

'Come here, my big African mama.'

He uses a cod black accent, which she's glad he's had the sense not to try in front of Simon or, in fact, the locals. As she moves towards him, his hand goes straight for her fanny, but, from long practice, she intercepts his fingers with hers and arranges their bodies into an embrace. In his kiss, she can taste the wine and roast almonds from the plane.

'Is it okay if I just clean my teeth?' she asks, hoping he'll take the hint as well.

'Have to? I'll take you as you are.'

His voice is muffled by sucking on one of her boobs through smock-top and bra.

'Can I, Jonny? Please?'

Disentwining, she grabs her wash-bag and manages to pee and be mostly done with the tooth-brushing before he walks in, now wearing only his boxer shorts, distorted by his stiffie. Libby has already dropped her skirt on the floor but Jonny pulls her knicks down from behind as she rinses and spits.

'Do you think the others are doing this?' he says in that throaty voice he always has when he wants it.

'I've no idea. It's not a competition, is it?'

'My bet is that Tom and Dr Em stopped years ago. With a doctor, at our age, you'd worry she was checking out your prostate. I never know about Tash and Simon but she always looks so uptight. Max and Jenno will be at it like rabbits on Viagra but, then, she's so much younger . . .'

'Thanks!'

She lifts her arms so that he can pull her top off, as he likes to.

'As Mummy always says, other people's marriages are a mystery.'

'Ooh, don't mention your mother, darling. You know it turns me on.'

Libby hits him playfully. And, although she sometimes worries what their marriage would become if she had a prolapse or even if the change is as bad for her as people say it can be, she feels the enjoyment of being wanted and of wanting him. She had always assumed, from novels and friends, that Jonny would stop fancying her one day, but it doesn't seem to have happened.

He's wearing one of his pairs of comedy boxers: Wallace and Gromit, smiling either side of the fly, oblivious to the unexpected protrusion now dividing them.

'Mrs Crossan, *please*,' he pleads.

Stooping to disrobe him, she hopes her back is up to it.

*

There have to be more ways of saying *four*. Tom calls up the thesaurus on his laptop but there's no entry for the problematic number, which confirms his fear that *quartet* and its variants – *quadrangular* and so on – are the only options. He goes back to the paragraph that stalled him:

> Among the most striking architectural features of Middlebury – mentioned in the histories of the county by both Arthur Mee (Hodder & Stoughton, 1945) and Nikolaus Pevsner (Penguin, 1961) – are the four almost-identical winged sandstone houses which stand on a . . .

Yes, it has to be quartet here.

> . . . a quartet of hills in the traditionally agricultural north-east corner of Middlebury, still called Cold Cotham, the name of the original mediaeval village on this site, although this name now survives only on a single signpost, dating from circa the 1940s. The houses are arranged in an almost formal clock or compass formation, standing within a circle in positions comparable to N, E, S, W or 12, 3, 6, 9.

Behind him, he hears a sudden snuffle–snort from Emily and knows what it will mean. The soundtracks of our families become as recognizable as favourite music. And a glance over his shoulder confirms that she is asleep. Her reading glasses skewed across her face, she looks like someone flattened by a punch. Poor Em. She generally does Mondays and Thursdays at the overnight service and this week covered Wednesday as well for Dr Rafi, who's skiing. If she's lucky, she'll have had a couple of hours kip on the callout centre put-up.

As he gently lifts the glasses clear of her face, she twitches, her vestigial cave-dweller's defence against predators, but he touches her hair and she settles again. He covers her with the embroidered coverlet and, lifting her paperback from the floor where it fell, saves the page with a bookmark.

Although the regular snoring suggests she's a long way under, he types more gently:

> This quadrangle of handsome Regency residences originally, in common with large areas of this part of Bucks, belonged to the estate created, at the turn of the eighteenth century, by Arthur George, fourth Duke of Grenville (1757–1841). Believed to have been built originally for occupation by relatives and trusted associates, they subsequently housed gentleman farmers and some descendants of the Grenville family, before passing into private hands in 1921, during the second of a series of sales of estate land and property, required to meet death duties due after the death of the seventh Duke.

He changes *parts* to *stretches* to avoid a repetition in the opening sentence, removes the first *death* for the same reason, then pauses because he has, as it were, bumped into himself, reaching the sentence that has already been much debated, with many suggestions offered, mainly satirically, during dinner parties attended by their octet.

> During most of the twentieth century, the Grenville Four, as the homes are locally known, remained working farms, with the south-facing house being owned for decades by Lord Crossan of Middlebury, who, as Timothy Crossan, served in the cabinets of Margaret Thatcher and John Major as Secretary of State first for Education and then National Heritage. The politician subsequently sold the house to his son, Jonathan Crossan QC, and so, at the time of writing, these imposing but elegant addresses, created for the cronies of an eighteenth-century landowner, now contain a rich variety of types and professions: a barrister and his JP wife; the CEO of a local luxury-gifts manufacturer and his wife; the Director of Public Relations for a leading bank and his wife, who runs a private catering

business; and a GP, a partner in Westbury's biggest medical centre, and her husband, who runs a private-security and risk-assessment business.

This reference to his own occupation will become ironic (he hesitates because the lexicographical columnist in *The Times* has recently addressed the misuse of that word) if any of the houses is burgled as a result of this pamphlet. Jonny has already taken to calling Tom's project 'the gangster's satnav.'

*

Many men of his age, he has read on the health pages, have trouble getting it up. But those guys must be smokers or married to porkers because Max has never been let down on parade. Just the sight of her walking naked from the bathroom, the flash of that black thatch, leave Brazilians to Brazil, and he's steely as a teenager. He pulls aside the sheet to show her: a magician-and-rabbit thing that goes back to the first time in the hotel at the Cheltenham conference. But he can't do that at home now, where they always have to fuck under the duvet in case of the kids walking in.

'Oooh. Hello, my old friend,' Jenno says, a regular line too.

'Not so much with the old, young lady.'

After fifteen years of sex, minus a couple of months either side of each child, the moves are well-rehearsed, but still work. She straddles him, leaning forward to kiss deeply while she hovers delicately above his cock, the still-thrilling sense of two mouths opening at once. Max grabs her hips and tries to pull her down but she resists. Knowing what she wants next, he gently licks her nipples, which she calls her launch buttons. Immediately, he feels her wetness, thinner and slicker than the spermicide she uses with the cap, and she lowers herself slowly until he is fully enclosed.

The best part always for him is this first moment of slippery admission, the privilege of being let in, where other men aren't. She bucks with a muscularity which would have finished off an early-shooter but Max is in total control of his body and hers. He pauses in the taut warmth before he begins to match her rhythm and make her come for the first time.

*

The idea of child-proof contraceptives is pretty bloody funny if you think about it, but Jonny at this moment fondly wishes he'd removed the shrink-wrap on the box before they started. He struggles to find the little rip-strip on the box.

Buying time his Walter really doesn't want to give him, he says to Libs: 'I'm afraid, darling, there are eighteen of them and it isn't sale-or-return. So you could have a busy weekend.'

'Are there always that many?'

'Good question. I don't think so. But everything's two for the price of three or 25 per cent extra free these days. The Great Depression, I know. And even I feel guilty about actually telling these shopkeepers that one doesn't need discounts. I suppose eighteen is a sort of family pack. As it were.'

The type he buys is pastel pink and printed with a picture of interlocking sun rays, presumably symbolizing simultaneous orgasm. He's found the tag but can't pull it. Problem is his fingers are too slick with love grease. He wipes them on the sheet.

Mrs Crossan is lying beside him, legs spread ready, one hand under her back, rubbing away the lumbago, or whatever, that she complains of these days.

'Jonny?'

'Mmm. Fuck *you*.'

'Excuse me?'

'I'm talking to the box, honey . . .'

'Do we absolutely have to use one?'

'What?'

'Couldn't we just try it once without?'

'Steady on, old girl.'

What's brought this on, then? Ah, doesn't necessarily mean she wants to . . .

'Oh, what? Are you just off the rag?' He doesn't remember any blood last time. 'Or about to go on it?'

Jonny first heard that phrase from a working-class Liverpudlian, *Educating Rita* type he briefly bonked at college. He loved the vivid physicality of it, from the days when women actually used scraps of flannel rather than the sleek and moulded shapes, described as if they were cars, you see advertised on television now.

'But the thing is, Libs, that calendar-shagging lark doesn't really work. It's why there are so many damn bloody Catholics.'

Finally managing to split the plastic wrapper – the sheaths' sheath – he is opening the box when Libby says: 'I'm forty-six, sweet. I'm so not going to get pregnant now.'

'But, if you did, toots, I mean, *five* kids . . .'

'We can afford them. And, anyway, more and more people have four these days. Four is the new three, for people like us. So five's not, like, *Bangladeshi* or anything . . .'

It always amuses him that the shelf at the chemists is still labelled Family Planning, the old-fashioned phrase a throwback to the days when politicians and clergymen had to be persuaded that they should be sold at all. But, actually, their own brood was pretty much planned: Hugo, Tilly and Plum at two-year intervals and then six years until Lucas, the result of Libby's visit during the fraud trial in Nigeria, where the rubbers on sale were thick and smelly and they chucked them in the Hilton bin.

'Ah. But you've just gone from saying you definitely won't get up the duff at your age to saying five wouldn't be a disaster . . .'

'Oh, Jonny Crossan, I'm not one of your witnesses at the Bailey.'

She reaches round and gives Walter a Dobson, which he needs, having struggled to keep up while he was wrangling the mackintoshes. When she stops, he turns and finds her kneeling on the bed, hands on hips, legs apart and . . . 'Oooh. What's up with you, Georgina?' He drops the box on the floor.

'Camella recommended it when she did my legs on Wednesday,' Libby says. 'It's called a landing strip. It's like having your fanny sandpapered, so I hope it's worth it.'

He thinks of an airport pun – about having a slot open – but his jokes have sometimes broken the mood before and so he pushes her gently back on the bed, lies between her legs and nuzzles her unexpectedly bald Georgina.

*

Murmuring in her sleep, the leading local family doctor prompts her husband to address the question of the effect the present residents have had on their environment:

> Both the perfect charm of their surroundings and the granting of Grade II Listed status to all four buildings by English Heritage mean that the houses would remain entirely recognizable to the ghosts of their benefactor and his architect. Discreet and appropriate changes have been made, though, especially by the current generation of mortgagees.

That may not be factually accurate – Max is far too loaded to have a mortgage – but the sentence sounds nice and a privately published edition to mark the two-hundredth anniversary of the date-stones on the Grenville Four, only of interest to those who live here, will not be subject to Google-checking and troll-correction.

> Barns have been converted into gyms, children's playrooms and guest flats. Three of the houses now have swimming pools . . .

The sounds from the bed tell him that Em is doing her big-cat wake-up stretch.

'Aye-aye-aye! I fell asleep . . .'

'Yes. You needed to.'

'Tom, do you want to come over here for a lie down?'

'I . . . I've sort of got going on this.'

'Oh-*kay*. Which bit is it?'

'The way we live now.'

'What?'

'Rebuilding and redecoration of the houses.'

'Oooh-er. Controversial.'

'Yes. I was thinking of putting in a graph of who copied who when.'

'Careful, darling. Remember Max is paying for the pamphlet.'

Settling for local history over sex with Emily suggests that his testosterone levels must be dropping, but he still feels a flash of resentment at the mention of Max as leader of the pack. He lets it go, though.

*

Feminists would kill her for thinking this but she feels complete with a penis inside her. Max isn't the biggest (although she told him he was, just as she had the other two of her ten who asked) but, though maybe that really matters to some women, at least if you believe what you read in *Glamour*, it never has for her.

For a tall, broad man, Max is surprisingly gentle. Only with him did Jenno really come to know why they call it lovemaking.

If anything, he can be too tender. Sometimes a girl just wants it quick and hot, especially when she's got a Pony Club event next morning or her book's at an exciting bit. But Max is the sort of man who, now he can't open the door for women or stand up when they enter the room, has transferred the elaborate social courtesies to foreplay and intercourse. If she starts to move down the bed, he'll always go down on her first, always lets her come before him, preferably several times. Nobody wants premature ejaculation, but overdue isn't always so great either. Perhaps it's how things are with an older man.

'Oh!' she gasps. 'You can come in me now.'

Above her – as she likes him to be when he finishes – his brow creases in concern: 'What about you?'

'I'm done. Seriously, Maxie, I can't last much longer.'

Concentration showing on his face like he is taking the world's hardest maths exam, he thrusts harder and deeper. Oh, slow, God, slow and deep, fuck, Jesus, what are you doing to me . . .

'I love you,' he grunts, as he always does, when she finally feels the hot splash deep inside.

'Ditto,' Jenno replies, as she always does.

Max tries to pull out of her.

'No. Stay.'

She wants to fall asleep with him inside her.

*

'Moo moo ma noo na.'

'Der da der da durdala.'

'Yer huh lur la lah.'

'Per perllula ma nah nana.'

Talking like Clangers goes back to when she and Jonny were first together as students. They save it now for hotels, in case the children overhear, although, when you think about it, even if they are listening, they're hardly likely to ask: what was that funny language you were speaking when you and Daddy were playing polish the candlestick.

'Ur hur huh HUH HUH HUH HUH,' says Libby, which isn't really Clangerese but she isn't really thinking about knitted lunar puppets at the moment, frankly.

*

There's no more guilty behaviour than blanking a screen when someone comes over, but he can't risk her asking what he's looking at. Simon just hopes he isn't blushing as well.

Tasha is pink and soap-scented from the shower, strands of damp hair struggling from a white-towel turban that matches the fluffy hotel robe: once, all erotic triggers. Once, he'd have pulled the bulky knot apart, pushed her back on the bed and tongued her cunt until she could stand it no longer, fumbling to pull his zip down to release his busting truncheon and pull him into her.

A cloud of steam that escaped before she closed the bathroom

111

door hangs in the room. His brain makes the connection and begs for a cigarette.

'I hope you weren't working, Simon Lonsdale,' she says in her joke–scold voice.

He has turned away from the iPad to face into the room. She sits on his knee.

'Just looking at some new apps.'

'Right-oh. I might have a better idea.'

Until the hell of the last two years, he would have been astonished at the idea that he might ever be pleased by impotence, but he is thrilled and relieved that her bum suggestively grinding into his bollocks goes for nothing. Prone, like some erotic statistician, to look back over the twenty years of their sex life, he is now darkly convinced that she had only ever come on to him when she was broody (such was her regularity and organization that Polly, Josh and Henry can be pinned down to a single night or, at most, a night and a morning) or, latterly, when his wallet wouldn't open. This is – transparently – the reward fuck for giving in on the weekend in Marrakesh.

'It's not your laptop I'm interested in,' she pouts. 'It's your lap.'

Like most women, she is bad at double entendre, sounding like a bad actress who doesn't really know the lines. Which, to be fair, is often a problem in porn as well.

'Actually,' he tells her, 'it's not a laptop. It's a tablet device.'

He was not sure he could be as cruel as this and feels the thrill of a singer who suddenly hits a note outside their range. There's a flash in her eyes that shows it has almost been enough to unwoman her, but Tasha is famous for her determination. Her parents, he always feels, are slightly scared of her.

But, hang on, she's getting off him. Maybe it's worked. She kneels beside him and reaches for . . . *oh, no, fuck, she's going to give me a blowjob. I've got to stop her.* Sentences the teenage Simon could never have envisaged being thought. Like an experienced felon accepting a numberless arrest, he lets his body go slack, trying to set an example of flaccidity for the rest of him.

She unzips him and splits his boxers, fishing out his reas-suringly limp dick. Thank God.

'Oh,' she says. 'Oh.'

He congratulates his cock for not cooperating.

What terrible parallel universe have they landed in?

*

When you've been doing it with someone this long – twenty-six years! – you know the moves, as champion ballroom dancers must. As Libby's knees lift and clamp his ribs, meaning she's reached her trembler, he takes his cue to stop and shoot. How strange not to feel the trampoline kickback of coming in a rubber.

Sometimes, Walter packs up as soon his job is done. Other days – today – he's up for overtime. Why does that happen? Jonny suddenly wonders if it means she's fertile, their bodies conniving at that level of hidden smells and messages there are articles in *The Times* about. He has read about tests where female students sniff the sweaty vests of the basketball team and instinctively choose the one who would give them the best baby.

But, in this glowing moment, he wouldn't really mind if there's a child, which must be one of nature's tricks for re-placing the race.

'Orr yessss!' says Libby in the northern voice of the dog on the car-insurance adverts.

*

At least one in four long-term marriages becomes completely sexless, Zelda has consoled correspondents complaining of bed-death, while suggesting ways to reverse the trend: date nights, weekends away, counselling.

Well, they've tried the weekend away and that's been a fucking (no pun intended) disaster. From Natasha's own expe-rience, and the sorts of conversations girls have, she knows of no known case in recorded history of a bloke actually turning down the old salt lollipop – the bane of many relationships is

113

that men want it – but Simon looked at her like she'd just offered to bite the thing off. Perhaps she should write to Zelda. But the reason she reads the problem pages – she sees – is that she feels superior to the dumped and loveless who write in.

One in four. But that's the problem with statistics. When the paper says that 10 per cent of women with a ginger-haired left-handed aunt will develop MS, you assume you'll be in the ten in a hundred, not the ninety. But, conversely, it's no consolation that a quarter of wives with time on the clock haven't been touched in a year, because she can inevitably only think of the 75 per cent who are presumably being humped by their husbands until they beg for a night off.

Shifting on her side of the empty bed, Natasha loosens the dressing-gown cord which she re-tied too tightly after the oral fiasco.

Simon has gone out for a cigarette. His laptop – *tablet device*, my God when he said *that* – is on the table. It will be PIN-protected, presumably.

*

'Oh, Libby and Jonny have had sex,' says Emily, putting her BlackBerry back in its sheeny sheath (he offered her an iPhone for her birthday but she's frugal) and picking up *Mister Pip* again.

'What? You heard her? Like in . . . ?'

Tom turns round from his village history. She likes him in his glasses, which soften the rugged face old soldiers seem to grow, but he wears contacts for work and the social circuit. The stuff so many of us do that we think makes us look younger. Who are we kidding?

'Hear her? No. There's a whole corridor . . .'

'Skiing that time, she could have been up the Matterhorn and still . . .'

'She Tweeted . . .'

Now Tom turns round fully: 'Libby *Tweeted* that they've had sex?'

'Well, not exactly. But . . .' Emily takes out her phone again and scrolls to the latest update, taking her glasses off because she can't read her book without them but can't read her phone screen with them, an oddity of the ageing body untouched-on in medical school. 'Here. *At the* riad *in Marrakesh: fun, sun and the usual stuff you do with no kids around.*'

Emily doesn't read out the *lol* at the end because she thinks the boys are probably right that Libby is getting that wrong.

'Right,' her husband says. 'Not exactly *Channel 4 News*, is it? I always wonder what historians of the future will make of Twitter. An age so obsessed with celebrity that everyone becomes an egotist, putting out press releases on the hour. Who are her followers, apart from you lot?'

'It's not about numbers.'

'No. Has she put *lol* at the end?'

'What? No.'

*

She is used to passwords. W-A-N-D-E-R-E-R-S and B-O-L-T-O-N were two of his favourites in the days – early in online technology, earlier in their marriage – when they gave each other access. She simultaneously hates and envies those couples who have a joint electronic address – Jonny and Libby, inevitably – although it's interesting that there are so few. An email address has become the room of one's own.

The iPad, though, throws up four empty spaces for something called a Passcode, which presumably could be numbers or letters. Knowing that it's stupid even as she does it, she flicks in T-A-S-H. There is no help in knowing that she can only be imagining that the security software rejects this possibility with insolent quickness.

Tasha has no idea if the iPad locks you out after a certain number of wrong guesses. One of the problems of spying on Simon is that he upgrades so rapidly to each new gadget. Which is another thing. He bangs on more than the Chancellor of the Exchequer about the need for them all to tighten their belts, but the budget for boys' toys seems to be limitless.

Simon is a slight man with a soft tread and so the minimal twitch of the door handle leaves her insufficient time for an alibi dash from the desk. The stench of cigarettes comes off him. Did he always smell like this or is it what happens when the body goes honest on you? At least she won't have to kiss him with that ashtray taste.

'You look guilty,' he says. 'Have you been wanking?'

Women, when asked about their first experience of sheer love, routinely compare it to the feeling of being about to faint. And Tasha has swooned enough in her life – periods before she got the hang of them, fasting for Communion – to recognize the signs. It was true of love but also applies, she now discovers, to hatred.

*

After the snowy A-Class (definitely king in the local hierarchy of cars, Tom notes) drops them at a junction, they are met by two burly men in multi-coloured robes and tasselled fezzes. Each holds, in one hand, a laminated sign showing the name of the restaurant chosen by the hotel and, in the other, a long cylinder topped with a slatted cage containing a live flame, blazing bright against a night darkness that seems remarkably deep to a visitor used to overlit cities.

Waving these brands, the guides lead them down streets of trampled, reddish earth. From doorways and corners, packs of young boys in odd combinations of traditional and modern dress – robes, replica football shirts, big trainers with the famous tick encrusted with dust – run towards them. The children, less committed to ethnic authenticity than the restaurant's staff, carry battery flashlights which they aim, like expert interrogators, straight in the faces of the tourists.

The pleas range from the basic ('Gimme money, mister'), through the emotionally loaded ('my momma real sick') to the obscene: Jonny Crossan claims that one of them has invited him to fuck his sister for fifty dollars. They stick to the agreed policy of the weekend, which is to ignore begging, although Jonny jokes that, if the pound was stronger against the dollar, he might have taken up the kid.

The food is decent enough, although they are alarmed by the menu's reliance on the tagine, the local cuisine's posh risotto, in which the only surprise is whether meat or vegetables stud the rice. Libby delivers one of her unstoppable monologues about a film she's seen on TV, which are always hard to follow because of her tendency to refer to several characters interchangeably as 'he' and 'she'.

Jonny notes Nicky Mortimer from the trains (and, now, the plane) at a table with his wife on the far side of the restaurant.

'*Zelig*!' says Tom and, for a while, they discuss their favourite and least favourite Woody Allen movies.

There's a row, initiated when Emily questions whether they really need the fifth and sixth bottles of expensive imported French red (Tom guesses that she's arguing on economic grounds, but it's inevitably taken as medical), about what Max and Jonny call the 'blame game'.

'You tell all your patients to drink less and eat less,' Jonny says. 'Because of the alleged national epidemics of alcoholism and obesity. But, at the same time, there are all these pieces in the papers about how life-expectancy rates are increasing. The Queen can't afford the stamps to send cards to all the centurions and so on. So beer and beef can't be that bad for you.'

'Well,' Emily tells him. 'We'll see. Middle-class problem drinking . . .'

'Do they mean us?' interjects Libby in another of the comedy accents to which she's prone.

'. . . is a recent phenomenon. We'll only know the consequences in a few decades. Stomach, bladder, pharyngolaryngeal, oesophageal cancers.'

'Cheers!' Simon raises his glass, and asks Tom, with typical snideness, 'Do you find she's a very popular dinner-party guest?'

On a management course in the army, they studied a list of personality types and one of them, an unfortunate metaphor in that workplace, was 'the sniper', someone who crouches unseen on the rooftops of the conversation, waiting to take out someone else's runs. Simon, especially when he's been drinking, is the sniper par excellence.

'The point is . . .' Max, like a politician in a debate, has lifted his voice above the others trying to get in. '. . . that we've become unrealistic about death. Take poor Bill Adamson.' As normal, when the dead member of their circle is mentioned, they look down, from respect or superstition, an indoor version of removing hats for a cortege. 'At the funeral, we were standing round convincing ourselves that, as his parents weren't there, they'd probably died youngish, which means that cancer probably ran in their family . . .'

'I can't talk about a patient,' Em warns, as normal.

'I'm not asking you to. I'm saying we're obsessed with finding a reason. If only that pilot had read the maintenance manual properly. If only the sniffer dog had twitched at that suitcase.' (Jonny says 'steady on, we're flying home' and Emily adds 'if only the GP had spotted the early signs of New Variant SARS', then says she's speaking generally.) 'If only they'd eaten less red meat. But random – in the proper sense, not the one our kids use – shit happens. It probably happened to Bill Adamson and it will happen to more of us. There isn't always a reason why people die.'

'Exactly. It's like conspiracy theories . . .' begins Simon.

Emily and Tasha both groan, seeing that a known conversational no-go area is about to be breached. But their discomfort only encourages Simon: 'Betty Blodge drives into a concrete wall at high speed and the people who know her send a condolence card and get on with it. Princess Diana is driven into one and the only thing that can explain her death is that the Duke of Edinburgh ordered MI6 to kill her . . .'

Tom is sick of being parodied like this again: 'Si, we've been through this before. You never explain how the driver came to have so much money in his bank accounts . . .'

'And I've never heard a decent explanation from you of how

Phil the Greek made sure the car would be driven by a secret agent who was pissed out of his head . . .'

'Boys, boys,' says Libby. 'You're getting boring.'

'I think it goes further than Max was arguing,' says Jonny, and you can see him on his feet at the Bailey, trouncing opposing counsel, one of those moments when someone's work shows at home; dinner parties have been ruined for Tom by worrying about people's window locks. 'It's not just the desire for death to be explained, but for it to be deserved. Against all the available evidence, we want life to be fair. He did A, so he died from B. Smokers maybe, but beyond that . . .'

'Alcohol is the new nicotine,' says Emily.

'Although you'd be unwise to light it in the same way,' Simon snipes.

Jonny waits, a professional trick, for silence to fall before completing his speech: 'The fact is that, beyond that, most deaths aren't deserved,'

'Except the death penalty,' Max cuts in. Jenno flinches, one of those moments when you sense a sore spot in a marriage.

'Oh, Lord!' Tom pleads. 'Don't get Max started on capital punishment.'

*

On the first morning at breakfast – thick, bitter coffee and rolls warm from the oven, eaten at canopied tables on the walled flat roof of the *riad* – Max mentions he's interested in going to the souk. Jonny says 'Poof!' and Libby 'Bless!', by which they mean pretty much the same thing. But Dr Emily turns to Jenno and says: 'You've got a gem there.'

There's inevitably some banter from the other chaps about his going shopping with the girls. Tom is planning to look at some Moorish tombs and clearly touting for company, but Jonny says they didn't sound very 'more-ish' to him and, as he and Mrs C have been at it all night (Libby hits him, but in that way that makes you think they may have been), he needs to replenish his juices. Simon mutters that he needs to put in some hours at the iPad on a brand remanagement document he is presenting to the board on Monday morning. Cue discussion of why men can't relax, with Tasha as counsel for the prosecution and Jenno as judge.

But Max isn't going to be a martyr to barter because he's a new man or a good husband. Although he'd never be idiotic enough to admit it to the womenfolk, this is a business trip. Just as Tom is obsessed with forms of transport (a hangover, presumably, from his army years, or the reason that he signed to be a soldier in the first place), Max loves to observe commerce in action. His entrepreneur's mind is always alert to display, pricing and signature product lines. As someone leading a traditional family business through a period of technological transformation and financial catastrophe, he loves to see examples of smart diversification: the blue-chip chocolate bars, for example, with their limited edition Easter and Christmas specials in recent years. What might be the equivalent, he's always thinking, for Dunster Manor?

And the Arab street-market is selling at its most elemental: the souk, although he obviously probably shouldn't say it aloud around these parts, is his Mecca. At first, he's disappointed, as the donkey cart they picked up outside the hotel dodges the bikes and clattering Ladas and Trabants down streets filled with shops, goods and logos you might see anywhere. But, eventually, they arrive at an interchange of narrow, cobbled paths crammed with shaded stalls.

On the surface, for the CEO of an outfit dealing in prestige goods, there's little to learn directly here. This is the birthplace of the principle of pile it high and sell it cheap, although, which is the lesson, the freshness and beauty of the products belies this.

The spices are piled in pyramids of vivid colours: nutmeg, cumin, cinnamon, he recognizes. But, looking deeper into the canopied stand, he sees the same flavourings in jars and bottles with gingham bonnet tops. So the canny Arab merchant is catering to two different markets – loose for the regulars, tweely potted for the passing custom – just as Dunster Manor has had to do, although in reverse, making products more spontaneous and less packaged for the online clientele.

At most of the concessions, the goods are arranged on wide, raking trays, with the shopkeeper standing at the top on a raised platform, like a croupier at a gaming table. Alongside the spices, shining inclines of fruit, vegetables and nuts create another fury of competing shades and, also here, shape: prunes, apricots, figs. Max marvels at black olives as large as marbles and walnuts like a giant's knuckles.

The sweet or sharp tangs of this multi-levelled plenty waft distracting perfume over the donkey piss and shit. A mortician's trick for which, in this culture, spices are also used. The basic business tactic of making your products look irresistible is well understood here, a modern website merely an extension of these street-traders' ancient wiles. This thought prompts him to capture the scene on his phone; he will surely be able to use it in a motivational blog or a talk to his staff.

'Maxie, how much is too much?'

Jenno's shout from the other side of the bazaar drags him from his reflections on the origins of business. His wife is with Tasha, Emily and Libby beside a stretch of bays containing clothes and household goods. From one stand, specializing in mirrors of numerous sizes and designs, fragments of the women's faces flash. In the neighbouring space, brass and copper ornaments – lamps and mobiles – hang and, next to them, racks of leather and animal skins – cattle, goat, camel – and then a tumbling array of shoes, belts and bags, which he guesses to be the target of their party.

He walks over and asks Jenno: 'What's that, darling?'

'We've got our eye on some bags and shoes but we don't really know what would count as a lot.'

'You know what? I've never really got the concept of too much,' says Libby.

Max is trying to remember the exchange rate from the *FT* on the plane but Libby already has her iPhone out ('Three signal bars here. Amazing!') and taps at an app.

'One dirham equals 0.0772086738 pounds,' she reports. 'Although I was always in the retard stream for Maths.'

'So that means what?' asks Jenno. '1 dirham is about 70p?'

'No. 7p.' Emily corrects her. 'So 100 dirhams is about seven pounds.'

They ask the stall-holder the prices of the bags and slippers they fancy and uncertainly translate them into sterling.

'Thank God,' Libby says, 'we don't have to do it in euros.'

'Okay,' says Emily. 'Let's offer him 10 per cent less.'

Tasha disagrees: 'No, fifteen. Let's go for it.'

Libby throws the face of an archbishop being mooned by a curate: 'What's this? Just pay him what he says. Simples.'

Emily looks dubiously at Tasha, who becomes spokesman for both: 'But, in places like this, they expect to be bargained down. You have to be mad to pay what's on the tag.'

'Look, guys,' Libby insists. 'In England, we make a point of paying as much as we possibly can for everything. I don't know about you, but I always assume the reduced goods in a supermarket have something wrong with them. So what's a few dirhams here or there? It makes us seem cheap.'

Max enjoys this clash between Western and Eastern traditions of consumption. Against some board opposition, he has always refused, through two recessions, to discount Dunster Manor prices, believing that the company's customers take comfort in belonging to a club others can't join.

The invariably caring Emily is worrying at the issue: 'I suppose, given the money we have, relatively . . .'

'Relatively,' echoes Tasha.

'. . . it's a bit, I nearly said *rich*, of us to be taking it away from a bloke who's probably trying to feed his family on a pomegranate.'

'Bollocks!' Libby's strong, confident voice – and perhaps the international currency of the word – causes adjoining stall-holders to turn. 'These guys are loaded because they set their profit margins so high.'

Max, as the group's resident business tycoon, feels he should contribute: 'Libby's right.' She punches the air and shouts 'Yessssss!' 'Barter is for their own people. This is more like Fortnum's. You're here because you can pay.'

'We've got it. Let's flaunt it,' says Libby, pulling rolls of notes from her handbag and handing them to the merchant who, though at first visibly surprised to be making a sale at list prices, smoothly produces from beneath the wooden table of his traditional Arab shack a payment terminal for Tasha, who wants to pay by credit.

Next, in a multi-storey woollen-goods warehouse, whose owner reacts to their transparent Englishness by claiming to have appeared in one of Michael Palin's travel documentaries, Libby and Jenno buy, again without tussling for a reduction, several carpets and rugs to be shipped to England. Visualizing the already lush, warm floors of both their house and the cottage in Somerset, Max assumes that the intricately woven coverings will have to, as they do in the shop, hang from the walls. But they have the money and so it is their moral duty to spend. He thinks of himself as kick-starting the Moroccan economy.

Tired from buying, they drink mint tea – sweet and glutinous, the texture more soup than beverage – in a cafe overlooking the central gathering place. 'It translates as the Square of the Beheaded,' Emily tells them from her guidebook.

Tasha dissolves a handful of sugar cubes in her already sweet drink.

'I can barely stay awake,' she explains. 'Could I be diabetic, Em?'

'People who think they are usually aren't. Funnily enough, the biggest risk-factor for most illnesses is thinking you haven't got them. Most of my hypochondriacs will outlive me. But come and see me when we get back and I'll test you.'

'Max got top marks in his Key Man medical the other day,' Jenno says. 'Didn't you?'

'Um, yes,' he answers through a mouthful of tea, the question unexpected.

'You're probably just shagged out from last night,' Libby

tells Tasha, who replies with real cat's claws: 'Oh, for God's sake, Libby. You're obsessed with sex. It's like being in the fourth form.'

'*Eet wurze a hoke. Can't Tasha take a leetle hoke?*' Libby tries to soothe her, in one of the silly accents she does, although one he can't place.

Weird. Because it suggests Tasha isn't getting any. Which is odd because, for Max at least, of all the women round the table, she's the one you would. Barring his Jenno, of course. Which just goes to show that you can never tell who's happy.

*

People think Emily doesn't drink much because she's a doctor. But she never has been one for the booze. As a 15- or 16-year-old at parties, she would often pretend that her orange juice had vodka in it. Even now – at dinners and on trips like this – she has a glass or two more than she actually wants, just so the others don't feel judged.

She'd expected it to be less of an issue in Marrakesh, assuming that a Muslim country (even though her guidebook stresses that the government is secular) would be dry. But a *riad* seems to have a deal like those private-drinking clubs in London. Every half-hour or so, the gangly African appears from the stairwell at the corner of the roof terrace, bows deeply and then beamingly accepts for replacement the empty wine bottle they hand him.

Even so, at 3 a.m., they're having guilty, slurry discussions about whether they can really expect Mohammed, as they've Christen— er, named him ('Be heavy odds on at Paddy Power, wouldn't it?' says Jonny) to bring them an eleventh and twelfth white Rioja.

'Mo seems perfectly jolly about it,' Libby says.

'Although he may be storing up resentments,' Max suggests. 'Probably has to be up for prayers in two hours. This time he might come back with a dozen sticks of Semtex stuck to his chest.'

'Sshhh!' she whispers instinctively, overlapping with the same warning from Tasha, who, she notices as a friend not a doctor, really is knocking it back a bit tonight.

'Are there terrorists in Marrakesh?' asks Jonny. The essy ends of both words come out in a slush.

In any group of friends, certain subjects are soon deferred, by unspoken convention, to certain people, and Tom is their security correspondent: 'Not in the sense you suggest it, Jonny, of their being harboured here. The king and the government know their dependence on western tourism . . .'

'People like ush keep it going!'

'In a way, Libs. In fact, a few of the post-9/11 Hollywood movies about Al Qaeda plots were filmed here, filling in for places where they couldn't be made.'

'Well that's good,' says Jonny, overemphatically, with the audible relief of the intoxicated at a run of non-slurry syllables.

'Yes and no.' Tom pauses, enjoying the superiority of knowledge. 'Some would argue that it makes them a target for AQ. Like Bali. Playground for the children of the Great Satan and so on.'

Jonny visibly whitens and looks sweatier than he should in the cool night air. Emily again thinks that she should maybe drop a hint about an appointment.

Tash inclines her head and eyes to the right and they follow her gaze to find 'Mohammed' in his dazzling white djellaba standing with gentle expectation in the corner. Sensing their attention, he lowers his head to the level of his waist. Emily experiences the unease she felt with the black waiters on Felix's school rugby tour of South Africa.

'Is everything satisfactory?' their host asks.

'Look, my dear chap,' says Max, 'We're terribly worried about keeping you from your bed . . .'

Max's half-smilingly guileless face and softened voice make her think of David Cameron in a crisis, but it's probably just standard public-school manners.

'Is no problem at all, sir.'

'Really? Well, if you're absolutely sure we're not completely ruining your life, then we'd take two more of these and absolutely promise that'll be the lid on it.'

Their host doubles over again, soon returning with, in each hand, an ice-bucket containing an opened Rioja. His leg muscles must be strong to manage the stairs without support.

Jonny operates as sommelier, although lacking the necessary steadiness of hand. On this round, he doesn't even try to refill Emily's glass and Jenno covers hers with admonishing fingers. Tom accepts a top-up from politeness but never even sips it, which is very him. The other five slosh and sluice as if these were the first drinks of the evening.

Providing further evidence for Emily's scepticism about her middle-class patients who insist that their drinking is restricted to a glass with dinner (beneficial for antioxidants and circulation, they have read in the papers), they have been drinking for eight hours now, beginning at the latest restaurant recommended and booked by their hotel.

Now, at 3.20 a.m. on the hotel roof, after what Emily calculates to be eighteen bottles between the eight of them, the conversation is flagging, reduced to travellers' platitudes: views, weather, what may be happening at home. Emily listens with the exaggerated clarity of the designated driver, noting the over-articulation and hasty corrections of false words. She remembers something she heard a theatre director say on Radio 4: that bad actors act drunk, whereas, in reality, someone who is pissed is trying not to act drunk.

'So dark,' says Libby, with the nervous care of someone in the early stages of learning English. 'And more starless than I thought.'

'Good cheese,' Tasha agrees, then corrects herself: '*choice.*'

Sensing the failing energy, Max and Jonny swap smirks, the latter taps his foot, counts 'one, two, three!', and they begin their party piece.

'*I want to live like common people,*' Jonny sings.

'*I want to do whatever common people do,*' Max joins in.

And, then, together, they continue: '*I want to sleep with common people, I want to sleep with common people, like you . . .*'

They tail off, from the effort of singing in their condition.

'Are you absolutely sure you should, darling?' Jenno asks. 'It's probably an offence to sing western pop songs.'

Libby stands unsteadily, her speech now degenerated to the level of an EFL student asking the class for the first time to improvise sentences of their own: 'I think I'd better go to bed.'

Jonny, at once, is on his feet, slapping his wife on the bottom: 'I'm right behind you, darling, though not in a gay way. We have un . . . unfin . . .' Three goes at that word until he gets out 'unfinished business before' and then a final sound so pissedly sibilant that Emily's brain doesn't process it until the Crossans are walking, with the cotton-wool steps of minefield-clearers, down the stairs: '*slumber.*'

Emily takes her cue to stand. Check-out tomorrow is 11 a.m. and she still hasn't got her sleep straight after last week's over-nights.

'I think that's me as well,' she says.

'*Us,*' Tom corrects her, rising and entwining his arm in hers, in a way she finds deeply touching.

'Oh, hello,' says Tasha. 'Someone won't be getting much sleep.'

'Oh, no. No, I . . .' Tom stutters, spoiling it.

Emily's about to do the round of goodnights when she sees that Jenno, quite unnoticed by Max beside her, is asleep on the table, having made a pillow of her arms.

'Max,' she whispers, nodding.

'Bless!' says Tasha.

Max puts his arms on Jenno's shoulders and trembles them slightly: 'Honey, you should go to bed.'

Jenno groggily rejoins them, her face and shoulders running through the stages of shock, wake-up sour mouth and middle-aged stiffness.

'Uh, what time is it?' she gruffly asks.

Emily, thinking that Jenno, as the youngest of them by far, should be able to do these pseudo-student nights, leaves them to it, descending the staircase from which their tourists' booze has obligingly arrived, her arm linked with her husband's.

*

As soon as the moralizing doc has gone, Simon gets out his coffin nails.

'Good man,' says Max, who is still holding on to Jenno, trying to keep her awake, like the parent of a sick kid in a film. Into a hand that briefly stops squeezing a comatose shoulder, Simon palms him a fag.

'Cheers, Si.'

'What about me?' Natasha wheedles, in that paedo-pleaser voice she keeps throwing. He offers her the packet, top flipped off.

'Oh my God,' complains Jenno, jerking to alertness. 'You're not all going to smoke all over me.' She's co-sponsor, with Emily, of the Clean Air Act. She twists round to look at Max: 'In a way, I wish that medical hadn't gone so well. You think you can do anything. But at your age . . .'

'Thanks for that, sweetie.'

Jenno stands, with a cartoon cat-stretch, and says: 'I've simply got to go to bed. Coming, Maxie?'

Simon can't imagine it's a dilemma. Drinking coffee that morning beside the pool in the *riad* courtyard, he and Jonny agreed how much they envied Max, having younger pussy on tap without having to risk his house and pension.

But the luckiest husband of their group (although Libby shows every sign of being a goer) lights his Light and says: 'I'll be down. I have to keep the Lonsdales company.' Jenno kisses Max (lips! now there's a second marriage) and leaves them, rattling the massive key-fob as she goes.

How ironic that he and Tasha should be the last pair here as he assumes them to be the least secure of the couples and is pretty sure they're the only two who didn't fuck in the siesta

128

gap. He also wouldn't have chosen to see out the evening with Max, who tends to preen himself as the senior businessman, although, personally, Simon doesn't see how the current business model of Dunster Manor is tenable.

'Is Sir Adrian showing any sign of humility?' Max booms, his cigarette, you feel, an unhappy stand-in for the cigar his demeanour really demands.

Simon buys a pause with a draw on his own fag. 'Well, I have to be a bit like Dr Emily on this one. I – and I know I sound like Blair on weapons of mass destruction here – I know more than I can necessarily say . . .'

'Swollen bollocks, Simon, it's all over the newspapers.'

'Well, what have you read?'

'Sir Adrian thinks Samson Brothers was unlucky with the global recession. He doesn't accept that bankers did anything wrong. He doesn't see why he should take a reduction in this pension. He doesn't, as everyone says these days, get it.'

'That's pretty much what he thinks, yeah. If he went on Desert Island Discs, every single fucking record would be "Sorry Seems To Be The Hardest Word" . . .'

'And do you feel that you, as Sir Adrian's PR man, have had any success at all in shifting him in the direction of contrition . . . ?'

Fuck you, Max Dunster, with your patronizing attitude. Simon stands.

'You going to bed?' asks Tasha, who has just lit another cigarette.

'I need a piss.'

On the staircase, he follows the signs, showing an arrow and a top-hatted man, but realizes that they are directing him to the ground floor. He feels for the hefty key in his pocket and decides that he might as well go to room 22.

He pees at a volume and intensity that feels almost sensual, congratulating his middle-aged bladder on dealing so efficiently with the long night's wine.

He actually has the door open, planning to go back to the

roof, but, as if in a government information film about the perils of the Internet, his eye is caught by the temptation on the table.

*

A late-night and holiday smoker – and Marrakesh at almost 4 a.m. qualifies on both scores – Tasha wonders, as Max chivalrously clicks her husband's lighter to another of his Marlboros for her, if one of the attractions of the habit is the ease with which it covers silences. The cigarettes give them something to do as they gaze out at an African sky that leaves nothing to describe except the already-exhausted subject of its darkness.

She contemplates the oddness of sitting in the middle of the night with Max. As with any set of friends, their group has its fixed formations. The basic eight for dinner-parties, holidays and theatre and movie outings also splits into various unisex foursomes: the girls for gym and tennis, the boys for rugby and shooting, although Simon blows hot and cold on those. By unspoken understanding of friendships and tensions, they even sit in a certain boy–girl order in restaurants and on planes and trains. So it's incredibly unusual for half of one couple to be alone with half of another. This is because, Tasha assumes, of the adultery taboo. Novels and movies from the Sixties astonish her with the constant swapping of partners, but she finds it impossible to imagine any infidelity in their circle.

Out of nowhere, Max says: 'Do you think we'll get into trouble for this?'

A clued-up woman is used to men saying ambiguous things just to see where they go, and so she takes her time before replying: 'For what?'

'Smoking up here. There aren't any signs. On the other hand, nor are there ashtrays.' They are using empty Rioja bottles for this purpose. 'But, from what we saw in the market this morning, it seems to be pretty much obligatory even for Muslims. Even so, since the bans started everywhere, you never quite know what you can and can't do.'

'I think our biggest danger is my husband going ape-shit that we've finished off his packet.'

Which reminds her that Simon must have been gone for ten minutes now. All wives have intermittent morbid fantasies of finding their spouses collapsed with a coronary, and she has a sudden image of hers slumped over the bog. The thought that widowhood might solve some problems brings a little shiver of guilt.

She locates her ancient Nokia (a clunky, big-buttoned museum piece compared to the phones the others have; she would treat herself to something better if Simon wouldn't pull his money face) amid the mess of bottles and glasses that makes her think of teenage parties. In both the restaurant and on the roof-terrace, the four mothers in the group kept their phones in front of them like bulky extra cutlery, in case of urgent messages from children or au pairs.

where U? she texts, then puts the phone back down on the table. She refuses fully to visualize what Simon might be doing but knows that it is likely to involve his laptop— forgive her: fucking 'tablet device'.

'You seem rather down in the dumps at the moment?' Max says.

In a movie, she would have flinched. 'Do I?'

'Sorry.' He holds up his non-smoking hand in apology. He's one of those men who tan easily; in his light-pink polo shirt (she'd never get Simon in pink), he's deep brown from his forearms to the fingers. 'Nothing worse than being asked what you're thinking.'

'No. You're okay. Things haven't been great at the moment . . .'

'Oh?'

Although she's been round the block enough to be suspicious of what might lie behind Max's sympathy, she's enjoying the sensation of being in a conversation with a man which doesn't feel as if it should end with judges holding up scorecards for effort.

Her phone vibrates on the table. She imagines her husband's irritation at having to reply. She reads his answer:

not up for Mad Max in his cups gone to bed door unlocked

No *xx*s. And you even get those from the MOT centre these days.

'The last two cigarettes are ours, apparently,' she tells Max.

'Good. Was there a machine in the lobby, did you notice?'

'A what machine?'

'Cigarettes. What did you think I meant, for God's sake, Natasha? Condoms?'

She had always assumed she would grow out of blushing, but apparently not. In their letters to Zelda the magazine counsellor, the forbidden lovers often say that they didn't realize what was happening until it was too late. But she has always been sure they did and is surer now, becoming absolutely certain when Max returns to the role of friendly confessor: 'You were saying . . . bad days at Black Rock . . . Tell me, if it helps . . . if it doesn't, don't . . .'

'Look,' she says. 'Simon's dealing with the whole Sir Adrian thing. He says it would be easier doing PR for the Yorkshire Ripper . . .'

He lights the final pair of cigarettes, first hers, then his. Can this be done unsensually?

'And how's your business going?' he asks. To the shock of being in an equal conversation is added the astonishment of being asked about Natty Cooking Ltd in a context that doesn't involve its possible contribution to the family's financial blackhole.

'Well, you know what times are like . . .'

'What? The recession? We've been very lucky at Dunster's, actually, but, as President Clinton used to say, *I feel your pain.* There'll always be a demand for food as good as yours. Remind me when we get back to sign you up for the office Christmas do again . . .'

'That'd be great. Some of my regulars have had their entertainment budgets slashed.'

'I know, I know. It's the first thing the finance guys put a line through. I think that's a mistake. If you've got it, circulate it. We shouldn't be ostentatious with so many people suffering but, in this of all times, the staff should be thanked for a hard-working year. Does Simon think he might lose his job . . . ?'

This is a fear she lives with daily, but the brutal expression of it, with so many of her defences down from the place and the wine and the hour and the afternoon's humiliation by her husband, bring hot tears as quickly as the flicking of a switch.

'Oh, Lord,' says Max. 'I'm sorry. There I go clod-hopping in . . .'

'No. It's not . . .'

People know what is happening. They know. Know that the next move will be the arm around the shoulder, then the stroking of the hair, the patting of the head and the gentle turning of the cheek. Then the lips meeting and retreating, repeating this ritual of resistance once more, and then a tongue in her mouth which, for all the sourness of stale wine and cigarettes, is the first for God knows how long, and prompts her body to ache at another lengthy absence. Tasha knows what is happening and she wants it to.

FIVE

NOTHING TOO GOOD FOR THEM

The flowers have begun to arrive. The ritual in England for the shockingly dead since Diana: the cellophaned arrangements lying wind-shivered on the ground. Bulging from the frozen earth, the bright blooms look incongruous, cheating the seasons. A line of poetry lodged in her head since English more than twenty years ago: *lilacs out of the dead land*.

But, these days, the floral tributes will already be a minor shrine compared to what is happening online: the Facebook pages, especially for the children, with their misspelled expressions of shock and, with depressing inevitability, some anonymous malevolence. Even four deaths as cruel and brutal as these will invite glee from online psychos; and the extremity of the killings may even inflame the response. Were such feelings created – or merely revealed – when typing replaced speech?

One of the squad is always designated to read all the pages and messages generated by a death: social networking can expose in moments a skein of connections and resentments that would in the past have needed weeks of door-to-door or subpoenaed telephone records. As a parent, Kate is terrified by the web's stripping of privacy; as a detective, she celebrates it daily. So often now, a victim turns out to have posted or tweeted the motive for murder and, frequently, the identity of the murderer as well.

Walking back up to the death-scenes, she turns to see the nanny and the coffee guy, their routine but mainly useless interrogations over, sitting next to each other on the fold-down steps of the support van. The girl is crying and her fellow bystander at this catastrophe rests his hand, tentatively, on her arm. At a murder scene, basic acts of human kindness are amplified.

Lorenzo has already changed into anticontamination clothes; Kate matches him. As they go through the front door, she notes the video entry-phone, the angled CCTV cameras and the laser trip-points.

'Impressive security set-up?' she says to Lorenzo. When someone is heavily protected, it can mean either that they're cautious or that they have enemies.

'Yeah, but it's like the babysitter, isn't it, guv?'

'What?'

'Urban myth. The babysitter gets a threatening call, rings the operator . . .'

'Oh, yeah, okay . . . who traces the call and says unfortunately the maniac is on the upstairs extension? Never made sense technologically; two calls on the same line. Might work better with mobiles. But the point being that the killer was already in the house?'

'That's what we're thinking, isn't it?'

'We urgently need to find E.'

The security notices stuck to the windows and speared in the lawns and drive outside bear the name Rutherford Secure and a phone number.

'From the number, it's local. Get someone to ring them and ask for the CCTV footage,' Kate tells Lorenzo.

The main door leads into a hall, which confronts her with the unavoidable poignancy of domestic investigations, although she has previously known it only in the cases of a single dead or presumed-dead child. She tries to look at, without really seeing, the lines of shoes and coats and schoolbags ready for the morning. They are still neat, so Kate could tell forensics for free that they have not been disturbed since the mother straightened them on the way upstairs the previous night, trying to impose some order on the teenage chaos.

The one convincing argument for naturism she has ever known is the pang of abandoned clothes, as final as the line of chalk around a corpse. After her father's death, the one time she sensed her mother about to crumble was when they took his suits to the charity shop.

In this place where A, B, C and D died, everything looks so expensive and elegant that she has a flashback to family and school outings to famous houses. The hallway is dominated by a wide dark-wood staircase, from which the sound of voices, cleanly muffled feet and camera flashes betray the major sites of investigations. She has been told already that the victims were murdered in their beds.

On either side of the hall are two closed doors. Liking to go clockwise, which imposes a kind of science on a search, she opens the first with gloved hand. It's a kitchen, bigger than her living room, with massive glittering silver sinks cut in. Between them are the equally sparkling facades of a double Aga and mirror-bright steel pans hanging from an overhead rack, sug-gesting the set of a TV cookery show. How many cleaners must it take to keep it as gleaming as this, and might they be witnesses? Along the walls are marbled, altar-like preparation surfaces, the central island unit with granite preparation slab neatly lined with spice stands, wine racks and the scarlet Italian coffee machine that inadvertently led to the discovery of the crimes.

'Nothing too good for them,' says Lorenzo.

'What? Oh, I see. Death at the Ideal Home Exhibition?'

Nothing too good for them. She flinches at something in the phrase that is judgemental and envious, perhaps because of the echo of expressions about hanging or prison being too good for someone.

Here, as in the hall, there is no suggestion of burglary or disturbance, which suggests a hired hit or what one of her lecturers at sleuth school used to call, scandalizing his students, a friendly killer.

Between two windows on the outside wall hangs a vast,

framed set of family photographs under glass. Children rise in size and reluctance to be snapped, their outfits graduating from babygros to suits and dresses at what look like family weddings. The parents beside them show the spread of flesh and retreat of hair, inevitable even to gilded families, but their smiling pride is constant. Several of the images are beach scenes, alluring blue seas and leaning palm trees in the background. Nothing too good for them. These will be the photos in tomorrow's papers as they take on the designation of a Tragic Family. Kate tries to match the portraits to their alphabetical victims, but then looks away. Although they draw the eye magnetically, the snaps are unlikely to be evidence.

One of the SOCOs – Henderson? – comes downstairs and pauses at the open kitchen door, nodding his respect for her presence. She wants to ask how bad it is, but never admit the work gets to you. 'Preliminary findings?'

'Pending official identification, mother and three kids, killed in turn. Doesn't look like the children even woke up.' They sleep so deeply, Kate thinks. 'The mother may have sat up in bed before . . .'

Conversation at crime scenes contains so many sentences no one wants to finish. The death of children is the greatest terror of a parent, and detectives are forced to watch others suffering it. She becomes irrationally concerned for the safety of Jack and Molly. When she can make an excuse, she will text them.

Henderson, carrying tagged evidence bags, heads for the front door, where he crosses with one of the DCs new to the murder team: possibly Warrington.

'DCI Duncan?' the newcomer asks her.

'Yes?'

'Ma'am, we've a first trace on . . .'

Lorenzo interrupts with the necessary ritual for new recruits: 'She takes "guv".'

Kate explains: 'The other one makes me sound like I should be opening hospitals and getting bunches of flowers from curt-seying little girls. This trace you say you've got?'

'Yes, uh, guv. The missing vehicle we think E took. It looks as if he drove from here to one of the other houses in . . .' He stabs a hand towards the window, gesturing outside. 'I suppose you'd call this a ring, would you?'

'Okay.' Fuck. 'And reports of further victims?'

'Nothing at the moment. But we're doing a safe-and-well check now . . .'

'Is the car abandoned at the other house?'

'No, we're tracking it. Workplace, contacts.'

'I know we shouldn't jump officially,' says Lorenzo. 'But it reeks of a classic multiple murder–suicide. Christ, what kind of fucker is it who can wipe out his entire family?'

'We don't close off roads as early as this,' she rebukes her junior. 'We don't know what happened here.'

She speaks for show, and possible case-review by an outside force. She already has a theory about why these four – and almost certainly five – people died, based on the way they lived.

Thinking that she will finally have to go upstairs and see her first spree, Kate is grateful to be delayed by the appearance of DC Taylor.

'Something from the local station, guv,' he says. 'Could be useful.'

'Go on.'

'There's a report of the perp – the *assumed* perp – being involved last night in a disturbance in a neighbouring village . . .'

Perp. TV has Americanized British detectives, which irritates her, but she lets it go.

'A disturbance?'

'He made a rather threatening visit.'

'Any casualties?'

'No. Verbal violence only, from what we can tell. But the recipient felt threatened enough to report it.'

'Name?'

'A . . . er . . .' He scrolls the memo function on his tablet. 'Nicky Mortimer.'

'Okay.' She turns to Lorenzo: 'Check the feasibility of seeing him.'

'Oh, and guv?' says Taylor.

'Mmm?'

'They've radioed from the tape. The local vicar's turned up.'

'What does he want?'

'*She*, actually. The, er, Reverend Sue.'

How shameful, when she always tells her own kids off for saying fire*men* and, indeed, police*men*.

'Why's she here?' she corrects herself.

'Says she wants to . . .' – a quotation voice, long polished in court – 'pray the area.'

'*Pray* it? Is that even an expression? Well, she'll have to wait until we've cleared it.'

SIX

AND HIS SHELTER WAS A STABLE

After the last and only time – which must be four years ago – Simon swore he'd never go shooting with them again. If higher-rate tax-payers need a Sunday-morning substitute for church-going, there must be better ones than standing in a ploughed field in a camouflage waistcoat blasting a midget discus into bits.

Lately, instead, he's been playing tennis with Tom: just the two of them on the Rutherfords' court in all weathers, it feeling almost adulterous not to be playing men's or mixed doubles with another two of their group. Tom's the best friend Simon has round here, never making him feel – as he does with Max or Jonny – that his balls are being weighed on a set of golden scales. Tom doesn't give the impression of laughing at your failure in not having a private All England Club of your own; his bashful manner on the subject suggests that he somehow won it in a lottery.

When they had finished playing yesterday – Simon winning two 6–6 sets on tie-breaks after losing the first one 4–6 – and were having a cold Bud in the kitchen (Emily was taking one of the Saturday-morning surgeries the government has insisted on to improve customer service), Tom said: 'Look, Si, are you okay and everything?'

'What? Has Tash put you up to this?'

'*No!*'

'Or Emily?'

'Absolutely not.'

He can tell from Tom's shock that he's telling the truth.

'I promise you, old mate, I haven't said anything to anyone, and wouldn't. Just you haven't seemed quite right since before Marrakesh. I know all that business with getting back was . . . If it's medical, then, yes, it's Emily's department. But, if there's anything you want to talk about, then tell a . . .'

Between two English men, the word 'friend' must lie undetonated. And, while Simon has absolutely no intention of telling his problems to anyone – although there is a brief moment when he considers confessing all, a human instinct that must explain how his wife's church became rich enough to settle all those law-suits from buggered altar boys – he's sufficiently touched by the other bloke's concern to be softened up for what comes next.

'Oh, I meant to mention, Si. We're going shooting as usual tomorrow at Northbury Farm . . .'

'Thanks for the warning. I'll be sure not to paraglide or fly a light aircraft over the area.'

'Seriously, it's unrecognizable now from the times you went.'

'Really? So there's no more Jonny and Max seeing who can shoot it higher?'

'I'm talking about the facilities. They've smartened up the whole operation. There's a proper club-house, not far off nineteenth-hole standard. Bacon sarnies before, pints afterwards. And the stands are way better. I've got really into fur-and-feather recently . . .'

'But enough about your fetishes.'

'Behave!'

Both Tom and Emily use that admonition; one of those things that couples share, like colds. And, though almost everyone Simon meets through business these days seems to shoot at weekends, which has given him a theory on the subject, he asks anyway: 'Why have they spruced it up?'

'Our old friend, demand. Andy Tonks . . .'

'Is he the ageing Bruce Willis lookalike who runs it?'

'What? Yes. He says he's never known so many people

wanting to shoot. And at least from what we see on Sunday mornings, it's all classes and ages, your proverbial brickies and baronets . . .'

'Great. Just what the UK needs in the age of road rage and recession, I'm sure: a heavily armed male population.'

'Oh, come on, Si, give it another go. With Max and Jonny I can feel a bit of a spare part . . .'

'There are three of us in this carnage, you mean? I can imagine.'

And the truth is that Simon can see some appeal in the idea as a vent for his frustrations, like smashing plates against a wall. So here he is the following day, picked up at 9 a.m. (Tasha says, in her most care-home tones, that it will be good for him, which almost makes him rethink) and driven in Tom's Freelander through the almost post-nuclear bleakness of a winter Sunday in the English countryside. The snows earlier in the month – catastrophically delaying their return from Marrakesh – have gone, leaving the best of winter; days that are chilly but dry and bright.

At the end of a long stretch of bare ploughed fields, he recognizes the approach to Northbury Farm, although, as Tom had promised, the site immediately looks changed. Beside the retro curly writing sign – advertising the farm and the sale of eggs, cheese and bacon – is another notice – straight black capitals on white – announcing a Clay Pigeon Shooting Range for four hours on both weekend mornings.

To the left, a field has been covered in asphalt, roped off and divided into white-lined parking bays. Tom's Land Rover joins a line that suggests the forecourt of an especially eclectic car dealer: neurotically new and polished 4x4s, BMWs and Mercedes alternate with battered flat-beds, paint-peeled jeeps and white vans advertising plumbing and electrical companies still showing 071 and 081 London phone numbers on their mud-splattered flanks.

The shooting costumes are equally contrasting. Two thin-faced wrinklies, in the old-English aristo mould, stand in tweed plus fours, deerstalker hats and thick brown hunting socks, as they lift from the boot of their Beamer scuffed metal gun cases that have doubtless been handed down through generations. But from the vans, trucks and jeeps come variously bulging (beer bellies, pumped muscles), sandpaper-scalped twenty- and thirty-somethings in army fatigues and boots, thumping towards the clubhouse with their guns already unsheathed and hanging from their meaty hands.

The rest – like Tom – resemble cover models for a Burberry Outdoor Range catalogue: multi-pocketed beige suede waist-coats – often matching the shade of the canvas gun bags strung across one shoulder – over polo-necked black or brown Arran sweaters, with chinos tucked into shooting socks. Dark beanies worn against the morning frost add a hint of guerrilla or commando to the outfit. Marching across the car park, the men give the impression of a private militia with an unusually broad social reach.

Simon is wearing jeans, trainers, the black Puffa jacket he used to use for junior rugby coaching, baseball cap and Bolton scarf. He hopes this get-up signals him as an irregular. The only other customer in such casual attire is a chubby man with wild grey hair whose T-shirt slogan seems to identify him as a farmer: *Happiness is a Tractor and a Big Girlfriend.*

He sees Max's sportster pussy-magnet parked as they reach the clubhouse. Jonny Crossan bawls across: 'Excellent work, Tom. The prodigal returns! Dunster's just getting in the pig baps.'

On cue, Max stamps down the steps of the wooden pavilion, clutching to his tummy, like a nervous fielder under a high catch, four steaming, napkin-wrapped rolls. Sartorially, Jonny belongs to the set recycling grandpa's wardrobe, Max to the high-street models. They dash through the pleasantries, shuffle off gloves and then eat. The bacon is microwaved beyond taste but, as with burgers and hotdogs at sport stadiums, tradition is more important than nutrition.

Ammunition next. They go inside the clubhouse. Last time Simon was here, the shells were dispensed from a box under a tree, but now there is a counter with lockable display cases containing tubes of graded explosives and a range of merchandise including sew-on patches, like scout badges, stitched with the letters DTL and then a number. At first, Simon wonders if some sort of private army really is being run from the farm but, when he asks about the insignia, Tom explains: 'Those? Oh, DTL means *down the line*. It's the number of birds you've nabbed in a row.'

Jonny, he now notices, has a DTL 50 patch on his gun-bag and Max a DTL 75 but Andy Tonks, smacking their boxes of shells down on the ledge, wears a DTL 500 sewn on to his shoulder, advertising his status as top gun, like a golf club pro playing off scratch. Tonks's chosen headgear is a beret. Ex-army, Simon guesses: Belfast, Falklands, then mercenary assistance on a couple of African coups before servicing the Sunday blood-lust of British businessmen.

Tonks – who, in concession to the temperature, is not today wearing the vest over bare skin that originally earned him the comparison with the star of *Die Hard* – notices Simon and says: 'New recruit today, gents?'

'A former player,' Jonny explains. 'Then picked up something nasty from the *Guardian*. But back on parade, I'm happy to say.'

Sensing the best approach to Jonny's metaphorical riffs, Tonks ignores the detail and responds generally: 'Well, he might use a recap of the rules. No alcohol – that incident with the hipflask is not forgotten, Mr Crossan. Guns broken at all times when moving between stands or waiting to shoot. Okay?'

'Broken?' Simon checks with Tom when they are out of the shop. 'That means snapped open between the barrel and the handle?'

'The butt and the stock, yes,' Tom replies, pulling language rank, as veterans in any field do.

The rest he more or less remembers. At regular intervals around the edge of a large wheat field – a few green buds showing in the rimy, corrugated ridges – stand olive-coloured bunkers, rather like bird hides, but from the roofs of which rise aluminium cylinders, angled in different directions, mounted on rotating motors.

Crouching in the grass behind the stand, Max, Tom and Jonny unpack their guns. There is general admiration of Max's, which seems to be new to them.

'Did you get yourself a bigger one?' asks Simon, but the intended sarcasm bypasses Max, who replies: 'What? The firepower's pretty similar. Twelve-bore. But I've moved from Browning to Beretta and – this time – I've opted for side-by-side rather than up-and-over.' Pointing to Tom's and Jonny's weapons, he establishes the difference between the two barrels being parallel or on top of each other. 'When you want to have a go, just choose the one that suits you, although, for my money, you won't do better than this one.'

'Although, as in so many other areas of life, what you're packing matters less than how you use it,' Jonny joins in, from ground-level, where he's assembling a gleaming Remington, a name that makes Simon think of westerns.

'Perhaps,' counters Max. 'Although the ideal is to have size *and* power.'

Simon enjoys the easy confirmation of the subtext he suspects in these Sundays.

The air is filled with the repeated sonic cough of lighted powder, sounding louder or softer depending on each shooting party's distance from their stand. The smell of spent shells wafts across the field like an odd pollen, though curiously reassuring in its reminder of bonfire nights.

Behind them is a railway embankment, intermittently shivered by the disturbance of air and earth from a Pendolino speeding to London. Tomorrow morning, before light, Simon will be on one: the last week before Christmas.

There's a queue at the first three shoots – 'People tend to do them in order, like a golf course, although there's no reason to,' Tom tells him – which confirms the popularity of the phenomenon, this chunk of rural Buckinghamshire now a Sabbath

Vietnam. So Simon watches, with Tom as his guide: 'Over there, that's called fur-and-feathers . . .'

'Ah, yes. You mentioned . . .'

'You get two clays at a time: bird and rabbit. The rabbit, as the name suggests, shoots along the ground. So you have to aim high and low in close succession.'

As they watch a group of the buzz-cut younger shooters in combat clothes, he notices the used cartridges spilling out of the side of their guns, whereas the older types are stopping to reload.

Tom follows his gaze: 'The camouflage lads use automatics. And they never pick up the dead shells. Sore point with the committee.'

'Probably the videos they grew up on. Clay Pigeon Rambo. You lot don't?'

'We're purists. Although Max might well go automatic one day, if he thought it would give him a competitive advantage.'

There is no discussion about order. As if by right, Max snaps his gun shut and walks towards the stall.

'Who'll pull for me?' he asks.

'But enough—' says Jonny.

'About your sex life,' Max and Tom complete the joke for him. Simon tries not to think about the extent to which life becomes repetition.

Tom joins Max at the stand, asking him: 'Do you want them together or on report?'

'Report.'

Max braces the gun against his shoulder and shouts: 'Pull!'

On command, Tom presses a small plastic device in his hand, from which a wire leads to the stand. Simon hears the click of the rotating cylinder and then the crack of the shot but doesn't see the clay at all.

'Kill!' shouts Max, then, in rapid succession, 'Pull! . . . Kill! . . . Pull! . . . Kill! . . . Pull! . . . Kill!', his words split by the whirr of the bird-launcher and the thunder of his gun.

Suddenly, Tom shouts 'Incoming!' and the trio of regulars cover their heads and crouch-run backwards, Tom pulling

Simon with him. When they straighten up, there's a semi-fractured clay lying on the ground where they were standing, resembling a shellac ashtray, warm to the touch from its explosive elevation.

'Sorry, guys,' says Max. 'We're shooting into the wind today.'

'Normally, they just fall in the field,' Tom explains. 'I wouldn't buy your Weetabix from here.'

Max kills another ten birds in a row – down the line – before swapping places with Tom, who asks for the pairs to be despatched at the same time. Tom doesn't call the hits but Jonny does it for him, although the shout is rarely heard because he seems to miss most of them.

'Ah,' he says, taking from Max a scorecard mainly pencilled with Xs, 'my eye seems out today.'

'Shocking, Captain Rutherford,' says Max. 'Absolutely shocking. No wonder we lost Northern Ireland.'

'Can former soldiers be court-martialled, is what I'm wondering,' Jonny adds.

Simon has a horrible feeling that Tom may have shot badly in order to make his reluctant guest's own impending efforts look better in comparison.

Jonny adopts a complicated wide-legged stance, side-on, like McEnroe's corkscrew serve. The commentary is monotonous – 'Kill! . . . Kill! . . . Kill! . . . Kill! . . . Kill!' – until a sudden variation: 'Smoked! Smoked! Kill! Smoked! Kill! Smoked!'

Simon looks questioningly at Max, who explains: 'It means the bird is shattered completely. Just dust. Only show-offs shout it, though.'

Jonny snaps his gun – the gunpowder stench so strong that it stings the back of Simon's throat – and holds it out like a torn French stick: 'Want to show us what you've got, Mr Lonsdale?'

On his previous visit, Simon refused to shoot. He feared it would be like porn: the browser who finds a site of hitherto-unimagined scenes and is startled by an answering desire.

This time – from curiosity rather than courtesy – he takes

the weapon. He is relieved that he feels no immediate urge to assassinate a politician or shoot up a high-school. The gun feels heavy, awkward, alien. And yet his mind cajoles him into believing that he may feel better for having fired it.

Tom, standing beside, shows him how to rest the butt on his shoulder at an angle that leaves enough space for the recoil: 'Most people new to it – they go home with a bruised shoulder.'

Tom is on the wire for him.

'Pull!' Simon shouts, the confidence of his voice surprising him. He hears the clatter of the contraption and is aware of a dark spec in the sky. He pulls the trigger, first too gently to engage it and then with compensating strength.

Few human occurrences now are genuinely fresh: the testimony of print or film previewing every action or emotion. Even a fresh generation of astronauts would only be comparing notes. Simon is ready to be shocked by the kick of the gun. And he is. It feels – again, a metaphor he has inherited from reading accounts written by other firearm virgins – alive in his hands, like an eel or a snake.

'Pull!' he shouts again and this time fires more quickly but with no more hope of contact. Two perfectly circular clays will lie between the buds of wheat.

'It takes some time to get the hang of it,' Tom says consolingly. But Simon's failure has been a reassurance. Initial disappointment that this simulated killing did nothing to slake his rages and frustrations soon gives way to relief that he has no violence – or, at least, not of this kind – in him.

*

Mumsie drives her their in the Golf that's going to be hers for driving practice when she gets to seventeen. They let her choose the colour – yellow, which meant they had to weight because apparently that's, like, a custom-something – but not the car. She really wanted one of those sweet little Beetles, like Rosie's mumsie has, but that became a federal case for some reason. Mumsie said it wasn't 'practical' to learn in. Troll!

She's already had a go in the Golf in the fields around there house. The first time, it just, like, stopped, and she sat their thinking *fuck* she'd trashed it and Mumsie and Dadsie would go all Prezident Obama on her about how lucky she is to have these chances. But Hugo, who was standing in the middle of the field like a horse trainer, just came over and, without needing oxygen or anything, taught her all about stalling. To be honest, she wishes Hugo could go out with her on the proper roads but it's gonna be Mumsie. Josh says she holds on to the roof-strap and keeps pressing her feet into the floor like she's breaking.

Tilly reckoned Dunster Manor would be a big old house like in *Rebecca* they were made to watch in English. But, when they get their, it's like an airport or whatever: low flat-brick walls and glass and stuff.

'Ask questions but not too many questions,' says Mumsie, being really bitchy, 'and try not to say "like" between every word. And, if you have to write anything for any reason, for God's sake use spell-check somehow.' Yeah, yeah, speling is for wimpz. 'Don't roll your eyes like that, either. And even though you've seen him in his swimmers in Barbados, call him Mr Dunster. I'll pick you up at six.' She pulls the Golf door closed and then opens it again. 'And it's *yes*, not *yeah*.'

'Yeah, whatever.'

'Tilly!' Gotcha, Mumsie. 'You're really lucky to have this chance. Oh, and you haven't got that wretched iPod, have you?'

'Nada.'

In reception, there's this cool smiley girl called Becky (plastic boob-badge), who's wearing a really nice dress she saw on the Abercrombie website, and goes, 'Good morning. How can I help you?'

'Oh, right.' Jeez, this is awks, like speaking in tutor group. 'I'm, um, Tilly Crossan. I'm here to, like, trail, Max, Mr Dunster for a day. Work Experience?'

Becky frowns. 'Really? I don't think I have anything down.'

Fanfuckingtastic. She's always been worried the rents had

fixed it up with the Dunces when they were all drunk one Friday or Saturday night. Or both.

'Tilly – was it? – do you know who this was fixed up with?'

'Oh? I, like, think my Mum . . . Mum and Dad know him. Libby and Jonny Crossan.'

Weird how it never feels quite right giving the folks first names, although there are a few at school who *Charlotte* and *David* theres all the time, even when there not, like, steps or Mummy's special *friend* type shit.

'Tilly, do you want to take a seat over there and I'm sure we can sort this?'

There are these, like, swing doors between the seats and Becky's desk and they swish open and this guy in a track-suit comes through. He's really old (thirty?) but dead fit and he definitely gives her the full body scan, even though Mumsie made her wear a body-burka and what she calls the Sensible Coat. Tilly was, like, I'll be inside all day but She was only on transmit, as usual. Troll.

Emily's speaking quietly on the phone – like the nurses on TV when someone's in a coma – but you can still here easily enough: 'Jackie? It's Becky. Max is in with Steve, right? . . . Just I've got a young girl . . .' – get her! – '. . . called, er, Tilly Crossan in reception. She thinks she's trailing Max for a school thing? . . . no, there's nothing on the master grid either . . . okay, you're an angel.'

Big voice now: 'Tilly, we're checking. This isn't your fault at all.'

No, we no whose fault it is, like usual. Needs to drink less. She and Hugo do a song: 'We say go to rehab but Mummy says no no no'.

'Thank you,' she says to Becky.

The walls around are covered in old drawings. Victorian or something, probably. The swing doors swish again and here comes Max Dunster with a big smile and his arms stretched out like that time he forgot to pick up Rosie from the gymkhana. 'Max is such a charmer,' Mumsie always says.

150

When she was younger and thinking that she really must have been adopted, her fantasy dad would have been something like Max. He has dark hair (not like Dadsie's ginge frizz that he's given to her, which was always a bit of a blow to the adoption theory), which still has hold and bounce, plus he's got a good tan and a not-bad bod for an old guy. Not hot but not totally not-hot. And you never feel he's perving on you, like some of the guys you see at Sports Day and Speech Day, who look at you like the paedos on *South Park*. Actually, none of the husbands in what Mumsie calls The Eight are really like that. In fact, strictly confidential, she sometimes worries that Dadsie is the one: the way he stares at Phoebe Rutherford's and Polly Lonsdale's boobs and (ew!) their wazoos when the whole gang get together for a barbecue-and-swim day.

'Tilly, Tilly,' he says, holding out his hand to shake, which is what he always does, not like some of the other dads slobbering at you on both cheeks with stinky drinky breath and leaning for balance on your bra-strap. 'This is going to be fine. Absolutely fine. We've got our diaries a bit crossed . . .' – Becky behind the desk lets out a bit of a grunt – 'My fault entirely, my dear Becky, no one else's. But we can make it work today still. Come with me. Becky, you have permission to horse whip me at the appropriate time.'

Omigod! Tilly's struggling not to giggle as he (these heels, these heels) sprints down a long corridor with more of those old pictures and now some new ones as well. There's an open door at the end of the corridor and he waves her in. He helps her off with her coat, like Grandpa does, and hangs it on a rack. Max's office is a bit like the ones in the interviews round of *The Apprentice*: desks, chairs, paintings and stuff. He waves towards a leather seat for her. On the table behind the desk are photos of Jenno (Hello? And you complain that we can't spell), Rosie and Jamie and one of another older boy she doesn't recognize. Plus some really ancient people, from before colour photos: probably his folks.

'So, Tilly, forgive me. Now I remember, there was a letter.'

Yeah. She can see her frigging pink paper on his desk and is going to show him when he puts on these big black spex and gets there. 'Ah, yes. I'm pleased to see your spelling isn't any better than my lot. I always think we should get a refund from Westbury Park's English department.'

She gives him the ha-ha-ha laugh she developed for Dadsie's jokes.

'This is some kind of school project?'

'Well, yeah. *Yes*. For Business Studies, we have to, like . . .'

'Study a business? Sure. Your letter said you need to observe, which you can certainly do this afternoon, though possibly not with me. I've got the last part of one of these medicals they make us have at our age. Your dad probably has them . . .'

At Family Sunday Lunch (which Mumsie makes them have), Dadsie claimed last week that some doctor in London had stuck a finger up his bum. Ew. The prostrate or whatever.

'Um, I think so.'

'And you also need to interview me about the business. Which we can do now. I've been able to cut short a routine with Stuart Pearson, our finance manager.' Routine? Are they, like, dancing? 'Do you want to record this?'

'Oh, yeah. If I . . .'

She puts her iPhone 3 into flight-safe mode and scrolls down to the voice recorder. In the pocket of the rancid jacket Mumsie made her wear, she finds her list of questions.

'Pink ink, Tilly? That's not what you get when you're interviewed by the *Financial Times*. Well, in a way, you do . . .'

She has absolutely no idea what he's on about. She straightens the list of questions on her knee, finding her special pink pen annoyingly hard to read. Before, she imagined herself looking him in the eye, like on television, but, now it comes to it, she reads them.

'You're, er, called Dunster and so's the company. How far back do your family go?'

'Oh? This has always been a family business. It was founded

in Manchester in 1803 by the first Maxwell Dunster, my great-great-great-great grandfather. Did you get all those greats, Tilly? Four of them. The name came down the male line. I'm strictly Maxwell Dunster the Sixth but it always sounds a bit American to me.'

Fuck. Praying the recorder is working, she forgets to ha-ha-ha him but he carries on anyway: 'Maxwell Dunster the 1st set up as a rival in the diary business to John - L-E-T-T-S - Letts. You probably know Letts Diaries? No, well he was a stationer in London who realized that the business people he was selling paper to were always looking for books to write down their meetings with merchants and suppliers and their addresses and so on. And so he came up with the appointments diary, as opposed to the sort of diary in which people wrote down their thoughts about the day. Like Peeps . . .'

WTF? She has no idea what Peeps is but, as long as the recording is working, can Google it later.

'. . . to this day, Letts remain our major rivals on the diary side. But, luckily for our shareholders today, the first and second Maxwell Dunsters – Jackie, my PA, can give you a family tree with dates and everything – diversified into the wider communication business: the nineteenth-century equivalent of social networking, I like to say. Business cards, gift cards, notepaper, calendars. You probably saw when you were sitting in reception, we have the original artwork from many of the early calendars. Victorians would actually anticipate every year who would be in the cartoon on the front of the Dunster calendar – politicians, society figures or whoever – in the same way people now speculate over who will be on, I don't know, *The Graham Norton Show*.'

The phone on his desk – an old-fashioned one on a big square box, with a sort of cord – buzzes.

'Tilly, I'd better take this.' He picks it up and puts on a posher, deeper voice, like when Mumsie is on the phone about Pony Club. 'Yes, Jackie? . . . is she? . . . okay, I'd better talk to her . . .' He covers the mouthpiece and whispers: 'Just got to take this quickly, Tilly, okay?'

Then he reaches across, picks up her iPhone and, sliding his glasses down his nose like old dudes do, finds Pause and presses it, which is all a bit Torchwood.

'Hi,' he says. 'Hi, Tasha . . . no, reception's very patchy in the office, which does at least mean the staff actually get some work done . . . yes, I was going to call back but an unexpected intern . . . no, not like *that*, it's Tilly Crossan . . .' Celebrity! Who's he talking to? Oh, *that* Tasha. 'Well, that's because Steve is saying there isn't going to be a Christmas Party this year . . . yes, I know I'm in charge . . . Tash, Tash, can I call you back after this?'

'Sorry,' he says. 'Do you want to switch your . . . ?'

She puts it back on.

'Was that Mrs Lonsdale?' she asks, feeling, for the first time, like a proper reporter.

'What? Oh, yes. She does our catering.'

'Wow. She's, like, a really amazing cook.'

'Yes. Do you want to get back to your questions?'

She runs her finger down the pink list and asks: 'Oh and is this, where we are now, like where Dunster Manor was originally?'

He laughs in that way that beaks and oldies do when you've made an arse-clown of yourself: 'Oh, I should have explained that. There never has been a Dunster Manor. Although your dad sometimes calls our house that, as a joke. *My* pa – that's him in the black-and-white photo over there – changed the brand from Dunster to Dunster Manor in the 1960s. He realized that there was a big American market for English nostalgia. People in Bumsuck, Kentucky' – omigod! Rude-word alert! – 'liked the idea that their diary or calendar or notecards came from some huge estate with a lord of the manor riding his horse past farm labourers and milkmaids. The Dunster Manor logo we still use – the big country house with vines and a cart outside – was knocked up by one of the calendar artists in about 1962.

It's one of those strange things about history. A lot of the specs – that's specifications – that were going out of fashion here in the sixties – ribbon bookmarks and . . .' – no fucking idea what he just said – '. . . you're looking blank – G-I-L-T F-O-I-L – gilt-foil edges – that's when the side of the book looks shiny, like a Bible – were suddenly all the rage in the States.'

'Wow!' she says, buying time, because she suddenly can't read Mumsie's handwriting on the next question.

'Interesting stuff, isn't it?'

Like, *no*. 'Oh, er . . .' She's got to what Mumsie called the killer question. 'Is it, like, difficult at the moment because people, like, don't use this kind of stuff so much?'

'This kind of stuff?'

Suddenly, he sounds like Dadsie with a strop on. Man up, Tilly.

'Well, yeah. Appointments . . .' The word sounds grown up in her mouth, going to see the doctor or the dentist. 'Thank-you notes and that. Don't people do all that on their smart-phones now?'

He leans forward, all serious, like when she asked Dr Rafi to go on the pill. Awkward!

'Well, I can see why you'd think that. But have you heard of something called Diversification . . . ?'

Yeah, I'm not a retard: like *Glee* doing the tour and the albums and the movie. The, like, top dude on the show said in *Closer* that multiplatform is the only way now.

'I think so.'

'Business is about adapting. Do you remember . . .' He says *fy-low*-something. 'Well, that's the point I'm making. Suddenly, in the 1980s, people were carrying round these, in effect, diaries with removable pages. Letts saw that first and got heavily into the – do you need me to spell it? – the F-I-L-O-F-A-X. Dunster's were a little slow off the mark then but not since, I hope. You probably don't remember electronic personal organizers either? But we found an American partner for those. And it's absolutely true that thank-you notes are a declining market, although your mum still always sends them, for example. So, in the nineties, we diversified into the neash luxury-goods business.' She can Google *neash* later. 'Dunster Manor chocolates, shortbread, fruitcakes. The Americans eat them as fast as we can make them. At the moment, we're developing Dunster Manor apps for mobile phones, Kindle's tablet devices: a twenty-first-century version of the diaries and calendars the first Maxwell Dunster made two hundred years ago. With which, Tilly, I think we've come nicely full-circle.'

'Thank you.'

She reaches for her iPhone and switches off the voice recorder.

'I hope it's recorded.'

'Yeah, I think so.'

'Because I'm not sure I could say all that again!'

She *ha-ha-ha*s him. He says he's got his medical appointment in the afternoon but Bobby Someone in Production will take her round the site and show her what's what, although a lot of it happens elsewhere now *lah lah lah lah lah*. Thank God Mumsie doesn't know you don't need an iPod once you've got an iPhone.

*

To be perfectly honest, he only came to the party because Monifa wanted to. Especially since they moved out, she suffers an insecurity about belonging – it's a subject largely undiscussed in their marriage, apart from her occasional jokes about being 'the only black in the village' – and somewhere secretly, he suspects, she took the invitation to the Crossans' Christmas Drinks as a sign of acceptance in the country. The country*side*, that is. As he has had to explain to more than one Ku-Bucks-Klanster out here, Monifa was born in England as much as they were.

He feels a pulse of protective love for her being – yet again – the only non-white face in the room. He can't imagine what it must be like. When they lived in London and friends would explain that they'd taken the kids away from the local state primary because they 'were getting a bit left out on the playground' (which was one of the accepted codes) they were talking percentage balances. But, at a social and professional level, Monifa is often literally on her own. At some bashes in the country, there are Asian nannies and au pairs but – here – the domestic help seem to be interchangeable Antipodeans, standing in one corner of the vast barn – a conversion on two levels – and refilling each other's glasses from bulky jugs of fruit punch. Their hostess – Libby Crossan, a small woman with dark ringlets, who seems to have spent the evening almost jogging between knots of guests, with a laugh you'd have to call a cackle – has explained more than once that these girls are the designated drivers, paid extra for the night to shuttle their families here and back in the fleet of showroom-glowing Discoveries lined up outside.

It wouldn't have worked for the Mortimers. They've left the kids with a babysitter: Hannah Smith from next door. The invitation didn't mention children but there seem to be dozens of teenagers – flirtatious, fashion-victim girls, boys standing slackly uncoordinated like puppets with broken strings – and quite a few younger.

Nicky looks around, hoping for someone he knows. Blinking in surprise at seeing David Cameron in conversation with the Prince of Wales, he squints across the crowd and spots David Beckham talking to Barack Obama. Both men, though, have clearly ceased their exercise regimes and, as the American president slides his face on to his forehead, in order to drink more easily, Nicky understands what has happened. Although the party wasn't advertised as a masked ball, several guests have brought those plastic jelly-moulds of celebrities that are sold in joke and gift shops.

From the middle of the semicircle of guests to which he is loosely attached, the muscular, grey-haired quiet guy he recognizes as the doctor's husband says: 'It said in the local paper they've got special patrols on the back roads, hoping to catch party boozers.'

One of the wives is coming towards him: tall, with shoulder-length chestnut hair, younger than most of the women here. Her dark-blue dress protrudes impressive cleavage which he tries, as a post-feminist man, not to notice.

'I think I remember you from Marrakesh Airport!' she says.

'Nicky Mortimer,' he replies, offering his hand, but she leans in for a double-*mwah*, with scents of perfumed ears and cham-pagned breath, identifying herself, thankfully close enough to his better ear, as 'Jenno Dunster'.

'Ah, yes, of course.'

Married – isn't she? – to the tall one: the calendar tycoon who's on the train less often?

'How long did it take *you* to get back?' she asks.

They're raising their voices over pounding music from giant speakers in each corner. The sound comes from an iPod on a wall-mount. He's too far away to see the display panel but the device seems to be on shuffle as the playlist jumps arbitrarily between Radio 1, Radio 2 and Classic Rock. 'Satisfaction' by the Stones is followed by a hip-hop track he doesn't recognize. Signs in childish felt-pen writing – a smiley face in the dot above the i – direct guests to DANCING UPSTAIRS!

'Well,' he tells Jenno, already feeling social throat from the effort of projecting. 'As it turned out, we were lucky. We'd opted for the lunchtime flight because Nina had her Grade-8 violin next day. We were diverted to Luton because Heathrow and Birmingham were closed and – according to what people in the passport queue said – we were the last to land at Luton. *London* Luton, as they call it now, though fooling who? What about you?'

'We'd gone for the 6 p.m. back to make the most of the time. The web junkies among the boys had seen stuff about snow closures in the morning but we sort of ignored it and shopped for England. When we got to the airport, it just said *annulé* in French under all the flights to the UK. And we were, like: *what?*'

'Crikey. Was there panic?'

'Well, most of us have live-ins, so the kids were fine. Bit of weepies down the phone because some of the online stuff was saying it might last all week and our Rosie's started reading news feeds. Jonny was due in court next morning but he rang that sort of spiv they have and got it shifted to someone else. How did people manage before mobiles? It was worst for the Lonsdales because Tasha's folks were looking after the kids and Simon's so tight and Northern that he didn't want to pay the extra hotel. I think he's still trying to get it back on insurance. The rest of us just enjoyed two extra days in the sun. Better hotel as well, as it happened. Max's PA found us one in the shadow of the Atlas mountains.'

Her eyes do the social slide. She mouths a hello at someone he can't see and says: 'Must circulate.'

Nicky wanders among the tipsily shrill mob, a roving microphone capturing fragments of speech: 'I finally eagled the third there for the first time in my life. The one with that bugger of a bunker . . .' And: 'The chemo was sixteen weeks. Her hair's grown back three-quarters now. Been an absolute trouper.'

He sees his wife on the far side of the barn talking to Dr Rutherford and, feeling socially useless (he has never been good at parties), crashes their chat. It slightly concerns him that Monifa has stuck with the one person she knew (and professionally, not socially) in advance. He flutters his fingers on his wife's back.

'Oh, hi, sweetie. Emily was just telling me about these houses . . .'

The doctor, it strikes him, stands out among this gathering almost as much as Monifa; she is the only woman in the room with grey hair. The Dye-Hard generation, as he thinks of them.

'The Grenvilles? Well, it's Tom's subject, really. He's literally written the book. Or is writing it . . .'

'I've heard bits on the train,' Nicky contributes, fighting, as usual, the sense of a social occasion as unwillingly improvised theatre. 'Are all four of the houses exactly the same?'

'*Were*. Tom's got a whole bit in the book about symmetry: both the houses individually and as a quartet. And they're listed now, so the basic shapes are the same. And I think they all already had Agas when we bought them. But everyone has done their little nips and tucks . . .'

'Do they all have a barn conversion like this?' asks Monifa.

'Three of them.' The doctor smiles. 'Jonny and Libby did it first, then Max and Jenno followed, although they'll probably both tell you it was the other way round.'

'Simultaneous inspiration, I guess,' says Monifa. 'I've worked some copyright cases. That's what people tend to say. You said three of them? So you, Emily . . .'

'No. We put in a tennis court instead.'

There's a silence – sipping and appreciation of drinks – which Nicky feels elected to end: 'The four of you – I mean the four couples – who went to Morocco, you seem very thick . . . ?'

'Thank you very much . . .'

'I mean close . . .'

'Mmm, I mean we drive each other crazy sometimes. And you still sometimes have to sweat about seating plans. But I was thinking in Marrakesh – life is about gangs. School, uni, villages. I read somewhere that nobody really makes new friends after the age of thirty . . .'

Monifa looks down, her manner when riding an insult, and, though he's sure Emily meant nothing deliberately, Nicky feels a vicarious sting, as he always does when the castle doors of England clang against his wife or their children.

'How's it hanging, you old banker?'

He turns to find Jonny Crossan, dressed in the full penguin rig.

'Jonny!' They shake hands and hold the grip, probably both considering a supporting arm rub or shoulder slap and then aborting it. 'Thank you for inviting us.'

'I guessed that our nation's financial community was

probably short of white card on the mantelpiece this festive season . . .'

Two teenage girls in white blouses and black skirts stop beside them. The elder refills their champagne flutes without asking, while the younger totes a silver tray of the *trompe l'oeil* nosh that has become more or less obligatory at such dos: bonsai fish and chips in tiny newsprint cones, shrunken toad-in-the-hole and meat pies the width of tuppenny bits. Such Lilliputian food suits both the aesthetic and dietetic aspirations of this set.

Jonny strokes the gingery mane of the younger girl – 'Nicky, this is Plum, my younger daughter' – and nods in the direction of the elder, blonde waitress: 'And Polly Lonsdale, whose mother is responsible for these exquisite nibbles. You met Tash in . . . ?'

'Yes.'

'You can rely on Tasha. Succulent, juicy and extremely more-ish. And her food's not half bad either.'

'Oh, Daddy, you're so embarrassing,' complains the Crossan girl. The cook's daughter drops her head as if hoping that her fringe will make her invisible.

The subject of this discussion – or at least Nicky thinks so – comes over to join them, although she looks different: thinner maybe, or her blonde hair fluff-cut shorter.

'Nicky? Tasha,' she confirms. 'Marra—'

'Of course.'

Tasha takes a dwarf canapé from the tray.

'Try and whizz them round while they're nice and hot,' she tells the waitresses. 'These are lukewarm.'

'What you get for employing slave labour, Mum,' says the one with the champagne bottles.

'I'm paying them the minimum wage,' Tasha says, her speech quite sloshy. 'By which I mean the minimum I could think of.'

Nicky, who can never quite switch off his business brain, wonders if she's catering the party at a discount for her friends or at the normal rates, but judges it too rude to ask. As close as he gets is: 'Don't you have to be in the kitchen, cracking the whip?'

'And miss a party like this? Rachel, my event manager, does all that.'

'This must be a busy week in your line?'

Through the natural undercurrents at stand-and-chats, the group they were in has fragmented, reshaped by someone seeing a friend or fleeing a bore, and merged with other huddles, leaving him alone with Tasha.

'Yeah. Christmas drinks and summer weddings are our biggies,' she tells him. 'But at the moment we're getting fucked – excuse me – like everyone else. I do this one at cost and good-on-yer . . .'

'Right.'

'And a lot of firms are playing the Grinch card this year . . .'

'The what? Oh, cancelled Christmas.'

'Yeah. My husband's at Samson . . .'

'I know . . .'

'And – two years ago – their Crimbo do was Will Smith DJ-ing and Paul McCartney running the tombola type of thing. This year, they sent round an email saying a donation will be made to the Red Cross Disaster Fund. Which is fine but – when everyone starts doing it – it's a fucking disaster for the piss-up support industry, like me.'

'Although I doubt Sir Adrian's Christmas lunch at home will be on an austerity budget.'

'Well, exactly. Apparently he's fifty on the 25th – wouldn't he just have to share a birthday with the Messiah? – and he was planning to fly a hundred people to Antigua in a chartered 747. When Simon tried to tell him it wasn't a good idea, he said it was a private occasion financed with his own money. He's from planet where, exactly . . . ?'

She takes another slug of Roederer Cristal and he's about to tell her that Robbins Schuster Geneva also has a global directive against Christmas parties this year but, with bubbles still on her lips, she carries on, though lowering her voice: 'Even my old friend Mad Max is doing the Scrooge thing. Previous years, the Dunster Manor bash in December has been my equivalent of Wimbledon to a strawberry farmer. The full Christmas dinner inside a baby baked-potato shell was practically fucking Heston Blumenthal. But, this year, it's a big box of Quality Street on reception and Secret Santa on the last Friday before . . .'

'Are they having a bad time?'

'What? Well, no, this is the thing. According to Max, Rudolf and the other reindeer are going to the court of European Human Rights because they're so knackered from carting retro Dickensian grub and stuff to North America. No, apparently the board feels that it would Send The Wrong Signal' – she snaps thumb and finger together to subvert the words – 'to be seen scoffing micro mince pies in the' – the hand gesture again – 'Current Economic Climate. And – if even Mad Max is worried about pissing off the poor – then the country really is buggered.'

This hurricane conversationalist – you'd think she hadn't spoken to anyone for weeks – takes a long reflective drink, which allows Nicky to interject: 'Our hosts tonight don't seem to be hanging the sackcloth. They . . .'

'No. Well, that's Jonny and Libby for you. They're what I call the megaphone wealthy. This is even more OTT than last year. And I mean they've invited pretty much anyone they . . .'

She tails off, sober enough to spot the offence. A taller girl with ginger hair stops beside them with a tray of what turn out to be minuscule cucumber sandwiches, the size of thumb-nails, complete with crusts. He takes three, then puts one back, fearful of seeming greedy.

'How's it going, Tilly?' Tasha asks.

'Fine.'

'How was your work experience with Max?'

'Fine. Actually, you rang up when I was, like, interviewing him?'

'Did I?'

In the next reshuffle – country party as country dance – they are nudged into another huddle.

'Hi,' says Tasha.

'Oh, hi.'

This exchange is with her husband – the ferrety little one who's the joker on the Pendolinos – although you don't need to be CEO of Relate to notice that they don't seem very thrilled to see each other. Dr Rutherford's husband is also in this pack and so is a big, red-faced lady in a green dress who keeps saying 'Pardon?' to the woman next to her. Although, embarrassingly, the conversation in the group seems to have been stopped by the inclusion of Nicky and Tasha.

'Oh dear, was my husband telling you all how wonderful I am?' she asks. 'Should I go?'

'Actually, Tash,' says Tom Rutherford. 'The chaps were discussing the best ever players and best ever managers at our football clubs.'

'Oh-*kay*. Well, I'd certainly be up for that. You all know Nicky Mortimer? Nicky, fire away . . .'

He isn't sure if she's joking and her manner gives no clue. So he says: 'Well, for me Peter Osgood and José Mourinho. Although, ironically, I'm not entirely sure the former would even have got into the latter's team.'

'And that would be . . . *Chelsea*!'

'Bravo, Tasha!' Tom Rutherford says. Nicky is also impressed. Though he is extremely married, any theoretical fantasies he has involve a woman genuinely interested in football.

'A lucky shot. Mums of teenage sons pick stuff up,' Tasha says. 'Which reminds me that I haven't spotted Josh in here for hours . . .'

She looks at Simon, who says: 'Don't look at me!'

'Oh, well, he's probably spliffing up or shagging the nanny. And, Simon, who have you gone for from Burnley, only joking, Bolton?'

'What's this about?'

'It's not about anything, darling. I'm taking an interest in your interests?'

'You've been drinking.'

'Sherlock Lonsdale cracks the secret point of Christmas parties. And you haven't been?'

'Okay, okay, darling. Take it easy.'

Tom Rutherford steps into the embarrassed tension created by a couple's public row: 'If you really want to know, Tash, Si went for Nat Lofthouse and Sam Allardyce.'

This pool of guests uncertainly disperses. Champagne and social discomfort telling on his bladder, Nicky asks: 'Does anyone know where the loos are?'

Tash points to another homemade notice – GENTS & LADIES – on cut-out paper finger-shapes pointing towards the main barn doors.

'I'll come with you,' says Tasha. 'I mean, I need to . . .'

There are so many interlocking knots of gossip, porcupined with elbows holding drinks, that they are forced to the edges to find a route through. Nicky finds himself, disconcertingly, with his cheek brushing carpet.

'Ah,' he shouts, 'did she bring these back from Marrakesh?'

'I think so. Most of them did.' She scuffs her feet. 'Check out the floor. I think Libs got rugs and cowhides as well.'

As they struggle through, comments drift from conversations: 'Last year was an absolute disaster. Jonty tore his spare pair of salopettes on the first morning. So I was spending every afternoon in a laundrette.' And: 'I'll give you the chap's card. Nothing illegal. Just a few back-doubles. This fiscal, I paid 30k tax on income of a mill six.'

Outside, his face smarts as the sweat from the party lights and body heat meets the biting night cold. Above the village, fireworks are fizzing, the celebratory seasons blurred by the moneyed seeking fun. They follow an illuminated path around a covered swimming pool to the house, its windows rectangles of warm inviting light. Lying on the ground is a trampled scattering of one of the shrunken foodstuffs – walnut-sized plum puddings topped with a tiny gelatine holly sprig – spilled by the under-age waitresses. At least two dogs are barking in harsh harmony, presumably in a kennel somewhere to the right towards the stables.

'What do they have?'

'A black lab and a little yappy one. That's pretty standard round here.'

He's struck by how frequently Tasha seems to speak as an external observer, a Carraway to the Gatsbys of Max and Jonny. The Rutherfords also seem to have some distance from the glittering centre of the circle, through Emily's professional exposure to the world from which these people's treasures separate them. Admitted by job and income, disinherited by his wife's skin, Nicky always feels ambivalence on such peacock evenings.

Inside the house, there are queues for the two downstairs loos so they follow another paper finger upstairs. Two doors on the same corridor are identified as BOYS & GIRLS but, when they try the handles, both rebuff them.

'There are never enough by this stage of the evening. We had Portaloos in the garden at our last one,' says Tasha. Nicky test-flies in his mind a joke about how full of shit these people are, but politeness overcomes his idea of himself as an outsider.

From inside the male facilities, there's a flush, a tap-splash and a click. Max Dunster folds himself through the door, bent almost in half to clear the nineteenth-century frame. Offering a hand still wet from the basin, he says: 'Ah, Nicky, excellent. Very keen to discuss with you the euro's future or not.' And then, seeing the other figure in the corridor: 'Tash! Smashing snacks, even by your standards.'

'Good. A lot of it's stuff I'd ear-marked for your do.'

'Oh, Tasha-basha, don't be cruel to me.'

Nicky enjoys a spectacularly sustained slash, happy at the lack of symptoms of the number-one male cancer. The walls of the lavatory are filled with framed photographs of Crossan-looking children of various sizes sitting or standing in lines of hooped-shirted students. He finds his own N.M. Mortimer in the Girls Under-13 Hockey next to M.P.R.V. Crossan. So Tilly is short for Matilda.

Walking back to the barn, he passes Tasha and Max, talking intensely by the poolhouse. Both are smoking, his free hand thrust into a jacket pocket, hers hugged under her armpit. Without coats, they must be perished, adding pneumonia to the potential deaths already listed on the packet.

As a reluctant socializer, Nicky knows that the two disasters at crowded parties are to arrive too late or to go out and come back in alone. In the hot, loud room, he wanders between tight throngs of gossipers and close-together duos whose body language repels interruption.

Looking for a group he can join, he catches more snatches of chat: 'I don't think an email is adequate. I still hold store by a proper thank-you letter. Or a note-let.' And: 'Have you seen that documentary about Enron? In the end, the whole thing unravelled because a journalist asked the simple question: what does Enron actually do to make its money? Exposed the whole thing as a fantasy?' And: 'I seem completely to have lost my knack with meringues.' Finally, the punchline of a joke: 'You get to smell the goods but not to taste them!'

That would be the one about what a pizza deliveryman and a gynaecologist have in common, then. A sign that the event has reached the stage of things being said that would never be spoken sober.

Trying to find Monifa, he comes across the Rutherfords instead.

'We're thinking of making a move,' she says. 'I've got surgery in the morning and with this bloody chest bug panic . . .'

The doctor's husband asks: 'I don't suppose you've seen Mad Max anywhere, have you? I'm supposed to be fixing a security review of his factory over the break.'

Nicky feels the little thrill of insider information: 'I just saw him outside by the poolhouse. With, er, Tasha.'

'Did you?' says Emily. 'Like guilty things!'

Nicky wonders what's being got at until she puts two fingers to her mouth and blows between them. He smiles at the mime.

'Oh, right. Yes, I'm afraid they were. Listen, is he "Mad Max" just in the way that women called Lucy get called "Juicy" . . . ?'

'Well, not entirely. When we were on safari, he actually tried to bribe the guide to drive closer to the lions.'

'That was Jonny, wasn't it?' says Tom.

'Was it? Could have been either. They egg each other on.'

As the Rutherfords leave, he feels a hand on his shoulder and turns to find a rather sloshed Jenno Dunster.

'Nick!'

'Nicky, by preference.'

'I was just talking to your delightful wife.'

'Oh, good.'

'Was Monica . . . ?'

'*Monifa.*'

'What did I say? Was she your secretary?'

'No, she's a lawyer. She was outside counsel for us on a really tricky acquisition.'

Just then, the music stops and, sensing the change in noise levels, the crowd tapers into surprised silence. The psychedelic party lamps are suddenly switched off and replaced by the hard white light of the strip bulbs in the barn's roof. It has the feel of a police bust. Adjusting eyes find Libby Crossan standing at the centre of the room, mobile in hand.

'I've just been called by Elsie Harper in the village,' she says. 'Apparently there are kids fuh . . . fucking in the graveyard.'

*

In these dry, silent months of their marriage, it has become common for one of them not even to know that the other has left the house. She'll get an *x*-less text from him about kids' pick-ups when she thinks he's at his computer in the Office but he turns out to be playing tennis at the Rutherfords'. Actually, in the worst cases, he is at his computer in the Office when he texts her.

But, this morning, Tasha is really *making an effort*: a key phrase on the advice pages. This project is helped by the fact that Simon is going in later. Rather than bumping across the bedroom in the dark before six, wakened by the humming and vibrating of his iPhone on the table, he was still there when her clock-radio woke her with the *Today* programme (the nice gay one and the Scottish one this morning) at 7.45. So they got up together or at least at the same time.

'Are you going in late today?'

'I told you.'

Did he? She does forget things (more so since she started feeling so tired all the time) but she is also convinced that one of his latest tactics is to make her think she has Alzheimer's.

'Well, can you tell me again?'

Are you proud of me, Zelda?

Simon sighs. 'I'm going to see Sir Adrian at home. *His* home.'

'Right. And where's that?'

'I told you.'

'I think that must have been one of your other women.'

'No. It's your early-onset Alzheimer's. Well, not *that* early. He's got this fuck-off mansion in Oxfordshire.'

'Oh, that's easy. M40?'

'Well, if not too many truckers have been playing chicken overnight. I sometimes think they should only have it on the traffic news when that road is *open*.'

So he will be gone for several hours; longer, as his mission (she vaguely understands) is to persuade Sir Adrian to make some kind of grand apologetic gesture (a foundation for dis-advantaged inner-city children has been mentioned) to the customers of his bank and the others.

'But you'll be back for supper?' is as far as she feels she can go.

'Well, unless the Highways Agency knows something we don't.'

When he comes into the kitchen – even now, there is something about a man just showered and shaved, somehow smooth and purified – she says: 'I could do you scrambled eggs or something . . .'

He looked less shocked when she offered him the blow-job in Morocco. 'What? Nah, I'll get a salmonella pasty or something when I fill up.' He checks his watch. 'Christ, Junction 8A will be . . .'

She watches him carefully as he gets ready to go. Sudden flashbacks of her dad gathering up umbrella, briefcase and (or has she imagined this?) bowler hat. Simon travels lighter, putting his phone in the inside pocket of his jacket and fishing the Audi keys from the pot on the far side of the fridge. (Tom Rutherford, in his most recent security review, warned against leaving them on the stair-post in the hall, mentioning gangs using fishing rods through letterboxes.)

'Okay,' he says.

'Won't you need your iPad?' she dares.

'What? I'm not a kid on a school trip. No, Sir Adrian's so completely paranoid now that all electronic devices have to be given to his goons at the door. He's convinced we're all secretly taping him, which must mean that he's been secretly taping us for years. The less I take the better.'

She fears that her face has given away her relief that he is leaving his machines behind. Covering herself, like a wife in a comedy, she crosses the kitchen and straightens his tie (he pulls away, as if anticipating a strangling) then extends the parody into a peck on the cheek.

'What the . . . ?' he says, swallowing the last word against the presence of Henry, hunched over the *Guardian* sports section, slurping down a brimming bowl of Coco Pops. (Polly and Josh are still dead to the world. Teenagers and sleep is a recurrent subject among the mothers over coffee.)

'Good luck with Sir Adrian,' she says.

'Well, if you see him on the 6 o'clock news in a sackcloth shift announcing an orphanage in Calcutta, it's all down to me.'

'Can I ring you if there are problems with Josh?'

'I guess. I mean, it's pretty simple, isn't it? Grounded means grounded.'

'On Facebook, he says he's going to a party in Winslow tonight,' contributes Henry, sending a spray of milk and half-chewed cereal across the table.

'Henry, it's not good to be a snitch,' she scolds him, finding a squeegee-cloth to clean up around him. The kitchen will need even more work before Irena the Cleaner gets here.

'The only way he'll see Winslow is on Google Earth,' Simon says, in a disciplinary voice that she hadn't heard from him until the graveyard business but which, against her inclinations, has impressed her.

Although Tasha has every box-set of *Spooks*, she doesn't feel entirely cut out for what she has to do. But, knowing that Simon is prone to wheel-screeching returns to the house to retrieve forgotten items, it seems an elementary precaution to wait quarter of an hour. She tries to read the *Guardian* – recession, killer-bug vaccination delay, *Britain's Got Talent* – and then to make conversation with her youngest.

'Sit up straight! It's bad for your digestion, eating like that.'

The slouching slurping continues.

'Henry, I mean it!!'

'Mum, don't be so stressy.'

'What are you going to do today?'

'Dunno. Not much.'

'Should I see if Henry Rutherford wants to come and play?'

'Yeah. If you like.'

'But I don't want you plugged in all the time. Will you take Ella and Clooney for a walk?'

'Mum, my leg's really bad . . .'

'What's wrong with it?'

'I did something playing football in the field with Josh.'

'Walking will be good for it.'

'Mum!'

'Are you sorted out for presents for everyone or . . . ?'

'Polly said she'd drive me to Aylesbury. If she ever wakes up. We gotta get Josh's stuff as well as he can't cos you've called in the feds . . .'

Tasha had been concerned, when they sent the children to Westbury Park, about the effect on their accents; that it might soon be like talking to Little Lord Fauntleroy. She needn't have worried. Though Henry is marginally the worst, all three speak like drug-dealers in *The Wire*.

Her watch suggests that Simon will be safely crawling towards the M40 now. With perfect timing, Henry stands and, without announcement, leaves the kitchen and bounds upstairs, where his PlayStation will nullify him for hours. For once, keen to get on with her mission, she doesn't summon him back to put his breakfast stuff in the dishwasher, confining herself to yelling 'clean your teeth!' after his retreating feet.

From the kitchen window, she can see no car approaching the house. There is more traffic than usual on the road at the bottom of the hill; no school-runs this week but more shopping trips, leaving early to beat the pre-Christmas crowds. So many black four-wheel drives in a line that you'd think Obama was on a visit.

The room they call the Office (years ago, they experimented with 'study' but Simon, in one of his Northern spasms, considered that too posh) is at the rear corner of the west wing. For someone who watches as much television as Tash does (even more since Simon stopped talking to her), there's a thrill in living in a house that incorporates the title of the presidential drama.

This, though, is mainly Simon's domain; she only comes in to do the annual accounts for her company and the VAT in the periods when she has earned enough to qualify, which seems unlikely to be a problem for a while. The walls are decorated with photos, posters and fixture lists relating to Bolton Wanderers. For various birthdays, she arranged to have framed pictures of the scoreboard at big games they won. Her only real contribution to the decor is a Dunster Manor calendar, printed with tweely archaic scenes of horse-ploughing and apple-picking, which she feels an obligation to Max and Jenno to display.

Among the aspects of her husband that have been reclassified from endearing to maddening is his messiness, and at first she fears that she will be unable to find the iPad in the desk's avalanche of Samson Brothers folders, crumpled newspapers and football programmes. But there it is, balanced on top of a stack of those hardbacks he's always reading, with titles like *What Billionaires Eat For Breakfast*.

The deal she has done with herself is that she will be relieved if it turns out to be women or even men. Only images of children will constitute a crisis. Although, even in setting these parameters, Tasha can see that the mere fact your husband is not a proven paedophile may not be an ideal foundation for a marriage.

She has decided to try the iPad first. The office also contains a flat-screen iMac – on which her own accounts are kept – but it was the newer machine he cradled so protectively in Morocco and which seems the likeliest to hold his secrets.

As preparation, she researched Bolton on the BBC site, surprised by quite how much stuff there was about a football team which, from Simon's habitual gloom after their matches, doesn't seem to be much good.

At the passcode prompt, she reaches for her football crib-sheet. Although several four-letter words relating to Simon come to mind, Tasha, used to longer passwords on the antiquated devices she owns, struggles to think in more truncated formulations.

She tries N-A-T-L, not for her own name, but for a club legend player, Nat Lofthouse (Christ!, did Simon pick her for her married initials only?). WRONG PASSCODE TRY AGAIN. Her next effort is S-A-M-A, the manager (the "Gaffer") he banged on about at Jonny and Libby's Crimbo bash. At Simon's insistence, their last-but-one labrador was called Big Sam.

But the device rebuffs her second guess as well. Although she manages her own computer transactions only with sarcastic back-up from the children, Tasha understands that a certain number of wrong log-ons might freeze the machine and even leave a warning for the rightful client. So this is serious, Jason Bourne stuff.

An iPhone site she consulted advised a combination of digits and letters. But the possibilities must be infinite without one of those whizzy clickers they stick on safes in heist movies. About to give up, she is staring at the wall above the desk, where he has hung the presents from the time when they were thoughtful to each other. The two scoreboards show Bolton Wanderers 2 – West Ham United 0 and Bolton Wanderers 2 – Manchester United 0. Cup finals, she dimly remembers learning in the days when his devotion to those men in baggy shorts seemed sweet.

Her first attempt – B2M0 – fails but the result of the older game – B2W0 – is successful. The benefits of all those late nights watching stored-up episodes of *Spooks* alone!

She's familiar from the adverts on TV with the lines of brightly coloured apps, labelled with names she expects: BBC, CNN, FT, *Guardian*, BWFC. No – thank God – KIDS R US.

The icon on one folder declares that it contains his messages. Zelda has often counselled readers that, just as few of us would want a microphone broadcasting from our minds all day, it's rarely wise to read a partner's diaries or emails. While the agony aunt never quite says that some secrets can be healthy, she certainly encourages mystery.

Polly is shouting from the landing. Tasha goes out before she comes to find her.

'Mummy, I've run out of pants!'

'I saw some drying on the Aga. Are you taking Henry shopping soon?'

'I guess.'

'Is Josh up?'

'No. But, like, he's under house arrest so . . .'

'He is not under . . .'

Like so many conversations with her 18-year-old daughter, this one is called off as pointless.

She resumes her spying. Her fear here is not porn but mistresses. *I found an email to my husband from my best friend.* Who is her best friend? Round here, Dr Emily, she supposes, although Libby is a laugh and Jenno grows on her, even if Tasha's brain still tries to spell-check that silly name every time she tries to say it. Which of them would Simon be shagging if he's shagging one? Jenno, she supposes, because she's younger, although what happened in Marrakesh (no, no, we're not going there) leads her to wonder if Mrs Dunster is quite the draw in that department you might think.

She recognizes the addresses of Simon's brother and mum and of Tom Rutherford (mainly headed: 'Tennis?'). The torrent from Jonny Crossan is, from the header lines, mainly forwardings of those sick jokes about dead celebrities or clips of obese American teenagers falling over. Hundreds have the suffix *@samsonbros* but none with a giveaway user-name such as *hottielottie* or the subject-line *room 46, door on latch*. There are masses from HSBC, looking like the bank spam (pretending that their pathetic interest rates are doing the customer a favour) that clogs up her Nokia.

Does the fact that she has found nothing mean that Simon is a better person or a better liar than she thought? She finishes and, in another tribute to her television education, wipes the screen with a tissue.

House-pride leads her to polish the front of the iMac as well, dropping the screen-cleaner into a bin brimming with crumpled tissues, before switching it on. The start-up screen offers her the names of the five members of the family with their separate admission boxes. Ignoring TASHA, she chooses SIMON and, happier with this era of computing, taps in b-i-g-s-a-m.

Tasha likes to be good at what she does and seems to be a reasonable spy. HELLO SIMON, she is greeted, and then asked: ARE YOU SIMON? Can this rudimentary security check ever have deterred a snooper? She confirms that she is her husband.

175

Many of the icons and folders are familiar from the other boy-toy but she is intrigued by a file identified as *Collected VAT Returns 1993–*. Simon, being a PAYE employee, isn't eligible for VAT. *I discovered my husband is running a secret company.*

Tasha missed the generation of women encouraged to aim a mirror and a flashlight between their legs for self-knowledge. But she knows what she is looking at, even without enlarging the miniaturized JPEGs: a gallery of fannies; disembodied pubic triangles with a border of thigh, the, er, labia stretched and sometimes fingered. The pictures seem, from the download information, to come mainly from a website called Gash.

Even now, though, she has a sensation of escaping the worst. These genitals are not shaven bald, vajazzled or – worse – pre-pubertal. They are adult women, not much more explicit than in the *Penthouse* and *Mayfair* she once found under her elder brother's bed. (Has she always been a sneak?) Zelda, she's sure, would tell her that there are worse things.

But does he sit here in front of the screen and . . . ? She can't think about it. A sudden flashback of Simon saying, in the days when they still did it: *babe, don't ever shave down there.* And perhaps there *are* worse things. Catching sight of the violet blur of her speeding pulse as her hands rest on the keyboard, she opens a file called *Regulatory Guidelines in Mergers and Acquisitions.* A distant memory of Simon telling her, when the Sir Adrian crisis began, that the worst stuff is always hidden in the most impenetrable documents.

Tasha realizes that she has involuntarily closed her eyes. Opening them, she finds nothing of concern unless some fiendish pornographer has constructed a code based on financial jargon and formulae.

In the bottom right-hand corner of the desktop, there's a folder marked PRUE.

Tasha chides herself for her easy understanding of her husband's masturbatory habits. Unless he can't spell the insurance company, this will be the floozy file, the smoking gun. She imagines Prue as an Australian, early twenties, blonde, with a huge bush presumably.

Her hand is trembling so much that it takes three goes to open the folder.

*

Every desk in the branch is busy and all the chairs in the waiting area taken, with a line of people waiting by the door. Rolls of spangled wrapping paper rise like periscopes from the bulging bags most customers carry.

This is Jenno's second Christmas as a volunteer and, standing in the middle of the high street like an admonition, the CAB draws in shoppers who know, even as they join the festival of over-spending, that they can't afford it. Only January is worse, when the credit-card bills and loans have to be paid.

She swaps goodbyes and happy holidays (she hates the phrase but, these days, better safe than suspended for racial insensitivity) with a couple whose builder has left the work unfinished, the second most common query after debts. She needs a wee, which will also provide the chance for another squirt of germ killer; she feels like a politician, forced to shake so many strangers' hands.

But, as she half-stands, Mandy and Danny are coming towards her. There is no buggy today; presumably the older children are looking after the younger ones. The woman is now so pregnant that her winter coat won't close over the bump.

'Oh, Hiya,' Jenno says. Mandy makes a sound with an 'h' in it, Danny flicks his chin upwards. Anger crackles between the couple like an electrical current and she surreptitiously checks for bruises on Mandy's face. It's terrible how suspicious this job makes you. Apart from trying to spot the beaters, they are always on alert, especially at this time of year, for those known as the 'ledgers', the clients at risk of throwing themselves off or under something.

Jenno mouse-manoeuvres their file on to the screen, uneasy as she feels Danny's raging gaze fall on her. She fears the confrontations there will be when volunteers have to start telling customers the government's new tests for benefits.

'Okay,' she says. 'Just refreshing my memory. Yes, now the good news is that we've been able to consolidate the loans into a single payment and agree a pay-back schedule. *But . . .*' – though she generally drops her 't's at CAB, she emphatically hits this one – '. . . we are going to have to cut down on expenditure . . .'

'Are *we?*' sneers Danny.

'Leave her. She's all right,' Mandy tells him, then turns to Jenno with a pouty, pleading look that suddenly makes her seem years younger. 'Thing is, Jenny, it's *Crimbo*.' She winsomely extends the final syllable. 'You know how it is.'

'I do,' Jenno lies, smiling. It is easy enough to be sympathetic, or to seem so, but genuine empathy is surely impossible. The Mandys and Dannys live on a different planet – where food and warmth and shelter are in terrifyingly short supply and the population expands at a bewildering rate – and it is mad of her to think that she can land here on Monday and Thursday afternoons and every fourth Saturday and depart without damage.

In desperation, she asks: 'Do you or any of your children have disabilities?'

'Yer what, love?' Mandy asks.

'I'm not being funny. If there was anyone in the family with a disability, we could claim for . . .' – *the only state assistance you don't yet have* – '. . . what they call DLA – Disability Living Allowance . . .'

'I could mek one or two of 'em disabled if it helped,' says Danny, who seems, at a glance, to have even fewer teeth than previously.

'Don't ever say that,' Mandy scolds him and Jenno is convinced she sees fright in the woman's eyes.

'It's difficult,' says Jenno. 'Especially at this time of year. But we can only try to help you if you are prepared to . . .' She pauses to find a kinder translation, but her bilinguality fails. '. . . if you are prepared to make some sacrifices . . .'

178

Mandy lowers her head, like a child being told off, while Danny's eyes remain level, staring scaldingly. So tall and broad that he seems as high seated as some men do standing, he sweeps his gaze from her breasts towards her waist, like a ripping zip, in a way that she remembers from her days of travelling on the Tube. Though wearing her cheap volunteer jeans, she pulls herself closer to the table, unsure what he could see from there.

'Bet you've got a nice place for yerself, have yer?' he sneers.

Is this bravado or a version of *I know where you live*? Jenno feels fear, but also anger. Offered, like Libby, the chance to be a magistrate, she chose not to lock up the disadvantaged but to help them. She sees now, though, that the idea was futile. While she suffers guilt at having what she has, the Dannys of this world burn with hatred at her having it and will one day come to try to take it away. England will end up like America and South Africa, with the wealthy living in fiercely defended enclaves. She must ask Tom to check the house as well as the factory.

*

They think of their own homes – each set on a separate hill – as remote, but Sir Adrian lives in a different scale of isolation. Simon hasn't passed another car for ten minutes now, which is a relief as the narrowing roads, heralding deepest countryside, only allow one vehicle to pass at a time. He has a sudden image of the banker blocking the way in a tank-like vehicle, scowling down the other driver to reverse.

Keeping below forty – both from fear of collision and the pulsing worry of being only three speeding points away from disqualification – he uses the remote pad on the wheel to skip between radio stations. Unable to settle on any music – Radio 1 playing stuff that feels too young for him, Radio 2 too old and Radio 3 too gloomy – he opts for an Agatha Christie serial on Radio 4. It's a Poirot he's heard before or seen on television – the one about Mrs McGinty being killed – but *Murder on the*

Orient Express and *Roger Ackroyd* are the only two in which he can ever remember who the murderers are. Mrs McGinty, he thinks, turns on a nursery rhyme.

He has the heating on full blast and the rear windows down. A smoker's winter compromise: he's on his third (is it? No, fifth. Fuck) cigarette of the journey.

On a distant rise to the right, he sees what he assumes to be Trimbury Manor, the only house within view. It's as if the owner knew that he might one day have to hide away, although the original motive will have been space: people use money to get as far away from other people as possible. In summer and autumn, the residence, despite its size, must be almost invisible to passers-by, the roads bordered by tall hedges and the estate ringed with trees. Winter, though, has thinned the screen, the leafless branches offering a peep-show of the imposing stone building.

'Turn right and continue for 2.8 miles on unnamed road.'

The voice on the satnav is the rather camp Australian man. Simon prefers the brisk English navigator called Emily, but Henry, mucking about with Plum Crossan on the way back from the school carol concert yesterday, had kept changing the settings, giving him a different accent or language at every junction.

All along the road with no name, on the side by the house, is a wall topped with twists of barbed wire and spikes. Simon wonders if it this has been added since the bank went bust. Large wooden signs – warning of rapid response with dogs – bear the familiar logo of Rutherford Secure. Go, Tom!

'Arrive at destination on left.'

The weakness of GPS driving – he has discovered, from taking Josh and Henry to various football and rugby grounds – is that a single postcode can cover a number of locations. But Sir Adrian King-Jones, inevitably, has a Royal Mail sector to himself.

A short white-gravelled drive leads to black-painted gates of prison-thickness, topped with whirring cameras on extendable arms which turn and swoop, like ostrich necks, towards Simon's car. Patches of the gate look uneven, as if frequently coated: covering angry graffiti, perhaps. He lowers the windows to speak into an intercom on a post.

'Simon Londsale. From Samson Brothers. For Sir Adrian.'

'Okay, mate.' The voice is slightly poshed-up cockney. 'Just hold there a mo while we scan your plates.'

With a gymnastic manoeuvre, one of the cameras on the gates swivels and dives to frame the front bumper of the car. Given the company Sir Adrian is (or at least was) known to keep – Oscar-winning actresses, Premiership football managers, supermodels, Brit Art superstars – Simon is concerned that the machine will be confused by the absence of personalized plates. But the nosey lens retreats and the disembodied EastEnder instructs him: 'All good. Follow the long drive to the top. If you think you're lost, you're not, it's just long. And we'll be watching ya.'

Despite their solidity, the gates open and close so quickly – presumably to prevent tail-gating – that Simon briefly antici-pates being mangled. He's grateful for the geezer's warning when, with more than a mile ticked off on the dashboard, he still hasn't reached the house, which seems to be receding and sometimes disappears completely. Then he sees again the arch of the portico and enters a stretch of gardens mown in two-tone stripes, with croquet lawns and peacocks strutting. Beside what looks to be a full-sized cricket pitch, a scoreboard still shows the final innings of last summer. The number 6 bats-man was undefeated on 46.

In Middlebury, Simon is considered rich (''im from the big 'ouse,' he overheard a farmer say once in the pub), but Max and Jonny and probably Tom are considerably richer. And, in the grounds of Trimbury Manor, he's a pauper. Wealth is a ladder which always has rungs above.

His progress is stopped by car-park-style barriers and a green hut from which a burly stubble-nut in a black bouncer's suit steps, stoops and waits with a bad-toothed smile for Simon's electric window to descend.

'Good morning, Mr Lonsdale.' The Londoner from the entry phone. 'There's parking to the right of the main house. Space 8, if you can remember. Space 8. You'll see two disabled bays. They're for you in case you take any pictures or recordings while you're here.'

Unsure of the hierarchy, Simon half laughs. The joker returns to his bunker and the barrier lifts. He has diligently memorized the bay number, but there's another reminder in a different suited bruiser standing on the grass verge beside it. This one is carrying a large transparent plastic bag – echoes of airport security – which he holds open as Simon gets out, wincing at his dodgy right knee's stiffness from the drive.

Clocking Simon's scarf, the bouncer growls, 'Be lucky to stay up this year', football the shared masculine language, except for rugger-buggers like Jonny and Max.

'Yeah. I know.'

'Phones, tablet devices, if you would. Anything electronic, basically, including car keys.'

'Seriously?'

'See anyone smiling?'

When Tom tells people his security staff are mainly ex-soldiers, Simon teases him that he means ex-cons; turf accountants would suspend bets on this one. From a jacket pocket, the Strangeways alumnus pulls what Simon at first fears is a cosh but which turns out to be an airport scanner-bat. Christ, the bastard really does think someone's going to kill him. Bugger, there couldn't be some gunshot residue on his scarf from the clay-pigeon shooting, could there?

'Okay, Mr Lonsdale, you'll be met at the steps at the front.'

He stops to take in his first full-on sight of the house. From a combination of schooling and Google, he knows that it's a Palladian mansion, although he would have personally described it as a private White House. A vast triangular central arch is supported by pillars rising from wide grey terraced steps.

The elegantly symmetrical wings look much as they would have done two hundred years ago, except for thickened glass (presumably bullet-proofed) and circuit boxes for the alarm system.

A more primitive signal – a stentorian cough – alerts Simon that Sir Adrian King-Jones is standing on the steps, posed sideways with his feet on consecutive levels, as if expecting his portrait to be painted at any moment.

'Simon Lonsdale,' says Sir Adrian, the use of both names a compromise between mistering and intimacy. 'I saw you on the drive.' Is this detail intended to suggest omniscience or a telescope? 'Beamer series 7. These stringent economies at SB I read about don't seem to be affecting the press office. First time you've seen the pad?'

His first thought is of the helicopter pad visible to their right, until he realizes that the tycoon is being matily self-deprecating.

'Yes. I've read about it.'

'So did I. That's why I bought it.'

Sir Adrian waves at the vast expanse of manicured grass, a personal Hyde Park complete with ornamental fountains.

'I understand why they sent you on "gardening leave" – now I see the size of the garden,' Simon risks saying.

'Hummmna!' The tycoon's menacing yelp of a laugh sounds as if a spike has been put through his foot. 'You wanna try stand-up if you ever lose your present job.'

One of Simon's problems is that he doesn't know how frightened to be. Sir Adrian is no longer his boss – and his mission today is to extend the company's distance from the toxic greed of its suspended overlord – but defeated chief executives often pile up bodies in a final shoot-out at HQ. And that would be in character for this man. A 'friend' of the financier once insisted, in a supportive *FT* profile early in his career, that the man who liked to style himself AKJ was otherwise known at Samson Brothers as the King. In fact – as internal emails released during some of the many malpractice cases against the bank have revealed – he was commonly referred to in written communications as 'King-Jones. Many former colleagues and business journalists insist that they were the first to insert the derogatory apostrophe.

'My preference for business meetings is the loggia,' the scandalous banker tells him. 'But it would be a little chilly today. I've had them light a fire in the Yellow Room.'

Turning abruptly, his host strides into the house at almost jogging speed, a signature trait which must have begun as a symbol of his busyness, but which he can't break even in the idleness of disgrace. They race past darkly varnished furniture and gilt-framed paintings of ugly men, pale women and maritime battles erupting in orange bursts of canon fire.

'Do you shoot, Simon?'

Surely to God, he isn't going to be expected to murder birds on this trip. He gambles that the question is simply manly small-talk.

'Not . . . a bit of clay pigeon on a Sunday morning.'

'That can be fun. But you want blood and squawks, ideally. What do you play off?'

'You mean golf?'

'What else?'

'Er, eight or nine, if the wind's kind.'

He hasn't played for months, since the time when Jonny accused Max of shifting a lie with his foot. Sir Adrian always reminds him a little of Max Dunster: a large-framed man who would naturally be fat but chips away some inches with strenuous exercise.

'Scratch, for my sins,' the banker boasts.

The gloomy corridor seems almost as long as the gravelled approach. Descending a corkscrew staircase is a slight young woman with waist-length black hair and a deep tan that looks natural rather than bottle-splashed. She's wearing a dress with one of those sash-belts that make women look like presents waiting to be untied.

Slowing almost to normal walking pace, Sir Adrian tells her:

'Honey, I've got to work for a while in the Jaundice.' His voice, generally at the harsher end of the Irish spectrum, suddenly softens into the celebrated mellowness, but is back to the default as he throws over his shoulder: 'Simon, you'll doubtless recognize Marissa from the stacks of mendacious newsprint you so assiduously accrue.'

Lady Marissa is the businessman's second wife, twenty-five years younger. It has become a cliché of the many pieces about the Samson Brothers collapse that the CEO's maniacal inflation of his salary and pension, even as the bank's customers lost their businesses and jobs, was encouraged by a divorce having divided his wealth. Simon tries to fight the sexual envy which rages in him these days as lust once did. He less envies Sir Adrian's income than the fact that it has allowed him to buy young cunt. (There are rumours now that a top-dollar lawyer has just got him an injunction over another office fuck.)

An open fire always takes Simon back to his grandparents' terrace in Bolton, although the nostalgia is not exact, the smell and smoke of wood quite different from coal. A tray with a cafetière, two mugs and a plate of shortbread biscuits stands on a low table beside one of a pair of leather wingback chairs at angles to the hearth.

'I went for coffee. And men use mugs, I think. If it's tea you want, I can always call them.'

'A mug of coffee would be great.'

Waving Simon to the further seat, Sir Adrian says: 'Shall I be motherfucker?'

They sit awkwardly in silence with their hands around the mugs. Perhaps both of them have read the same business books about the tactical power of pauses.

The elder man blinks first: 'So the Ruling Revolutionary Council have sent you to negotiate my surrender? We both know it's going to end as a compromise, so you scratch your line in the sand first. What are that new gang of decaffeinated, wind-turbined, hysterectomied bankers going to offer me?'

Simon saw enough of AKJ in negotiations – including the

disastrous North American expansion which triggered the near-obliteration of the bank – to anticipate that it would be like this: his severance as the greatest deal of his life and pursued even more keenly than the others. In previous contracts, he was only dealing with other people's money, while, here, he's fighting for cash he considers his own.

'The figures are on paper for you, Sir Adrian. A very generous pension . . .'

'The *full* pension? Plus the lumper?'

'Look, er, do you read the papers?'

'Would I? You come into a room full of people shit-bagging you, don't you walk away?'

'But you'll know that the scale of your, uh, compensation has created an image problem – both for the company and for you . . .'

'Image? *Image* is for retard soccer players with tattooed arses.' Simon flinchingly anticipates the inevitable next sentence. 'With Adrian King-Jones, what you see is what you get.'

'Yes, well, the point is, Sir Adrian, that now that people have *seen* what you're *getting*, they don't want you to have it . . .'

The tycoon's hands shake so much that the gold-and-emerald pattern of the plush rug at their feet is threatened by splashes of coffee.

'Mr Lonsdale, let me ask you a question . . .' A favourite technique of Sir Adrian's; during his disastrously belligerent interview on the *Today* programme on the day of the government bank bail-out, a columnist calculated that the guest asked more questions than the presenter. 'Are *you* paid too much?'

Which is exactly what he said to John Humphrys. Simon can only attempt the same reply: 'This isn't about me.'

'Oh, but it is. It's about how we decide the fair price for a man's work. Women too, God bless them, in the workplace now. You're pulling down Beamer company wheels plus how much . . . ?'

'Our contracts have a confidentiality clause, as you—'

'Hah. I'd show you mine, but you won't show me yours. Point is, are you getting too much as Head of Public Relations at a bank that's scuttling round the world sourcing stronger glass because the public keeps smashing its windows in? Or is it the right amount? Do you think it's the right amount?'

'Well, obviously, I . . .'

'Go and stand on the road down there – the *public* road – and stop a few cars and it won't be long before we find someone who reckons you're obscenely over-paid. If we happen to meet a nurse or a teacher driving to Poundland, is it called?, you are *fucked*, sir!'

'Yes, I know, I'm aware that, by the standards of most people, we . . . I'm . . . very lucky. But the point is that you, Sir Adrian, you were – are – paid thirty, forty times more than most employees get, including bonuses . . .'

'And how does one get a bonus?'

Bully your shooting buddies on the remuneration committee to vote it through. Simon just lets the monologue continue: 'My lack of languages is one of my educational regrets, but even I know that words beginning in *bon* generally mean something good. I did good work until the world – the *world* – ran out of money. And, Simon, how many press offices are there at SB?'

'Well, in the whole division, including press and public and corporate, I suppose . . .'

'And how many CEOs? Are you a Marxist?'

'No. I, er, of course . . .'

'No, you strike me as one of those types who voted Lib Dem so you could feel like a nice little lefty while benefiting from the low tax rates of the parties that could actually get in.' This analysis is so accurate that Simon is reduced to muteness. 'And now you shout it out at dinner parties about the Lib Dems propping up the coalition but secretly hope the Tories will strike down the 50 per cent income tax.' A second bullseye. 'But my point is that only a Marxist would think that everybody should be paid the same. We're both inequities. Sure, I'm a bigger one than you, but neither of us would be wise to walk our dogs through Crack Alley Estate late at night. We're in a country where everyone is paid too fucking much – except the prime minister, apparently, and what I'd give to have his trust fund – so why am I the only one to take a cut? Especially as I find myself on the dole at fifty. I didn't get my pension pot by holding up post offices with a shotgun, you know . . .'

No, Sir Adrian, by robbing a bank. This is pure AKJ: superficially convincing, unless you keep remembering that he's quibbling over quantities of millions.

'But, Sir Adrian, the point is, isn't it . . . ?' Durham University Debating Society, 1982, the Oxbridge rejects braying at the tongue-tied northerner. This House Maintains that Charity is a Luxury. 'Whether it's fair or not, the issue is appearances. What happened at Samson's has swung the spotlight on you, *your* severance package and pension . . .'

'Well, as you say, spotlights swing. Where might the beam fall next? Remind me, Simon, of your job title . . . ?'

A trap, obviously, but his feet have nowhere else to go: 'Director of Public Relations . . .'

'And did you – ever, in all the time you were taking your contractually confidential whack to advise me on my relations with the public – did you ever come and tell me to tone it down a bit? That maybe you and I should both be paid a little less? That the SB Gulfstream should be put on eBay? Against the day when the public, in a shit-storm of hypocrisy, would decide they wanted Adrian King-Jones's head in a bucket? Because if you didn't – and I think you didn't – then it strikes me that you weren't an especially good Director of Public Relations . . .'

Fear is a natural condition for an employee, but Simon has the bewildering impression of being sacked by someone who is no longer his boss.

'But it's the context, isn't it, Sir Adrian, that has changed. There was a time when slave-trading . . .'

'What the fuck has that got to do with the cost of gorgonzola?'

'We cancelled a big dinner, didn't we?, on 9/11? It wasn't

wrong to have arranged it; it just looked different after what had happened. Same with this. The level of security you have here now – I don't suppose you had it before the bank crash?'

'Didn't I? People like me have always been at risk of envy and . . . greed.' The fractional hesitation before attributing avarice to others is the tycoon's single flash of embarrassment so far.

'But you're more . . . recognizable now. I'm sure you've had to take extra precautions.'

'Maybe. So what you're suggesting is a symbolic sacrifice of a slice of the pension to which I'm legally entitled?'

'Yes. You're right that this is gesture politics. But it would be a popular gesture.'

'It might get a few of the hacks off my back. But I'll still need bodyguards for the rest of my life.'

'Security isn't my area. I'd also strongly suggest a public event or two that shows you in a philanthropic light . . .'

'Hummnh! What, a Fun Day here? Bouncy castles for chemo kids?'

'Something more lasting, I'd suggest. Put some of your money into a trust or foundation . . .'

'Like the Prince's Trust, you mean?'

'Well, I . . . along those lines.'

'But all those years of being pictured hugging black girls in youth clubs in inner-city no-go zones – what has it actually done for old Charlie? All the opinion polls I've read say he's a clapped-out bark-sniffer who should hand over the throne to his oldest and go and fish in Scotland with the one he'd apparently rather shag than Diana. I could be photo-opped playing ping-pong in Willesden until Shergar comes home and I'd still be spending the same percentage of my pension on keeping my wife and kids safe. I'm damaged goods. What I'm going to—'

A gentle knocking at the door is followed by the entry of Lady King-Jones.

'Darling, cook is asking numbers for lunch.'

'Well, I'd hoped you'd join me.' Simon is surprised until he realizes Sir Adrian is looking at Marissa. 'So just the two of us, I'd tell her, honey.'

'We don't seem to have got very far,' Simon concedes. 'I'll report back to the interim board. Obviously there'll be a lull over Christmas. But—'

Sir Adrian cuts in: 'I actually found our conversation useful in consolidating my views. I'll make a proposal to my usurpers in due course.'

*

Since a Man in a Van started bringing her shopping, Jenno has forgotten how cold supermarkets are, even in winter. But she's doing Nigel Slater's Goan Fish Curry tonight and found herself completely out of garam masala and coconut milk. She can't wait for the next Ocado delivery and the food bit at the petrol station wouldn't have them.

She's surprised to find that even Waitrose is full of posters saying how cheap everything is. There's a line of own-brand stuff in basic packaging, presumably aimed at refugees from Tesco. There really must be a recession on. *Essential*, the cheaper tins and packets are called. She files this away to tell Max, who, with his business brain, likes to know what other companies are up to.

But also, which is more her Waities, there are lots of posters of a beaming Heston advertising his seasonal specials. Some of his stuff is just too you-know – the anti-freeze ice-cream or whatever – but he's made a special Xmas pudding, with a whole orange in the middle, which, according to the paper, sold out in a blink. Jenno had hoped she could nab one online but was beaten even there. Just in case, she checks the shop's festive dessert section, but there's a polite sign explaining that Heston's strictly limited edition has now sold out.

The stacks of puddings that are for sale – all those bowls in shiny crinkly paper, like giant Quality Street chocolates – whizz her back to Christmases when she was little. Even when she's with Max, who can't be offered a free sliver of Stilton by a teenager in reindeer ears without giving her a lecture about seasonal marketing strategies, she's a sucker for shops at this time of year: the tills draped with tinsel and the ladies on the till seeming a little too jolly from a bottle of something in the staff-room locker. She thinks of that phrase from Christmas hymns or maybe Dickens – *good cheer* – and how nice people can be to each other when they want to be.

Although Max always says that they change round the aisles to make you buy things you didn't come in for, the World Cuisine section is exactly where she remembers it being, although possibly longer, as the British palate expands.

Moving sideways to see if there's anything interesting on the Thailand shelf, she bumps into a lady with a trolley and has done the *sorry sorry* before she realizes who it is.

Generally, in this sort of weather, Tasha wears a black fleece with the logo of that bank her husband works for. Typical of her that she's happy to be seen in a golf-day freebie, as long as it's warm. Very Welsh. Jenno tried three different outfits before settling for her knee-length purple woollen coat over trousers and angora sweater, with the scarf Maxie bought her for her birthday. It's ages since she's seen anyone in a duffle coat: back-of-cupboard desperation, or perhaps Tasha borrowed it from Polly.

'Tash! I didn't recognize you without your fleecy thingy.'

'What? Oh, I always wear the same clothes, do I?'

Oh, dear, Mrs Chippy, here we go.

'Actually, you know what?' Tasha admits. 'I have stopped wearing it. I mean, Lehman Brothers is more famous, *infamous*, but even so. I have visions of being pelted with baguettes . . .'

'I know!' Jenno tells her. 'Max says we all need to keep our heads down. He reckons, when the public-sector cuts start to take hold, there are going to be attacks on the rich. We're getting Tom Rutherford to give our place the once over again, although it already feels like Fort Knox to me.'

'Well, in our case, it won't be because we're rich but because, in all those pictures of Sir Adrian ducking into cars with a briefcase across his face, Simon is usually behind him. But what you're saying . . . did you see Libby's tweet?'

'I've been busy. I've got a few to re- . . .'

'Apparently Jonny's Bentley was scratched at the station.'

'Oh my God! Exactly the same thing happened to Maxie's Porsche. It's called *striping* apparently. They take the keys of whatever they drive and . . .' Jenno makes an imaginary vandalizing slash across the packets of Organic Ramen Noodles and jars of Mikawa Mirin. 'Max is going to London a lot more at the moment for meetings – I think the company's expanding further into America – and I've told him it might make more sense to have a chauffeur. Unless he takes the shopping Beetle, pretty much any of our cars is going to antagonize the . . .' – she isn't sure you can say chavs in public now – ' . . . *have-nots*.'

'Well, you can understand why people would hate – not just Max, I mean – all of us these days . . .'

Jenno is conscious that Tasha seems a bit off with her. And, in fact, she's looking pale and even shaky.

'Tash, are you going down with something?'

'What?'

'No, just you're looking a bit off your oats.'

'Am I? I thought Emily was the only doctor . . .'

Turning away, Tasha takes a packet of couscous from the shelf and zaps it with a little grey thingy.

'Hey, Mrs Skywalker or what?' Jenno says, trying to lighten the mood.

'Oh, these,' Tasha replies. 'They're quite good fun.'

The handset is flashing and bleeping. 'Ooh, it's talking to you, Tash.'

'It does that.' She brings the machine right up to her face: somebody needs to make an optician's appointment! 'Telling me couscous is three for the price of two.' Tasha adds another two packets to one of the green canvas bags she has in her trolley. 'Of course, it makes you buy more than you need.'

'It wouldn't be worth it for me, the few times I come in here,' Jenno responds, more for something to say than anything else, and suddenly worrying that Tasha will think she's sounding like Jackie Onassis – when, in a flash, she realizes why her friend is – what's that Aussie expression the au pair has? – coming the raw prawn with her: Max's cancelled Crimbo thing.

'I expect we'll see each other in church on Christmas morning,' Jenno tries, for something innocuous to say.

'Why wouldn't we? I don't think I've been excommunicated for anything.'

Grow another skin, Jim. But she has another go: 'I've told Libby to ask the vicar if we can drop that awful Peruvian Gloria this year. All that chanting makes me feel like a Moonie.'

'Oh. They have to change. They can't just have music for old farts.'

Jenno tries to touch Tasha's hand but strokes the zapper instead. 'Look, Tash, I know there's some stuff between you and Max . . .'

Hello? Now you'd think she had grabbed the price wand and actually tasered Tasha with it, like those splat guns the Henries are always playing with. What's that all about?

'Jen . . .' begins Tasha, who has started calling her that for some reason, but she doesn't really feel she can say, *Oi, where's my 'o'?*

'He was as pissed off as you were that the Dunster Bash was cancelled . . .'

'Oh!'

'But it's the new FD, Stuart Thing. He's always going on about prudence . . .' Christ, she wonders if Tasha is actually going to faint. 'Thought we had enough of that with One-Eyed Gordon. Sweetie, are you sure you shouldn't run yourself along to Dr Em? You might have picked up a bug or . . .'

'What? No, look, Jen . . .'

The Christmas crush starts earlier every year, as everyone tries to avoid it by shopping sooner. She and Tasha keep having to flatten themselves against the shelves, as heaped trolleys bump like dodgems. 'Oh, hello there,' says a quiet voice, edging politely past. Who the hell? Oh, the, er, black lady at the Crossans' party, from Morocco. Not *from* Morocco. They *hello* her back.

'Jen, the thing is, I guess I just feel awkward because of the graveyard thing. We've only really spoken on the phone and . . .'

Jenno laughs: 'Oh, *that*. I mean, we're a score-draw on that one, aren't we? We've both got a randy adolescent . . .'

'I know. I suppose I feel worse because it feels as if Josh was leading Rosie astray . . .'

'Oh, Tash, don't be so old-fashioned. Girls like sex as well.'

'What? Yeah. But, Jen, they're under-age. They were *breaking the law* . . .'

She's about to say *darling, it's the twenty-first century* but remembers that Tasha is a Catholic, where the only sex allowed is between priests and choirboys.

'Sure, Tash. But it's like speeding limits, isn't it? Mummy's the only person I know who drives at seventy. These days, fourteen is the new sixteen, in the sort of schools they go to. Be even worse if they were boarders. You just hope they'll be sensible. Which they say they were. And, if Elsie Harper really found what she says she did on the gravestone, they definitely were . . .'

'Sensible! How sensible is it to be shagging on dead bodies when it's minus three?'

'They were wearing Puffas.' She finds herself giggling. 'Sounds like a euphemism, doesn't it? But, yeah, Max and I have talked about that. It would be better if they thought they had a safe place . . .'

'Jen, they're fifteen.'

'How old were you when . . . ?'

'Excuse me! I hardly think . . . Eighteen or . . . first year uni . . .'

'Really? I was fifteen. But then I'm . . .'

Oh, Christ, she keeps doing this.

'A younger generation?' Tasha completes the sentence. Jenno feels the quick burn of a blush: the only second wife among their set, she is always aware that age and infidelity are touchy subjects.

'No. I don't mean . . .'

'Josh is grounded until New Year's. Have you grounded Rosie?'

No. 'She knows what we think about it. It's funny, though. If this was fifteenth-century Italy or whatever, we'd be desperate to get our kids together . . .'

'Would we?'

'The top families all intermarried, didn't they? Unless they were like the Montagues and Capulets or whoever.'

Deep within herself, Jenno is so proud of her children that she finds it very hard to disapprove of anything they do: even al fresco sex on the bones of the Middlebury dead. She sometimes worries she's going to end up like those mothers you see on American television, standing with a candle outside death row insisting that their boy was framed.

'Er, ladies . . .'

They turn round to see the tall, good-looking young man in the apron – a special one, with holly and ivy, for the time of year – who greets you as you come in: 'Madam and Madam, the aisles are pretty busy today and you're causing a little bit of a logjam. There's a very nice coffee shop beyond the tills, if you want to continue your conversation.'

It's just like when a teacher said that Rosie or Jamie might benefit from being read to more at home or, when you're standing in the aisle of a plane or a train and someone says *excuse me* in that snotty voice: a flash of anger at being criticized by an inferior. This jumped-up johnny in his silly costume: what school did *he* go to? which university will *he* get into?

'Sorry,' Tasha says and moves away towards the breakfast cereals, making the phone-mime. Is she being paranoid or does Tasha seem glad to get away?

Although Jenno only has two items – which becomes five when she adds three bars of Green & Black's on a 3-for-2 offer

– even the baskets-only checkouts have a queue far down the aisle, this close to Britain's blow-out.

'You'd think they'd put more staff on at Christmas!'

The elderly voice – slushy with cheap dentures and the growly county dialect – comes from in front of her.

'What?' Jenno says.

'Them being over-run and two empty tills thar!'

'Yes.' Smiles. 'I know. I know.'

So her initial instinct – partly because, with the Antipodeans running a shuttle service, they were all pretty pissed – was to treat the whole thing as comedy: Libby stopping the music and announcing the morbid orgy, the frantic texts and phone calls to children who couldn't be located, the eventual revelation that Hugo Crossan had driven one of the Discos down the hill to the village churchyard, where it seems that Hugo and Tasha's Polly went at it on one slab and her Rosie with Josh Lonsdale on another.

Elsie Harper, church warden and chief of the Neighbourhood Watch, claims to have found 'several cigarette butts and a used prophylactic' around the Crossan vault. In the absence of DNA testing, which Mrs Harper at first seemed keen on, the single contraceptive might confirm the claim of the 15-year-olds that they didn't have 'full sex', although not necessarily, as Tasha thinks Polly is on the pill now, which Dr Emily, typically, wouldn't tell them.

Being so grown-up about it makes Jenno feel, well, grown-up. But Max, when she tried to say something wry in bed about how odd it was to think your little girl might be doing this as well, actually lost his erection and couldn't get it back. Perhaps, in the end, all fathers are Muslim when it comes to their daughters. She remembers her own dad squirming and busying himself at the drinks cabinet when they showed him the foetal scan of Rosie, apparently horrified at the evidence that his princess had been penetrated.

'Oh dear, Jen, you'll be here until Boxing Day. You want a queue-buster!'

Tasha flourishes her scan-gun as she wheels the trolley past, leaning in to its weight, the green canvas bags piled high.

'I'll stick with the man in the van, thanks! Oh, Lord, which reminds me. I need to be back for the coffee guy . . .'

'Oh, yes, I got the text this morning he was coming.'

'Have you ordered the Natale Intenso? The website says it's perfect after Christmas pud and dessert wine.'

'I got some of the special Christmas one, yes.'

Actually, when she thinks about it, she and Max haven't slept together since that time. She should do something about it tonight – perhaps she'll make the curry less smelly than Mr Slater recommends – because, from her history as a mistress, she is convinced that men need to be stoked regularly, like fires.

There's a commotion to her right, where Tasha is at the Shop-and-Scan stand. Her zapper is flashing red and bleeping furiously. The chap in the apron says: 'Nothing to worry about, madam. You've been selected for a random hand-check of your shopping. If you just hand me the scanner and the first bag . . .'

For the second time this morning, she worries that Tasha is going to faint. Except that now she is not pale but red-faced and sweaty.

'You know what?' her friend tells apron man, 'I've completely forgotten to get a couple of things on my list. I'll be back in . . .'

Like a rider trying to turn a spooked horse, Tasha hauls the trolley round, bent low against the handle, and forces herself, against the tide of impatiently waiting shoppers, towards the fresh-vegetables section. Looking down, she does not acknowledge Jenno.

*

'What then?' asks Max Dunster. 'Art thou Elias?'

The sonorous voice is suited to these words, his height enhancing their projection.

'And he saith,' Max continues, 'I am not. Art thou that

prophet? And he answered, No. Then said they unto him, Who art thou? that we may give an answer to them . . .'

With the old words, a lot of people go all hammy and spitty, like Tony B Liar reading lessons at memorial services. And there were rather a lot of such events, weren't there, Tony? But Sue has to admit that John 1:21–23 couldn't be read much better than this – clear and crisp, with subtly different voices for the to-and-fro of Jesus and his questioners – if you have to have it. Which she has to. The KJB is the Koran of Middle England. When Libby Crossan, chairman (she insists on the *man*) of the Parish Council, telephoned after the third interview, the call began: 'Reverend Susan, we've come to the conclusion that Middlebury is ready for a lady vicar. But we're not ready to drop the King James and the prayer book. Can you meet us halfway?'

'I am the voice of one crying in the wilderness,' Max continues. 'Make straight the way of the Lord . . .'

The morning dawned as what she thinks of as a false white Christmas: deep frost but no snow. Even with four services in four different villages, she enjoys this day. The extra relatives and guests are good for her diocesan headcount and collection – most pews have a granny and/or grandpa added to the usual pack – and there's a special atmosphere in church: not just the bright but tired eyes of the younger children but the sense that the adults as well have won a lull in their lives. Her only worry is that her sermon may prove rather controversial here.

'These things were done in Bethabara beyond Jordan,' Max concludes, 'where John was baptizing.'

Unwinding himself from the pulpit, the reader nods to her and then bows deeply to the altar, like an old-fashioned actor at the curtain call; another of their High ways she's getting used to. For the last three years, Susan has been taking worship in a prefab round room in a Leicester shopping centre, shared with all the other faiths except the Muslims and Jews who prefer their own places, and so this ancient building, its stones stained with 800 years of prayer, demands some adjustment.

A short, wiry guy she's never seen before – Mrs Lonsdale's husband, it seems – keeps hiding yawns behind his hands.

'And now please stand, if you are able,' she tells the congregation and begins the Collect: 'Almighty God, who hast given us thy only-begotten Son . . .'

*

Apart from following the others' Amens, and sitting and standing – presumably they now say *if you are able* because of the disability lobbyists – Tom isn't listening to what the Rev has said or to Maxie belting out the Bible. In what he hopes will be taken as repose, he gazes at the roof, its curved wooden beams giving the appearance of an upturned boat, where glowing electric heaters are suspended at intervals to discourage any locals from using the cold as an excuse for not saving their souls. Festive sprigs of holly and ivy have been twisted around the pillars.

In his head, Tom is road-testing sentences for his pamphlet.

At the north end of the village green, the thirteenth-century church of St John the Redeemer, though its numbers of Sunday worshippers have fallen in line with the rest of the Anglican communion, increasingly attracts architectural pilgrims drawn to see some of the oldest surviving ecclesiastical wall paintings in the UK.

He probably won't mention that these sacred images, faded by age to the diaphanous trace of a watermark, are currently threatened by bat shit. White bed-sheets drape several of the benches in the left-hand transept, spattered with the droppings of the traditional church vermin. Determined to call in an exterminator, Chairman Libby was horrified to discover from her husband that bats are a legally protected species.

A classic example of a crowded English country churchyard contains both crumbled moss-covered tombstones of forgotten Middleburyians and lovingly preserved tombs, frequently marked with fresh flowers, containing the remains of several generations of major local families.

As Em says, remember Max is paying. In which connection,

it will be politic not to mention that the more unconventional tribute of a used Durex was recently laid on the lovingly preserved tombs by two local children. Jonny, of course, as the clans all arrived under the clanging bells this morning, bawled across the courtyard: 'Slippery as it is, kids, try to keep on your feet!' The looks from Tasha and Jenno could have roasted in a moment the birds that have been slow-cooking since before dawn in their country ovens.

Never detached from the wider world, Middlebury appointed its first female . . .

A sharp dig in the ribs from Phoebe, to his right. He looks along the bench past Felix and Henry, lankily bored in the suits they wear like prison outfits, and sees Emily pointing at him. His daydream has been noticed. Ah, a hymn. Phoebe, with that mock-maternal manner girls take on so early, sighingly places in front of them *Hymns Ancient and Modern Revised*, open to number 432, parentally placing her finger on the line the congregation has reached.

'*Where a mother lay-aid her baby,*' he joins in. Who cares if I'm singing or not? But Emily lives her life as if everyone is watching all the time and, in this village, she may be right.

*

In school choirs, Simon was usually instructed to stand at the back and goldfish-sing. For the first three years at his secondary modern, teachers would console him that his voice was breaking, until they concluded that he was naturally tone-deaf and croaky. And here he is, at forty-seven, still miming roughly in time.

Next to him Henry – God or Darwin knows where he gets it from – is fluting away like one of the cute acts on one of those shows Natasha says the family should watch together.

And through all his wondrous childhood
He would honour and obey . . .

Simon smiles (visibly, he fears) at the irony of this applied to Josh, lolling and scowling at the fact that this will be his only outing of the holidays. Personally, he thinks they were too tough on the boy, but Tasha went all Taliban, especially about the scumbag on the grave-slab. Some Catholic throwback, maybe.

Polly is giggling and nudging Henry at Libby Crossan's colossal, wobbling soprano tones, soaring above the ragged racket of the congregation. Simon looks around, the church perpetually unfamiliar to him because he comes less than once a year – the Christmases they've been here, minus those spent skiing or in Mauritius.

Although not officially Jewish, unable to be bar mitzvahed even in their reform synagogue, the matrilineal qualification feels to him as ludicrously manmade as the cooking rules, and he considers himself a Jew or at least Jew-*ish*, as Jonathan Miller brilliantly put it. Churches unnerve him and this one in particular, shadowed by the memory of his dad's refusal to attend their wedding, which leads to thoughts of his father's funeral, the unfamiliar scratch of the yarmulke on his scalp and his desperate generalized muttering and turning during recitations he no longer recognized.

Where like stars His children crowned,
All in white shall wait around . . .
around . . .
ound.

'Once in Royal David's City' finishes, like a horse race, at three different speeds.

'Let us pray,' says Rev. Sue.

Christ, this is the bit he really dreads, when they leave you alone with the inside of your head, no MP3s allowed. Catholics, his wife once told him, were taught to examine their conscience every night before going to sleep. In which case, there must be a lot of papist saints, insomniacs or liars. The Jew in the pew, he idly rhymes to himself.

Simon tries to make his mind a blank sheet of paper but it fills with unbidden writing. Printed sentences. An email, dropping into the inboxes of SB staff at 18.47 on Christmas Eve.

Burying bad news. Simon had written and approved the fucking thing (he flinches internally at even thinking the word in church) but he still received it on the global mail-out, vomit returning to the dog.

> In solidarity with the economic situation of the nation, the bank and its customers [in other circumstances, Simon would have been pleased with the phrasing], Sir Adrian King-Jones has agreed to a 50 per cent reduction in the lump sum and a 30 per cent reduction in the final-salary pension payments to which he was contractually entitled. In recognition of Sir Adrian's gesture [that loaded word the closest Simon could get to editorializing], the board of Samson Brothers has agreed that all senior staff will take a decrease [he had wanted to write hit] in their salaries and pensions, according to a sliding scale. Newly appointed CEO Alex Manning-Williams said: 'I am deeply grateful to Sir Adrian and my senior colleagues for making the company leaner and fitter and better-positioned to action our recovery plan.'

Simon was too shaken by the news he was disseminating to tell AMW (why do all these bosses want to be number-plates?) that action isn't a verb. In his own case, the reduction will be 20 per cent. Sliding-scale seems apt. For forty-eight hours, since the arrival of AKJ's proposals for a severance deal which will also neatly penalize despised former employees, Simon has had an almost physical sensation of slipping from the life they lead. He is glad his dad is dead, rather than having to admit to him how bad things are or, more likely, lie that everything is fine.

The deals will be officially announced in January, making more impact on a parliament and media back from holidays, but AMW wanted to tell staff first, poisoning the season of theoretical goodwill but ensuring they didn't get the news first from, as he put it, that stuttering bugger on the BBC. 'A perfect piece of PR, don't you agree?' said AKJ, and Simon was coerced to concur.

His feeling of failure is visceral: the cave-man who was too weak to kill the bison. But he has not said anything to Tasha, their now habitual distance making this omission seem almost normal. Their impending poverty is thrown on the heap of unsaid things, dislodging at the top his certainty that Tasha hacked his iPad and iMac when he was in Oxfordshire; the giveaway weakness of the spy-wife the clearly wiped screens and tidied desk. He is sure that she has opened PRUE but, true to the rules of the house, neither of them has revealed their dangerous information to the other.

He looks along the pew (Josh sullenly playing pocket billiards) and sees Tasha standing bowed, eyes tightly closed, deep, presumably, in prayer. He envies her such faith.

*

Please Lord, adulteress and shop-lifter though I am, take pity on me, a sinner, and keep my children safe from danger. Although the nuns and her mum were hot on 'intercessionary prayer' (where, in Catholic doctrine, you pray to Jesus, Mary or one of the saints, who fast-tracks it to the big man, a sort of religious equivalent of Shop and Scan in the supermarket, no don't go there), Tasha has always prayed directly to God.

When she was younger (from seventeen to twenty-five-ish, the age when she stopped going to Mass on Sunday morning and favoured staying in bed to have sex with Simon instead), she used even to ask Him (memories of the red-pen capital correction when she forgot in Scripture essays at school) to save a parking space close to uni or work (which, on a significant number of occasions, He did), until she felt guilty at distracting Him from war and famine with her selfish transport problems. On several occasions, she prayed that her diaphragm hadn't failed, although knowing in her heart that the Catholic God would logically have urged the angels to use the pins whose heads they danced on to stick holes in it. In the run of miscarriages between Josh and Henry, she asked that He might make her pregnant, though obviously via Simon rather than the Holy

Spirit. Her mum would say these prayers were answered. Even now, every time she takes a flight, she adds her own precaution to the safety drill: *Please Lord, sinner that I am, let this plane land safely, for the sake of my family.* The sins used to be vague but are now all too specific. She talks to Him in archaic language ('*Please Lord, let me be / not be with child . . .*') because Bibles and prayer books suggest that's what He likes, although she can see the illogic of this. If there really is a heaven, then Shakespeare, for example, is more likely to be chatting to Darwin and Elvis in a brummie whine than iambic pentameters. God doesn't speak King James.

She still sees Him, childishly, with a cloud of ancient hair around his mouth. When she *does* see Him, which increasingly she doesn't. For most of her life, prayer felt like a conversation, although one-sided: she imagined a giant, kindly ear, hovering above the horizon, like a sunrise, sifting wishes. But speaking to God, for at least a year now, has felt like yodelling in a canyon. For most of the time, she is convinced that there is no one there. Her atheism is only dented when Professor Richard Dawkins turns up on television, his sheer certainty against eternity instantly reconverting her.

A sudden flash of her and Max on the roof in Marrakesh. His hand against her. Her mouth around his. No, no, stop. In recent weeks, she has come to understand the phrase about putting something out of your mind as a physical reality, imagining a ladle spooning a sticky reminiscence from the brain.

But, without sounding too Clintonian about it, does once actually count as adultery? Another unwanted image (the silent emptiness of prayer becomes a wall on which the worst thoughts are daubed): the meeter-and-greeter in the supermarket, standing at the end of the Fruit-and-Vegetables aisle, watching with a frown as she stands, cheeks blazing as they haven't since she was thirteen, scanning the unregistered items in her bags. Returning to the checkout (Jenno, thank God, gone), she expected to be arrested. The handset still marked her for a random rescan, but it came out perfectly. All the smart young man had said was:

'If you ever find an item isn't scanning properly, Mrs Lonsdale, you can always ask us for help.'

So not really an adulterer, then; not really a shoplifter. *OH, YEAH?* the voice of God rings in her ears. She once read a book by a man who stopped believing as a teenager, so that his dead grandparents wouldn't see him masturbating. And perhaps her own loss of faith also comes from shame.

A bout of coughing signals that the silent prayer is over. She opens her eyes as the vicar announces the second reading.

Jonny Crossan, walking slowly and carefully (perhaps he put a bit too much away last night), approaches the altar and (yes, he must be hung over) leans heavily on the edge of the pulpit as he goes up the steps. He's in a black pinstripe suit and his Garrick Club tie. Never knowingly under-dressed, our Jonny. The Christmas service always has two readings, so both Max and Jonny can claim the title of local squire. The smaller performer has to pull down the bendy microphone from the position in which Max left it.

'The epistle is from the Book of Hebrews,' he begins. 'God, who at sundry times and in divers manners spake in time past unto the fathers by the prophets . . .'

She drifts off, hoping for a short service. She's using Jamie Oliver's Christmas Goose recipe, adapted to slow-cooking in the Aga, and is nervous of his urgings to check frequently that the bird isn't drying out. She got up at six to put it in and, by 8 a.m., the kitchen was filling with the smell of Jamie's flavourings of orange, ginger and spice, which she thinks of as Dickensian.

Tasha tries to focus on what she was brought up to call the Word of God. But the old language is too much like ploughing through Anglo-Saxon in the first year at Birmingham. As Jonny gives it the full Olivier, she prays to the God she has lost, a plea that takes her back to the years of her deepest belief: *Please Lord, let me not be with child.*

*

Can one go down with late-onset dyslexia? The words, in heavily leaded gothic script, swerve and shimmer as he tries to read them. *When he had by himself purged our sins, sat down on the right hand of the Majesty on high . . .* A gallon of toxic porridge is sloshing in his gut, as layers of perspiration on his forehead are blast-dried by the suspended heater and a heavy drop of sweat sploshes from his armpit and hits his shirt like paint thrown by a left-wing demonstrator.

And again I will be to him a Father and, and he shall be to me a Son?

And again, when he bringeth in the first begotten to the world, he saith . . .

His voice in his head feels echoey and toneless, like speaking to the follow-boat on a diver's talk-back. He wonders if he could skip a chunk. The words are not printed on the service sheet and only his pa and those ancient spinster Durham sisters are following in their own black, battered BCPs.

Fainting, Jonny has always thought, is for girls, with their lower blood pressure and monthly haemorrhaging. But, for the first time in his life, his legs feel bouncy on the ground. He grips the rail of the lectern but his slicked hand slips and the fist he makes to steady himself increases his awareness of a thumping pulse. He panics that this is the heart attack he has long antici-pated, but surely there would be chest pain.

They shall perish but thou remainest; and they all shall wax old as doth a garment;

And as a gesture shalt thou fold them up . . .

He said *gesture* instead of *vesture*, whatever that means, but only the three keenies will know. Bile splashes the back of his throat, so that the next words come out croaky and he has to cough the frog away. He can feel a double pulse in chest and neck and his voice sounds strangulated to him, like those trainee newsreaders you hear on the wireless, who rush and stumble through the bulletin, desperate to get it over.

They shall be changed: but thou art the same, and thy years shall not fail. This is the word of the Lord.

The congregation responds, 'Thanks be to God', and Jonny silently seconds them. He has avoided the irony of dying while reading the Bible. He tries to back down the steps but his feet are bean bags, like the time he had a trapped nerve but worse. He shuffles away and more blood flows into his limbs and he makes it to his seat, grateful that, by tradition, the Crossans occupy the right-front pew.

'You all right, sweetie?' Libby asks. 'You look a bit sweaty.'

'Fine, Toots. Coffee on an empty stomach. Should have had some toast.'

The Vicaress comes down to the front of the altar – she has told the parish council she considers the pulpit 'hierarchical' – and holds out her arms.

'Did we all get what we wanted this morning?'

Libs touches his arm and winks; they got a quick one in after sending Lucas back to bed at 5 a.m., with a warning not to return until his clock clicked six. To be honest, Jonny could have done with the kip, but he always thinks that, in the rest home at the end, you'll regret the sex you didn't have.

Lucas and Jamie Dunster, from The Eight, are shouting out the video games and phones they got, as are the younger kids of the newcomer couples further back in the church. Mainly phones and tablets; it sounds like an Apple sales convention.

'What we get is very nice,' says the Vicaress. 'But what's even nicer . . . ?'

There's one of those excruciating silences that general-public questions always get. Jenno Dunster whispers in Jamie's ear and he says so quietly that the Vicaress has to double over like a bishop's crook: 'To give?'

Libs nudges him again, triggering a pornographic flashback. Surreptitiously, as if scratching an itch on the inside of his wrist, Jonny takes his pulse, two fingers flat, like a watch-strap, as Dr Em once showed him. The runaway horse is a docile pony now.

'There's an expression we often use, isn't there?' says the Vicaress. 'Give-and-take. It's important in any relationship that we aren't taking more than we're giving . . .'

He really daren't catch Libby's eye. He drifts off, not listening to the blah blah blah. He no longer thinks that he is dying, but begins to understand what the problem is: he is thinking about death. Churches spook him. Walking past the gravestones, sitting in the pews, he finds it impossible not to think that this is where – barring a plane crash with no remains, or the reasonable historical possibility that he outlives the Church of England – his funeral will be.

Looking at the altar, he tries to imagine – and then not to imagine – his corpse in its casket. The horse is galloping through his veins again. Religion makes him ill. But the problem is easily resolved. As a Holiday Anglican, he wouldn't be expected here again until Easter, when they will be in Barbados, anyway. So at least he won't have to go through this again until next Christmas. He tries to listen to what the Vicaress is saying.

*

Jenno wishes it wasn't a Eucharist. Although no one has ever said anything, she feels uneasy, going up to Communion as the second wife of a divorced man. She also knows that Mummy and Daddy will not be too keen on a woman priest. At home in Hampshire, they have resorted to driving to a distant corner of the county to locate a male vicar. She can imagine her father's reaction only too well if the Reverend Sue, as she is prone to, goes off on one about the gap between rich and poor. As it is, there will be a scene over the Kiss of Peace, which Daddy considers a happy-clappy abomination.

'I don't plan to detain you long this morning,' the sermon promisingly starts. 'Presents to be opened and relatives to be fed, I know. So I just want to talk briefly about two particular phrases we've heard in the service this morning. The first is from the epistle, so nicely read for us, thank you, by Jonny.'

Biased as she is, Jenno thinks that Max read better (Jonny sounded as if he'd been on the sauce) and feels a tremor of resentment that the other lesson has been singled out, like seeing someone else's child receive a prize at speech day. She glances at Jamie and Rosie, sitting between her and Max in some of the clothes they got as presents: selections from the Hollister collection. So well behaved, bless them. In the pew behind, she distinctly heard Emily hissing at Phoebe and Felix to stop texting.

In this moment, she determines that she will not let Max send the children away. In contrast to her own generation, the roles are reversed, with the children (because of *Harry Potter*) wanting to go, but the parents largely resisting, although the Crossans' oldest three weekly-board now. Max is making noises about Eton for Jamie, but she will stand up to him. Agonizing about putting their dogs into kennels for odd weeks, the moneyed English happily despatch the children for two thirds of the year.

'I want you to hold in your head,' the vicar says, 'this sentence: *Thy throne, O God, is for ever and ever.* And this one, from the carol – I never think Christmas is Christmas without it, do you? – that becomes such a part of our lives: *And his shelter was a stable.* And isn't that the truly amazing thing about the child whose life we celebrate today? He was entitled to sit on a *throne* but he was happy to begin his life lying in a *stable*! And remember, not even a stable in the grounds of some huge house – where a rich man keeps his horses – but in the stable beside an inn, a place where ordinary people – workers, travellers – tied up their horses for the night . . .'

Jenno wonders where exactly this is going. As does Max, who, at the bit about a rich man keeping horses, does one of his neck-jerks of surprise, like he's just sat on a spike. And Daddy starts gripping his hymnal very tightly, as if he for some reason fears Mummy means to steal it from him.

*

To be honest, she was always slightly worried that they'd appointed a closet lesbian, but it turns out they've got an open bloody Marxist. If she didn't want a parish where the people live in big houses, she shouldn't have taken the job. Libby, who went out on a limb at the parish council for the Reverend 'Sue', sticking up for the general rights of women without ever actually using the f-word, listens with horror as the Red Rev goes on.

'A throne and a stable. Keep those two pictures in your mind. We all think, don't we, in our heads, that we deserve to sit on a throne?' Apart from anything else, the lavatorial double entendre is rather unfortunate. 'But maybe a stable would be better for us. I don't know if you saw it but there was a rather good TV series this year when, for charity, a top comedian went to live in a hut in Ethiopia. He said it changed his way of thinking completely.' Yeah, right. And now he's advertising cheap hotels on telly. 'I'd be the first to admit that the Church itself hasn't been perfect in this regard. Bishops' palaces, lavish rectories. But we're making progress. In the parish of Middlebury, it's a parishioner who lives in the rectory, not the rector.'

Like a soldier in the trenches, Libby enjoys the relief of the shells falling further down the line. She sneaks a glance back at Toby and Alison Rawlinson, who own the Old Rectory. Ali's looking fit to be tied.

'But, when I parked outside the Old Rectory this morning, did I feel envy and resentment that the living of Middlebury no longer comes with that magnificent house thrown in?' Betcha did, Mrs Mugabe. 'No, I didn't. Because, if my boss was born in a stable, why should I be living in a house with six bedrooms and who knows how many bathrooms?'

Toby R is making noises somewhere between a cough and a growl. 'Frankly, I'm more aware that there may be people living in council houses who think that the vicar is lording it a bit by living in a semi-detached in East End Lane.'

Libby enjoys the fact that she and Jonny are the only couple sitting side by side; most parents book-end their kids, which makes her think about people using their children as buffers. She tries to catch her husband's eye, but he seems in a dream, probably thinking about some trial, or sex!

'There's a bit of a fuss going on at the moment – isn't there?

– in the local papers and on the radio about the travellers who have set up home in Eastbury Woods? And there's a bit of a campaign going on, to get them to leave?'

Jonny's Pa doesn't give much away in his expressions – which was probably why he was one of the few ministers who flourished under both Thatcher and Major – but his foot has started tapping on the hassock. Perhaps he used to take it out on the carpet under the cabinet table. Presumably the Red Rev realizes she's got a Tory Party grandee in the congregation? Of course, she does; it's moistening her gusset.

'It's not right for me to take sides in this dispute, although I'd just say that they are living on what is actually common land, meaning for everyone.' Yeah, Susie Marx, for everyone, not for pikeys with their bear-like dogs on chains. 'And I just wonder if maybe the travellers, in their living arrangements, aren't a little closer to the spirit of the baby who lay in the hay than some of us are. We probably think – don't we? – that we wouldn't want our own children born in a stable? A bit beneath them.'

This reminds her to check on her brood. She leans across Hugo and whisper-hisses: 'Tilly, tell Plum to stop mucking around with Lucas!' Her two younger children are playing a sort of ping-pong with hymn books as bats and Plum's rolled-up mitten as a ball.

'But our Lord Jesus Christ didn't think it was beneath him. As we go back to our big, centrally heated, double-glazed houses to sit at a table groaning with food and drink, just keep remembering that line from the carol: *And his shelter was a stable*. The retiring collection today would generally be for Church Fabric Fund but there are greater needs elsewhere at the moment. So I have decided to donate all the money collected at the four churches in the Middlebury Mission on this Christmas Day to the Somalia Famine Appeal.'

Which just about puts the tin lid on it as far as Libby is concerned. Nobody wants to see little African kids with their swollen bellies, but the church roof is like a Swiss cheese and bats have colonized the building. The next meeting of the PPC is going to be bloody.

*

The rising, triumphal organ notes at once transport Max back to earlier performances of this most seasonal of tunes, boomed out in school chapels and the old stone churches in the two villages where he has lived for the longest stretches of his life. Even played so slowly by old Mrs Pennington that the congregation has to keep stopping for her to catch up, it is as familiar as the national anthem.

'*Hark the herald angels sing!*' Max begins, cough-clearing his throat, and realizing, in one of those ridiculously late flashes of understanding about something one has always said and done, that the singers are supposed to sound like the angels singing. Fat chance of that here today, even with Libby trilling like Dame Kiri Te Kanawa. This carol should clearly be sung by sopranos, although Jamie and Rosie beside him, who have the necessary voices, are refusing to use them, from teenage (well, Jamie isn't quite a teenager) fear of being conspicuous.

Perhaps the words mean more than ever before to Max because he is a changed man. Just like anyone else, he has read the articles and seen the TV programmes about people who claim to have 'found God'. He has always imagined the moment as a sort of ethereal orgasm, warmth coursing around the brain or the heart. And this is not what has happened to him; he is not sure what has happened to him. But something undoubtedly has.

For all of his fifty-six years that he can remember, he has been the sort of chap who goes to church twice a year, to hear about the baby in the manger and the saviour on the cross, because his parents always did and because it seems as much a part of living in an English village as cricket in July and a bonfire on the green in November. A few baptisms, weddings and funerals in between and that was your lot, from font to coffin. It has nothing to do with 'God', who is for Catholics and

Americans. At Bill Adamson's funeral, the last time he was here, Max felt blankly incredulous as Mrs Vicar promised that his former FD, consumed by a tumour at forty-five, would even now be introducing improved financial systems to Heaven PLC.

But, this morning, during the 'let us pray' bit, when Max generally thinks about foreign markets ripe to be exploited or the next time he might have sex, something disconcerting occurred. He knelt and placed his face in the bowl of his hands, as the God-botherers among them like Emily and Tasha do, and it happened. Not a vision exactly, no burning bush or voice out of the clouds, rather an internal churning, which he thought at first was acid reflux, but soon settled into a certainty of the presence of his dead father. And the shade of Maxwell Dunster is not a cajoling or admonishing force, as he had been so frequently in life, but a source of reassurance, who suddenly understands and supports his son in a new way.

Max feels another tremor in his torso but immediately realizes that it is his iPhone, vibrating silently with a message. Even allowing for time differences, markets and factories are closed everywhere today, so it is unlikely to be an urgent, work-related call. He doesn't check the message, as he did at Easter, leading to an editorial in the parish newsletter about attention during services, from that old bag of a locum they got between Canon Ashby and Mrs Vicar. It won't be his mother, who will know he's in church, so he can be sure who it is. He will find a time between opening presents and sherry to ring back. He winces as Jamie, not quite knowing his strength, elbows him in the ribs.

'Dad, I've gotta go up.'

Oh, yes, the bidding prayers, of course. Max slides inelegantly sideways and his son clambers past. The choice of the children to read the petitions closely resembled the selection of the South African cricket team in the post-apartheid era, so many special-interest groups needing to be appeased. The final squad comprises Jamie Dunster, Plum Crossan, Henry Rutherford and Henry Lonsdale. Libby says Jenno was holding out for two of hers to read – using Lucas as well or, alternatively, stretching to five prayers – and Ali Rawlinson apparently sent an email about 'the usual carve-up by the four holy families', but the fact is it would have been terribly difficult if anyone from their quartet had been excluded.

Lined up on the altar, the boys look like they're facing a firing squad, the girls as if they're being presented at Buckingham Palace. At eleven, two years younger than the two Henries, Jamie already dwarfs the older boys. The gift – or sting – of genes.

'We all get a day off today,' says Mrs Vicar. 'Well, except Muggins here. But at least I know my boss is at his desk as well, still listening to our needs. God is even busier on Christmas Day. By what I understand is a tradition in this parish, the prayers of intercession have been written and will be read by some of the young people in our congregation.'

The priest smiles and nods at the children. Henry Lonsdale takes his at such a lick, and with such slovenly pronunciation, that it isn't entirely clear what he's asking for, but it sounds as if he's got the boring school-register one, invoking help for Elizabeth our Queen, Rowan our Archbishop and Alan our Bishop. Alan!

Plum Crossan, though a blush burns under her freckles, reads hers slowly and clearly enough to be up for a Poetry Cup come speech day: 'We thank you for our families and pray that we can fully understand what our grandparents, our parents and even our brothers and sisters . . .' – the Reverend Sue leads a splutter of indulgent laughter – 'do for us. We think also of those who are missing their loved ones this Christmas Day.'

Henry Rutherford – Emily's gentle manner in Tom's soldier's body – invites blessings on all those in the medical profession, the emergency services, the army and the police. The prayers are like coursework at school, Max thinks, actually written by the parents. He certainly assumes Jenno wrote Jamie's.

Watching his son, he feels, as at a school play, a combination of pride and fear of being let down or of someone else's child shining.

'We think of those who do not have the chances and advantages that we have,' reads Jamie, quietly but audibly. 'We ask that you protect those in need and distress and that we will always be appreciative . . .' – a stumble on the long word – 'of our good fortune. Lord in your mercy, hear our prayer.'

Max joins in on the response, although his own view is that we make our own luck. There wouldn't be any money for the welfare state to hand out without the hard work and tax yields from the top half per cent of the country.

'Thank you, Jamie, Plum, Henry and Henry,' says Mrs Vicar, a politician's aplomb in using all the names, you have to hand it to her. 'And now let's take a few private moments to reflect on what God has given us and what we would like to ask Him for.'

Glowing like a filament in one of the overhead heaters, Max's father is with him again, smiling benignly at the surviving generations of his clan. Max lowers his head and closes his eyes and is filled with a sensation of absolute contentment.

He is a successful businessman with a thriving company, a happy and loving marriage and smashing children. He does not consider this the result of luck but he is profoundly thankful for it.

'God, we thank you,' he begins confidently.

'Dad!' hisses Jamie beside him and he realizes that he has just boomed out one of the responses restricted to the vicar.

*

Is this the last Christmas they will all be together? Ever since Felix was approaching sixteen, Emily has been sadly anticipating the collapse of their little quintet, expecting the older children to start skipping the twice-yearly church turn-outs and trips to see her mother, or even making their own arrangements for holidays.

Felix and Phoebe, though, continue to come willingly to events that Henry is obliged to attend. On these occasions – the line of towels on the beach, hot chocolate in the ski-slope cafes, her mother's Sunday roasts, these candle-smoked benches – Emily has a sense of the five of them seen from outside, like a photograph, and feels a fierce sense of pride in their family. The thought of Felix leaving home next year (he has offers to read Medicine at Leicester and Nottingham) is almost unbearable to her.

She secretly gloats about how well-behaved her own three are, compared to Jonny and Libby's four, who are tussling like puppies in the front row, although it doesn't help that you can't really fit a family of six into one of these pews. She sees the problem, though: you want them all next to you, this day of all days, not one stuck behind with Granny and Grandpa.

It's only in church, now, that she really thinks of Tom as a soldier; turning up with his medals on Armistice Day and, even today, standing with his hands cupped backwards at the end of perfectly vertical arms, as he must have learned at Sandhurst.

Emily isn't sure what she believes, although, in common with most doctors, she has attended enough deathbeds to accept that human existence is on two levels: the body and something else, whether we call it the soul, the spirit or the life-force. The contrast between the person and the corpse is so extreme that it is easy for her to understand why so many have concluded that something is thrown free from the car-crash of mortality. Her medical training tells her that the difference between the two states is simply cardiac and cerebral electricity but her instincts intermittently question this explanation. And, if the Crucifixion is a fairy story, then it is a brilliantly clever one in addressing the fact that most lives end in pain and suffering.

She glances at her mother at the end of the pew, worried about how she'll be, this first Christmas without Daddy, although so far Mummy has shown the impressive resilience of most of the elderly widows she has treated, telling stories about her late husband with no visible trace of grief or tears, even though her children tense at the uneasiness they always project on to her. Mummy's single visible sentimentality is that, at both her house and the Rutherfords, she has taken to sitting in the chair that Daddy favoured, an assumption of his role that has several times made Emily fear weeping. Mummy's church-going, always well beyond Anglican habit, also seems to have helped her.

Emily enjoys church when she's there, especially the silence; often she wonders if Quakerism might be her ideal religion. But, as on planes, she cannot relax entirely. Twice in previous years, she has had to go to work during the service, when elderly worshippers swooned in the pews. They've had to get up in the morning more quickly than usual, rushed or skipped break-fast, giving their Amlodipine and Bendroflumethiazide less time to kick in. And the constant sitting and standing doesn't help, subjecting blood pressure to unusual fluctuations. Both occa-sions turned out to be simple faints, thankfully – an actual death in church just feels too weird, like an over-eager funeral – but a corner of her eye is always checking people's steadiness, like a woodman must watch trees.

There were times during the second lesson when she was worried Jonny was in trouble: as white and shaky as a sail in a gale, like he had been in Marrakesh a couple of times. Some-thing digestive, she'd guess; he definitely drinks too much. She's thought of mentioning it to Libby, but she'd probably just do that snooty stuff about his 'doctors' being on the case.

'The peace of the Lord be with you always,' says the vicar.

'And also with you,' Emily replies, conscious of her own voice sounding strongly in the apologetic response.

'Let us offer one another the sign of peace,' the Reverend Susan instructs them.

Emily has Jonny's parents directly in front of her. Lord Crossan turns smartly to take her hand with a wide grin and a crisp 'Peace be with you'. Even retired politicians can never stop campaigning, she supposes. He still has that slight glow of people used to being known, the expectation of recognition, although only serious political junkies could possibly remember him now. She receives from Lord Crossan's younger second wife an almost contactless handshake.

As she takes Felix's awkward paw and Henry's silly effort, pumping her arm like a gambler emptying a fruit machine, she feels a hand on her shoulder and turns to find Jonny, who has walked back two rows, manoeuvring round the vicar, who always comes down off the altar to work the whole church and is now testing the diplomatic skills of the former Tory minister.

'Peace, Doc,' says Jonny, kissing her full on the lips, as is his way. Emily turns to make the gesture to her parents and then poor Becca Adamson and her kids. She catches sight, on the other side of the aisle, of the vicar enthusiastically pressing the flesh of the rather frosty Rawlinsons, whose rectory she doesn't covet.

Tasha, on the inside edge of the Lonsdale pew, extends her hand across the nave. Poor thing, she looks worn out. Emily, in a flash of friendly sympathy, feels moved to hug her but settles for the standard C-of-E hand-squeeze.

The flaw of this symbolic greeting, she reflects, is that church-goers generally sit next to their families and friends, with whom they ought to be at peace anyway. But perhaps, when she is an old and lonely widow one day, subscription copies of the *BMJ* stacked unopened on the hall table, she will be glad of the contact.

*

What Sue likes to do is to invite those who aren't receiving Holy Communion to come to the altar for a blessing. All she asks is that they carry a service sheet or hymn book so she doesn't suddenly wave a wafer at them.

The Church very much encourages this approach as part of the ecumenical effort to reach out to those who are not (for whatever reason) communicating Anglicans, or to spiritual browsers. Otherwise, the risk is a sort of sacramental South Africa, with a queue of a few regulars for the Eucharist while the unconfirmed young and partners of other faiths cool their heels in the pews.

If she's honest, it's also a sort of test, a way of taking the temperature of faith in a congregation. The people who won't accept even a blessing are the atheists who have been pressured into coming for social show or because they're chasing a place in the local faith school, although you also get Catholics who have married out but still hold to the old sectarian ways, and Jews and Muslims in mixed marriages, for whom she understands it would be a big deal to come and kneel in front of her. Those are the usual reasons people opt out from the altar, although she sometimes idly speculates that there might be a murderer or adulterer out there, who takes religion seriously enough not to risk offence to God.

But today in Middlebury, she's close to a full house. Admittedly, the white-haired smoothie she recognizes as one of Thatcher's gang rather spoiled the effect by glaring at her through narrowed eyes as she said 'the Body of Christ'. With the seasonal worshippers, she's only previously seen them at Easter, so doesn't really know who they are, apart from the Dunsters and the Crossans, who boss the PPC. Except for a couple of elderly parishioners, who might have mobility issues (she must put in the next newsletter that she's happy to come down to them), everyone joins the queue today for at least a blessing, even the small intense one, who stank of fags when she exchanged the peace. But his wife or partner, the exhausted-looking blonde, who explained in the porch at Easter that she was really a Catholic and so not sure what to do about Communion, folded the service sheet into her pocket as she knelt at the rail and took the bread and wine. By the end of the line, Susan was breaking the hosts in half to make sure they went round.

Used to parishes where the collection is taken between the sermon and the consecration, she has written on her service sheet in biro: RETIRING COLLECTION! It's one of the parochial rituals here that the bags go round at the end. Possibly some former rector was concerned to keep God and Mammon as far apart as possible. *Retiring collection*: one of those old bits of language that hang around Anglicanism, like

President for the celebrant, which always make her feel as if she's running a country.

So she says: 'Don't worry, you'll soon be going home to your turkeys!' For some reason, Mrs Dunster and Mrs Crossan in the front pews exchange a smile at that. 'But, as I said earlier, the collection today will be in aid of the Somalia Famine Appeal.' She checks another note in the margin: 'Er, Rosie Dunster and Tilly Crossan have kindly agreed to take the collection today.'

The two teenage girls in brightly coloured winter coats have been prodded out into the nave early by their mothers and start with their own families in the front row. In his church, they use those green leather purses with a thin slot on top, which are regarded as best practice these days, reducing the risk of a collector or a worshipper palming some notes off the plate, although there probably wouldn't be much chance of that here.

What did concern her about this parish was the risk of a backlash against her chosen cause from the mob who argue that money sent to Africa is wasted by Marxist dictators blah blah blah. But she needn't have worried, for it seems that different political pressures are at work.

Each of the girls begins by sliding what Susan can tell (and fears she is meant to see) is a folded twenty into the purse. Then each of their siblings, it seems, makes a matching donation. Susan has never previously seen a fifty, but guesses those are what the parents are putting in. Is she imagining that Mr Dunster and Mr Crossan, the two readers, are looking across to the other side, like rivals in an auction house, to check what the other is bidding.

And, yes, now, the very tall one, Max, takes from his wallet a second of the denominations she doesn't recognize. She fought a losing battle in the PPC to encourage envelope giving, with its possibilities for Gift Aid. Now she thinks the opposition came from rich parishioners determined to flash their cash. She feels her Christian charity being severely tested.

*

Simon is confused. Half-Jew, whole-agnostic, he was suddenly moved, during the part the service sheet calls 'The Breaking of the Bread', to follow his Catholic wife to the altar. She turns towards him in alarm, like a woman hearing footsteps in the street at night. Her shock almost prompts him to turn back but he is propelled by some mysterious instinct to be helped or cleansed.

He kneels, the service sheet held across his chest like a breast-plate to avoid becoming an accidental communicant. The heat of the priest's hands on his scalp, cupped into a soft skull-cap, surprises him. Although it is so long since he was touched by a woman, there is nothing sexual or even maternal in the gesture. But he has a definite sense of what feels like a soft warmth being drawn into his body, under the cover of firm words to which he feels the pressure to surrender. He returns to his seat with a nagging sensation that a transaction has occurred. He is not able to believe that he has experienced *grace,* but nor can he attribute what happened merely to a trick of bodily contact.

'Make a Christian of you yet, will we?' Jonny bawls at him now in the porch, as they move in the slow queue of worshippers falsely complimenting the vicar on the service.

'What?'

'Aren't you normally sat back there like Billy No Mates while the rest of us hit the chalice? I mean, hand-job only this year, I know, but even so.'

'I know it amuses you to act like I'm the Chief Rabbi or something. But I've told you before I'm not even really Jewish . . .'

'No skin off mine if you are, squire.'

'Beautifully read, Jonny,' Emily luckily interrupts from behind.

They turn ('The King James is so poetic, isn't it?' Jonny acknowledges the compliment) and she's in a line with Libby and Jenno, looking like a girl band of unusual variation in age and weight. Simon has no idea where his wife is. At the end of the service, she knelt, bowed forwards with her face flat against her hands on the pew as if she'd fainted. This cage of faith is a place she sometimes goes and where he thinks it best to leave her.

'I had to smile,' says Jenno. 'The vicar going on about us rushing home to our turkeys. I'm not sure she'll ever *get* Middlebury.'

'We're doing Heston's goose this year,' says Emily.

'You can't go wrong with that,' Jenno tells her. 'We had it last year. I've plumped for a three-bird roast this time.'

Libby giggles at this and Simon wonders if she's maybe found something funny in *plumped* applied to game birds, until the laugh is revealed as one of triumph: 'We're having a five-bird roast.'

'Five?' Jenno challenges her. 'Supermarket, presumably?'

'No. Middlebury Butchers. Either the father or the son did it. I mix them up.'

'I'm sure Harry told me three was the maximum they ran to. Which five?'

'Oh? Goose, pheasant, poussin, definitely. Two others. I leave it to the experts.'

'Wow. I'm surprised there are enough left for a dawn chorus round here,' Simon attempts, in his role of group joker. 'You'll probably find sparrow in there somewhere.'

But only Libby, the victor, laughs. 'Anyway,' she says, 'lunch is going to be completely ruined by Jonny's Pa going on about the sermon. What can I say? If I'd had the first idea I was hiring Martina Luther King, I wouldn't have.'

Simon doesn't hear the rest of the conversation. He's noticed a bunch of fresh flowers in front of one of the mildewed, tilting headstones; a long connection between two relatives or friends. He thinks about how long we can expect to be remembered.

SEVEN

THE THIN PINK LINE

As often happens in houses, the kitchen has become the centre of operations. Lorenzo points at a big cylindrical plastic tank, like an aquarium with no fish in it, which stands beside the glistening machine that the caffeine mule had driven here to feed.

'Water-filtering system as well,' he says to Kate. 'It's a miracle they agreed to breathe the same air as the rest of us.'

The super rich, she thinks, are the only victims cops would now risk criticizing. She rehearses a rebuke about how Lorenzo would be much more careful if the dead were travellers or sex-workers, but even to introduce these groups as a comparison might cause offence to some. And for her to complain would also be hypocritical; she is fighting the temptation to see the murders as a parable.

They are waiting for the police surgeon, who has been delayed at an RTC. The dead are given every chance of life. And so, although the bodies were almost certainly long cold when the coffee guy raised the alarm, it's now statutory procedure to call paramedics to the scene. Once they have ruled out the possibility of resuscitation, the doctor comes in to do the certifications.

'Guv, look at this,' her junior says. 'We've lucked out on identification.'

At one end of the restaurant-size kitchen is a darkly varnished wooden table, set for a breakfast that will never now be eaten. Beside one of the five places is an iPad and, on top of it, a neat stack of instantly familiar booklets with burgundy covers. Death-scenes teem with the sadness of unfulfilled plans, spoiled appointments. Kate guesses that the mother was due to book airline tickets or complete some online documents.

With gloved fingers, Lorenzo picks up the first passport. 'Full names, ages, photos, guv. I know we'll need to get official IDs done. But if I get these details back to the murder room . . .'

'No. No!'

'Guv?'

Kate is remembering a rookie mistake she made and the denunciation from a DCI that still shapes her actions on a case.

'I think you bunked off too many lectures, Rob. Fires, sprees. Never assume that everyone from the family is in the house; never assume that everyone in the house is from the family.'

'Oh, Christ, yes I'm . . .'

'Life isn't like the electoral register. Relatives, houseguests. Didn't you have sleepovers when you were a kid?'

'Yeh. Stupid, guv. *Sorry.*'

She hears footsteps and crackling phones in the hallway and the kitchen door is pushed open.

'Police surgeon,' shouts her Crime-Scene Manager, Sally Burden. An Indian man of medium build, with darkly luxuriant beard and hair, enters with paper-muffled tread. He's a new one to her.

'Surinder Rafi,' he identifies himself and, when she has done the introductions, says: 'Nasty one, this, then?'

Kate nods. 'Four dead upstairs. All look like shootings. Ballistics are on it.'

'Intruder?'

'Unlikely. Neither the dogs nor the alarms went off. The man of the house and one of the cars are missing.'

'I see.' A good non-committal, professional, time-winning phrase; she has used it herself. 'So are we thinking . . . ?'

'We'll decide what we think when we know what people like you think.'

The SOCO Henderson comes in to escort the doctor upstairs and is followed by DC Taylor, who's carrying an evidence bag.

'Guv, something in one of the bathrooms might be interesting . . .'

Although she has used them only a few times in her life (twice for ecstatic reassurance, two or three times for relieved failure), Kate immediately recognizes, in the sealed plastic wrapping Taylor hands her, a pregnancy-testing stick. Thinking how rare it must be for a woman to look at one that is not her own, she turns the thermometer-like instrument to the light and is certain she can see the thin pink line that indicates confirmation.

'Guv?' Lorenzo asks. 'If a murder victim is pregnant, what's the . . . ?'

'I was just trying to remember. It came up at a course I went on. In America, it's double homicide in most states, no question. Here, you have to have been born before you can be killed. The CPS has brought an add-on charge of manslaughter in some cases. But you have to prove the perpetrator knew of the pregnancy and intended to end it . . .'

'So E finds the plastic piss-stick and . . .'

'Yeah, perhaps.'

'Have we ever had a white-on-white honour killing?'

'Rob, I told you about speculating. I shouldn't have to tell you why else that comment . . . So, it couldn't be any worse than it is. But it looks, from this, as if the mum was pregnant . . .'

'Guv, you keep doing me for jumping to conclusions. But one of the other victims is a teenage girl . . .'

But these are the middle-classes, she starts to think, then stops herself.

'You're right, Rob. I've internally bollocked myself.'

Lorenzo smirks. Could a pregnancy, though, have led to all this, or is it just collateral damage?

The door swishes softly back and the doctor comes in. She wonders if he heard any of the previous conversation. You judge the seriousness of a crime scene by the scalded look of shock even in the eyes of those whose job is seeing stuff like this. Dr

Rafi contemplates her warily as if she's his patient and he's breaking terminal news.

'My age,' he says. 'You think – hope, anyway – you've seen the worst you're going to see.'

'Yeah,' Kate acknowledges. 'Anything of relevance for us, you think?'

'The certification part was easy. All long dead, gunshots. There is one thing . . . look, they weren't my patients – most of the people round here go private for most things, frankly – but I know the family. A little bit, anyway. The people in these four houses were a bit of a village within a village. They'd never invite me to anything. But I'd come across them at the golf club, Christmas drinks, one or two friends in common. And I've been out here a couple of times to the kids when I've been on out-of-hours service. And, the thing is, one of the kids up there, I'm sure I've never seen him before . . .'

'Thanks. That's interesting.'

She throws Lorenzo a told-you-so look, her lecture on a household's possible subtractions and addictions perfectly vindicated. As the doctor leaves, she says: 'Thanks. Odds are we'll have another body somewhere. So . . .'

'Let's hope not, but yeah . . .'

Dr Rafi leaves. 'Rob,' Kate says to Lorenzo, 'it seems a bit like Monopoly . . .'

'You mean unreal money?'

'No, I mean these four houses as a sort of set. Send a car to the other three. See if there's a friend of the family who can ID them at the morgue. Although tread carefully. From what the doctor says, we could have someone else's kid in here as well . . .'

'Sure. This, er, Nicky Mortimer might help. We're making arrangements to see him now. And I've sent someone to talk to the other au pair. She's insistent, which is interesting, that everyone was terrifically keen that she went to the theatre last night. Practically begged her to be out of the house, is how she puts it . . .'

A murder investigation, she has had to learn, is the opposite of a maths problem: the more complicated it gets, the closer you may be to a solution.

She needs to go upstairs to see the murder scenes, get it over with. But as she's crossing the hall Taylor calls through the open door from the courtyard, in the tone of controlled excitement that she has come to recognize and welcome in investigations.

'Guv, we've just got . . .'

She beckons him across, pleased to defer again the sight of the dead children.

'Yes. What?'

'We've found E. Place of work.' A classic pattern in two-site killings: work and home. 'Suicide, it looks like.'

'Can we jump to conclusions now?' asks Lorenzo behind him. Answering with what she calculates as her scariest glance, she looks through the window down the hill. At the gates, the massive metallic mushrooms of satellite dishes rise from branded vans in what is already a substantial media encampment. Kate clicks to the news-feeds on her mobile and has the disconcerting experience of seeing the reference points around her – the house, forensic vans and white-suited SOCOs – as the background to the reports live from the scene. The news crawl bawls: BREAKING NEWS – AT LEAST 4 REPORTED DEAD IN BUCKS SHOOTING SPREE.

When she began as a detective, only the killing of a celebrity would have brought coverage like this. Now, though, anyone who dies in an interestingly violent way (at least if they are white and middle-class and paid their taxes) becomes famous, with a vigil at their gates, interviews with those who at least theoretically knew them, ridicule from online trolls and wild conspiracy theories about how they died. Everyone is a Kennedy these days.

EIGHT

DEAD ANTS

'The one playing the husband – the main husband – he was in something, wasn't he?' asks Libby Crossan, during the first interval.

Nicky is about to answer when Dr Rutherford gets in first: '*Jewel in the Crown*, wasn't it?'

'Oh my God! Of course, Em. The baddie with the, er, *black* glove.' Strange how terrified people become of the word in Monifa's presence, even hesitating when ordering coffee. 'I had such a crush on him when it was on.'

'Oh, no, honey, don't make me wear the glove again tonight,' mock-pleads Crossan, the stocky ginger QC, son of the politician, from the look of him.

'Why are women so attracted to bastards?' wonders Nicky.

'Are they?' asks Monifa, rapidly overlapped by Jenno Dunster.

It is several years since Nicky went to the theatre. Apart from a few dutiful trips to Shakespeare with his parents and school, he has always preferred movies, first cinemas, then video, then DVD. But, in common with so many of life's compromises, his play-going came from falling in love. Monifa, a good enough actress at school to have been in the National Youth Theatre, playing Desdemona in a race-reversed Othello, had posters of NT and RSC productions on the wall of her Hackney bachelor-girl flat and stories of queuing from dawn on the freezing concrete beside the Thames while a law student at LSE, to pick up the cheap day seats the National sold at 10 a.m. On early dates, he had required all a young trader's bullshitting skills to affect more familiarity with the names she mentioned – Richardson, Ashcroft and Schofield, or was it possibly spelled Scofield – than he possessed. These days, Google must make emergency cramming before an assignation so much easier.

'I'm not really quite sure what to make of it,' booms Max Dunster, handing round the glasses of Chilean Sav Blanc that he, as notional host of the evening, has poured from the two bottles waiting for them in an ice-bucket as they came out at the interval. 'Why has the other couple turned up at the house?'

'Well, as they say in the play,' Monifa explains, 'they were suddenly too frightened to stay at home, so they came round to their friends.'

'No, no, no, I got that, Monica . . .' – a twitch of his wife's lower lip her only reaction to this misnaming – 'But why were they so terrified?'

'I expect we'll find out in the next bit,' predicts Libby.

'Well, er, Libby, not necessarily.'

'Oh, Lord, it's not going to be one of those clever jobs, is it?' says Max. 'That just, you know, stop, instead of ending?'

'You've seen it before, then?' Emily asks Monifa.

'Yes. And studied it, actually.'

'The pissed sister's in *Harry Potter*, isn't she?' asks Libby. 'Professor Umbridge?'

Nicky senses Monifa's frustration at the level of the discussion, but their group well represents the general mood. All around them, people are debating which movies and TV dramas they might have seen these actors in. Perhaps it would be easier if the cast had their previous credits printed on their costumes, like sponsors' names on footballers' shirts.

The Almeida is one of the places the Mortimers used to come to during their North London years, but it has been substantially renovated since then, although what seems to him to be the curse of all theatre – insufficient bar space – remains.

The word most frequently heard is 'sorry', as drinkers knock their elbows against the huddles behind and beside them. With people trying to drink and eat, while squeezed into tight circles, their arms are as busy as a rowing crew. On the chest-level round table are white plates of tapas-style snacks: tiny sausages with dipping bowls of mustard and ketchup, spatchcocked prawns with a cup of mayonnnaise, potato skins filled with melted cheese and bits of bacon.

Trying to nibble a too-hot sausage, Nicky hits himself in the nose with it instead, when a big man behind him steps back suddenly.

'Is it too cold to stand outside?' Nicky asks.

'Ugh!' says Emily. 'There's practically a mushroom cloud over the door.'

'None of our party outside smoking furtively, for once,' says Tom, the doctor's husband.

'What?' Max barks. 'Oh, bloody Simon, yes.'

'Absent friends!' toasts Libby, raising her glass.

Nicky is aware of a minimal widening of Monifa's eyes. The Mortimers are uneasily aware that, tonight, they have replaced one of the couples in this ruck of chums he likes to think of as the Famous Eight. The invitation came at Euston, hot off the Pendolino, when Crossan suddenly dashed across to platform 16, the one that puts you on the street without going through the barriers (a curious move, but would a QC really be involved in a ticket scam?), and left him alone with Max Dunster, who was coming up to London for some kind of appointment in Harley Street. Nicky had no interest in going but correctly predicted that his wife would say: 'Oh, we haven't been to a play since we moved out!' which was true, the bank's corporate jollies involving opera. He wonders, as he often does, if her acceptance is affected by insecurity about inclusion. He had assumed, though, that their presence would swell the party to ten.

'What was the Lonsdales' excuse for flunking?' asks Jonny.

'Simon just said they were busy,' Dr Rutherford reports.

'Tash was a bit vague about what they're actually doing tonight.'

'Playing marinade the bratwurst, I'd imagine,' says Jonny Crossan. Libby hits him but adds: 'You know what? I did wonder if they might be trying to sneak in another bambino under the wire. Four is the new three and so on.'

At this, the one who calls herself Jenno looks a little wistful. Nicky tries to remember how many children she has.

The tannoy coughs: 'Please return to your seats in the auditorium. Act two of *A Delicate Balance* will begin in three minutes.'

Nicky begins the precautionary sprint to the Gents that becomes such a feature of the social life of a middle-aged man, finding Jonny, Tom and Max at his heels.

As his wife warned, the second half contains no explanation of why the scared pair have taken refuge in their best friends' New England mansion. The multiply divorced daughter of the house becomes more of a character, shouting at the refugees to get out. In the dark warmth of the auditorium, Nicky feels the slumping body and flickering vision that is always his fear in the theatre. In his dating days with Monifa, he used to sleep as late as possible in the hope of later making it through three hours of Shakespeare. Just as he feels himself going under again, he is jerked to alertness by the snoring of Tom Rutherford, who is nudged awake by Emily.

Perhaps this is suggestibility, because the characters in the play are getting ready for bed, exchanging good nights, until the main husband and wife bid each other farewell, presumably intimating that they have separate bedrooms?

The lights come on and the applause spreads through the auditorium.

'You were right, Max,' Jonny says. 'Just stops! They aren't even coming out for a bow. I suppose that's the trendy thing.'

Monifa's apologetic smile tries to slighten the bite of what she has to say: 'Um, it's only the second interval. This is a three-act play.'

Max does an exaggerated double-take face: 'Really? Is that normal?'

'In American theatre of the time, yes. In fact, you know that expression – there are no second acts in American lives?'

'You know what, people say it all the time in Waitrose,' chirrups Libby.

'Yes. I . . . I just read it in a biography of Kennedy, I think,' says Tom Rutherford, more pleasantly.

Monifa is clearly considering abandoning the conversation, but goes on: 'It's often misunderstood. People think it means that there's early success, followed by nothing. But Fitzgerald, who said it, was thinking of three-act American plays: from development to destruction with nothing in between, no second . . .'

'Oh my God, it's like the Open University,' says 'Jenno'.

'No, no,' says Max. 'If you'd only told me before, I'd have ordered a couple of bottles for this one as well. Now, it's going to be a Moscow bread-queue at the bar. Any fundamental objections to Sav Blanc again?'

Nicky holds up a hand. 'Thanks, but I'm driving.'

'Oh, Christ, yes, Libs, who's our designated breathalyser?' Jonny asks his wife. 'Bit of a novelty for us, tonight. Without Tash and Simon, we can fit everyone in one Disco.'

'Okay, I'll drive, honey,' says Libby. 'But I can have another little one, can't I?' *Liddle*, he has noticed the women in this group say. 'I've only had one . . .'

'Be careful,' warns Emily. 'I know an awful lot of people who've been flashed on the M40 recently.'

As Max pushes towards the bar, past sarcastic squawks about turns, Nicky, although he feels no need to pee, decides to avoid any possibility of distraction during the third act by giving his bladder another chance to drain. There must, he thinks, be a seven ages speech in a man's relationship with his penis from cradle to grave: beginning and ending with unpredictable pissing, with that other journey in between from being unable to stop hard-ons to being unable to start them.

The angles of the lavatories mean that, coming out, Nicky

passes the inevitable winding line outside the Ladies. As he waits for the complicated contraflow to clear, the frequently replenished stream of leaving and arriving men crossing the static snake of waiting women, he briefly finds himself behind Libby and Jenno.

'I think she's one of the ones that have a bit of a chip on their shoulders,' the former is saying. 'Desperate to show how much she knows.'

'Mmm. I know what you mean.'

Ah, the protrusion on the clavicle: another of the agreed codes. Tested again by English racism, Nicky either fails or passes the challenge (he is never sure which) and lets it go. They will return to the auditorium as if the women never said it and he never heard it, and perhaps that is the way it has to be.

He fights his way back through to hospitality base-camp, where Max Dunster hands him another tulip flute of chilled white. He is pleased to see that the Rutherfords are having what sounds to be an intelligent conversation with Monifa about the play, or at least the playwright.

'You might know *Who's Afraid of Virginia Woolf?* better,' his wife is saying.

'Oh, yes,' Dr Emily agrees. 'Well, the film, Liz Taylor and . . .'

'Married couples getting drunk and fighting,' Tom Rutherford says.

'I get enough of that at home myself!' declares Max Dunster, putting an arm round Nicky's shoulder and edging him as far away as the competing throngs permit.

'Nicky, really pleased you and Monica could come tonight . . .'

'Mon-*ifa*.'

'What? Oh, I see. But it's an odd one, isn't it? I worked for years with a Stephan we kept *Stevening*. Max is a bit of a no-brainer.' A joke occurs to Nicky which he suppresses in the interests of social harmony. 'So how are tricks at RSG, these days, when every quarter is the worst one since the one before?'

'Well, to be honest, we feel a bit guilty . . .'

'Guilt from a banker? Hold the Bloomberg feed.'

'Well, it's the old paradox that, in the corporate finance side, slumps are good for us. I mean, it's the insolvency practitioners who are really laughing. But we're the paramedics of the economy as well, and the telephones are burning. Restructurings, fire-sales, rescue investment.'

Always sensitive about client privacy – perhaps he could discuss this issue with Dr Emily – Nicky dislikes talking work and so changes the subject: 'How are things on your side of it?'

'Ha! The undertaker getting out his tape-measure?'

Nicky sometimes thinks that everyone is missing a skin nowadays, the simplest comment interpreted as insult. His standard sand-bag phrase: 'No, no, not at all!'

'Good, because you'd be wasting your time. Actually, I know what you mean about guilt. I've got to the stage where I don't like talking about our results because they're up in pretty much every column . . .'

'That's good. Have you analysed why? I mean, good products and . . .'

'I think, in the heritage-gifts sector, there's a certain reassurance – this calendar on the wall, that diary in the handbag – that people are keen to hold on to. But you're right, the way things are in most places, it feels like laughing at a funeral—'

Interrupted by the warning that act three of *A Delicate Balance* will begin in three minutes, Max waves a long arm in the air and shouts: 'My party, this way! Where's Crossan? Oh, out there. Passive smoking, or whatever.'

Their host gestures outside, to where they can see Jonny standing among the banished nicotine addicts, though not smoking himself. With an unwelcome tremor of the social uncertainty that Nicky always supposed would disappear as he got older, he worries that the lawyer dislikes him or resents the Mortimers' apparent usurpation of the Lonsdales.

Feeling a duty to oppose those who have mocked his wife's seriousness about the evening, he concentrates fiercely during the final act. And, either because of this mission or the script, finds himself tremendously gripped. It's revealed that Tobias and Agnes had a child who died, which prompts a graphic but all too credible conversation between them about the times they subsequently made love and he spattered her belly rather than risk impregnating her again. And then a magnificent three-way confrontation between the couple, their daughter and the alkie sister about whether or not they have an obligation to take the terrified friends into their home. The 'terror' or 'plague' that drove the fleeing couple from their own residence is never specified but Nicky feels he would be disappointed if this fear were revealed to be of nuclear war (the play was premiered, the programme says, in 1966) or death or debt. What the drama-tist is surely getting at, he feels, is the abyss that we ignore to go on living; the looming blackness from which money, sex, drink, children and evenings at the theatre try to distract us.

'Amazing play!' he says to Monifa. A perjurious phrase from their dating days, but tonight he means it.

'Oh, good. I've always thought it was saying something.' Under the cover of a kiss, she whispers in his ear: 'So I wanted to see it, even with this lot.'

Nicky's guilt about suspecting her of social neediness is covered in the bustle of the whole row standing up and rucking for scarves, hats and bags on the floor, while the impatient people further down the row nudge impatiently towards the aisle.

'Well,' says Jonny Crossan. 'It definitely got better.'

'I thought the black-glove guy was *fantastic*, especially when he lost it at the end,' concedes Libby. 'But you know what, though. Maybe I'm just dim, but I still don't get why the other couple came round . . .'

'Really, darling. Well, it's the 3 a.m. terrors, isn't it?'

'Is it, darling?'

'I think so, yes. That moment in the night. Of course, we English just get over it and get on with it. But trust the Ameri-cans to . . .'

An elderly man being helped by his wife down the theatre stairs turns, presumably to identify the voice libelling his tribe. 'Jenno' puts her arm round Jonny and coos, pseudo-maternally: 'Don't worry, Jonny, if you and Libs ever turn up on our doorstep terrified, we'd take you in.'

'The thing about sleepless nights is you've got to make use of them,' says Jonny, elbowing his wife in the ribs, his brief philosophical interlude now apparently over.

'But I think that is one of the things Albee wants us to think,' Monifa says. 'What would we do if we got the knock on the door?'

'What it made *me* think,' says Dr Emily, 'probably from the people I see at work . . . is whether we'd have the courage to admit things have got that bad?'

Although he rationally knows that this cannot be the way in which the world works, Nicky always feels a superstitious shiver at visions of future doom. When he was a kid, his Granny Mortimer used to scare the bejasus out of him with a terrible expression about someone walking over your grave.

His shoes slip on the pavement as he comes out of the theatre. People theatrically clap their gloves and rub their cheeks as they sense the temperature. The night freeze combines with a whipping wind that keeps the pavement farewells blessedly brief.

'Really glad to have seen that,' he tells their host.

'Yes, a real treat,' Monifa adds.

'Well, if you're ever up for another one.' Barring, presumably, the return to the fold of Tasha and Simon. 'Pendolino bush telegraph, or do you have a . . . ?'

Fumbling off one glove, the cold reddening his knuckles at once, Nicky unsheathes his iPhone, ready to give or receive electronically, but Max hands over a little stiff business card. Ah yes, of course, a Dunster Manor product line.

'Oh, okay. I'll send you an email tomorrow,' Nicky tells him.

'Splendid. Although I vote for something a tad lighter next time,' says Max Dunster. 'Are there any good new musicals on?'

Social farewells have the intricacy of synchronized swimming. The Mortimers circle the other couples like visiting Royals, Nicky shiveringly exchanging handshakes with the other three men and minimally lip-brushing the three women on both sides, while Monifa kisses all twelve male and female stranger cheeks.

The traffic out of London is light, but the road so slippery that the Discovery at times auto-selects four-wheel drive. A fog is building and, as they clear the city, the Hoover Building, its greens and pinks shimmering in the security lighting, looks even more than normally like a Disney castle.

'Do you ever feel like the people in the play?' Monifa asks him.

'What? Smug and rich, you mean?'

'No! Terrified?'

'No. Well, sometimes. Don't we all? Never that bad. Do you?'

'Well, I . . . you'll groan but . . . I think my faith helps. One of the things about that play, it's a completely Godless world.'

'No, I won't groan, Mon. I wish I shared it . . . actually, I did think that. Don't Americans go to church all the time?'

'Nicks, why do you think they invited us?'

'I don't know. I think the gangleader – *Max* – I think he – you saw him in Marrakesh – I think he enjoys showing off, like an emperor. He wouldn't accept any money for all that endless wine or for the tickets, though I offered. I think he's one of the rich that needs to be seen to be rich, isn't he?'

*

Almost as soon as Max shouts the code phrase, he and Jonny are on their backs on the floor, their legs waving in the air. Most of the other men dive sideways from their chairs with equal speed. To Tasha, the scene resembles a playgroup of gigantic toddlers pretending to be beetles. In the part of the bar their group has commandeered, she is one of only two people who remain seated. Even Emily, surprisingly, has thrown herself prone, air-pedalling.

The only other chair-bound parent is (at least Tasha thinks he is) Kevin's dad, a bearded and surely clinically obese man who (she guesses) feared that he would have trouble getting up again. With the sixth sense of a woman in a pack of men, Tasha has a sudden suspicion that Matt Collingdale's dad is taking advantage of the angles to look up her dress and quickly locks her knees together.

'Thompson! Thompson! Thompson!' Jonny starts a chant from the carpet, which is soon being howled by the crowd. Max hauls himself to a standing position, grabs the empty plastic wine bucket from the table and holds it in front of the seated behemoth now confirmed as Kevin Thompson's father.

'Forfeit! Forfeit! Forfeit!' choruses the gang of dads.

Their victim holds up both hands, palms outward, in the body-language short-hand of common sense. 'Guys, guys!' he pleads, 'I've got a dodgy knee.'

'Lard-arse! Lard-arse!' begins Matt Collingdale's dad, despite a substantial beer-gut of his own straining his replica England rugby shirt, but this shout finds only a couple of supporters from the floor and is rapidly abandoned as the chanters sense the unease of the others.

'A pound coin, Mr Thompson. No euros please!' demands Max.

Shuffling his bulk, Kevin's dad finds the coin in his pocket and drops it in the drinks cooler where it chimes against the deep layer of fines already accumulated on the tour. Most of the parents are now sitting again, thirstily returning to their drinks. Emily mutters to Tash: 'They're not going to keep this up all weekend, are they?'

Max is loping back to his place and Tasha thinks she's escaped. He has been nervous of her since Marrakesh. But Jonny begins banging on the table with his beer-glass, establishing a rhythm that now becomes a lyric: 'Tasha! Tasha! Tasha!' Matt Collingdale's dad is soon duetting and the din quickly builds into a beerily loud slurred choir. Max silences them with a conductor's shushing hands.

'Oh, oh dear!' he says in the Shakesperean actor's voice he has assumed as tour leader. 'There's a swell behind Mrs Lonsdale!'

With their gender's astonishing speed at detecting innuendo, the men guffaw and bang their tankards on the wooden surface. She cannot imagine that Max, who has acted as if Morocco never happened, intended the double meaning.

'I promise you, Mr Dunster, it's just the wallet in my pocket!' Jonny yells, encouraging more suggestive thumping of mugs.

Max, carefully lifting his long legs over the jumbled feet, a man permanently fearful of tripping, comes towards her, rattling his punishment fund.

'Tash,' he begins. 'There's a general feeling . . .'

'Not me, sir! My hands are on the table!' bellows Toby Remington-Jones's father. Having managed to avoid boys' public schools and rugby clubs in her life so far, Tasha is receiving a rapid crash-course in their atmosphere. A depressing feature of the weekend for her already has been the easy revelation of the schoolchildren and students these adults would have been. A rule, she realizes, that also refers to her: still the snotty one rolling her eyes at the sexual baiting from the boys.

'Oh, put it away, Max!' she hears herself saying.

'Not the first time she's said that,' howls Jonny. Tasha flinches, as she does at any shagging banter these days, but convinces herself that the laddishness is generalized rather than personalized.

'Pay! Pay! Pay! Pay!'

The chant, underscored with foot-stamps, expands to include everyone except Emily, to whom Tasha looks for support. But her friend is glancing down, her focus turning out to be a purse, from which she takes a pound coin and lobs it into Max's penalty collection. The rebel that Tasha was in adolescence feels disappointment at the intervention of the peacemaker the young Emily would surely have been.

Jonny jumps to his feet, the Apple Tree Motor Inn in Gloucester suddenly a high court. 'Mr Dunster, sir, is it acceptable that forfeits should be paid by another party?'

'Objection sustained, Mr Crossan,' Max says. God, what will they do to her next? Water-boarding? But then Max adds: 'Though, in this case, the bench makes an exception.'

Tasha exchanges with Max the glance of the mutually blackmailing. The ringleader returns to his seat and the separate clumps of conversation resume.

'Jesus, Em,' she says, taking, then regretting, another glug of the linctusy pub red. 'Was it as bad as this last year?'

'Oh, yes. I think the Westburyians Rugby Tour is like Christmas. Everything's the same except the numerals in the year. There were more mums last time. But it probably won't surprise you that they only come once. Except me. Curse of being a GP. Surinder Rafi used to do it, but his boys are through the system now.'

'*Little girls' room*,' mutters Emily, getting up and leaving Tasha alone, half of a tour-clique of two. What is she doing here? she thinks, a question she is not alone in asking. On the motorway – with just Josh and the two Henrys, it made sense to use one Disco and share the petrol – Emily had expressed amazement that Tasha had come on the trip.

'Oh, Simon's done it every year since Josh was in the under-10s. I thought it was my turn,' Tasha lied, hating the *bless*-face Emily gave her, a fellow veteran's tribute to a marriage of give-and-take.

Emily's next question – 'Should I turn down the heating?' – baffled her until she understood she must be red and quite possibly sweaty at the memory of the real reason she was on the rugby tour. Even now, two weeks on, she still relives, several times a day, and more often during broken nights, as survivors of life-threatening accidents must, the moment of impact.

'I've been thinking. I don't think we should see Max Dunster for a while.'

Simon, after a typically silent and wine-anaesthetized supper in the kitchen, has his back to Tasha when he says this, having filled the dishwasher, his only real concession to joint domestic chores, and so could not have seen her panicked reaction. She is relieved he isn't standing at a window, with its possibility of background reflections: the sort of thought that has been routine since paranoia became a habit.

'Why?' she replies, her voice feeling as tight and dry as when she did the eulogy at Dad's funeral.

'What? We always seem to see the same people: like Siamese – conjoined, we're supposed to say now – um, octuplets. I just think we could use a break from him.'

She has, in general, become used to her husband saying things that are vague and incomplete. But is he trying to trick her into admitting the reason she might be relieved not to see Max? Has he picked up on some history between the two of them and is fishing? For the character in an espionage drama that she has inadvertently become, such frenzied self-interrogations are a regular occurrence.

As in public speaking, she is conscious of exercising almost a star soprano's control over her tone: 'Well, yeah, he can be a bit of a . . .' – her brain instantaneously saves her from the Freudian *prick* – 'prat sometimes . . .'

'Sure. Yeah. No, Max is just, well, Max. It's more than that . . .'

No high notes, no high notes: 'Really? What?'

'Oh, you know, like he's the Warren Buffet of Buckinghamshire and I'm some jumped-up bank clerk. He's always asking me how things are going, in a loaded way, and then boasting about how Dunster Manor is beating the trends . . .'

Her newly trained face hides the relief she now feels as efficiently as it disguised the fear. Simon hates Max for being rich and securely employed – not, unless he is being extremely Machiavellian, for any other reason.

'He was banging on about some theatre outing on the train this morning,' Simon continues. 'But I said we were busy . . .'

'Oh!'

'The coven will probably put pressure on you to go, next time you see them, but I'm serious: I'm maxed-out on Max for the moment. Oh, and . . .' He's lighting a cigarette; she has had to let him smoke in the kitchen since it became too risky to confront him over anything, even if she does have her knowledge of the PRUE file to use in any nuclear stand-off scenario. 'I am not going on that fucking rugby tour this year . . .'

'Really? But Josh and Henry are both desperate to go.'

'Tough. I am not sitting there watching Flashman having flashbacks to public-school pranks for another whole weekend in some pissy motel . . .'

'Well, you can fucking tell them they're not going . . .' – hiss-whispering because it has always been her pledge to herself that the kids should never hear them arguing – '. . . and you're always complaining about money these days and we've fucking paid for Josh and Henry and *a parent* . . .'

'Why don't you go with them, then?'

'What?'

Her genuine surprise has, she hopes, disguised the elation she feels. Simon must suspect nothing, or he would scarcely suggest that she spend a weekend in Gloucester with the man who (mentally whispering now) fucked her on a balcony in Marrakesh.

A flashback within a flashback. The thundering voice of Matt Collingdale's dad releases her from it: 'The compound-inflation-adjusted equivalent of a penny for your thoughts?'

Emily is not back from the loo. The usual problem, she assumes – with the exception of their group, the pub is filled with young women, out this Saturday night as part of couples, or in work or uni groups.

'What?' she says to Rick (is it?) Collingdale.

'You seemed kilometres away.'

'What? Oh, no, just Emily's gone to the loo.'

She realizes how weird this sounds, as does 'Rick': 'Oh, I'm sure she didn't mean it personally.' Then he adds: 'Tash, would you mind if I slide in?'

While lacking a cigar to waggle suggestively, Matt Collingdale's dad easily communicates with his eyebrows and voice that he is talking about more than moving his stool (Christ, the English language is a minefield of innuendo) closer to hers and Emily's.

'LEFT-HANDED DRINKING!' Max, without warning, roars across the bar. Instantly, Tasha's new companion switches to the unfamiliar grip, sloshingly lifting a pint of beer, while using his right hand to shift her wine-glass to her left hand and raise it to her mouth. Instinctively, she tries to shake the attentions away but his hold is strong.

'Who was the last to get it up?' Max bellows, receiving the desired gleeful hooting.

'Thompson! Thompson! Thompson! Thompson!' comes the answering chorus.

The resentful but resigned eyes of a man accustomed to bullying blink from the fleshy, reddened face of Kevin's dad. When the shouting has died down enough, he pleads: 'Guys, guys. Listen, I am *left-handed*, naturally. So it's ambiguous.'

'Ooooooooooooo!' the mob immediately mocks the fancy language, in a reaction Tasha remembers from A-level English.

'Big guy, big word,' Matt Collingdale's dad sneers, beerily close to her face.

'A lefty in the camp,' Max says. 'We hadn't reckoned on that. What do you rule, Mr Crossan?'

'In these circumstances,' Jonny says, 'it is clearly indicated that the defendant should have drunk with his right hand instead of his left.'

'But then you'd still have said I wasn't drinking left-handed!'

'Ooooooooooooo!' the men shriek again, encouraged by the petulance in their victim's voice.

'FORFEIT! FORFEIT! FORFEIT! FORFEIT!'

'The bank of shame,' says Max, rattling his collection. In

groaning slow-motion (Tasha tries to resist a mental metaphor of Sumo wrestling), Kevin's dad stands and faces Max.

'FIGHT! FIGHT! FIGHT! FIGHT!'

And, like a gunslinger in a shoot-out, the challenger does swing his hand to his hip, but pulls out a crumpled ten-pound note, which he flutters into the bucket.

'Take that for the next ten and maybe you can leave me alone. Goodnight!' he says, turning and trying to force a path through tables overlapping like Olympic rings.

Jesus, Mary and Joseph and all the Saints. Tasha feels and then sees the Collingdale guy lifting her hand and stroking it.

'It's a point, I suppose. I should have checked if you were a cuddy-wifter before I helped you.' She shakes him away. 'Cuddy-wifter is what my nan always used to call them. I always thought it sounded a bit rude, like *cunnilingus* . . .'

He slowly rotates his tongue outside his mouth. Aren't blokes unbelievable? Off the leash for the weekend from Matt Collingdale's mum or possibly step-mum, he really thinks he has a chance of sleeping with her.

Thank God, Emily is back. 'You okay?' she says, 'there seems to be a bit of an atmosphere.'

'Have you got your gelding irons in your bag?' Tasha whispers. 'The boys' games are getting out of hand.'

'DEAD ANTS!'

Alcohol and adrenaline make Max's voice even louder than usual. On CCTV footage, it will look as if a bomb has exploded in the bar. All the men crash to the floor, with squeals of pain as they hit themselves on table edges or other falling bodies. Successfully capsized, they thrash their limbs around, until Max, from his prone position, shouts 'At ease!' and lifts himself up on his elbows.

'Who's out?' he asks, looking up. When he sees that Tasha and Emily have not moved, there is a moment in which his fury is visibly exposed and then controlled.

'GIRLS! GIRLS! GIRLS! GIRLS!'

Matt Collingdale's dad, who starts the chanting, also jabs

his finger at Tasha. She feels in her pocket for change, identifying through everyday Braille a clot of pound coins. She brings one out and flicks it into the bucket. Satisfied by the silence that results, she repeats the action, the clunk resounding in the room, then smiles at Emily.

Tasha stands up. 'I think I'm going to go to bed.'

'So am I,' says Emily.

'Can we come and watch?' shrieks Jonny and the first trumpet notes of male sexual speculation begin to rise in the room again. But, this time, they are quickly silenced, like a mobile phone in a theatre, because Max says 'Leave them!'

'Our apologies, ladies, if the entertainment may have gone too far,' Jonny says, sounding like someone from Jane Austen. Even now, at least within their circles, a woman holds over a man the power of what she might tell his wife.

The two women wait for the lift but the red number 4 glows unchangeably in both indicator panels and so they walk, Emily impressively unpuffed while Tasha fights to silence a wheeze.

'Thank God I can take this bloody headband off now,' says Tasha, snatching her Minnehaha feathers from her scalp and tucking it under the strap that attaches her quiver. 'You cowboys lucked out, I can tell you.'

'Mmm, although the squaw was getting all the male attention, I noticed.'

Emily is wearing a checked shirt, neckerchief, jeans and boots, which, unlike the outfits of the Indians, pass without comment in Gloucester on a Saturday night. The two costume options – selected by Max as tour captain and to be worn on all public occasions under pain of fine – were chosen by ballot at the previous Sunday morning's game. If the draw had come out differently, they would now be dressed as witches or wizards, tarts or vicars, roundheads or cavaliers, ghosts or ghoulies.

The Apple Tree Motor Lodge – a two-storey yellow-brick building in an industrial cul-de-sac under a motorway bridge – is not the sort of place Tasha and Emily would ever have expected to stay in. But Westbury RFC Sunday rugby clubs include children from state and even special schools and so the tours must find the economic lowest common denominator, subsidized by some discreet grants. The green paint on the hotel's stairwell walls betrays several summers' fading and the smell in the no-smoking rooms suggests that some of the weekday clientele of stressed-out salesmen risked the £100 Deep-Cleaning Charge threatened in a red-lettered poster on the wall. The joke among the group already is the receptionist's blank reaction when Max Dunster asked if he could upgrade to a suite.

Pushing open the scuffed double-doors on to the fourth-floor landing, Tasha and Emily see immediately why the lifts were stalled at this level. The bleep warning that the doors are jammed can intermittently be heard between the shrieks of dozens of the younger boys. Jamie Dunster and Kevin Thompson are using their front-row forwards' bulk to force back the doors, firing from those massive plastic guns they all have at packs of other boys who, shooting back, are trying to enter the elevators.

The floor is littered with what look like orange-coloured tampons, which Tasha identifies, from many shouting fits outside her son's bedrooms on the day the cleaner comes, as the ammunition for those bloody nerd guns.

She sees her younger boy among the squad bombarding the lift that Max's Jamie controls.

'Henry!' she yells, and, dog-like, he responds to the disciplinary voice even in the melee.

'Oh, er, Mum.'

'What the hell is going on? You know we said no nerd guns on the trip.'

'*Nerf*, Mum.'

That adolescent head-shake at the idiocy of old people.

'Chill, Mama Bear.' The name he uses to wind her up. 'It's just a bit of fun.'

Tasha wins the struggle not to become her mother and

rejoin: *until someone loses an eye*. The noise and shooting stops as the presence of the parental police force is gradually noticed.

'Step away from the lifts and let them go,' Emily says in an impressively commanding voice which may well draw on similar stand-offs on night call in tower blocks where the menace of the youths is unpretending and their guns are not orange-and-blue plastic.

Jamie – already a beanpole from Max's genes – scowls savagely at his godmother but he and Kevin Thompson obey her order. Tash briefly wonders why Kevin's dad, coming upstairs earlier, permitted the riot to continue, but realizes that the children will have victimized him just as their parents did. Looking around, Tash sees Lucas Crossan lying still beside the wall. She checks her watch: 23.23. The boy is eight years old. The minefield of disciplining other people's children: she would be careful even if they hadn't done *The Slap* in book club.

'Lukie, what are you doing?' she asks softly, bending over him. His eyes blink open under the feathered head-dress. A gappy smile of recognition.

'I'm dead,' he says.

'The game's over. Everyone's going to bed.' She turns and raises her voice to take in the whole crowd: 'Everyone back to the rooms, please. And we don't want to see or hear a peep until eight at the earliest. And pick up the . . .' – she has always flinched from the word bullets – '. . . *pellets*, please.'

The boys collect the tangerine foam cylinders from the floor. The Indians, carrying bows and quivers alongside the toy rifles and machine-guns, look like guests planning to attend two rival fancy dress parties on the same night.

Instinctively, Tasha and Emily both move towards their Henrys to kiss them goodnight but the maternal embarrassment radar installed in 13-year-olds as standard kit efficiently senses the threat. The boys dash off down the corridor with ambiguous flat-hand gestures of farewell.

All down the long, mustard-carpeted corridor, latches click shut. A flashback to school trips, followed by age's painful incredulity at the distance of these memories: at least three decades.

'Bloody hell, was it like this last year?' she asks Emily.

'Well, the splat-gun craze hadn't started then. But yes. The dads just don't notice it's going on, like dirty houses, which may be the best way. Actually, I find this one relaxing. When I went on the Italian art trip with Phoebe's year, we spent most of the time trying to stop them bonking each other . . .'

'Yeah,' Tasha risks saying, 'not much risk of that on this tour.'

'Oh, I don't know. Robbie Collingdale was all over you . . .'

'Oh, Robbie, is that what . . . ?'

'Isn't it . . . ?'

'Rick, I thought he . . .'

'Maybe it is. I told Max we should all wear badges.'

'Anyway, behave. It was beer-goggles.'

For Tasha, there is an excitement to hotel rooms, however drab. A shrink (if she believed in shrinks) would doubtless link this to the much-repeated family story of how, taken to a bed-and-breakfast in the Dales aged four, she asked, after saying her prayers: 'Mummy, is this our new house now?' In the late eighties, when she and Simon got gazumped on the Hammer-smith house, having already sold the Battersea flat, they had lived in hotels for three months and, though Tasha loyally echoed the dismay of her husband and their friends, she relished the little rituals of lining up her toiletries on a different sink, choosing from another room-service menu. Sometimes, driving, Tash has imagined taking a room at a Days Inn beside some smut-smudged motorway service station: not for sex (although that must be a large part of their market) but for sleep, defiance of the diary's hourly demands, no one knowing who or where she is.

In room 426 of the Apple Tree Travel Motel – chessboard bedspread in light and dark green, framed print of children fishing beside a stream, liquid soap in upturned bottles and loo paper shaped into an arrow as if targeting your arse – Tasha sets her hairbrush, paperback (swotty Emily has chosen *Hard Times* for book group) on the pock-marked blonde-wood bedside table (will *pock-marked* one day leave the language as a result of better vaccination?). In the bathroom – so tiny that Max, an example used purely for his size, would surely struggle to shower – she wees, then touches herself inside, hoping for the dryness that sometimes means she's coming on, but she really doesn't know enough about herself down there to be sure. Maybe she should ask her husband, presumably an expert from the compilation of *Collected VAT Returns 1993–*.

After the inevitable lengthy struggle to turn down the heating, apparently default-set for visiting Hawaiians whose clothes got lost at Heathrow, Tasha changes into her jimjams, chains the door (fearing prank-raids from the dads) and loosens the hospital-tight sheets (imagining immigrants making the beds for sod-all per hour) enough to slide down the left-hand side, always the left, even when she has the choice. She can remember when to fill half of a hotel double-bed seemed a waste but it feels a treat, a relief. Her boarding pass from Marrakesh marks the Dickens where she left it at page 178 . . .

Natasha has borrowed Nicky Mortimer's car – a top-of-the-range Mercedes – and is driving it up the M40 in the fog, past the Hoover building, when the dashboard starts to rattle. She is panicking about how to tell a man she scarcely knows that she has wrecked . . . Her phone is trembling on the bedside table. Her sleep-stuck eyes blearily make out the flashing rectangle edging towards *Hard Times*. Away from home, she always keeps the phone on vibrate overnight in case of the children or her mum. The brutal red of the plastic motel clock-alarm says: 03:11. A bad-news time only. With sudden nervous alertness, she grabs the hand-set.

Against the bright shimmering light, the word: Maxmobile.
Christ, silently, and then: 'Christ, Max, what the . . .'
Whispering, because: 'I'm outside, T, can I . . . ?'
'It's 3 fucking a.m., Max . . .'

'Tour time, sweetie, tour time.' Perky as ever, though slurred. 'That's, what?, afternoon *tea*. We need to talk . . .'

True, but: 'Go to bed, Max. I'll see you in the morning.'

She kills the call and, sitting up in bed, turning on the light, ignores the repeated calls and 901s. Then a text: *T, what do you think I am? M xxxxxx.*

Only once in her life, in New York, when she and Si were doing it in the afternoon, and a maid tried to get into the room, has Tash heard the scrape and rattle of a chained door being forced.

'Tash, I'll be a perfect gentleman.'

The sound of his voice is in the room. Fuck. How did he? Out of bed with a speed she has not risked since her bulging disc, ridiculously glad of her pyjamas, Tasha sees, in a slice of bright light from the corridor, that the chain, though straining, is holding but that he somehow has the door open.

'Max, please,' she pleads, 'I'll tell Jenno.'

'Tell her what exactly?' This quiet voice of his, though reasonable, is surprising, frightening.

'Tash, I'll wake up the whole corridor and then we take our chances with the village gossips.'

At the third fiddling attempt, she slides the silver circle into the same-shaped hole and shakes out the chain, aware of this being a moment of decision.

Blinking in the low light, he looms over her in the confined space, flushed, clearly at least a little drunk, jerking out an arm for support against the wall.

Still keeping her voice soft, conscious that the only sound at this time is the muffled static of the motorway traffic: 'Did anyone see you come in?'

'My dear girl, if they did, your reputation . . .'

'Ssshh!'

'Last man standing. Drank them under the pool table. Crossan disappeared twenty minutes ago on the pretext of checking on Lucas and never came back.'

'And how did you get the door open?'

Max holds up the white plastic card with its black magnetic strip.

'And how did you get that?'

'As Tour Leader, I have the room list. I told the polytechnic halfwit at reception I was Mr Lonsdale, locked myself out. Shockingly lax, places like this. At the Paris Ritz, I saw a poor sod standing stark bollock naked with a tourist leaflet over his meat and veg while they carried out 'security checks' before giving him a new room key. Gone for a piss in the middle of the night, he took the wrong door out of the bathroom, found himself in the corridor, I suppose. Traveller's nightmare. Ever happened to you? No, you sleep in PJs. I guess I imagined diaphanous nighties.'

'Max, this isn't right.'

'Banter, Tash, banter. Might I avail myself of your facilities?'

He side-steps her and ducks into the bathroom. She is relieved that his call of nature gives her time to think, but then is ambushed by a vision of him washing his equipment as a prelude to seduction, as Simon used to on their early weekends away, panicking now at the thought of him coming back into the room.

Tasha has, in the past, had sex when she didn't want to (which woman hasn't?), because it seemed easier in the end than a boyfriend or her husband getting the grumps, but has never, thank God or whatever, been raped. Much as her conscience tries to argue otherwise, she knows that what happened in Marrakesh can't be put into that category. Although she tries not to replay images of that night, and mentally pixellates any images that arrive instinctively, Tash imagined, in the days immediately afterwards, a court-case in which defending counsel (a version of Jonny Crossan at his worst) gleefully established through cross-examination that she had unzipped the trousers of her assailant before he pulled down her knickers, and that he had asked 'Is this okay?' and 'Are you protected?' (the question of a man with a fertile younger wife), to both of which she had answered 'yes' (one half-truth, one age-related gamble), before

251

he pushed himself into her, an easy entrance, not because of passion or desire but the novelty of being wanted after her long drought with Simon and the feel of a different man (a hot shoving urgency long forgotten) after twenty years, although her certainty that Mohammed would reappear on the terrace, leading to her being stoned to death and pilloried in the UK newspapers as a feckless posh bird, stopped her much enjoying it. He came too quickly for her to have a chance herself, although the lack of an orgasm subsequently allowed her mind to argue that it hadn't really counted, like Clinton with Monica. At breakfast on the terrace next morning, her gaze was relentlessly drawn to a stain on the wall at a compromising height but Max (is this just him or all men?) was able to behave as if he had spent the night in his wife's blameless embrace.

The sound of flushing and then splashing taps. The bathroom door opens, releasing a curried stink which, though revolting, at least innocently validates the visit.

'You need to go, Max.'

'I needed to come' – Christ, does he mean? – 'to talk to you. Tash, do you think anyone ever reads the Bibles?'

'What?'

'In hotel rooms . . .'

'Sshh!'

'*In hotel rooms.* A business course I went on, there was a guy who used to ring up in advance and tell them to take the Gideon out of the drawer. I don't think he was a Satanist or anything, just didn't think it should be forced down anyone's throat. As it were.'

He has moved into the main part of the bedroom. She follows him. By the window beside the radiator, there is a table with a laminated leaflet about WiFi connection, and two chairs, in one of which Max sits.

'Because, if you think about it, anyone who was really into the Bible would bring their own. And, presumably, there's a Scripture app now. I just wonder if anyone ever, in the middle

252

of the night, depressed or whatever, has ever taken out the hotel Bible and read it.'

Her bed-things feeling flimsily intimate, she pulls her big blue touchline jumper from the top of the overnight bag and shrugs it on.

'Max, it's twenty past three in the morning. We're playing Gloucester Grange Under-13s at ten. You can't be here.'

'I thought we needed to have a chat.'

'Do we?'

She sits down on the bed at the furthest edge from him.

'Don't we? I just feel there's a *thing* between us . . .'

Is he mad? 'Are you mad? Look, what happened happened. It shouldn't have happened but it did. And now we just have to be like grown-ups – *be grown-up*s, I mean – and pretend it never happened . . .'

Max looks baffled. 'What? No. I don't mean a *thing* thing. Look, Mrs Lonsdale, I'm not a book-worm and culture-vulture like you. Words aren't my oyster, onion, whatever the expression is. When I say there's a *thing* between us, I mean an atmosphere, a . . . there's a French word . . . .'

'*Froideur*?'

'That's the one. You go, girl, as my Rosie says. Brains as well as beauty.'

'Stop it! And are you surprised it's a bit off between us? Or are you in the habit of, er, pouncing on your best friends' wives on rooftops in Morocco?'

'I've really no idea what you're talking about.'

Tasha has known clients who point-blank deny that a price has been agreed or invoice sent, but the phenomenon is new to her private life; perhaps it is a trick that men in business learn.

'Glad it was so memorable,' she says. 'Which it wasn't for me, incidentally.'

'There was a moment of connection that night. I don't deny it. But I love Jenno too much to cheat on her.'

Thrown by the progress of the conversation, she is suddenly

conscious of the circulation ceasing in her feet and huddles herself in the cheap lumpy duvet.

'So what did you want to talk about then, Max?'

'Oh, the – insert that French word here – I'm talking about is the Christmas Party thing. It's clearly not an ideal situation and I completely understand your feelings. But it wasn't me. My new FD was adamant that we couldn't be seen to be nibbling while England burns or whatever . . .'

Blood and tears: you can feel them coming, a warning sting just before, but can do nothing to stop them, the body calling the shots. She sniffs in an attempt to pass it off as tiredness or the beginning of a cold but feels the waterfall on her cheeks.

'Oh, whoah, Tasha, whoah. This isn't what we want at all. What's brought this on?'

Max stands to play Samaritan.

'*Stay there!*' she hisses, the vehemence and fear of being overheard combining to make her voice sound foreign in her head. But she has been a woman long enough to know where the comforting of tears can lead. Max compromises by sitting on the opposite edge of the bed. Tasha tightens the padded white cocoon around her.

'Will it help at all if I get you a glass of water? There's tea but it's those damn sachets. In this situation, one always wants to say: *there, there*. But I don't suppose it ever works for anyone. Children, maybe . . .'

'Max . . .I've got a bit of a problem . . .'

'What? You're not . . . ?' His fear – she sees triumphantly – is that she's pregnant, but the detail contradicts his rewriting of events. 'You're not *ill*, are you, Tash? Ever since Bill Adamson came to ask me for time off, the word *problem* . . .'

'What? No. No, it's not that. I . . . it's . . . what the English don't like talking about . . .'

'You mean God? Not your chap for that, really. Oh, *money*. Cripes! Jenno did say something funny happened at the supermarket . . .'

Fucking nosey spiteful cow. 'Did she?'

'Credit card refused or . . . I'm not sure. I get accused of that man thing of not listening properly . . .'

'Oh, I just had problems with the new scanner system. I'm not talking about that. Max. *Marrakesh* . . .'

They are risking normal voices now, although they sound boomy in the deadened night.

'Tash, I've just—'

'No, not the . . . the three days we were delayed getting back by the snow at Heathrow? You booked that hotel in the mountains . . .'

'Yes, we landed on our feet there, didn't we?'

'It was nice but it was five hundred dollars a night . . .'

Flashing fragments of those three days with Simon, mainly silence with occasional shouting, incredulously triple-checking their currency conversions before slipping the sliver of plastic inside another folded-over bill.

'Was it? I'm afraid I just pay off the balance without looking at the debits. Silly, I know, because of fraud . . .'

'I put it on my card because Si was already giving me grief about the cost of the flights on our Visa and . . . now the bill has come in and . . .' – the tears threaten again – '. . . I can't pay it . . .'

'Pay the minimum. That's what a credit card is for. I know the APR is . . .'

'But I can't, Max. I've . . .'

'Maxed it? Ah! Well, you need to be extra nice to Mr Lonsdale, don't you? A T-bone and a blow-job on a Friday night . . .' A flood now: our helplessness when emotions take control. 'Oh, Tash, now, look, you've really got to stop the waterworks. Money's what I've got. Money's what I do. It's not worth this palaver. We'll sort something out . . .'

This seems the perfect opening to say, firmly through the snot and splash: 'I just need a loan, Max. For a couple of months at the most. Bookings always pick up in the spring, with weddings.'

'Ah. Now. No. That isn't what I meant. One of my pa's

better sayings was that, if you make a loan to a friend, you tend to end up losing one or the other or both. Let's imagine you're a business in trouble and war-game this. Cash reserves? Simon must be pulling down a fair whack at Samson's – there are surely bonds and ISSAs tucked away . . .'

'The thing is . . . Simon's under such strain at the moment that I'd really rather leave him out of it. Look, between us?'

'Of course . . .'

'He'd be too proud to say anything to you boys but – in this restructuring thing at the bank – he's had to take a 25 per cent cut . . .'

'I saw a piece in the *FT*. I asked Simon on the train but he said it didn't affect him . . .'

'Yeah. Why do men need to lie all the time?'

'I don't think we do, do we? Christ, 25 – that's some haircut, more a cut-throat shave. So you need to keep all this behind his back?'

Still enclosed in the bedclothes, stretching, she reaches the pack of tissues on the bedside table and blows her nose with therapeutic deepness.

'I need a loan, Max.'

'It's not a good idea.'

'I'll tell Jenno about Marrakesh.'

His face takes on a look of steely calculation, the businessman again. 'You got drunk and, er, tried your wiles with me but I said no. My wife will believe me. But, if Simon believes you, it doesn't really help you . . .'

'If I can't pay this bill, I'll have to get divorced anyway.'

She dabs her eyes and nose with an already-sodden hankie. Max is still, blank-faced.

'A loan is the wrong solution,' he says. 'But we may be able to find a compromise.'

Her relief is brief before the terrible realization that he intends to offer her money for sex.

*

On any given day, it's close between them: most sets are won to 4, with several turning on the tie-break that kicks in at 6–6. But, this morning, Tom takes the first set to love and only some over-confident shots in the second – the size of the lead encouraging him to try for baseline-smudging lobs and backhand volleys rather than the cautious keep-in-court pushes of hobby tennis – allows Simon to claim one game and avoid what they call on the Wimbledon radio commentary a pair of spectacles.

Now, though, Simon serves, a first with no more strength than a girly second, a good foot in but bouncing low. Tom hits a whippy pick-up, cross-court, which Simon just meets with a scuffy back-hand, looping up invitingly for a smashed forehand into empty court.

'Game, set and match to Mr Rutherford,' Tom says. '6–love, 6–1.'

He keeps the score in an approximation of the Edwardian drawl of Dan Maskell, the commentator on the first tennis he watched as a kid, although he's probably the only one to get the joke these days.

They play best of three and have always needed it, so there's an awkward moment now, like the time when the Australians and West Indies were winning test matches in less than three days and England would come under pressure to play a quickly scheduled one-dayer to make up the beer receipts.

'What do you want to do, Simon?' They meet at the net. 'Another set? Or just a tie-break?'

'Know what, mate? I might just leave it. I'm not really feeling it today.'

'Are you carrying a knock?'

A slight Cockney inflection; it's a shtick between them to speak in sports-page phrases.

'Playing through the pain barrier?' Simon responds in kind. 'No, I give it 110 per cent but I just had no answers for my opponent in this kind of form. But I have to look to take the positives from this and kick on.'

Non-ironically, they shake hands on today's pasting.

'Come on,' says Tom. 'Let's go and scarf some bacon sarnies.'

Because of the direction of the wind, they can hear the guns at Northbury Farm. Tom suggested they went shooting this morning, but Simon pulled a face and said last time was enough.

As they walk back to the house, Tom loosens and ripples his legs and arms, surreptitiously, so he won't be noticed, in the warm-down exercises Em showed him. As soon as he stopped moving, he felt his hamstrings and lower-back protesting at the confusion of temperatures: the sweat on the skin under his tracksuit (their winter tennis gear) meeting the biting air. At fifty-four, with tennis and sex (which, in fact, they managed rather nicely the night before Em left for Gloucester), every success is haunted by the thought of when the body will rebel.

The kitchens in almost all the houses he visits for security reviews have a powerful sense of female domain, the heart of a home, and he always feels an intruder in his own, grabbling and rattling for pans in cupboards too low for him. Agas also alarm him, not merely as a cliché of his class, but because the four different ovens of modulated hotness bear no obvious relation to the cooking times on the ready-meals he relies on when his wife is away or doing nights.

He arranges six rashers on a silver tray and, though the concept of baking bacon still seems alien to him, puts them in the top right quadrant, then takes two rolls from the bread-bin and places them in the upper left to warm. He fills the water tank of the CappucinGo machine, switches it on and asks Simon: 'What's your favourite colour? We've got all the usuals plus a Brazilian Capoeira that's Flavour of the Month – literally . . .'

'Oh, I . . . think I generally have the green? Is that the Carretta?'

Tom opens the lid of the compartmentalized wooden box, removes three capsules – lime, asparagus and emerald – and holds them out on his hand, like a jeweller.

'We have three greens: Moresca, Fuoco, Moneghina . . .'

Simon peers and points to the darkest: 'It's that one, I think.'

'Moresca? Mmm, the aftertaste's a bit treacly for me. I'm going to have a Capoeira. Do try a sip, if you want. The Specials tend to be at least interesting . . .'

Although Tom has never believed that the old trick of baking bread when showing prospective buyers around a house can actually work – at least not since it became a top-ten factoid – kitchen smells are undeniably seductive. Sizzling bacon, warming dough and roasted coffee collect as a scent that could be bottled and sold as Home.

He checks his BlackBerry, neatly lined up on the work surface beside the car keys pot. The red alert light is flashing. A text:

Surviving. Even boysier than last year. T and I keep being fined by M for breaking tour rules. No medical skills necessary yet though M has hangover from hell this am. See you 4-ish. lol. E xxxxx

Archaeologists of the future will surely be astonished at the existence of this strange sect that spelled and punctuated texts, while also being made to 'laugh out loud' by things that weren't obviously amusing.

'Emily,' Tom glosses for Simon. 'Max is being very Max apparently . . .'

'Yeah. It was the Dead Ants thing that finished me last year . . .'

'Are they still doing that?'

'Yeah. You have to decide whether to wreck your bank balance or your back.'

'I remember. Thank God I married a doctor, which gets me out of it. Have you heard from Tash?'

'We're not big texters, really. Polly said she Facebooked Henry and there was some stuff about how pissed the grown-ups were getting in the bar.'

'Ha! Em says Max is pretty wasted . . .'

Tom replaces the handset beside the neatly folded *Observer* he collected from the mailbox after letting out the dogs. They look down at the headlines. More Transport Chaos and Cancellations. Censors Defend Rape Film Certificate.

Tom flips over the paper to show the bottom of the front page. Government Targets Welfare Cheats.

'Not before fucking time,' says Simon, as Tom passes him his coffee and drops into the machine the shiny silver capsule for his own drink.

'Said a spokesman for a bailed-out bank,' Tom replies, smiling to lessen the potential offence.

'Well, yeah. But that's the point, isn't it? We need to sort out the state-subsidized scum at both ends and leave more room for us poor hard-working buggers in the middle.'

Checking the top oven, Tom finds the bacon curled and crisping on the tray, takes it out and rests it on top of the cooker. He suddenly sees himself as a contestant in Masterchef. Opening the other oven, he tests the temperature of the rolls with his hand and, satisfied, scoops them out, tears them open and layers the sizzling strips inside. On the tray, each piece of meat leaves an outline of its shape, like the lines showing where the victims lay at a murder scene.

'Sauces and so on against the wall,' he tells Simon, placing the aromatic bap on a plate and handing it over.

'Actually,' he resumes the interrupted discussion. 'I think we should all be grateful to the welfare state . . .'

'Seriously, Tom?' – muffled by a munch of brunch – 'Families where no one's had a job since 1926? Council employees on long-term sickies with supposed bad backs who are running removal companies for cash on the black . . .'

Tom delays by savouring the guilty Sunday morning treat, probably knocking out the calorific benefit of the tennis. It is a difficult calculation how far to disagree with friends. Among their group, there are a number of subjects now avoided by common consent because of scars from dinner parties: capital punishment (Max and Jonny fiercely pro, Emily and Tom anguishedly anti), God (Tash thought to be a bit of a left-footer still), Palestine (they are never quite sure if Simon is Jewish or not), teenage sex (since Rosie Dunster and Josh Lonsdale in the graveyard) and Tony Blair (Emily now his only defender). Which leaves them to talk about taxation, education, television and scroungers, on which they pretty much agree. Except . . .

'The thing is, Si, the more I check out the houses of these people who are terrified someone's going to come and rob or rape them for being rich, the more I see the welfare state as a sort of Peace Tax . . .'

'Come on!'

'Seriously. A lot of the people who live on hand-outs – take the cash away and they'll come looking to make up the short-fall. Have you ever heard Jenno on some of the people she gets at Citizens Advice?'

'Well, Jenno, yes. There's that guy she's convinced will come after her.'

'And imagine if he didn't get his benefits. A war on spongers would be good for my business. But you'll – *we'll* – end up spending everything we save on welfare, trying to make our-selves feel safe.'

'No, no. I . . . is there a . . . a . . . ?'

Tom correctly guesses the missing word as napkin and passes Simon one to wipe away the floury goatee the roll has given him.

'Ta. So you're admitting, Tom, the work-shy are potential murderers?'

'Well, hang on. Work-shy is your term. And, obviously I'm not saying that. My point is that we can't just pretend that other people are nothing to do with us . . . Do you want another coffee . . . ?'

'No. Okay, yeah I will . . .'

'Another Moresca or why not try a Capoeira? . . .'

'Whatever this one was, I'll stick with . . .'

As Tom scans the tray for another emerald pellet – they are low on several colours, he'll need to get online and put an order in – Simon says: 'Anyway, you're bound to be soft on spongers. Emily's got one of those massive public-sector pensions we keep reading about . . .'

If his wife were here, there would be a warning glare or an old-fashioned kick under the table; the diplomacy gene given to women in general and Emily especially. But she is away and, thinking that he is being sympathetic to his friend (he has been worried about Simon for some time), Tom says: 'Yeah, I know. Guilty as charged on that one. She actually got a letter from the NHS a couple of months back, saying that her fund had reached the maximum limit and there was no point paying in any more . . .'

That awful sensation of telling someone what a crashing bore Colonel Duggett is and realizing, halfway through the story, that the someone you are talking to is Colonel Duggett. There is a savage accusation in Simon's look that Tom has never seen before, although Em says Tasha sometimes talks about his moods.

'I know, I know,' Tom says, softening his voice as he would with one of the kids in a strop. 'That was my reaction too. We private-sector workers, who'll have to warm ourselves on the ashes of the stock market. All I'd say is that Em's a bloody good doctor . . .'

Simon's hand goes to the pocket of his tracksuit, as if for a weapon, but comes out jangling car keys.

'Oh,' Tom says. 'I'm just about to do your second Moresca . . .'

'You know what, mate? I'd better be getting back. I'm under the cosh from Tash to get Polly out of her pit and doing some revision . . .'

'I've got to take the dogs out later if you want to tag-team . . .'

'Nah. That's a Polly job as well. And I'll be hunched over a keyboard all afternoon.'

'Look, don't tell Em I told you about . . . she'd be embarrassed . . .'

'Yeah? Don't worry. What happens not on tour stays not on tour.'

There are men who felt like blood brothers in the army,

with whom Tom doesn't even exchange Christmas cards now. We shed friends painlessly, like snakes' skins, through moving houses, changing jobs, the great division between the parents and the childless. But not since school, with its spiteful shuffling of cliques, has he had so strong a sense of being present when a friendship cools.

'Okay,' Tom says. 'I expect the girls will arrange something for next weekend. Or give me a bell about tennis.'

'Yeah. Whatever.'

To the list of subjects not to be risked socially, Tom adds, alongside God and politics, pensions.

*

Quite shockingly in need of a shot of vitamin C before the lucrative but monotonous labour of a con on Dept of Transport v Middlesex District Council, Jonny detours to the fruit stall on the Euston Road.

He got some money at the Euston cash-point, where the withdrawal options screen offers buttons up to £500. The one at Middlebury petrol station stops at £60. Even machines are judging how much cash they think we have.

He hasn't felt this ghastly since the fourth and final morning of the bender in Biarritz for Dunster's fiftieth, and Gloucester brings fewer compensating memories. He only managed four hours sleep on the Saturday night and woke with a mouth like a whore's hole, from the blackcurrant antifreeze that passed for Merlot at the Bates Motel, before Lucas was banging on the door to go to breakfast. There were others in worse nick – Toby Wallace's dad was seen throwing up into a bush before refereeing the first game of the Under-8s triangular – but they must all have been over the driving limit and he was glad Dunster had grabbed the chauffeur's cap for this trip. And even Max VI must have been worried about getting bagged and pointed, because he was unusually quiet on the run home. He still looked a bit off his tucker on the Pendolino this morning; he's going up to London a lot more these days, possibly got a lady tucked away

263

there, although Jenno looks as if she'd have the moves to keep him on the ranch. Mrs Lonsdale and Dr Rutherford, of course, were smugly Sancerre-wouldn't-melt, having turned in early. Last night at home, Libby was up for a comeback shag, which was just what BUPA ordered, but then Jonny couldn't get to sleep again and is convinced he heard the church bells at every hour.

The womanly whiff of plump, ripe figs cuts through the petrol stench.

'Four figs, please,' he asks Geezer 2, the words suddenly sounding unlikely, like an EFL test-sentence. Geezer 2 flaps a brown paper bag at him and asks a question that requires native knowledge: 'Do you want to, or . . . ?'

'Oh, I'm sure you know more about fruit than I do.'

Jonny believes in professional expertise – it hasn't been the same since solicitors got pleading rights – but internally winces at his posh platitude. He sounds to himself like Princess Margaret visiting a market town.

Geezer 2, who may suspect a test of his probity, deliberates hugely before dropping the four biggest and least blemished figs into the bag, deftly tying its corners into a Bridlington sun-hat.

'Anything else with that?'

Shopping here is inevitably influenced by fragrances that beat the fumes, and the scent of nectarines prompts him to take four of those as well. Jonny hands over the two coins with his ungloved hand and receives the standard 'Thank you, young man', an ancient sales trick that strangely never fails to flatter and amuse the customer.

He is resting his briefcase on the stall's wooden edge, shuffling space for the bags among the case papers, when his iPhone rings. With the wrong glasses on, he has to move the screen close to his face to see the icon: PHome. A call from this number, at unexpected times, is one of his burrowing fears: *Pa's had a bit of a turn . . . The doctor says they want to do some . . .*

'Hello?'

'Jonathan?'

The name he is now called by only one woman and one man; on this occasion, the latter.

'Pa? Is everything all right?'

'*Comme ci, comme ça*, frankly, you know, old boy. Is this a good time?'

'Depends what for, I suppose.' Jonny's laugh – guffaw, Libby calls it –another inheritance from his father, unusually finds no echo at the other end of the phone.

'Jonathan, I just wanted to give you the heads up on something before it's in the public prints . . .'

Jonny has moved against the wall, away from the whipped-up wind and the unbroken column of early morning workers heading from or to Euston and Euston Square stations.

'What is it, Pa, you jammy bugger? A portfolio in the Lord's? You said Cameron had been talking about it . . .'

'No. No. That was just paper talk, Jonathan. Look, son, there's been a bit of a bish over my expenses . . .'

The word falls as heavily on the conversation as the *cancer* he had half-anticipated.

'Christ, Pa, a brief I know has been instructed for one of the first ones they charged and he says he'd have a better chance of getting babysitting work for Ian Brady. What have you done?'

'Ah, well, in my defence, Jonathan, these are predominantly sins of omission rather than commission. A certain blurring of purpose on some overseas trips, some gaps in the filing cabinet when it comes to receipts and cash advances. It's possible that Marjorie may have been distracted, during the quarters in question, by her mother's illness.'

'Have you been charged, Pa?'

'No, no, no. That's some time hence, if at all. I am submitting to questioning at a police station, *voluntarily*, at a time and place of my own convenience . . .'

Communal wisdom and the anecdotes of friends have prepared him for this destabilizing switch in the balance of power between parents and children, the reversal in the person calling for help, although the stories have always involved illness. In this case, the question Jonny asks exactly echoes the one that came in the other direction when he was arrested for possession at uni.

'Are you being interviewed under caution?'

'I think that's the procedure, isn't it, Jonathan? However, Wilkinson . . .'

'Huh! Wilkinson couldn't have got Mother Theresa off a parking ticket! Do you want me to get you someone who can get his wig on without assistance?'

'You always say this. I have always found Wilky perfectly efficient. He, anyway, has warned that there is a public mood for making an example of those in *parliament*.' The word stretched out over four syllables, a generational relic of speech. 'At best, it's going to be heads down and tin hats on for a bit!'

'But, Pa, why did you do it . . . ?'

'Steady on, Jonathan. Not a question one expects from either a barrister or a son . . .'

'I mean it. You're a non-exec of every company that's still got a stiffie for the Thatcher years . . .' He's conscious of passing pedestrians turning in the direction of the raised voice, mobiles making every call a party line, so shrinks towards the wall. 'There are people all over Europe who'll still pay money to hear you saying how much better the country was when you lot were running it. So why did you need to put your hand in the cash tin?'

'Ah. Well, as I say, the discrepancies most likely lie in the ledgered record, for whatever reason, rather than the transactions themselves. And it's important to remember that *most* of the cases have been Labour . . .'

'Fucking hell, Pa . . .' Even as a teenager, he never had the balls to swear at his father, but does not apologize. 'Do they install some kind of button when they choose you: if in doubt, blame the other lot . . .'

'No. Well, yes, one obviously had to look into the old soul to a certain extent during this. All I can say is that one may have become a little, ah, fiscally insecure after the split with your mother. Don't get me wrong; she deserved every penny of her settlement, but one comes out of it feeling a little light. It's a relief to me that you and Elizabeth seem so solid . . .'

'Yes, well, I think we might skip the marriage guidance, Pa.' The sarcasm card now also passed from father to son. 'Let me know what happens or if you want to be put in touch with a proper lawyer. Now, I've got a case conference . . .'

'God bless,' Pa ends the conversation, as ever. The shock of what Jonny has just been told – the thought of the renewed headline presence of a surname he was claiming as his own, the cosmetic sympathy in the robing room, the jokes from Dunster and Lonsdale – combines with the weekend's toxic residue.

He feels cold beyond the effect of the January temperatures, but feverish as well. His heart is as fast as a teenage boy's obsoning hand. He is desperate for a Smedgewick. On the far side of the road, he can see the gleaming frontage of the new hospital, the smokers huddled outside even in this weather. For a moment, he thinks of presenting himself at A & E, exaggerating the symptoms, maybe adding chest pains.

But being let down by his father is no excuse for letting down himself. As is his habit in moments of weakness, Jonny scolds himself silently, as if his resolve were a stubborn dog: *Come on, Crossan, don't feel sorry for yourself, get on with it.*

Fumbling off his gloves, he clicks open the briefcase, clumsily extracts a fig from the bag and takes a bite, imagining the bitter-sweet juice swirling recuperatively through his blood, like insulin, although he isn't a diabetic. Although, Christ!, perhaps diabetes is what he's got.

He crosses the road, clogged with the impatient traffic of a new year's London business, but walks, without hesitation, past the hospital and to work.

*

The really smart marketing move, it strikes him, would be to put a special chemical in the pellets so that CappuccinGo customers piss a different colour. Even the most exclusive of the coffees – a Carinosa Deluxe, supposedly available in a run of only 1,000 capsules, first come, first served – goes down the drains looking no different from instant. But add a simple marker substance to the brew and the clientele would be able to prove their exclusivity at the urinals. Because, let's face it, this is more about what people think than what people drink.

Jason pulls into a lay-by outside Aylesbury to reset the satnav. Months ago, he used the Via facility to programme a loop between the four houses on the hills in Middlebury but, unusually, he is delivering to only one of the addresses today and so needs a simpler route.

He still struggles to distinguish between the houses, wives and dogs. But, as he turns on to the rising gravel drive, Jason thinks he recognizes this delivery as the hot one with the strange French name – *Jenaux,* or something, is the way she says it – and, as he pulls into the courtyard at the top, she is waiting at the main door. She might have seen him on the CCTV pictures – there's a swivel camera on every outside wall – or, more likely been tipped off by the mutts, who are going mental at the window.

Jason waves to her as, from the back of the van, he takes the package, swathed in tape printed with the words EMERGENCY DELIVERY, as if a surgeon waits with gloved hands.

'Good morning,' she shouts as he approaches, then, behind her, 'stop it, you stupid, stupid dogs!' She closes the door behind her and stands on the front step. 'Sorry about them. They're hopeless with strangers, although you don't really count as that . . .' – a not-discreet-enough glance at his name badge – '. . . *Jason.*'

'Don't worry,' he smiles. 'Dogs have boring lives.'

If this was a porn film, she'd reply 'not just dogs', but it isn't and she doesn't. Jenaux – brown shoulder-length hair, teeth flashing like a laser pen – is hugging herself against the cold, although she's wearing a fluffy black sweater with jeans that emphasize a tempting v from which he tries to keep his eyes. For all the gossip at the depot about couriers fucking customers, the company is so tight on delivery times that it would have to be a cum-and-run and, anyway, even Jenaux must be early thirties. It's those luscious Aussie nannies you get at these houses – sometimes, he sees one struggling past with a basket of washing – who he'd do if he got the chance.

Jason recites from the printed label: 'Emergency Overnight – 200 Carinosa Deluxe . . .'

'Oh, gosh! We got them!'

'Sixty Allegrezza, sixty Nizzarda and twenty Amoroso De-caffeinato.'

'That's great,' says Jenaux. He offers her the receipt screen and the wand for her squiggle. Handing it back, she says: 'I guess we must be your best customers round here?'

Jason isn't sure what to say. He has no reason to believe that coffee deliveries are, like medical records, subject to strict confidentiality. But clients must be entitled to some discretion.

'Go on, Jason,' she says, 'you can tell me. There are no secrets between us round here.'

Jason flicks his head towards the hill to their left. 'They probably order the most, I suppose.'

Her eyes follow his. 'The Crossans? Really? That surprises me. If I remember correctly, we were in the club long before Libby.'

'You *are* my only delivery here today,' Jason says, which seems to please her. There's a knock on the door from the inside, which he's trying to work out how the dogs have done, when it swings open. There's a bloke standing there – stocky, wind-burned face, short grey hair – who says: 'Oh, there you are, Jenaux. I've shut the dogs in the kitchen . . .'

'Just talking to Jason.'

Induction Course, day one: *our coffee is only as good as our relationship with our customers.* 'Oh, hello, are you Mr . . . ?' Jason begins, but can't remember the surname on the manifest.

'No, this isn't my husband,' Jenaux says. 'Oh, I realize that sounds . . . this is Tom Rutherford. He's doing a review of the house for us . . .'

A review? Does she mean, like, writing it up online? Best

Fuck-Off Houses in Bucks? This Tom offers a hand to be shaken and says: 'We're customers of yours, actually. Over there. Matter of fact, got a bit of a bone with your people. Email this morning to say we hadn't got any of the Limited Edition. Bid the minute I saw it, so must have gone like manure off a shovel . . .'

Jenaux does a little dance on the doorstep, clenched fists in the air.

'Oh, you buggers! You didn't!' the Tom one blurts.

'Don't worry! We'll do you a cup next time you come to dinner . . .'

Jason feels he should be shooting this scene as a commercial.

'Actually, Tom, we were trying to get everyone together on Friday but the Lonsdales have cried off again.' A little-girl voice. 'I don't think they like us any more.'

'M said Tash was a bit down on the rugger trip.'

They suddenly remember the tradesman is there.

'Thanks for this, Jason,' says Jenaux. 'I imagine we'll be seeing you in another couple of weeks.'

How much coffee do these people drink? They must spend most of the day buzzed and in the pisser.

Another 4x4 draws up and the little blonde Aussie gets out. Oh, Jesus, *sweet*. Jason throws his best thong-popping smile but only gets a flicker back. The passenger door opens slowly and a teenage girl with a cute – no, don't be a paedo – hauls herself out with the long face and cautious walk of the school-kid who's swung a sickie.

Jenaux's little voice again: 'Oh, Rosie-Posie, are you going down with something? Let's get you under the duvet with a hottie.'

Jason tries to get another look at the hottie he'd like to be under a duvet with, but only gets a glimpse of the au pair through the kitchen window, laughing and smiling as she's monstered by the dogs.

*

Carefully, looking at his fingers on the keys, like when he decided at fourteen to become a journalist and taught himself to type overnight on his mum's old Smith Corona, Simon types in R-A-F-N-S-T-E-I-N-S-S-O-N. Unless he's unlucky enough to be hacked by another Bolton nutter, no one would guess his latest password (or his iPad passcode, now derived from a little-known cup defeat) and certainly not Natasha, who he is convinced is the cyber-criminal. The only other suspects – the kids – lack Tasha's obvious motive of pure hatred. At least she's seemed a bit more cheerful recently, so she can't have found anything very hardcore.

The Scandinavian full-back's name grants access to the files. Sipping from a mug of coffee from the dark-green slug, Simon scans the emails first. Between the spam offering him the Nigerian lottery jackpot or a bigger cock, there are two globals from SB's HR department headed PAY REGRADING and PENSION CHANGES. Other communications this morning are a forwarded YouTube clip from Jonny Crossan (probably, on past form, animals fucking or children swearing), a message from *mandjdunster* (trust Max and Jenno to have a joint address, emailing's simultaneous orgasm) headed DINNER?, several from Tom Rutherford with variations of *Hi?* and *Hope You Okay?* and one from Dr Emily Rutherford, or strictly Westbury Medical Centre, advising him that, as an asthmatic, he qualifies for a free flu jab, which it is still not too late to take up this winter.

He ignores them all, wondering how many people are stupid enough to go after the African cash or a longer shlong.

Collected VAT Returns 1993– teases in the corner of the screen, promising a brief release. Tash has taken Josh and Henry to buy new rugby boots (a naturally masculine duty she took over when Josh, at nine, was cripplingly blistered by his father's purchase) and Polly has just left for what will be at least an hour's riding.

Simon double clicks on the dull phrase, then cruises the cursor over folders. Increasingly, he thinks of these documents as a monster in the cellar of the house, swelling between the neat lines of wine-racks and the child bikes saved for charity or grandchildren. Occasionally, he unbolts the lock and, through half-closed eyes, sneaks a look at how the creature has increased in bulk and fierceness.

*

Often feeling like an imposter among the others, Tom worries about being caught out and fears that the mechanism of his exposure will be opera or wine. In neither case is he sure of what he should be appreciating.

To his palate, the French white that Max served with the starter – pancetta and chestnut salad, attributed by Jenno to Nigella – tasted rather acidic, although that could have been the lettuce, which had a bitter tang. The leaves, their hostess said, were from a variety that sounded like *escarole*.

Even Tom, though, can tell that the red is something special. Max sees him lifting the label close to his face, trying to read it without glasses.

'Pomerol, 2006,' their host glosses the bottle. 'Seventy-five per cent Merlot, twenty-five per cent Cabernet. With something like wild duck, you need a bit of welly. The theory is that the berry notes complement the blackberry sauce in chummy's . . .'

'Raymond Blanc's,' Jenno fills in.

'That's the chap. His recipe.'

'And this is celeriac puree, Jen?' checks Libby.

'That's right.'

'Delicious.'

During the first two courses, they discuss the older children's college applications and then the men's various plans for nabbing Olympic tickets, despite the irritating democracy of the application process. But just as, ten years ago, their conversations, however based, always seemed to reach property prices, now they head unstoppably towards pensions. And, calamitously, Jenno's placement has Emily next to Simon at one end of the Dunsters' great, Henry VIII-ish wooden dining table.

'It's all right for you,' says Simon. 'You're laughing.'

'I don't think I am, am I?' asks Emily, with her most severe expression, which makes everyone else laugh, although, poor thing, she doesn't understand why. Tom loyally tries not to join in.

'Yeah,' Simon boozily continues. 'All the way to the . . .'

It is impossible for Tom to subtract from his personality the fact of having been a soldier, so he cannot be certain that his fast, sharp sense of a bomb that is about to go off is a consequence of his former job. But, as he interrupts Simon – 'I got an email from Edgbaston about the test tickets. Should we be planning one of our Saturday specials?' – he has a fleeting feeling of stopping a convoy in the Borderlands because of a gut twinge that the lane to the right is even quieter than it should be.

'Bugger is, we're spoiled by MCC,' Max Dunster says. 'Edgbasters would be seats, not a box, wouldn't it? My legs, no thank you.'

Tom thinks that he has achieved the diversion, but Simon, after a fuelling slosh of Pomerol, resumes: 'Odd, isn't it? We think of the retired doctor as someone living quietly in a cottage, still getting eggs and jam from mothers whose children they miraculously delivered. Possibly doing a spot of locum work if their successor has accidentally killed someone.' Unfortunately, Simon is one of those people who are made aggressive but not incomprehensible by drink. 'We never really thought about the dear old doc on a yacht in the south of France, cheerfully trying not to come up with a cure for elephantiasis of the pension!'

'Leave Em alone. She's a . . .' Tasha has some trouble revealing exactly what her friend is, but eventually settles for *saint,* although in a pronunciation heavy with 'h' sounds.

'What would I know as a yid?' Simon carries on. 'But is it common for saints to call it a day on a screw not far short of what Sir Adrian Fucking-Jones is getting?'

'I think that's a lidd—' Emily begins.

'It's pronounced with a "t",' her accuser corrects.

Libby gives her train-brake sigh. 'What on earth are you on about now, Simon Lonsdale?'

'She said *liddle*,' Simon persists. 'All of you girls do. Which is a supermarket, not an adjective.'

'I don't think I did, did I?' asks Emily.

'I don't,' say Libby and Jenno together, while Tasha, who has been threatening the global supply of grapes all evening, swings her husband a look like a baseball bat and enunciates carefully: 'It's a word that seems to hurt him for some reason.'

'Anyway,' Emily picks up the conversation. 'My pension is fairly little.'

Hitting the *t*s so hard, she sprays spit, which nearly reaches Simon, who says: 'No, it isn't. It's so big you've had to stop putting in.'

'Now where have I heard that said to me recently?' clowns Jonny, but there is no time for anyone to groan before Simon fires the double tap: 'Emily, Tom *told* me.'

The look from his wife he always most fears, as he once did from his mother. 'I'm sure he didn't. ' But his face betrays him. 'Oh. Oh, dear.'

'Awks!, as Rosie always says,' laughs Jenno.

Resolving to drink no more, Tom is composing his apology for the drive home, but Emily, who he expected to fall silent and reflective, looks around the table and begins a speech that gives him a sense of her lectures at those medical conferences she goes to: 'Well, okay. Suppose it's *true*. Suppose I *have* put away as much as I can afford every month since I qualified? We have eight thousand patients in our practice. I provide night cover two nights a week. If I make a mistake, it's not about losing money, it's about losing lives. And the government isn't going to come along and say: *don't worry about the one you lost, here's another life to bale you out.* Why would it be so shocking that I get a better pension than a banker . . .'

'A: I'm not a banker, B: I've had mine cut by 25 per cent,' Simon comes back.

They brace themselves for what they know Jonny is contractually obliged to say: 'I hope you're talking about your pension, old boy!'

'Or whatever it is the rest of you do,' Emily goes on.

'Now steady on, old girl,' Max chides her, but Emily – and not because of drink, being as ever the designated driver – is on the sort of roll Tom has never known from her at an Eight night.

'Whatever you say about Tony Blair . . .' she relaunches herself, sounding like a politician beginning a new section of a conference speech.

Max and Jonny form their fingers into crosses and become a pair of vampire hunters.

'I don't think the worst thing he did,' Emily finishes, 'was finally paying doctors properly for what they do.'

'And maybe, in return, you should have offered to go and treat the wounded in all those countries he invaded,' snaps Libby.

'Don't mention the wars!' pleads Jenno, in a voice that is jokily singsong but alludes to a previous dinner when Tom was isolated, no almost ostracized, as the only supporter of Blair's foreign adventures at the table; sometimes, it now seems, the only one in Britain apart, presumably, from the former prime minister himself. So he can see the dangers of what he is about to say, but feels a duty to provide covering fire for Emily, not just from marital loyalty but guilt over having been exposed as a snitch.

Tom manages to cut in: 'As I may have said before—'

'We've told you, Tom,' Simon interrupts. Widening his mouth to lift his voice over the others, he shows a tongue stained almost black by the heavy wine. 'Leave Cherie to suck it for him.'

'Ew! Don't be such a schoolboy!' Tasha scolds her husband.

Tom has to shout so loudly to be heard that he feels a catch of soreness in his throat: 'The point is that the wars he fought saved us from much worse ones. Better that America went into Afghanistan and Iraq as part of a coalition . . .'

'Oh yeah, they're always such a good idea,' Simon sneers.

'Yes, as part of a coalition with constraints . . . better that, than America bombing – *nuking*, even, which is what the neocons clearly wanted – Kabul, Baghdad or Tehran. After 9/11, America was always going to demand a bloodletting of some kind. And Blair kept it within reasonable bounds . . .'

'Letting the blood of *liddle*' – Jenno clearly does say *liddle*, leading Simon to cheer and punch the air – 'Iraqi and Afghanistani children just like ours . . .'

'Well, not terrifically like ours,' Max heckles, wrapping a napkin round his head and adopting a cod Arab accent to say: 'It's camel club after school, Leila, and remember Mohammed's staying for Debate: This House Maintains that Having Two Hands is Over-Rated . . .'

'Don't be such an idiot, Max,' Tasha tells him.

'I say!' Max blinks.

'At least my husband's got a sense of humour,' Jenno joins in and then the women make noises at each other that you would have to be the most perfect liberal feminist not to compare to cats.

'Bitch fight!' squeals Jonny.

This is the worst it has been among The Eight since the Movie Character theme party, all those Christmases ago, when Max and Jonny came as officers from Colditz.

'Come on, people!' Libby pleads. 'We're better than this.'

She claps her hands until the hubbub is subdued.

'I'm sorry,' Jenno says. 'I've had a tough week at the Bureau. But I shouldn't have taken it out on you, Tasha.'

'Oh, poor you,' asks Emily, inevitably. 'What happened?'

'The two I think I've told you about? Mandy and Danny . . .'

'Maybe you shouldn't use their real names, Jen?' Em, just as typically, worries. Jonny's response is equally characteristic: 'Probably *aren't* their real names, if they're claiming welfare. Mr and Mrs Michael Mouse.'

Jenno's face twitches with the impatience of someone who has launched a story and been stalled: 'She's kicked him out, for reasons unspecified but probably not hard to guess: violent and unfaithful, I expect. But, of course, he hasn't taken his lot of kids with him. Which leaves her as a single mother of six, nearly seven. We were trying to come up with a revised weekly budget without his benefits when he came into the branch, shouting the odds. Fucking this and, uh, cunting that . . .'

'Oh, I love it when you talk dirty, Jen . . .'

'In a gentle and loving way, shut up, Jonny! He blames me for turning Mandy against him. Looked like he was planning to hit one or both of us . . .'

'Oh my God, he didn't . . . ?' asks Libby.

'No. The supervisor got the police in straight away. But . . .'

'I don't know how you stick it,' says Libby. 'At least my lot I can lock up . . .'

'No. You know what? Actually, I feel – and don't harrumph, Jonny – a sort of bond with her. If I have a, without sounding pretentious, theory of life, it's that sport is what men have in common, motherhood is what women have. It's a bond, what-ever the . . . *differences*. I look at a Mandy and I see a woman trying to do the best for her children, actually some of them not even hers . . .'

'But what about this . . . *Danny*?' asks Libby. 'He's in custody, I hope, is he . . . ?'

'Ha! Can't even slap their wrists these days because of elf and pastry,' says Tasha, with a spray of red droplets from Pomerol she hasn't swallowed.

'A caution,' Jenno continues, bringing a slushy shout of 'Told you!' from Tasha.

'And a warning not to approach you or his, er, partner, I hope?' frets Emily.

'Oh my God!' Jenno's hands, in their gesture of emphasis, narrowly miss the paper-thin Grand Cru wine glasses. 'What if he comes after you here?'

'Let him damn well try,' booms Max. 'We've had a review. Captain Rutherford has done us up like an Israeli embassy . . .'

'Well, I, er, hope so,' Tom says, realizing that he has spoken even less during this evening than most. He fears Emily thinks of him as boring; that perhaps they all do.

'I hate to say this,' Max carries on. 'But friend Danny would be a perfect candidate for the disciplinary system I occasionally . . .'

'Oh, God, not fucking boot camps,' Simon interrupts him. Tom also tries to think of something to say that might divert Dunster from another lecture on his vision of shipping the workshy and socially disruptive to the wastes of South Africa for three months of brush-clearing, loo-cleaning and forced-marching in the purgatorial sun. But it is Jonny Crossan who stages the distraction.

'What Mrs Dunster's experience demonstrates is the risk of mixing with a certain stratum of society . . .' Jonny taps a soft-leather slipper on a cross-strut of the dining table. 'One, two, three . . .'

Whooping with laughter, Max understands the cue and they duet:

'*I want to live like common people,*
'*I want to do whatever common people do . . .*'

The seating plan has put Tasha between Jonny and Max, so that her eyes are at risk from the pointing and punching gestures with which the two of them, especially when as lubricated as this, enliven their recital.

'*I took her to a supermarket . . .*'

Bouncing forward, Max delivers this line almost into Tasha's face, and she is almost kebabed when the singers spear pointing figures at each other on:

'*I said pretend you've got no money . . .*'

Tom is torn between the uncomfortable boorishness of the evening and the pleasure of hearing, even in such a rough rendition, a song he would take to the desert island without hesitation.

'*I want to sleep with common people,*
'*I want to sleep with common people*
'*Like you . . .*'

At this line, Tasha, looking near tears, starts to stand and is grabbed by the two crooners, whom she tries to slap away.

'Boys, leave her alone for God's sake!'

The voice is so strong and forceful that Tom turns first to Libby on his right, until he realizes that it has come from Emily on the other side of the table.

'*You'll never fail like common peop—*'

The cacophony stops as suddenly as a paused CD.

'I'm going,' says Tasha.

'You'll miss some really rather special cheeses,' pleads Jenno.

'Do you think you should be driving?' asks Simon.

'And *you* think *you* should?' Tasha snaps back.

'I can drop you both back?' offers sober, sensible Emily. 'Leave yours here and pick it up in the morning.' She glances at the grandfather clock in the corner. 'Later *this* morning.'

'Oh, you really are Saint Em,' says Jenno. 'After the way that Simon went for you over the . . .'

'Don't mention the pension!' Surprised by the rhyme, Jonny beats the rhythm on the table with a dessert spoon. 'Hey, Dunster, maybe we should switch to . . . I believe it's called rap . . . *hey, because of my station, I deserve my superannuation . . .*'

Emily stands, car keys already in hand, clicking out the silver prong like a tiny sword.

'Come on, Thomas,' she says, the long form of his name ominous. He dreads the conversation in the car after they have dropped the Lonsdales. Perhaps even more frightening is the thought of what she might say to Tasha and Simon on the drive to the next hill.

Max knocks one of the empty wine bottles on the table. 'Chaps, chaps! It's all gone a little bit . . .'

'*Blair*-shaped,' Jonny finishes the sentence for him. 'No offence to his keen supporters among us.'

'Knock it off, Crossan.' Jonny, as usual, does what Max tells him. 'Is there any possibility we could sit down and start again, like the civilized people we are? Jenno has got some excellent . . .'

'Lincet Brillat-Savarin,' she prompts.

'Thank you, sweetie. Easy for you to say that . . .'

'I think it's better if we leave it for tonight,' Emily says.

The goodbye kisses are stiff and flinching. What always had the potential to happen within The Eight, Tom thinks, has happened.

NINE

A FRIENDLY KILLER

She has an odd thought about the house carrying on, like a riderless horse, without its occupants; light, warmth and water still being paid for until someone freezes the accounts. Most of the dead – she knows from executing her dad's estate – are granted a short financial afterlife, money still coming in and going out, until the paperwork catches up with their status. Murder squads dissuade relatives from cancelling credit cards immediately because the pattern of transactions before and sometimes after death can be revealing.

Kate keeps her tour upstairs as brief as she can make it without igniting gossip about the girl cop chickening the job. The hardest sight is in the younger boy's room, where one of those plastic zapper guns they have is crunched into pieces, presumably by the feet of the shooter arriving or leaving; the latter, she hopes, or the child might have woken up before it happened. The shooter has used pillows to muffle the blasts, which would once have been evidence of a professional but, these days, such knowhow is probably available to anyone on Massacre dot com.

Having confirmed that they are investigating four murders in the house, she returns to the comforting warmth from the Aga, although its glow is not enough to overcome her body's natural shivering response to what she has seen. The death of children should not be worse but always is.

All murders come back to either money or sex. This motto

of her first DCI (who taught her much about the motives of murderers and of men) seemed too simplistic at the time for so complex a crime, and Kate has spent her career trying to disprove it. But all the murders she has worked so far have led back to debt, infidelity, greed, jealousy; almost every case reducible to the victim having something or someone the culprit wants.

She has mentally concluded that her mentor's theory holds for most cases except racial killing – rape–murder and homophobic killings are covered, involving motivation which, though warped, is sexual – but, even there, hatred of another person's skin may be driven by financial disadvantage or resentment.

But *this*: a case in which an apparently prosperous, respected man (she fights the temptation to include *middle-class* in the list of mitigations, while knowing the media will not) seemingly kills four people in his own home and then himself? When Kate first saw the house on the way up the drive, she suspected a new class of hate crime to which the country seems inevitably to be heading – the poor killing the super-rich from resentment of what they have – but her apocalyptic imaginings were soon challenged by the evidence that these killings come under the category of rich-on-rich.

So money is an unlikely cause here; the house drips wealth. Sex is a possible explanation. Two years ago, she was lead detective on a case in which a woman, after a row, had changed her Facebook status to single, this simple click of a mouse being enough to persuade her partner to kill her, or at least proving to be the final trigger for his psychopathic jealousy. But, in what the 24-hour-news channels are already calling the BUCKS FAMILY MASSACRE, why would the shooter take out his children (one possibly not his own) and himself as well? In the domestic sprees she can reference (reading, conferences), the cases of total wipe-out happened when the mother introduced a new partner to her life, leading the father to resent another man's influence over his children. So the state of the dead couple's marriage will be a vital area of inquiry. And what, in that connection, might be the relevance of the First Predictor kit they've found?

'DCI Duncan?'

The guv-less greeting signalling someone from outside the team. Thirty-something shave-head, piercing blue eyes. She scans her mental files: Lorimer, the force's media-relations manager.

'Yeah?' she says. 'You want to throw me to the dogs?'

'They're getting twitchy for a briefing. And the trolls have already got the case solved online, give or take the occasional wrong name and cause of death . . .'

'And you think anything I say will stop them? But okay . . .'

Though shamed by her vanity, she checks the state of her face in the entrance-hall mirror. *Saw you on telly*, neighbours and shopkeepers tell her with proprietorial pride after such appearances, as if she had croaky-karaoked a ballad on *The X Factor* rather than reported a slaughter.

As she's shuffling off the pyjamas at the forensics van, Lorenzo appears.

'Guv, I've fixed for us to go and see this Nicky Mortimer. He's waiting for us whenever . . .'

'Okay. I've got to go down the hill and appear on *Only Fools and Corpses* . . .'

'Yeah. The spin-nurse said.'

Lining up her reflection in the shiny side of the van, she hand-combs her hair. A shadow blocks out her impromptu mirror and she turns to see DC Taylor. She checks if he is smirking at her vanity.

'What is it?' she asks. 'I'm due to do a presser.'

'Another interesting call-in, guv. Apart from the Nicky Mortimer one. A friend of E's, from one of the matching mansions . . .'

'Really? With what?'

'Email, middle of the night. Only read it this morning.'

'Saying?'

'*Sorry*. Just that.'

'Oh-kay. Do we know what the apology was for?'

'He isn't sure.'

'We'd better see him.'

'Low priority, though, isn't it?' Lorenzo interrupts. 'We're still thinking classic friendly killer?'

'Oh, they're still using that phrase, are they? My point is that we still don't have an ID on one of the victims. That comes first.'

As she approaches the taped-off gate at the bottom of the hill, the heaving heap of media is suddenly flooded with brightness, like the action of a play moving to a different section of the stage, as the lights of the TV crews are fired up. Requests for names and details – but, above all, the number of the dead – are yelled from all directions at escalating volume, a few deep male voices dominating.

'Can you confirm five dead?' / 'Do you have any idea what caused . . . ? / 'Was this a family slaying?'

A *family slaying*: real murder as movie of the week. Seeing Kate, the media bloke, his yellow vest bouncing back the TV lights so sharply that some of the reporters shield their eyes, conducts the press gang into silence with his hands and says: 'DCI Kate Duncan, who is leading the murder investigation, will give a brief statement on the progress so far. You will understand that certain details must be withheld for operational reasons . . .'

Yeah, like men understand you're sometimes too tired for sex, or dogs that you're too busy to walk them.

'I can confirm, with regret,' Kate begins, 'that four bodies have been found at this scene: an adult female, two younger males and a younger female. A fifth body has been found at another location. The incidents are being linked.'

She is immediately interrupted by a rush of overlapping shouts – the words 'recession', 'marriage', 'shotgun licence' sounding out like spoken capital letters – from which she waits for an identifiable question to rise.

'Can we have names and ages on the dead?'

'No, no formal identification has taken place yet.'

'Do we assume the body at the second site is the killer?'

'We are unable to say at this stage.'

'In the village, the family is being named as . . .'

Cut in, before the name goes out on air and starts those rats running. 'Obviously, that must also await formal identification.'

'Land registry documents show that . . .'

With a crime-scene that's ever been bought or sold, a name is circulated within minutes, but there have been enough cases where victims were identified as suspects and vice versa – in early reports of the London transport attacks, the suicide bombers were included in the count of passengers dead – for it to be sensible to hold the lonely line of anonymity.

'I really can't help with identification at this stage,' she says.

An overcoated old bloke she recognizes as Delaney, one of the last of the old-fashioned fag-and-backhander crime-corrs, out-shouts the yapping pack to ask: 'Do you have reason to believe the gunman may still be at large?'

'At the moment, we are no longer looking for anyone else in connection with the killings. The major investigation is restricted to the crime-scenes here and at the second location.'

'And the second location is . . . ?'

'That's all for now,' she drowns out Delaney, before he can name the other place, although it will be all over screens now. But they have their story, or enough of one to feed the hungry gullet of public interest for the next few hours. The media guy steps across the camera shot to end the press conference. Kate goes to find Lorenzo to drive across the county and ask Nicky Mortimer what he knows.

TEN

CATASTROPHIZING

The douche catches her on the landing and comes right out with it: 'How do you feel about some dirty dancing?'

TBH, she's been waiting for this. On the Slave Girl site, which some au pair in Melbourne set up to vent and has become a sort of Fuck-YouTube for dudes on munchkin duties overseas, there's shitloads of stuff about the daddy in the family suddenly showing you a boner or dry-humping your butt when you're bent over the dishwasher. One slave-girl was offered double money to give the bloke a hummer when the mummy was at church, although they always reckon, in England, the danger time is when the wife is out at book club. Abby wouldn't mind being in the reading circle herself – she's starting English and Drama at UNSW in January – but the mummies don't think you've got a brain and the daddies only see snatch.

'Excuse me, Mr Crossan?' she says. OMG, isn't Libby at book club now? *The Pilot's Wife* on the kitchen table, a bookmark at page forty for two weeks now.

'I think we use a Jonny by now, don't we? Abby, I'm offering you a night of dirty dancing in London . . .'

She's always thought this one was a cock waiting to go off. He *accidentally dropped* the towel once, coming out of the bathroom, the oldest perv-swerve in the book, giving her a first, and please sweet Jesus last, flash of ginger knob. She thought she might be safe here because these two are, like, always fucking. Her first live-in gig, in London, him-and-her closed the bedroom door with a big click maybe one Sunday morning a month, and she knew to keep the midgies watching Cartoon Channel; but the Crossans' mattress seems to twang like a banjo day and night.

'Say again, Mr Crossan?'

'I am offering you two top-price stalls tomorrow night for what is by all accounts – at least our friends the Rutherfords enjoyed it – one of London's hottest musicals.'

Oh, yeah, *Dirty Dancing*. She saw it on buses in London. Maybe the douche isn't putting moves on her. But . . .

'But, yeah, but, I mean, why do you want me to go?'

'These tickets came into my possession. Don't ask how but perfectly legal, officer.'

'But why don't you take Mrs Crossan?'

The daddy in the London house was always trying to take her to the opera. Three hours of foreign singing and then trying to get his dick down your throat, no thank you.

'What? Oh, there are other things we could be doing here.' Fuck, he actually winks. 'And I wouldn't have thought it was our poison, frankly. Wasn't it a movie with that Patrick Swayze chap?'

'Who's he?'

'Bloody hell, you colonials! I suppose you do know who the Rolling Stones are, do you?'

No, not really.

'It's really sweet of you, Mr Crossan. But it's pretty intense here on a Friday night, with Plum's cross-country and Lukie's chess club. Libby needs me . . .'

'We'll sort that out.'

This is pretty weird stuff. Most of the time, they're getting you to work days you don't, rather than telling you to fuck off and have fun. He'll have some creepy reason, like wanting to do Libby on the kitchen table or whatever, but if she can get one of the other slave-girls to go with her . . .

'But Abby . . .'

'Yes?'

'There's just one little condition . . .'

Jeez, here we go.

*

Max refuses to admit how bad he's feeling. Each time his right knee hits the ground, there's a flash of pain, which he visualizes as a spiked line on a share-dealing screen. The bugger of running on winter nights is not the cold – within two miles, his tracksuited body is a cocoon of damp warmth – but the shock of the ungiving ground.

Barry has set them a new route tonight, starting with a loop around the disused railway line from Chapel Tewsbury, behind the business park. Dense clots of fog have dropped into the cutting, almost touching the rigid earth, perfectly dressing a set for the discovery of a body in a television mystery. Behind a fence, to their right, in a siding, at the blurry limits of vision, there's even a ghost train: an abandoned, smashed-windowed carriage, spectacularly vandalized with swirls of shiny paint.

'Gloves not enough? Want one of those fucking *snoods*?' Barry shouts over his shoulder, noticing that his client has fallen behind.

'No,' Max says. The strange sense in winter of words and air as something solid, swirling out of the mouth like regurgitated candy floss.

'Are you in pain, poof?'

'No. *No.*'

'Runners always hurt somewhere,' screams Barry. 'If you ain't aching it, you're faking it.'

Almost every car space in the business park is empty, except for the occasional Merc in a bay with a nameplate. Some CEO troubling over the numbers in the recession. They'd be better off exercising, keeping their brain sharp.

'Let's sprint, wimp,' instructs Barry, accelerating up the incline, as they pass Dunster Manor to start their second circuit. His next remark – 'Is that your fucking cardiac monitor?' – throws Max, until he understands that the trainer's younger ears have been first to hear the ringing of the iPhone in his hip pocket.

Max stops and, with clumsily gloved hands, gropes out the phone and see the ID: *Steve Pearson*.

'Phone is for home,' Barry barks.

'Look, I'm really sorry, but I have to take this one.'

'Okay, you fucking iPhoney!'

Max pulls up the rim of his black woollen cap to free an ear and wriggles off his running gloves. His FD asks if he's Max and he confirms that he is.

'Right. You sound breathless?'

'No. No. It's just I'm with Barry. That sounds wrong but . . .'

'What happened? Your girl said she'd make sure you dropped by at close of play.'

Across the park, the glass frontages of the factories and offices are mainly dark, except for the yellow rectangles where money or love is being made. Max has the luxury of both. He's happy to be running a company that doesn't have to scratch for every saving, although Steve's generation of FDs look for them instinctively, like dogs licking their balls.

'I'm so sorry, Steve. I took a call from Rosie – some horse she's scouting – and then Barry got his hooks into me . . .'

'Look, Max, what's the deal with this, er, Natasha Lonsdale? . . . *Max*?'

'Yes. Er, she's a chum and she's done grub for us in the past for this and that.'

'But not last Christmas?'

'Er, no. No we – *you* – cancelled the bash.'

'Yeah, what I thought. Max, is this Natasha close to anyone else in the company?'

'What? What do you mean by close? I've no idea. Could this wait, old boy? I've got a psychotic Springbok panting to kick my arse . . .'

'Too fucking right, posh boy,' interjects Barry, filling the gap with energetic running on the spot.

'Look, Max, I'm concerned about an irregular cash move-
ment . . .'

His knee feels as if it's going to explode. Must be the muscles
stiffening up in the cold. Another of Barry's workout nursery
rhymes: 'running or cumming – you don't want to stop halfway
through.'

'*Max?*'

'Yes. Go on . . .'

'On January 16th, Natty Cooking Ltd sent in an invoice for
party catering. Around 10k. As far as I can work out, that's the
same amount as last year's plus a rise roughly in line with inflation . . .'

'That's odd. How did . . . this invoice . . . where was . . . ?'

'I was doing the quarterly cash flows. But this is the fucker,
Max. The amount was paid on January 18th. By BACS transfer. From Dunster 4? The Supplier account?'

What's the recovery period from knee surgery? Most of the
people he knows have at least one bionic joint these days.

'I don't know what to say, Steve.'

'Whichever way we cut it, mate, I think we're looking at
fraud. Listen, is there any way someone else could have got hold
of your passwords and your verify device? This Natasha or her
husband or . . .'

'She's a *friend*, Steve . . .'

'Recessions make people desperate, mate.'

Barry would have rhymed it: *slumps* something something
dumps.

'I'm sure there's an explanation, Steve . . .'

'Well, I've tried to think of one . . .'

'Maybe the bank somehow thought it was a regular payment and just rolled it on?'

'I did think that at first. But why would they give her a little
bit extra for RPI?'

'I'll talk to Tash.'

'When?'

'As soon as I can . . .'

'You need to. If there's any suspicion of irregularity, the directors have a duty to act immediately.'

'Yes. Yes, I know.'

'Max, I'm coming across some quite troubling numbers. I'm beginning to think that your Bill Adamson may have been a bit of a crook.'

'Well, steady on. You have to remember that Bill was scarcely in for the last six months or so, with the treatment he was having, and then, well, the end. Isn't it most likely things went a bit spastic during that time?'

Bugger. He has said one of the words he's not supposed to say nowadays, although Barry is probably the person in the world least likely to object to old-fashioned language and Steve is preoccupied, saying: 'It's possible. Did you bring in an acting FD?'

'What? No, everyone mucked in. Nothing like the word *cancer* to make people do the right thing. But I suppose I did most of it myself . . .'

His hand is so shaky from the cold that he struggles to get the phone back into his pocket. Barry, high-kicking step-ups on one of the stone benches, sees that Max is finished and runs over, knees pumping high.

'Stop–start is like you never started. Clock back at the top.'

'I'm sorry. I think the business may be getting a little bit too big for my finance chap. Penalty of success.'

'Come on, we're back to zero miles, doughboy!' bawls Barry, setting off like a greyhound chasing steak. Max braces on his screaming knee and follows.

*

A teenage memory. He's seventeen or eighteen, going for his interview at LSE. The longest train journey he's done on his own – Bolton to Manchester to London – with both him and his parents pretending to be cooler about it than they are. Simon can see his younger self quite clearly, like a clip from one of those music-and-news compilations: *The Rock n Roll Years – 1980.*

The oddness of wearing a tie – borrowed from Dad – that isn't the school stripes, and that fancy shirt he got for Christmas: blue with white collar, a type fashionable at the time, and (the circularity of age) again now. He remembers Frank Bough wearing one on *Nationwide*.

Their family had a thing about being early – hours sitting in departure lounges for the package-holiday flight even to appear on the flicker screens – and so he has a long wait before his train. He's eventually persuaded his mum it will be fine to leave him. There's time for one of those breakfasts you only have when travelling – a sausage roll, a cheese toasty – even back then, before the chains with the French names had stalls on every station. But he's nauseous with nerves and worried about the lunch money Mum gave him holding out in London, from where northerners return with appalled stories about the cost of everything.

So he goes over to John Menzies, checks to see if there's any interesting injury or transfer stuff on the back of the News, which there isn't, then heads to the book section. There's a new James Herbert, but only in hard covers, so he'll have to wait for the paperback. He flicks through, checking for the ten-page sex scene Herbert usually inserts (the word itself almost giving him a hard-on) amid the horror, and which has taught him most of what he knows about how girls work, handbooks that have not yet been put to practical use. His eye expertly finds the give-away words on the page – *wet*, *hard*, *glistening* – which can sometimes leave you reading about a rainstorm but will generally get you to the right part. His prick fattens massively against the fly of the scratchy M&S suit they've bought for the university interviews.

Self-conscious about his erection, he swings his shoulder bag (thermos of hot chocolate, *To The Lighthouse* for the essay due soon, asthma inhaler, one of Dad's folded linen handkerchiefs) in front of his crotch and moves to the magazine racks to see if the new *Disco 45* and *The Cricketer* are in yet. And it's there that he notices Joey Delahay's dad. He and Joey, classmates at both primary and secondary school, have 'played' at each other's houses over the years and both fathers take their sons to Burnden Park on Saturdays.

Whenever he rescreens this scene, Simon realizes that it sounds like the prelude to a scene of sexual corruption and perhaps, in some ways, it is. Mr Delahay has his back to him and, while Simon's looking for the pop section, he sees the tall, thin man reach to the top shelf and take down a *Penthouse*. There's just a flash of a cover girl with legs spread wide before Joey's dad slides the shiny periodical inside the *Daily Express* he's holding and goes over to the counter.

The internal ayatollah that every teenager deploys against the older generation is outraged at this evidence of parental perversion – what could an old man want with wank mags? – then rapidly overcome by the sexual Machiavelli who is also on permanent duty: here is clear evidence that there must be a horde of porn somewhere in the Delahay house. Joey, when Simon tells him at school next day, is shocked and shamed for longer, but reaches the same conclusion. Their guess at the garden shed proves correct and, by the next Monday, Joey is bringing in thick Manila envelopes which they slip between their briefcases in the Sixth Form common room, like spies.

There were the usual kerfuffles caused by unexpected knocks on the bedroom door – cover pulled up, mag under mattress – but Simon was never caught at home and Jack Delahay either never noticed the ambushes on his stash or recognized the impossibility of discipline.

Simon's eyes and cock popped out at the split beavers, jelly-fish nipples and girl-on-girl embraces, and he must suppose that what happened on Bolton station is his equivalent of the sip of granny's sherry at Christmas which the addict tearfully recounts at their first AA meeting in those TV movies about drunks.

Are there support groups for porn addicts? And, if so, should he be looking for the phone number? Five years ago, a newspaper report about the risk of uncontrolled porn on the Internet led him to take the risk. He was astonished at the fannytasia he found there: first live vaginas winking at the lens and then, with a few quick clicks of slippery fingers, live streamed footage of couples fucking and sucking in every possible combination of genders and ages.

He can see that the risk of this pornographic free-for-all is that a viewer will release a desire he (and it will invariably be he) didn't know he had. But a gay site he found by accident did nothing to take him beyond his liberal belief in others being free to do it. And, with absolutely no interest in paedo, anal, snuff or vet (the categories divided with the precision of a spinster librarian), he never, in a market driven by perversion, has to pay for any of the straightforward stuff he watches and so leaves no giveaway credit-card details. He even prefers real bushy women, like the *Penthouse* spreads of his adolescence, to the vajazzled pseudo-schoolgirls that dominate online. This feels to Simon like a moral code.

Even so, he is clear-eyed enough to understand that there has been a shift in his relationship with the stuff. Jacking off to Joey's dad's mags made him want to have sex with real women, but his sessions on the Internet now are a favoured substitute for fucking. He knows that this cannot be good.

It concerns him as well that Josh and Henry have had access from the time they could type to images for which, at their age, he would have needed a brown-paper account in Amsterdam. What breed of men will be raised in this sexual manure?

But, like the boozer who will definitely quit tomorrow, he has spent another night on the sites, even taking the risk on this occasion that his wife, who surprised him by not going to book club (saying she couldn't stand the bloody novel), is watching TV on the other side of the hall. *The Killing*, he thinks, which, in another of their separations, he watches himself later on iPlayer.

He needed sex tonight, though, to stop him thinking about money. For weeks, he has been dreading the arrival of the credit-card bill for the extra hotel in Morocco. He doesn't understand why it has never shown up. He mentioned it to Tasha, who said she thinks she may have paid it, but he has no idea why she would or how she could.

The incoming ping of his email startles him. Seeing Rutherford in the header-line, he ignores it but then realizes it's Emily, not Tom. Is she hassling him over the flu jab?

Hi, Si. We're not seeing much of you guys. Is everything okay? Em xx

No reply necessary or, at least, possible. Deleting the XXX sites from the browser's memory, he double-clicks the hard disc, finds and opens PRUE.

*

He has heard and read stories of the later generations of families almost vying to die first because there is limited space left in the family plot or vault. And, suddenly, for the first time, it strikes him that they will come to this in Middlebury.

> Poignantly, as with many crowded English country churchyards, the length of local and family history represented here is becoming an issue. Estimates suggest that there is perhaps room for four or five more burials. Beyond that, current and future generations of Middleburyians will have to settle for the civic cemetry or cremation.

The red squiggle underline of the spellcheck questions cemetry. Only now has Tom found time to write the St John the Redeemer section he sketched in his head during Christmas service. The months of escalating panic in Britain – economic, environmental, now medical – have been good for business. His diary contains double last year's bookings for security reviews; such is the demand that he has even, for the first time since they set up, helped out on installations.

Are those thoughts too morbid for a local history pamphlet? Too junior to serve in the Falklands, and on civvy street by Iraq and Afghanistan, Tom belongs to a lucky cohort of British soldiers who faced real danger only in some corners of Northern Ireland. Cremation was requested on his next-of-kin forms and his thankfully rare involvement in the repatriation of fallen comrades confirmed his ambition to end as ashes, finding the reduction of a corpse to dust a gentler end than being planted in the earth like a barren bulb. But the Dunsters and the Crossans have lain under the church green for more than a century and, sticklers for tradition that they are, surely imagine this arrangement continuing. Terrified of starting a bidding war for the remaining graves, Tom deletes the precise prediction of how many more berths are left in the earth. It is his secret that he sees himself and Emily in retirement somewhere else; perhaps France. They only came to Middlebury because it was the one among her fourteen job applications that proved successful. How vain we are to claim our lives are planned.

The landline on the desk rings. He recognizes the number on the ident panel as Em's mobile. She's in Aylesbury at the out-of-hours centre.

'Hi, darling,' he says.

'Hell-*oh*.' It's her theatrically sighy voice, signalling exhaustion and boredom. 'You're up late?'

'Oh, I'm just doing a bit of my pamphlet . . .'

'That's good because you haven't been able to . . .'

'No. What's it like there?'

'Oh, everyone's convinced they're dying.'

'This new flu?'

'Mmmm.'

'And are they?'

'Not mainly. I got one admitted with suspected pneumonia. And a case of palpitations which is probably panic but you have to rule out a rate or rhythm disorder. Most of the rest are just lonely people ringing up because they want a chat. Like me to you.'

'Aah!'

'Tom, I'm worried about Tash and Simon.'

'Right? As a doctor or a friend?'

'I'm just worried. She hasn't come to the gym with us for weeks. And when was the last time you played tennis with him?'

'Well, er, Pensiongate, won't it be?'

What would we say for scandal if the documents that Nixon wanted had been in a building called the Tower?

'There've been flare-ups before. They pass.' Em should really run the UN. 'We got over the Colditz thing. Why don't you fix tennis with Simon?'

'Oh, this weather, our age, our backs . . .'

'Rubbish. Do you good to keep moving. I'll ring Tash. Can you try Simon?'

'I'll have a go.'

'Have you done the dogs?'

The darkest part of marriage for him has always been the lists of things to do and then the checking that they have been done.

'Phoebe did them.'

'Good. And she went to bed at a decent time?'

He, in fact, has no idea of his daughter's whereabouts since he heard the kennel gate slam. 'Yes.'

'Do we need milk? I can stop at the garage on the . . .'

'I've no idea.'

'Do you want to look in the fridge?'

'I'm in the study . . .'

'But you could . . . *okay, I'll just be* . . .' Another voice in the background. 'Darling, we've got a suspected MI.' Heart attack. 'Check the milk and text me.'

'Okay.'

With no medical professional present to make a questioning face, Tom splashes out another half-glass of Cab Sav. He closes GRAVEYARD and double-clicks the inbox. Jonny: SHOOTING? Jenno: RE: SECURITY REVIEW ESTIMATE. There is no reply to any of his messages to Simon.

*

297

Without bigging herself up, Jenno thinks she was star student at book club tonight. It helped that Emily, who's generally the boff, was working, and Tash, who maybe mentions just once or twice too often her degree in Eng Lit, texted Jenno to say that she was feeling fluey.

The Pilot's Wife was chosen by the Red Rev, her first time as picker. The usual rule is that the chooser hosts the group, but the three-bed semi that's now the rectory is too small for their turnout, so Jenno stepped in.

Jenno has read a few Anita Shreves on holiday. They're in the line of Jodi Picoult, who she also likes. Women facing moral dilemmas that would probably never happen to you but make you wonder how you would behave if they did. Suppose you had twins with kidney disease and could only donate to one of them? What if you were running for President and had a secret love child? Or were a heart surgeon who fell in love with a patient? Or your son was accused of murder? Or, in this case, after a plane crash, a widow who discovers that her husband was living a double life, with another home and family in London.

Libby said the book started well but lost its way, which is what she says most months. Ali Rawlinson complained that she wouldn't want any of the characters as a friend, which she says every month. Old Mrs Pennington, who still comes, bless her, got in a bit of a muddle and thought the pilot was divorced from the woman in London, which would have made it a less interesting book and a bit close to home for Jenno. Becca Adamson got weepy every time she said the word 'widow' and the regulars simultaneously realized that the vicar, being new, wouldn't know that at the moment they avoid novels involving bereavement for that reason. Jenno passed round the posh crisps (the parsnip with black pepper were a big hit) as a distraction, while Becca gathered herself.

Ali Rawlinson argued that the story was dramatizing every woman's fear that there's someone else, at which point the discussion got a bit eggy because her Toby is rumoured to be a bit of a swordsman. The Red Rev saw the novel as a parable about human selfishness, but without bringing God into it, and Libby said *male* selfishness, which started a debate about whether women were morally better people than men; a motion that was carried 20–0, with even Andy Topping, their token bloke, voting for it.

Jenno, though, took the discussion into an area the others hadn't thought of, by arguing that the book was questioning the whole concept of romance. What was interesting was that the pilot didn't find a second woman because he was unhappy with the first, but that he lived almost identical lives with both. So Shreve is questioning – she nearly says *subverting*, but fears it will sound pretentious – the idea of the One. As soon as she started speaking, Jenno appreciated that she hadn't considered the implications of this reading: she deeply believes that it was her duty to save Max from the always angry, rapidly frigid Hilary and show him what love could be.

'Ooh, Jen, are you advocating bigamy?' squeals Libby and they do a round about the possibility of the one and only. Old Mrs Pennington and Becca Adamson say they can't imagine being with anyone other than their dead husbands. Libby – after Jenno has stared down the joke about necrophilia that is obviously being planned – agrees ('Although, I mean, Jonny's alive!'), while Jenno keeps quiet. She is spooked by a thought she has somehow staved off until now: marry a divorced man and you always know that there was a time when he said to someone else the things he says to you. She has to hold to a romantic applied maths in which the second One has a higher value than the first One.

For the March meeting, it's Old Mrs Pennington's turn to choose the book and she goes for *The Way We Live Now*, to Trollope jokes from Libby and groans about its length and antiquity from a few. Jenno is infuriated when Libby announces that box-set groups have been trending on Twitter and that they should do *The Killing: Season 2* next month. Luckily, literacy wins the day.

When the goodbye kissing and gossip (Andy Topping has heard that travellers have applied for a permanent encampment at Eastbury Farm) are taking place in the hall, Becca Adamson seems to be hanging back and eventually it is just the two of them.

All the women are uneasy around Becca, from the primitive superstition that young widows will bring bad luck, that they resent your happiness and that they will steal your man. And, for Jenno, there's the additional complication of being the wife of Bill's boss.

Jenno feels bad for noticing that grief has aged the woman by at least a decade. She has the flat eyes and flushed cheeks of the tranquillized, and her sweater dress hangs baggily.

'Becca, I'm sorry if that book was tricky for you. I don't think the vicar . . .'

'Oh, I'm not worried that Bill led a double life.'

Jenno bristles at this insensitive response to her sensitivity, but grants Mrs Adamson the licence due to those whom life has treated cruelly.

'How are things, Becca?'

'People always say the nights are worst and they're right. I can't fault Dr Rutherford, though. And Dunster's looked after me well. Bill had a good pension.'

Feeling too much like the lady of the manor receiving the pathetic thanks of the peasants, Jenno tries to change the subject, but Becca carries on: 'Jenny, look, bit of an odd one, this.' Jenno magnanimously doesn't correct her. 'I had a call today from the chap who took over from Bill.'

'Really?'

'Steve, er . . .'

'Pearson.'

'Yes. He asked if Bill had any "work files" at home, anything on the computer. "Anything related to Dunster's", is what he said.'

'Did he say why?'

'He said he's doing – I think he called it – a "total retro audit" and he needs "all available paperwork". Is Max here?'

'Er, no.' Although she heard the dogs barking half an hour ago at the back of the house. 'I'll ask him if he knows anything when he gets in.'

'That would be kind. I've pretty much left Bill's study as it was, and I really hadn't been planning on going in there yet.'

Jenno stays in the hall, listening to Becca taking three or four attempts to start the car outside; she's 'scattered', as Granny used to say. Jenno waits until she can no longer hear the engine noise going down the hill, then finds Max in the family living room, supposedly watching *Newsnight* but playing on his bloody football game.

'Hiya,' she says.

'Hi,' he replies without looking up.

'Max?'

'Wait.'

Instantly, his face is clouded with a grimace of pained humiliation she has never seen before. He throws back his head and lets out a moan that causes Beauty to stir on the sofa in confused animal sympathy.

'Fuck. *Fuck.*'

'Maxie, are you okay?'

'I lost to Cheltenham. So I'm bottom, if the late kick-off goes against me.'

Jenno laughs in genuine relief. 'Oh, I thought it was something important.'

'Ha bloody ha, darling. How was the *South Wank Show* tonight?'

'It was fun. Penny Pennington rather got hold of the wrong end of the stick. Poor Becca Adamson is all over the place, still.'

'I know, I know. People's lives. Do you want to get yourself a glass?'

'No, I'm all right.'

She has been trying to cut back these last few weeks. And, anyway, it looks as if there's barely an inch left in the bottle of red on the sewing cabinet beside Max. She sits on the sofa, pressing her leg against the thick heat of his. He is always so toasty.

'Maxie, Becca said something . . .'

'Bad luck! I usually just tune out and try to look sympathetic.'

'Steve Pearson rang her up . . .'

'Mmm?'

He is already fiddling again with the PPS or whatever it's called.

'Some sort of audit of the company he's doing?'

He keeps pressing the buttons on the toy.

'Max?'

She's surprised by his huge smile, so completely the opposite of his earlier expression that she wonders for a moment if he's scored a goal on the silly game.

'Ha!' he says, facing her, still beaming. 'Frankly, I'm not surprised. He's turning out to be a bit of an old woman about the books. The problem is they din in to them all this stuff about due diligence and corporate malfeasance these days. I'll talk to him tomorrow and tell him to call off the dogs.'

Jenno yawn-talks that she's going up to bed now, with just the slightest seductive inflection which used to be enough, but Max says he's got to read some stuff for a meeting tomorrow. Both the kids still leave their bedroom doors slightly open – how long before they start pulling them closed? – and so she goes in to check them: when will they stop her doing that? Jamie has kicked off his duvet, as usual. Rosie, though old enough to have sex in a graveyard, is cuddling Rupie, the giant teddy bear that the Crossans gave her when she was born.

It's another half hour before she hears Max spitting and swilling in his bathroom. He comes in wearing both halves of his pjs, which means he hasn't taken the hint. Left insecure by the subject she stupidly brought up at book group, she wants to make love, as a charm against his past. It's at least two weeks since they did it, which is a bad sign in itself.

302

'Do you want to take those bottoms off?' she asks as he lifts up the duvet.

'Oh? Crikey! But it's a weeknight.'

'Maxie! You should make a Dunster Manor Married Sex Calendar, with the occasional Sunday picked out in red. Get them off!'

He wriggles out of the stripy trousers as she turns the light off. She lifts her nightie and cuddles up to him. Oh. She uses her hand to make him hard enough, then has to hold him against her like an applicator. Maybe he's drinking too much.

'Have you got your thing in?' he asks her.

'What? Oh, yes.'

'You don't sound very sure.'

'I wasn't sure what you meant . . .'

'So you've really come prepared?'

'What?'

'I don't want any more kids, Jen.'

'I know.' I just want to feel you inside me. 'I just want . . .'

But he's limp again and she has to do another Aladdin's Lamp. She rolls on to her back, he moves on top of her and she reaches for him. Getting him inside her is like a stuffed courgette recipe she once gave up on. But neediness speeds her responses and she doesn't mind too much when she quickly feels him thickening, until he starts to pull away. She tries to hold him where he is but he's too strong for her and gushes on her tummy.

'Oh,' she says. The deliberately disappointed voice she's polished on the children.

'Oops.'

'It doesn't matter.'

'Sorry, honey. I was going to give you some Irish airline but then I couldn't stop . . .'

She's holding her nightie away from the cooling pool of stickiness.

'It's okay. I've got to go and . . .'

Crab-walking to the bathroom, trying to catch the drips on

her thighs, she's nagged by a familiarity in this scene. But surely she can't have had a conversation about it. Not even Libby would. As she leans against the freezing edge of the sink and splashes hot water against herself, she remembers. That play they saw.

*

How long minutes and even seconds seem when you are counting them. He watches the shimmering red countdown: 5:29:58, 5:29:59. As the three zeroes roll into place, like catching a mileometer at the changeover moment – he always trades in a car when it's done 10,000 – he presses the top of the radio alarm to stop it going off. Libby, without waking, rolls towards the impression he has left in the bed. He kisses the top of her head and she briefly wriggles recognition.

Dead man walking. From nowhere, the taunt jumps into his skull and reverberates there like an echo in a cave. A trick of a tired mind, he tells himself. As has happened for as many nights as he can remember, he has heard the church clock striking every hour.

In the shower, Jonny fears he's going to faint and tries to steady himself against the wall, but his hand, slick with shampoo, slips and his toe slides into the tiled rim at the base. The shock of the blow triggers shivering and, for a moment, he considers going back to bed and calling Victor to cry off with flu. But trying to lose himself in the working day seems more sensible than lying awake for longer. Flinching from the chill of the lavatory seat, he endures a disappointing wind-Smedgewick.

As he gets into the car, perfectly on the quarter-hour, the news headlines are beginning. *Markets around the world have reacted nervously.* Until recently a news junkie, he now frequently seeks the rehab of Radio 3 as the news stations sound increasingly like readings from the Book of Revelations. He tunes in as the announcer is introducing a Schubert piano sonata, which calms him, until, on the outskirts of the village, he sees a rabbit in the headlights' beam too late to steer away and splatters it beneath the wheels. The music briefly soothes him again, until, on the dual carriageway to the station, he thinks he's been flashed by a speed-camera. Twelve points and a certain suspension this time. But, as the road curves, he realizes that the blaze of light behind him was just the brightness of the moon in the last darkness before dawn.

The omens further improve when his favourite parking space – number 8, on the ground floor next to the exit – is free. In the station newsagent, he plucks his usual two newspapers from the rack and puts them on the counter, folded so he cannot, for the moment, see the front pages.

'Selected confectionery for a pound?' the check-out Brenda says, gesturing at a stack of slabs of chocolate. He has never understood why sweets should be cheaper with newspapers, as if there were some secret government initiative to make the morbidly obese better informed or the better informed morbidly obese.

'No. No, thank you.'

The girl gives him the look, so common these days, that says he's an arse to turn down a bargain. But she reaches behind her and slaps what looks like a plastic jeroboam of Evian on the counter.

'There's a free bottle of water with this one,' she says, as she now seems to every day.

Jonny is increasingly bemused by the paper's apparent campaign to rehydrate the nation, a mission oddly never mentioned in editorials. He isn't thirsty (indeed, is calculating if his bladder will hold out until the train) and his briefcase would scarcely close when he left home.

'No thank you,' he says again.

She scowls at him like he's asked for a quickie round the back. 'Pudden?'

'I'll forego the water if that's all right.'

'Pudden?'

A sudden memory of his mother telling him how vulgar

'Pardon?' was, although his children's favourite deaf-aid is the dreaded American 'Say what?'

'I'm going to pass on . . .' – he stumbles on the looming double entendre – '. . . I won't take the water, thank you.'

'Wot? I fink you have to have it,' she says in her slovenly way.

Unless she is appalled at his turning down a free gift in such hard times or genuinely fears that he will be found licking the Milton Keynes concourse for raindrops, he assumes her shock is simply worker-ant conformity.

'I'm sorry. I simply don't have space in my briefcase.'

Although, in fact, a slug of cold *eau* might just hit the spot. The inside of his mouth has a thick sour coating, only thirty minutes since he cleaned his teeth. But it's the principle of being forced to take the water, as if in some capitalist parody of communism's insistence on the acceptance of provisions offered.

'Wot?' says the shopgirl. 'I'll have to check with the manager.'

He senses the tension and resentment in the growing line behind him, the line of looming times on the flicker-board inflaming impatience. Like the burn of bile that precedes being sick, he can almost feel the words pooling in his throat before they pour out: 'Young lady, you do not have to check any-*thing* with any-*one*. I am one of the country's leading barristers, a Queen's Counsel. And I can assure you that – if there existed on the British statute books a law making it a matter for the courts that a free citizen of the realm wishes to peruse the *Daily Telegraph* without first taking acceptance of a litre of free spring water – then I would most certainly have been informed of this offence. So I *think* we can consider it safe for me to leave without the *drink*. The correct cash for my newspapers is on the counter! Good morning!'

As he turns and sweeps away from the counter, there's applause from a couple of chaps he knows from First Class, although a black guy is making the Dobson sign and two young women in Russian hats are aiming faces at him like he's flashed them.

He has three minutes to make the 6.13 – two, in fact, because regulations make them close the doors sixty seconds before departure now. Just in front of the ticket barrier, a young couple are entwined, kissing goodbye, pressed tight against each other, Walter to Georgina, the last clinch of a weekend together. He tries to fight the resentment that increasingly rises in him at seeing young lovers together.

On the platform, he unfurls the folded newspapers, but wind makes sails of the pages and he has to move to the shelter of the footbridge. The *FT* has nothing on the front, but there it is on the *Telegraph*. He swallows, dryly, grindingly. Perhaps this is why they force water on the readership:

FORMER MINISTER CHARGED
WITH EXPENSES FRAUD

Tory grandee Crossan faces four charges of false accounting

Though far from being a McCartney or a Branson, Jonny long ago developed a familiarity with his surname in the newspapers: initially at second-hand, through his father, who, for a while in the eighties, would be mentioned as a possibility in discussions along the lines of 'if Margaret got hit by a bus'. Indeed, Pa had been credited with joking that 'the bus hasn't been built yet that would dare', leading to a Garland caricature of a Routemaster humanized with the minister's features veering fearfully away from a zebra crossing printed with the words Poll Tax, Unemployment and Riots, which the prime minister was stomping unblinkingly across. This cartoon is framed in the loo of the Wiltshire rectory. Then came his own mentions in reports of big trials – 'Jonathan Crossan, QC, for the prosecution, told the jury that the defendant was a calculating manipulator' – first with the thrill of recognition and distinction (in two senses) from Pa and then with irritation at the sensationalism of newspaper law reporting.

And now this. The .13 is a snail-rail with three stops (Bletchley, Leighton Buzzard, Watford Junction) but taking it means he won't have to face the jibes (or, more likely, and worse, the silent knowing smirks) of Lonsdale, Rutherford and the gang (Dunster is in and out of London like a fiddler's elbow these days), as they read of his shame in the newspapers.

Another entry for the superstitious debit column: the door of the First Class compartment lines up with the platform a yard from where he gambled on standing and he has to wait behind a queue of more prescient commuters to board.

*

Although the weather forecast on the car radio warned of snow in the north, the 6.38, which originates in Liverpool, is running to time. As others in the Gold Zone section of the platform struggle to read papers gusted by the wind, Tom smugly scrolls the headlines on his iPad, using his overcoat sleeve to wipe away the rain spits from the screen.

The familiar voice, high and loud behind him: 'I'm thinking: do we give old Gingernuts a sick-chit over this or do we rag him?'

'Morning, Max,' says Tom, turning round. 'I think the poor man deserves a break, doesn't he? Just be glad we never had dads who could embarrass us like that.'

'Ha! There have been board meetings when I've been thankful mine is safely under the Middlebury sod. No sign of Crossan this morning, I notice. Do you think he's keeping his head down? I guess it's like doctors, is it? I mean, JC can't defend him? And what's up with our other compadre?'

Tom follows Max's nod to a crowded stretch of asphalt to their right, where Simon stands looking fixedly at a new advertising hoarding, a watercolour of a horse-driven wagon in rocky terrain. *If There Are No Profits In One Place, Strike Out For New Territories.*

'Your tennis friend seems set on travelling among the mortals,' says Max. 'Should you persuade him to return to the faith?'

'Oh, look, leave him, I think he may be economizing.'

'The traitor! It's our patriotic duty to spend our way out of this recession.'

Max strides over to the lower-price zone, his smile igniting. 'Mr dear Simon, you seem, as it were, to be out of your comfort zone.'

Several other travellers swivel their heads in the direction of the theatrical declamation before Simon eventually acknowledges Max.

'Oh, hi. Do you know what? I've got a lot of stuff to look at, before a meeting. I've reserved a seat in G.'

'Right. Right, okay.'

Alarmed that charm – his reflex weapon – has failed him, Max looks like a father whose son has answered back for the first time. 'I see. It's just that – and obviously don't take this in a gay way – we were missing you.'

Tom can feel the class hatred radiating from the bystanding passengers. Max could never be a politician, because he doesn't see his poshness as a problem.

'I do wonder,' asks Max, coming back, 'if he should perhaps be consulting Dr Rutherford professionally?'

'I don't think a phobia of overpriced rail tickets is a recognized condition,' says Tom, who knows that he could never afford the luxury of First unless Emily earned such a whack.

Just as the Pendolino glides in, Japanese in its sleekness, Nicky Mortimer joins the file behind them. Having guessed the stopping spot exactly, they get a four-with-table and no stranger claiming the spare window seat, which is more comfortable but draws attention to the absence of Simon, or Jonny, depending on your perspective. For Tom, it's Simon who's the ghost.

'So, Max, becoming quite a regular?' Nicky says.

'I suppose I am. A lot of stuff in London at the moment. We've got a big deal going through.'

'Intriguing. Not by any chance a merger or acquisition?'

'I couldn't possibly comment.'

'Because Robbins Schuster Geneva is widely regarded as a leader in this line.'

'So I've heard. And may perhaps be called on. Who knows?'

The train, after going through Buckinghamshire at full tilting sprint, has squealingly decelerated to a halt.

'In fact, Nicky,' says Max. 'Do you know which one you're getting back?'

'What? No, you know how meetings grow. Particularly with the amount of compost some participants throw on them. You're thinking of a drink or . . . ?'

'Sure, if we bumped into each other. But no big deal. Some other time.'

'That might be best. I promised Mon I'd try to get back early. The kids have got the lurgy.' The click of the tannoy being activated, followed by an apprehensive exhalation in the carriage. 'Though, at this rate, we may not even be getting there . . .'

Tom recognizes the train manager as the Scouse joker who likes to turn the health-and-safety announcements into stand-up. But today he has a grave intonation: 'Ladies and gentlemen. You've probably noticed we've come to halt. And we could be held here for quite a little while, I'm afraid. The electrical current has had to be switched off because of a customer under a train at Watford Junction.'

Max bangs his hand on the table in frustration: 'Oh, Lord! You do wonder – don't you – if there'll come a point when we just have to leave them as jam on the tracks?'

Tom, though, is more struck at even suicides being described as *customers* these days.

*

Everyone assumes they are doomed. The car park outside the medical centre is full. There are even some vehicles perched perilously on the grass verges, slick with ice, beside the entrance. Emily is fully committed to the practice's seasonal influenza plan, although, if the vaccines had been available, she would ideally have preferred to inject all the under-fives as well as the traditional at-risks. But now the media have convinced people that they are certain to develop New Variant SARS and then will inevitably perish from it.

Each morning, her emergency surgeries are filled with men, women and children who could have been toured round the teaching hospitals as examples of optimum temperature and healthy respiratory system. It's infuriating because the succession of the *worried well*, a phrase that defines the twenty-first century for Emily, risks dulling you into missing the genuinely sick. Doctors are like the security staff at airports; perhaps one in a whole day's torrent will contain the ticking time-bomb and, if you miss it, the rest is hearings, lawyers and regrets.

Even with her reserved space, it's fiddly to get the Disco in because patients unable to find a free bay have double parked between the legal cars. Judged by traffic flow alone, the panic is worse than the 2009 pandemic, although she doubts that this reflects the clinical reality.

Speeding through the reception area, with the zoned stare she has perfected to avoid queue-jumping by the self-important or hypochondriacal, she catches sight of Tasha, sitting by the soft-play area, reading one of the star-and-bra magazines. Emily flutters her fingers as she passes, a compromise between ignoring her friends and scolding glares suggesting favouritism.

In Consulting Room A, she logs on and scrolls down the appointments for morning surgery. Top of the list is Becca Adamson. Tasha is 8.20, her third. Tasha? Although the software makes no distinctions in the list, two sets of patients – cancer remissions and friends – always shiver as if in italic.

'Becca, what can I help you with?'

At the start of her career, Emily took years to abandon the opener 'How are you?', which, as in social life but to the power of a thousand, invited either pointless pleasantries or unstoppable physical detail.

'I'm sorry to be bothering you again, Doctor . . .'

'Not at all.'

'But I had a really bad night last night . . .'

Listen to the patient's story, a lecturer in diagnostic medicine used to say and it is advice that has saved her from a GMC summons on numerous occasions, spotting the giveaway symptom in a thicket of everyday aches and, increasingly, theories cobbled together from online *What Am I Dying Of?* sites. But the problem, in general practice, is that the stories come round and round, often involving the same characters, like plots in soap opera. Mrs Adamson's is the narrative of savage grief: shock, insomnia, borderline anorexia, loss of confidence, hopelessness.

There is one new twist in the tale – a call the previous day from 'the company' about some paperwork – which is the detail she needs to hear. She visualizes Becca lying awake all night, calling the surgery the moment the lines opened. The receptionist will have asked if it is an emergency and she will have replied yes, which, to her, it is. A little flash of triumph – perhaps – at getting the first slot.

'Well, that's bound to have . . .' – don't say brought it all back, it won't have gone – '. . . to have made the loss even more raw . . .'

She's on 10 mg of paroxetine for anxiety. Initially, zopiclone at 10 mg as well to help her sleep, but withdrawn after four weeks in line with the practice's anti-dependence policy.

'Could you put me back on the sleeping pills, Doctor?'

'Becca, I explained that there's a risk of addiction.'

'That couldn't be any worse than how I feel now. I just want to *sleep*.'

What their lecturer had not mentioned was the necessity of not listening to the story sometimes, refusing to be moved by desperation. Venlafaxine, perhaps. But the practice manager will rant about the cost and . . .

'There's another treatment for anxiety I want to try. But we'll have to give you an ECG first because it's quite a strong drug.'

'Can't you give me something *now*?'

'Becca, there aren't going to be good days at the moment. You'll just have bad and better. You had a bad day and night yesterday – because you had a reminder – but today can be a better one.' She might have a quiet word with Max about whether the stuff that Dunster's needs to know is really important. 'I'm going to give you a slightly stronger version of the pills you're on to see if that helps. And if you make an appointment at the desk for the ECG at a time that suits you.'

She ups the paroxetine to 15 mg and sends it through to the dispensary. Becca is her first patient for days not to express concern about having This Flu, a perfect illustration of having worse things to worry about. The next patient – Nina Mortimer – does think she's got it, or at least her mother does, and it's possible she has, her temperature significantly escalated. Checking on the file that Nina is at least thirteen – yes, born 1997 – Emily prescribes oseltamivir phosphate in a 12.5 ml oral suspension. From their meetings at the Dunsters' party and the theatre, she suspects that the Mortimers are the sort of sharp-elbowed middle-classes who, if they don't get it from the doctor, will buy on the Internet something claiming to be Tamiflu, which might well be fertilizer, so better that they get the real thing.

Nina and Monifa are out of the room in two minutes, so she has saved six on the eight they allocate per patient. Showing them to the door, she leans out into the waiting room and calls 'Natasha Lonsdale?', calculating that the formal name will bridge the transition from friend to patient. Tasha, in turn, nods and says 'Doc' as she comes in, but looks pale and doesn't even try a smile, which leads Emily to suspect a lump or show of blood.

'What can I help you with?' she says.

'Doc, I think I might be pregnant.'

Crikey. She slides one eye to the file. Tash is forty-six, so the odds are against her, but the body sometimes wins unlikely bets. During her first year in general practice, Emily beamingly congratulated a mother of four who turned out to have come to arrange the termination of the fifth, and has never made that mistake again.

'And – if you were – would that be good news?'

The vicious, silent shaking of the head leads her to reinterpret Tasha's pallor, which she had question-marked as possible nausea gravidarum, as fear.

'Okay. The first thing is to ask you a few questions. And remember – in this – I'm a doctor and you're a patient.'

'Ooo-er. I remember my elder brother saying something similar once.'

This flash of the everyday Tasha lifts the mood in the room.

'Do you remember when your last menstrual period was?'

'Yeah. I think. Seven, eight weeks maybe.'

'Right. And are you generally pretty regular?'

'Yes, I think so. I mean you lose track more, once . . .' The pauses in the story, the lecturer had also said, could be as important as the story. 'Once you've had your children. I used to have red Xs in my . . . pocket diary. My mum had a late menopause and I read an article . . .'

'Okay.' The friend would ask: *have you and Simon . . . ?* The doctor asks: 'And have you had unprotected sexual intercourse since your last period?'

'Oh, er, yes. *Once.* Not that we . . .'

'And do you remember when that was?'

'Probably six, seven weeks ago . . .'

'Oh, right? A Marrakesh surprise?'

'What?'

Tasha's anguished grimace makes Emily think that she should have sent her straight next door to Dan or Rosemary. There are rules of clinical distance for a reason.

'Oh, yeah,' Tash recovers. 'Round about then, I suppose.'

'Tash, have you done a home test?'

'No. I . . . stupid, isn't it? Like you think if you don't actually look at your overdraft, then . . .'

'Quite understandable. Look, I know what it is that you're worried about . . .'

One of Tasha's faces of actressy exaggeration: *whaddaya-mean?*

'Your age and you're being . . .' Whoah, whoah. If this were your previous patient or the next one, you wouldn't know they were Catholic. 'At this age, there are all sorts of worries. But the tests are more and more precise. You would be making a decision . . .'

'Emily . . .' Tasha cuts in.

'Yes?'

'If I am . . . could I . . . sort it out without Simon having to know?'

The doctor comprehends what the friend wants to ignore. The doctor says: 'Have you had any abdominal pain or tenderness?'

'Would that be a good thing or . . . ?'

'Have you?'

'No.'

'Good. It might have indicated an ectopic pregnancy. In which case, we might have done a blood test. Because they sometimes don't show up in urine. I'm going to arrange for you to see one of the nurses now to take a test.'

'Oh. Can't you?'

'Tash, it's way below my pay grade to sit around while people widdle on sticks. But, promise me, if it's positive, you'll come straight back in here. I'll get you in between appointments.' Emily borrows an accent vaguely from ER. 'Trust me, I'm a doctor.'

'Thanks, Em. You're a friend.'

*

The results of Jonny's soothsayer game are coming in mixed. An 'incident' at Watford Junction – either a suspected bomb or a jumper, although, for once, the tannoy-boy didn't say – delayed the 6.13's arrival into Euston by forty minutes, which might easily be taken as prima facie evidence of the gods mocking him, although Jonny had left so early to avoid the shame of Pa in the papers that he still had time to spare. And the train pulled into platform 16, allowing him to leave the station without crossing the concourse, which was definitely a ladder not a snake.

Even so, his mouth still feels painted with wallpaper paste. At the fruit stall on the Euston Road, he judges the produce on its likely juiciness, eventually rejecting bulging figs for a bag of busty plums. In this temperature, it's like eating them from the fridge, but he enjoys the sweet wetness sluicing his gums, the sugary taste like medicine in childhood.

His phone bleats and he juggles it out with chilly, sticky fingers.

'Good morning, sir.'

'Victor.'

'Our good friend Hannah Dunn at Burlingham Marsham Fitch has got another anonymized emergency injunction application. Something of the flavour of the month, it seems. High Court, 11.45. Seeks to retain you on the usual arrangements?'

He has a horrible instinct that the applicant will be Pa but Hannah would surely be too canny for that, and Victor would know the name on the application.

'Do we know the client?' he checks.

'Oh. Er . . . client wishes to remain anonymous until acceptance of brief.'

A politician or a paedophile, then, probably. Or Pa. 'I've got a con on Middlesex District Council at 10.30, haven't I? Could I move that?'

'I'm sure they will understand the diary of someone like yourself, sir.'

'Okay. Fine.'

'Miss Dunn will be in touch about meeting you with the bundle.'

But, as Jonny returns the phone to his anti-theft pocket and shuffles on his glove, he feels a coldness even lower than the weather, shivering as his stomach gives a cement-mixer groan, protesting against his breakfast of a plum chasing two cups of strong coffee. The self-employee's need to be wanted – or greed to be paid – has already destroyed his strategy of invisibility:

a day in chambers among colleagues and clients who would not dare to be sarky about his father. In the corridors of the HCJ and Court 13 itself, no such proprieties will apply. Yet he cannot resist adding to the already pumped green cushion of money underneath him.

He has at least an hour free before he needs to head for either court or the set, depending on the instructions from his flattering employer. In a life timetabled like a train, this gives him on odd sensation of holiday. A walk will clear his head and settle his digestion.

'Plums too sour, young man? Choose some more.'

Geezer 1 has been watching him, surprised to have such a static customer among his rushing clientele.

'What's that? Oh, just thinking.'

With a feeling that his feet are being guided by some inner compass, he is turned, rather than consciously turning, left, back towards Euston. For a moment, he wonders if he is going home, but carries on, past what used to be the women's hospital, where he remembers, on a family theatre trip to London, giggling with his brothers (Christ, almost forty years ago now) at the unwisely worded notice PLEASE GO QUIETLY, aimed at drivers and pedestrians rather than patients. He checks the portion of the wall where his memory places the sign but there is no trace of it.

To the left, the pink-brick levels of the British Library. Reading, he always thinks, will be for his retirement. Although he prides himself on his memory – a barrister's asset – he can summon no picture of what was on this site before the BL. He crosses Euston Road at the junction where, in his college days, the student-insurance company stood, and, with an understanding that he is resuming routes programmed into him long ago, heads between the gardens and the halls of residence.

Jonny had come to London as a reject, disappointing Pa by failing to follow him to Oxford. He remembers being ragged at Wellington that he must be truly stupid if his father, already a shadow minister then, couldn't swing him into the alma pater.

317

Hughes-Parry, on the left, where he had sex for the first time. A third-floor room, he thinks, facing the gardens. He stops and looks up and, if this were a film, the bricks would shimmer and dissolve, revealing younger, unknown actors playing Jonny and Harry (for Harriet) Fraser-Lewis, a Geography fresher he'd met through the UCL Tory Soc. The shock of her black-bearded Georgina, marine tang and hot, slippery hollow, where he spilled within seconds into the sheath she'd insisted on, even though she was also on the pill. Blood on the rubber when he pulled out of her; his first and only virgin. Harry had always been organized. She had chosen him to pop her – perhaps because he'd pretended to be an experienced lover from a fictional summer romance – and then announced that she was ready, after three months, to move on to a second-year mathematician she'd met in Drama Soc. Jonny had Dobsoned and cried himself dry for two weeks, until he met Vicky Bellows, a Historian who introduced him, miraculously, to Mivvies and to cowgirl, driving against him as she sat astride.

He used to smuggle Vicky into Commonwealth Hall, at the far end of the gardens, where Jonny's haunted walk has taken him now. It was an all-male residence and girls had to be signed in and out in a ledger with a biro tied by string to the wooden entry hut, containing a revolving squad of hairy-eared blokes assumed to be war veterans. But visiting sisters, Christian Soc celibates or Commonwealth fellows going to spend the night at their girlfriends' more liberal residences could be prevailed upon to scribble a false out-time for surreptitious stopovers such as Vicky. In the second year, he met Elisabeth ('Libby to Everyone') Pardoe at a hunt ball in Dorset, disengaged himself from Vicky after a two-term overlap, and the rest is their story. Two years ago, he looked up both his UCL girlfriends on Facebook, our dangerous wormhole to the past. Harry was married to a diplomat and had four children. Vicky had vanished into a husband's surname, offline anonymity or, a statistical possibility, death. How different – he is not saying better – would his life have been with either of them?

Apart from more window bars and security cameras, the buildings are as he remembers them and still house students, though the racial mix seems greater, he notices, from the early risers unchaining bikes at the racks outside. Looking up at the sites of his sensual education, he thinks that there ought to be blue plaques.

At the end of the street, he glances left to the concrete terracing of the Brunswick, with that cinema where he watched French films to impress Vicky, then turns right, his old route to lectures, past the turn to the Law faculty building in Endsleigh Gardens, with its moot court, where he discovered the desire and vanity to be a barrister, confirming his intimation, from school and varsity drama, that he turned into a preferable person when he raised his voice in public.

Lazily taking taxis means he rarely walks in London and, if he does, on a court day, heads straight down Upper Woburn Place to the Strand. The last time he was in Gordon Square was a memorial service, at the chapel on the corner, for their class's most influential professor.

The junction has been pedestrianized now, with wooden seats and benches, a version of the urban beachfront in Times Square. Three classic red call-boxes stand in a line. Were they here before? He has memories of telephoning Harry and Vicky to make arrangements after lectures. But why three? Although, in those ancient-history days when people clocked the position of the nearest telephone like the weak-bladdered seeking public conveniences, he remembers long impatient queues to use the scarlet Tardises, the communal wail of dismay when the occupant pushed more coins in.

In sardonic comment on his nostalgic flashback, the iPhone bleeps inside his coat. He's set the tone to loud for the solicitor's call. But when he knocks his glasses on to his forehead and squints at a screen dazzled by low winter sun, he sees an email. It's from Plum.

Dadzee, you're a sleb. C this xxxxxx

Thirty grand a year on their education and they couldn't be

more illiterate if you'd just left them on a curb in Westbury Flats when they were five. Beneath his daughter's line of crosses and hearts, there's one of those blue strings of symbols and numbers that he knows to click.

If he'd been sent a shot of himself Dobsoning or in the middle of a Smedgewick, he couldn't have been more shocked. A reddened, twisted face he reluctantly identifies as his own is seen in profile screaming at a teenage girl who looks terrified and near tears. By pressing several buttons in succession, he cancels first the sound and then the picture, but not before he sees that the video has been given a title line in fancy writing:
GINGA WHINGA – WATER DICK!

His phone bleeps four times as he holds it: Tilly, Hugo, Simon Lonsdale, Tom Rutherford. From the question- and exclamation marks in the headers, he can see that all are forwarding film of his strop in the shop. Does no one in the world do any fucking work any more? Do they just wing humiliating videos around the globe?

Counsel in his own defence, he understands that, for the moment, outside of his children and supposed friends, he is just an anonymous posh twat confirming centuries of class prejudice. The crisis will come when the papers spot the connection between the fuming QC and the disgraced Tory grandee.

He fears he might actually be sick on the white stone of the pedestrian zone but, by tensing his belly, he turns the rictus into a burp that shudders his torso. Clearing the screen of the breeding sneers against him, he returns his last-received call.

'Mr Crossan!' says Victor, in a voice that always suggests a spine of parade-ground straightness.

'Look, Victor, bit of a squiggle on the injunction one. Just cracked a crown on some bloody breakfast bap. So detour to Harley Street, find out if my chap can see me pronto. But going to have to write off the morning anyway.'

'Sorry to hear that, sir. Teeth can be a bit of a circumstance. I'll make the necessary rearrangements. Maybe give me a bell later when you're back in circulation.'

'Yes. I'm sorry.'

With a sudden worry that his legs are going to buckle, Jonny shuffles, on numb feet, towards the wooden chairs. In relief at reaching them, he sits down with a speed that jars his spine. The phone again. *Hannah Dunn*, obviously not intercepted yet by Victor. He allows it to ring out and go to voicemail.

In the thirty years since he graduated, he can never remember being in London without an appointment to keep. Is this how it feels to be sacked or retired? Flexing feeling into his legs, he stands and walks slowly past the English building towards Tottenham Court Road.

He plays age's mournful game of what used to be there in his day. The long glass frontage of the bookshop is unchanged, although Waterstones now, not Dillon's. He remembers getting hammered on nearly intravenous Boddingtons in the pub on the left. The American Church, with its concrete garden painted with graffiti, is a fixed landmark and Heal's, among the retailers, has survived the many recessions. But the Jonny Crossan who walked here most days between the ages of eighteen and twenty-two could not have imagined the colonization by coffee shops: rival brands side by side by side, like banks.

The luxury of having time to look tussles with the pain of totting up times lost. Another long sequence of bleeps from his chest, like a heart monitor. A stream of emails with attachments and hyperlinks. Tilly, Lucas, various barristers with whom he fights a not-entirely-jokey rivalry. The only surprise is that Dunster hasn't twitted him yet. Ginga Winga, Shop Bloke, Waterman, Queeny Counsel is how he will be known for ever now online. And the worst is yet to come. He is astonished that most of those forwarding the film seem either pleased or at worst mildly teasing that he is being ragged internationally as a prat. He is sculpting an opinion about the impossibility of shame in the modern world, until he remembers that his father has disproved this view.

Jonny swivels and walks, quicker than his body's spirit-level wants, back towards the places that taught him law. He turns left down Gordon Street, passing the chapel and the Williams Library, where the brainy totty went, alongside the Bloomsbury Theatre (the Collegiate then), where he played a doddering nobleman in *Volpone* (always cast far in advance of his years), past the Department of Nanotechnology, an unknown subject when he was here, and the Student Union, a den of undergraduate Trotskyism he rarely entered.

Now Euston Station, for the second time in two hours. To avoid the concourse, he puts on his long-distance goggles and, through the sun-sparkled glass, scans the departure boards from the burger-and-pasty court outside.

Apart from the snow delay coming home from Morocco, which he considers an act of God, he cannot remember missing a day of a case, the result of a sense of duty combined with a robust immune system, although admittedly assisted by judges' short hours and long holidays. So, for the first time, he can apply to himself a phrase he has only used mockingly of others. Crying Off.

The three next trains all stop at Watford Junction. How odd that Watford, a place that he has never visited nor would ever want to, has come to play such a significant part in his life.

*

On their holidays in America, crossing a border always felt like a big deal, the state-lines firmly marked on the rental car map. But then people there wore their addresses like a badge – 'We're the Jacksons from New Hampshire,' strangers on trains and planes would identify themselves – and ran the states like little nations, with their own taxes, police forces and sports teams with silly nicknames. 'Hiya. We're the Lonsdales from Buckinghamshire' seems an impossible English phrase.

Tasha has driven the Disco through three counties in a quarter of an hour and, although each has a road sign welcoming her to the new territory – Buckinghamshire, Oxfordshire, Northamptonshire – there's no sense of being somewhere else: the same farmed fields, bypasses and signs at roundabouts pointing to superstores.

In the local shop last week, she noticed for the first time a line on the Shop-and-Scan stand saying that her registration details would be recognized at any store. So she asked Bruce to direct her out of state and, after following his confident Aussie directions, now pulls into another red-brick bungalow with green-on-white signage, almost indistinguishable from the one two miles from her house. And the check-it-yourself welcome board, with its hanging handsets, is also identical. Max Dunster would bang on about brand familiarity.

Even so, she swipes her card in the expectation of being prevented, but the screen quickly blinks WELCOME, MRS NATASHA LONSDALE and a zapper in the top row flashes. Almost three decades previously, the first time she bought a pregnancy-testing kit, she chose a chemist miles from home and filled the basket with innocuous smellies first. She adopts the same strategy now, piling fruit and vegetables into her jute bag before sidling into the Health and Wellbeing aisle and slipping a Blue Line Predictor under the bags of apples and potatoes.

The first of her secret missions accomplished, she slightly relaxes and finds herself in the World Cuisine aisle. After packing neatly in her bags previously unfamiliar pastas, pancakes, spices, rices, dried fruits and roots, she heads to Fine Wines. Retail Therapy.

*

Jenno is about to turn the ignition in the shopping Beetle when, remembering the show-off contest over clothes and cars that events at the school tend to become, she switches to the newest Freelander.

On the tuner, she chooses Radio 2. Ken Bruce. She's moving away when she sees Alice scuttling across the courtyard, having just come out of her hutch. Jenno winds down the window.

'I've left you a note on the kitchen table, Alice. I've got to go to the children's school.'

'Sure. Just checking you know I'm away after lunch today?'

The roster is on her diary app, so she can't be sure, but they generally don't let the girls go until after they've done the children's tea on a Friday. 'Did I know that, Alice?'

'Yes.' *Yees*. The value of Antipodean nannies in not giving your kids foreign intonations works fine except for positive responses. 'I'm going to the theatre?'

'Really?'

'Yes. With Abby? Who Mrs Crossan has? Mr Crossan got the tickets. Mr Dunster said it would be fine.'

'Did he?'

The help learned the same tricks as the children: if it's anything controversial, ask absentminded Daddy.

'Okay. Well, I suppose it's fine. There's a stew in the freezer I can heat up for tea.'

When Dr Welling's secretary telephoned to ask if she could drop by in the next couple of days, she was convinced it would be about Jamie, whose homework has become a battlefield each weekend. He has stopped bringing home the diary that lists assignments by subject. Now what he's due to do by Monday morning is only tearfully revealed deep into Sunday evening when she questions how he has so much time for the PS3.

Then what should be early bath and bed before the return to school becomes a tortuous two hours of English, or sort-of-English ('Write a letter from one character in *Romeo and Juliet* to another') wrenched from him as if he lacks the native language, then French reading delivered as if the words are poison pellets that might burst on his lips.

Jamie complains that everyone in his class is cleverer than him and he's probably right. He owes his place in the top stream not to examination scores but to a theory, advanced by his father and for the moment agreed by the head teacher, that he might benefit from being stretched. But this academic elasticity has not paid dividends and Jenno increasingly feels that he might benefit from lower expectations.

After a status game of whose diary was the biggest nightmare, they settled on Friday at eleven. As when ringing the surgery to arrange to discuss test results, she gave Mrs Diamond opportunities to reveal how serious the problem was, but she proved smoothly neutral, a veteran of discretion.

Jenno has not told her husband she is going to see Dr Welling. Max is exhausted and distracted at the moment, the company's North American expansion taking all his energy. Some mornings, she has to shake him awake after the back-up alarm has gone off. In truth, she is happy to be discussing Jamie's academic record alone, sometimes worrying that Max is too tough on their son, as his own father probably was on him. It is her job, she thinks, to break this chain of testosterone intolerance. But, if Jamie has to drop into what her husband calls the 'dunce dump', this demotion will be easier to sell retrospectively. In Welling's office, Max's bullish insistence on his children's possibilities might earn another term's reprieve. As a precaution, she scheduled the head for a morning when she knew he'd be in London; another meeting on the US drive.

Although Westbury Park lacks quite the history or buildings of an Oundle, Dr Welling's office seems closely modelled on Dr Thomas Arnold's, at least as Jenno knows it from the TV version of *Tom Brown's Schooldays*. It is dominated by an open black-iron grate, once presumably for the barbecuing of juniors, stacked with a smokey wood fire this still-cold morning. The three walls without windows are jaggedly crammed with various sports teams – mainly rugby, except for a few netball and hockey – peering with teenage gawkiness through picture-glass that flames with late winter sun. Jenno wonders if the squad-photos are rotated to include the offspring of visitors to the office who might prove lucrative to the school.

A desk with the heft of a high altar stands opposite a nook of four over-stuffed armchairs in fabric striped at the gentle end of the blue spectrum. These seating arrangements must be intended to allow the head to consult with a child and both parents but are only half-employed in this conference. Is it a bad or good sign that Jamie has not been asked to join them?

Dr Welling is late forties, with the firm face and body of a jogger. This tightness emphasizes his eyes, giving him a look of constant slight surprise that he doubtless puts to disciplinary advantage. Libby, who is chair of what Jonny calls the Pov Com, has described him as fanciable. To Jenno, the general effect is managerial rather than donnish, but education, like all businesses these days, is most keen to project efficiency.

Mrs Diamond serves scalded, scented tea (supermarket Lapsang?), in thin china cups with fiddly handles, then retreats and leaves them.

'Thank you for coming in, Mrs Dunster.'

'Mrs Diamond didn't say what it was about.'

'No.'

'To be honest, I have been wondering for some time if Jamie might be struggling . . .'

'What? Really? No, he's a great kid.' She tries not to flinch visibly at the goat-word. 'Rosie as well. Don't quote me on this but it would be a major surprise if they both left prize-giving empty-handed in July.'

Jenno has never imagined circumstances in which the news that her children are doing well at school might be ominous. But, if everything is tickety in that department, why is she here?

'Frankly, we've tried to contact Mr Dunster using most of the communication methods yet devised: paper and cyberspace. Actually, not all, I admit. Does it make me a bad person that I prefer to leave *tweeting* to the birds?'

Jenny tries to remember how she laughed at favourite Victoria Wood routines and to reproduce the sound perfectly.

'Though, joking aside, Mrs Dunster, we did need to have this conversation. So, when your husband failed to reply, over quite some time, we eventually tried you.'

Her inner feminist protests: 'Do you always talk to the father first?'

'Oh, well. Look . . .' In the conversational ping-pong, she has won the point. 'It was simply that Mr Dunster had been the point of contact on a couple of other matters. And, in as much as this matters, his name is on the bills and the cheques.'

Even though the head's authority has been challenged, his voice and eyes are kindly. She is frightened by the sudden feeling that she is someone who merits gentle handling.

'I wondered if perhaps you and Mr Dunster were having *difficulties*. It's something we sometimes have to be aware of, dealing with so many family units.'

Another yuck phrase. There is a smug game she has played with the school handbook: noting the pupils whose parents have two separate addresses. Ridiculous, as a second wife, but she regards hers as the only family Max has had.

'Oh, do you mean . . . ? No, no, not at all. I think Max has got his head down with his business at the moment. The children always say you could . . .' – she is going to use a metaphor about a naked woman walking past, but the beak's office always feels like a kind of church – ' . . . you could wave a giant slice of cake in front of his face when he's hammering on his laptop and he wouldn't notice.'

'Ha!' The spoken-out laugh of someone whose job involves pretending to be amused. 'And how *is* your husband?'

The emphasis is unsettling.

'Oh, he's fine, I think . . .' She instantly regrets the qualification.

'*Really?* Oh, good.'

'It's just, as I say, that he tends to get a bit caught up in the business. I've actually offered my services as an unpaid secretary but Maxie' – she calculates that the pet-name might make them sound closer – 'has never been much of a delegator.'

'Right? He's obviously been able to do more work than he thought he would. And I always feel I would want to if it happened to me. When staff have been affected, they've tended to take extended leave. But then teaching gets you in the balls of the feet and the back of the throat.'

She has always assumed that this predicament – in which

another speaker assumes she knows something – would involve the revelation that Max was having an affair. So she has no mental protection against this misunderstanding. As a viewer of the scene on TV, she would scream at the screen 'the husband's secretly ill!' but, finding herself inside the dialogue, is still driven by the demon of appearances.

She needs time and information and the best way of achieving both is to let Welling go on speaking.

'My mother-in-law, in the same *situation*,' he says in soft tones perfected by a profession in which death stalks students or their parents, 'had chemo followed by laser surgery. To no long-term avail, unfortunately. But there's so much more they can do now than there used to be.'

She has practised many times – which spouse hasn't, especially after Bill Adamson? – being told that Max is seriously ill but, in these rehearsals, the news has always come from a consultant or her husband.

'In a school of so many students, there will be *occurrences* of this kind, statistically if nothing else. We make psychological and, to a degree, financial provision. In fact, as you may know, there's a deal with an insurance company to offer a tailored fee-protection policy to all new parents, but Mr Dunster was not one of those who took it up. And it's clearly right that we offer the flexibility of fee deferral. But, even in the depth of sympathy we feel, there comes a point when we have to look again at what can only ever be a temporary arrangement . . .'

Jenno tries to remember, from the articles in the paper about miracle recoveries or tragic deaths, which one was chemo followed by laser. Pancreas? Kidney? He has been looking tired and possibly thinner, but Max has always been one of those slightly nervy fat-burners, and she put it down to how hard he's been working. And, though there's been a bit more distance recently in bed and elsewhere, she would surely have noticed if he was being attached to a bag of poison every few days.

Does tea, the fabled English remedy in these cases, actually work? She never takes sugar but should she now? She gulps some down – *aagh!* – before it is cool enough to be drunk so quickly.

'Oh dear, Mrs Dunster. I fear your husband hasn't told you . . .'

'No, he has. I just . . . I didn't know how much *you* knew.'

'I don't mean that he hadn't told you about the cancer. *Obviously*. I mean about the little deal we did. I'm not entirely surprised. Pride shouldn't come in to these things but it does.'

Dying and a double liar.

'No. Tell me.'

The head teacher's manner changes to that of a witness in court: 'In October, I asked Mr Dunster to come to see me. He'd missed – by quite a distance, actually – the deadline for the first term's fees for Jamie and Rosie . . .'

'We always pay annually, don't we? Upfront.'

'You had, in the past. Not this year. But we offer a termly option, and so someone who misses that first payment is technically only in default for Michaelmas. After a few emails had gone astray, he came in to see me. Sitting in that chair where you are now, I believe.'

Is that supposed to make her feel better? Your husband might keep tumours and bankruptcy from you, but, when it comes to choosing furniture, you have a telepathic understanding.

'When Mr Dunster told me that his income was interrupted and explained the sad reason, I gave him the option, which we always keep in the kitbag for such cases, of paying for that term backwards, rather than forwards. I'm afraid he's now missed that deadline and is also in default for the Lent fees. As I say, the school tries to do everything it can . . .'

'Yes, thank you, yes . . .'

Like a singer struggling in the wrong pitch, her voice seems strained and unfamiliar to her. This is a tune – subservient, on the verge of begging – she has not used since, well, since that time she thought that Max was going to break off the engagement. Having money means being on the top in conversations.

'But, with your husband ignoring messages . . .'

'Yes. I think you're right, Dr Welling, it will be pride with him. With a lot of men, it's a big thing to be . . . the . . . provider . . .'

'I want you to know that these conversations are one of the hardest things I do . . .'

'Thank you. Yes.' The desperate punctuation of another gulp of tea she doesn't taste. 'What do we do now?'

'Is your husband responding to the treatment?'

'I . . . look, I . . .'

'These are difficult things to talk about, I know. I should say that my office is a confessional, in the strictest Roman Catholic sense. The arrangement we made is known only to myself and the bursar. Jamie's and Rosie's teachers don't even know their dad is ill.'

'Look, what can I say, Dr Welling? To look at him, you wouldn't even know he'd been having treatment.'

'That's very hopeful. And, from what you say, he's managing to get back to work. Mrs Dunster, can I leave you to talk to your husband about how to proceed? If funds are still . . . stubborn, there is a Hardship Committee, run by the Friends of Westbury Park. Appeals are discreet, grants speedy and secret. You'd be amazed if I told you some of the kids who have had them. Although, of course, you'd have to shoot me if I did.'

Her stored Victoria Wood laugh again. But this lifebelt is thrown on to a dangerous undertow.

'Yes. I'm vaguely aware that a friend of ours might be on it?'

'Names and addresses withheld, as I said. But there'd be a lot more painful conversations without them. It's not giving too much away to say that they dip into their own pockets. One of the leading lights said to me recently that those who have had good luck with money should help out those who have been unlucky.'

She can almost hear Libby Crossan saying it.

'I'll talk it over with Max. I'm really sorry about this, Dr Welling.'

He spreads his hands in the don't-mention-it gesture. As Welling shows her out, she notices that the hands of his fancy grandfather clock are joining neatly at noon. A meeting that had seemed to run as long as she needed has lasted the length that he planned. She speed-walks to the car, in case Rosie and Jamie, switching lessons or heading for lunch, see her.

In the car, she texts Max, experimentally: *How are you feeling? xx*

Almost immediately, the incoming ping: *In meeting. But I'm good. Why? xx*

The trembling in her fingers making it hard to type: *I love you xx*

Again, the signature sound-effect of the twenty-first century: *Me too, silly xx*

She knows the school route well enough to find home by instinct, and to think. Twenty years earlier, Jennifer Timms had been handed by her headmistress a silver cup, acned with verdigris, for Practicality and she remains a champion of the craft.

On a trembling shelf beneath the chaos in her brain, she places the two possibilities. Either Max has been pretending to Welling that he has cancer or pretending to her that he hasn't. As it is clearly preferable for a man to lie to a slightly creepy head teacher than to his wife, she favours the first explanation, but knows its implications are hardly reassuring.

In sickness and in health. For richer and for poorer. In her dilemma, the words of the marriage service resemble a multiple-choice exam. Tick one in each box: poorer and in health, or in sickness and richer.

No, that is the point. Sickness and richer. If Max really has cancer, there would be no immediate financial implications; they have private health insurance and his colleagues could cover during treatment which, anyway, he would need to have received in conditions of extreme secrecy.

There can only be one reason that her husband is lying about dying. Poorer and in health.

*

Even the front-of-store staff seem to have a corporate uniformity. The lanky grinner in the striped apron at the Shop-and-Scan desk could plausibly be the brother of the one in her branch.

'Everything scanned all right this morning, madam?'

Tasha pats one of the four scratchy bags in her trolley and meets his gleaming eyes.

'Yes, thank you. Fine.'

She hands him the scanner, which he pops into the port beside his till, with a languorous smoothness in the flick of his wrist that feels mildly flirtatious. But instead of the display panel on his till filling with the green total of the prices she's tapped in, the handset shakes and flashes in its scabbard.

'Oh, dear. Not your morning, madam,' frowns the boy manager. 'Nothing to worry about, but you've qualified for one of the random tally scans built in to the system. Have you had one before?'

Almost. 'Er, no.'

'I'm afraid it's a bit of a bore because I have to rescan everything by hand. So if you can bear to keep me company for a while. Or there's a seating area over by the cafe. Entirely up to you.'

A globule of sweat, feeling like a bursting boil, rolls from beneath her bra-strap and splashes against the band of her pants.

'Entirely up to you, madam,' he repeats.

'Oh. You know what? I've just remembered there are one or two things I've forgotten. Stupidly. Why don't I just go and get them now and come back?'

The brightness of his smile surprises her. 'Well, that's perfect, then. You go and pick up the bits you've missed – basket over there, if you want – while I do this. I can scan the rest in for you at the end.'

Tasha reaches for the trolley but he's already pulling it to his side of the counter with one strong hand. *Please, Lord, let me be not afraid.*

*

The final ten appointments of the morning are all with patients who believe that they have The Killer Bug, only one of whom possibly has. Showing out Ali Rawlinson, who has resentfully accepted the refusal of a prescription for Tamiflu, Emily is surprised to see Jonny Crossan sitting in an otherwise-empty waiting room, distractedly flicking through an old *Hello*. She has no memory of ever having seen him as a patient and assumed him to be on Surinder Rafi's list, if he stooped to the NHS at all.

Jonny doesn't spot her, which she marks as significant. She has talked, on emergency call-outs, to cops, who agreed that, in these jobs, training gives way at a certain point to instinct. A detective, interviewing a suspect, develops a sense for whether someone is lying. Her own sensitivity is to the dying. She won't, at a glance, go that far with Jonny. But his waxy skin and skittery eyes signal that something is wrong.

Emily goes over to Gabby at the desk and in her long-polished mutter says: 'I had Mrs Rawlinson down as my last.'

'Yes.' An equally practised whisper. 'I told him you were fully booked. When I asked if it was an emergency, he said it "might be". I don't like to . . .'

The dread of not anticipating a catastrophe.

'No, no. That's fine.'

'His name's—'

'I know.'

Walking out into the waiting area, she lifts her voice to the other end of its pitch and calls: 'Jonathan Crossan. Consulting Room A.'

Eyes that seem almost teary look up at her from an article about the wedding of two people with implausibly orange skin and impossibly white teeth.

Jonny follows her in and seems unsure what to do. He is probably used to the sort of doctors who come to him, or to those who will have plump sofas in third-floor drawing rooms. Emily has to point to the hard-backed chair and say 'sit down'. Doing so, Jonny fusses with balancing his briefcase against the wall.

'Thank you for seeing me, Doc,' he says, in a voice far short of his typical vigour. 'I promise it's not my Walter.'

'I lose track, Jonny. Is that what we doctors call a penis? I get confused.'

'It's terribly simple.' But there is a disconnect between the familiar words and their delivery, like a dissident singing a national anthem. 'A Dobson is what I do before breakfast – if Mrs Crossan is away. A Smedgewick is what I do after breakfast, regardless.'

'I feel sorry for your matron at Harrow. Did you all have different words for everything?'

'I think it was a me thing really.'

'Anyway, whatever you call it, and whatever it's got, is irrelevant to the NHS,' she says, softening her own voice to meet his unfamiliar vulnerability. 'Now, Jonny, I can swing it either way, but are you actually on our list?'

'Oh, yes. We're registered. It's true I've never actually been in here. To be perfectly honest, I have always been rather of the opinion that, if one can afford to throw money at the problem, one should.'

'Okay. That's fine. And what problems have there been?'

'What?'

'I need to know if anyone is treating you for anything at the moment? Or has recently?'

'Oh. Ah. No. Not really. I'm one of those chaps that just gets on with it, I suppose. The set, er, chambers pays for an MOT once a year – drink a bit less, exercise a bit more, which

334

I expect they say to everyone – and arranges a flu jab every winter. Same logic, in both cases. Never good to change horses in the middle of a trial. Spot of acid reflux, occupational curse, apparently, of people who stand on their hind legs for a living: teachers, actors, silks. Chap in Harley Street gave me some pills and told me to go easy on rich food. But I find poor food doesn't really agree with me.'

The last line the authentic Jonny Crossan. But. 'But you're here today. And you don't look yourself. So what is it?'

'Doc . . . I rather feel I should call you Doc . . .'

'Lots of patients do. Sure.'

'It's a few things, really, coming together. And not in a good way.' As a friend, she would have rolled her eyes; as a doctor, she's impassive. Listen to the story. 'Sorry. The last few weeks, I've had trouble sleeping . . .'

Rest seems to be one of the few human activities he doesn't have his own word for.

'Trouble falling asleep? Or waking up and not being able to . . . ?'

'Both. Neither. I mean, some nights I'm not convinced I sleep at all.' Generally an exaggeration: sleep-clinic trials have shown that some 'total insomniacs' are averaging four or five hours. 'Funny thing, until recently, I had absolutely no idea that the church clock tolls every hour of the night.' Well, okay. 'And I – oh, Lord, you're going to go and get a jacket that ties at the back – I, well, I keep having this feeling that something terrible is going to happen . . .'

Which it generally will, with the world as it is. 'Tell me how that feels.'

'Oh. Utter funk. Heart banging like it wants to be let out. Sopping armpits. Spaghetti legs. This morning, on the station, I had a panic I was going to faint and go under the train . . .'

The GP's two daily nightmares: failing to spot something that will kill someone, failing to spot patients who will kill themselves.

'Faint?'

'What? Oh, yes. That I might fall on the track. Don't worry. I'm not going to throw myself under a Pendolino or something.'

Anxiety / Suicidal? Emily pencils on a pad in her deliberately incomprehensible scribble.

'And, when you have these feelings, do you worry that you're going to die?'

Jonny's mouth gapes open.

'Bloody hell, Doc. What do you think I've got?'

Emily laughs genuinely: a rare event in a consultation these days, when everything said has to be legally defensible if necessary.

'No, Jonny. I'm not suggesting you've got anything. I need to know if fear of death is one of the anxieties you've been having.'

'Well, we've all had the 3 a.m. heebies, haven't we? Got to be damn religious or bloody thick not to. But, yes, this has gone beyond that. I've started trying to get trains that come into a special platform – Harry Potter or what? – because there's one where you don't have to come out of the main entrance.'

'Oh, right.' *Tom said something*, no, no, 'And is that so you don't have to mix with other passengers?'

'What? Oh, I'm not that much of a snob, Doc. Someone told me – in fact, it might have been Tom – that the next big terrorist threat was a Mumbai-style massacre, machine guns at a railway station or shopping centre. Which is half good news because I wouldn't be seen dead in a shopping centre. But the word *concourse* . . . I don't know. Suddenly I couldn't walk across one. Damn stupid stuff but . . .'

'No. If it's what you feel, it's real.'

Jonny's uncharacteristic failure to snort at this liberal sentiment is perhaps the most alarming symptom so far. She underlines *anxiety* on her pad. And then writes: *catastrophizing.* This is as clear a case of cognitive distortion as she has seen. She experiences the guilty relaxation and relief that come from a quick and unambiguous diagnosis, regardless of the discomfort to the sufferer.

'Jonny, I just wondered in the church on Christmas Day, when you did your reading. Were you feeling anxious then?'

His face telegraphs methodical flicking through a mental calendar. 'Yes. Damn good. Can't hide anything from you. Yes, I was pretty convinced I was going to keel over in the pulpit.'

With dread, she asks the next question, framing it as clinically as possible: 'Any episodes of sexual dysfunction?'

'Hardly, Doc.' He laughs. 'With the emphasis on the *hard*.'

Emily waits.

'Well, actually a few times recently, I've, you know, wondered if we had to. Or, to be completely honest, if I could. Don't tell Libs, for the love of Allah.'

'You know me. I don't tell anyone anything. Look, Jonny, I just need to do your blood pressure . . .'

He offers his right arm with a childish compliance, again unlike him, although he is more his old self in clocking her cleavage as she leans over.

'Do you happen to know what it generally is?'

'Ye-es. These Top Man MOTs at the set, they send us a folder afterwards. Liver, ticker, all these numbers. The BP, as you lot say, I always think of as a bit of a thrashing in a 20-over game. 126/78. That sort of ballpark.'

138/82 today. Better than she might have expected, with him so visibly agitated. She deflates and releases the sleeve.

'Okay, Jonny, we can start doing something about this today. You've been experiencing what we colloquially call panic attacks. Anxiety is a natural human response to danger or challenge. If we didn't have any anxiety at all, then we'd be . . .'

'Max Dunster!'

'You said that. I was going to say reckless to the genuine levels of risk around us. But, in some – actually, *many* – people, that natural response gets out of hand, becomes what we call an anxiety disorder.'

She decides not to use the word *catastrophizing* to Jonny. Recent human evolution has caused skins to get thinner, patients taking diagnosis as criticism.

'I see, Doc. And can anything be done for me? Locked up? Lobotomized?'

'Don't be silly. I think, longer term, we might need to look at CBT . . .'

'Christ Almighty!' Jonny looks as if he is having a distress episode in front of her. 'Coronary Bypass . . .'

'No, no. That's CBG.' But a serious hypochondriac, clearly, his memory filled with medical acronyms. 'CBT is cognitive behavioural therapy. With a counsellor, you identify situations that cause anxiety and learn coping strategies. Fears aren't facts and we can teach your body that.'

Jonny makes his nasty-nappies face. 'Sounds a bit Islington placenta-eating, all that.'

'You need to do something, Jonny. How long have you been having these feelings?'

'You're so different from us briefs, aren't you? You can actually ask questions to which you don't know the answer. I . . . Christmas comes round every few minutes when you get to our age, doesn't it? Certainly, to be perfectly honest, several months.'

'Why didn't you see – someone, it didn't have to be me – earlier?'

Jonny leans forward, staring at the floor, a reprimanded child. When he looks up, his face bears the twisted rictus of recognition he adopts when Libby rebukes him for rudeness.

'Doc, bloody silly, I know. But my licence.'

A daily curse of her surgeries. Diabetics lying to her about hypos, patients with blurred eyes or slurred words desperate not to be diagnosed with a TIA – all in case the DVLA takes away their car keys. But. But.

'But we're nowhere near – not remotely – your being declared unable to drive.'

'What? Oh. No. I can get a chauffeur if it comes to that. My *weapons* licence, sweetie. You think, one hint of being a nutter and Plod's at the door demanding the keys to the gun cupboard.'

'You're not a nutter and . . .' A nudging worry: would she

give this much leeway to a stranger? 'Unless your hands shake on the . . .'

'Never an issue. Shooting's my relaxation. It's work and so on seems to bring this on.'

The diagnosis is over. A Peter-and-Paul morning: she will start introducing Jonny Crossan to the drug she has been weaning Becca Adamson off. *Zoplicone*, 10 mg, short term, with an encouragement to CBT. But there is one more area she wants to explore, based on her knowledge of the patient.

'Jonny, how much coffee do you drink on an average day?'

'Crikey. It was a bashing on the claret I expected. Well, I . . . more since we got the eyetie machine, I suppose. Have one after my shower in the morning before I leave. A cup of Virgin juice on the train, generally. We've got a Berlusconi brewer in the set as well, so I get through a few pellets there. At the courts, when the jury's out, we're in the caff. Couple more Italianos after dinner at home . . .'

'Okay. I think we're talking ten, twelve cups, are we? I might want to take a peek at your urine . . .' She sees Jonny thinking of a gag and then abandoning it. 'Caffeine can worsen symptoms of anxiety. You might think about cutting back.'

'Ooh-er. Mrs Crossan won't be happy. I think she's got a thing for the coffee guy.'

'That's a bit of an epidemic round here.'

She struggles with whether to introduce private knowledge, then does. 'Jonny, is any of this brought on by the video?'

'Bugger! Libby's shown you our videos?'

'No. The—'

'Yes, I know. The shop. I suppose there was bound to be an actual *water*-gate eventually. You've seen it?'

'The kids sent . . .'

'I'm not going to deny that it felt as if I'd been . . . I'm not going to say raped.'

'Good.' Which she wouldn't have said to a mere patient. 'Look, I'm going to give you a small dose of something for a short while to take the edge off this. Can you take it easy for a couple of days?'

'I suppose so. Let Britain descend into feral lawlessness.'

'Good. You should. Jonny, it was brave to do this.'

'Bollocks, Doc. How can running to the pill cupboard be brave?'

'Because you have to be strong to admit weakness.'

But she sounds to herself like an American motivational coach and so turns away and emails his prescription to the dispensary.

'Thanks, Doc,' Jonny says as she shows him to the door. Looking out at the empty waiting room, relieved to have completed a long morning's work, Emily remembers that Tasha has not come back. Good. So she isn't pregnant.

*

Max can't believe the bastards have sacked him. Wetness blurs his vision. He turns away, staring through the train window at a smeared, speeding England, flashes of green fields defying the muddied dullness of winter. The header of the message throbs at the top of his inbox:

MAX DUNSTER FIRED DUE TO POOR RESULTS

It's a lunchtime train north, the lull for business travel, so he is one of only three people in First Class. But he checks that none of the others has a line of sight to his screen before clicking open the brutal communication:

Max Dunster has been sacked by the board of directors because of a poor run of results and the club's current league position. The job will now be advertised.

Ungrateful fuckers. League 2 to the Premiership in three successive promotions and only six points off the Europa League qualification places in March. But his mistake was to spend too much money. There's a cheat that Jamie taught him, called Sugar Daddy, which lets you bring in tens of millions of investment, even to a minnow outfit. Max has spent £120 million in three years, against an income of £300,000, and *Football Manager* seems to be calibrated to punish you for such expenditure, even though the game permits the cheat.

In real life, he has never been fired or, really, hired, inheriting Dunster Manor through the inevitability of the sperm circuit. When Max began playing football-management simulation games – because both his sons had them and they seemed a sort of super-Subbuteo, which a man in his fifties could more or less plausibly be seen playing – he never imagined how realistic the emotions would be in steering a virtual version of his nearest proper local team (he considers MK Dons an abhorrence, a London club ludicrously transplanted to Milton Keynes) through the leagues. To his amazement, he has felt sick with nerves before and during games and after defeats. And now this sacking – previously, it has always been his own decision to find another team – feels as he imagines it must do when someone is, in that absurd euphemism, let go. Max cannot remember ever sacking anyone significant himself. He had been reaching such a level of irritation with Bill Adamson's grannyish attitude to corporate finance that a difficult conversation might have been necessary but then his FD's blood cells did the job.

His iPhone vibrates and flashes, the light reflecting in the train window. Beside the icon of a telephone trembles the name: Steve Pearson. Too distracted by the outcome of his fantasy managerial career to address the demands of his actual job, he watches until the name vanishes and is followed by a silent reminder of a voicemail, which he also ignores.

Max flicks back to his final match in charge: a 3–2 away defeat at Newcastle. The match took place on March the 27th, 2015. By using the Super-Fast facility, the seasons speed past. But, playing in the future, there's always a little shiver on your birthday. Getting ahead of yourself. The fateful fixture against the Magpies was played on the day that Max will be sixty. He tries to imagine himself at that age.

He turns to the window again but, as they come into Buckinghamshire, the frosted fields disappear. The pea-souper he drove through in the morning has never properly lifted. At the station, the platform lights glow fire-bright in the haze. On the platform opposite is an advertising hoarding with an oil painting showing horses and wagons striking out towards the mountains. The caption: *If There Are No Profits In One Place, Strike Out For New Territories.* A clever line, he has to admit, making every punter feel like a pioneer. But, in business, you've either got it or you haven't.

*

Dogs are jolly clever. After shouting all around the house, she finally finds Scruff upstairs in the spare-spare bedroom, a place she has never known him go before. He's lying upside down on Hugo's old bed, paws outstretched, bathing in a shaft of warmth. The brainy little thing has worked out that this is where to get the best of the sun, which is finally burning away the morning's fog.

He comes straight round from his dreams of chasing bunny rabbits as soon as Libby says his name and, the minute he sees she's wearing her walkies Puffa and woollen hat, he's off the bed and doing what Jonny calls his porn-star whimper.

'Shhhhhh, poppet!' she says in her doggie voice. 'Master sleeping!'

Scruff looks confused, as well he might. As they tend to go away for every holiday, she can never actually remember her hubcap being here during the day. When the dogs suddenly started their master's-car yaps during lunchtime – another example of canine IQ, this ability to distinguish between different vehicles – and she saw the sportster coming up the hill, her first thought was that he'd lost his job – although could barristers actually get sacked? – because of that hideous shop film people keep sending her. She's had to come off Twitter. But Jonny, when she mentioned it, breezed, 'Oh, that. That will pass. Attention spans are as brief as IQs are low,' which made her worry he had come home sick. Which he is, although thankfully just a 24-hour bug, which the quack at the set has told him he can knock out with sleep and a couple of days off the sauce.

She's been worried that he hasn't been sleeping. Several nights, when she has got up for a 3 a.m. pee – she loves a Nizzarda Limited Edition after supper but it goes right through her – Jonny has been lying awake, although not, as usual, because his telescope is up and ready; he pretends to be asleep, which isn't him. Secretly, she wonders if their swanky coffee machine has made him an insomniac. CappuccinGo has learned a trick from sweet-shops. Humans are in some way rainbow-coded: if offered a variety of colours, they will want to try them all, or most of them, except for browns, brown not being a problem with coffee obviously, but the pellets come in such a lovely range of shiny shades and, some nights after dinner, he's getting through three or four.

When she and Scruff come downstairs into the hall, Colonel is waiting, his tail flapping like, as Jonny says, a dominatrix's whip. Imprinted with the household routines, the dogs are acutely attuned to the possibility of a walk. Once, when on the way to the big deep-freeze, she stopped to pick a mud-turd off Lucas's wellies in the utilities room, both dogs were immediately at her feet, whimpering, knowing that boots meant walkies. Although when she shared this story with The Eight, bloody Simon Lonsdale said that, as the boots were Lucas's, if the pooches were really clever, they would have known he was at school and couldn't take them anywhere. She scribbles a note on the fridge pad – *dog walk with girls XXX* – in case Jonny wakes up while she's gone.

Although they definitely said 2 p.m., and it's not even ten to yet, the other three are all waiting with their dogs straining at the leash – 'Jenno' even looking pointedly at her Patek Philippe – when she pulls into Emily's courtyard. The hill from which they start the walk is decided by an unofficial revolving roster.

'Wait!' she commands, opening the door. Scruff considers ignoring her but eventually settles for just bouncing up and down on the seat. He's becoming almost tameable. Colonel, as ever, waits patiently until she comes round to his side. It's a constant mystery to her quite why he failed Blind-Dog Academy, docility and obedience being his defining characteristics, but the fact that he did has been a sighted family's gain.

'Wow! Another new Disco!' says Jenno, as Libby gets out. A score because, among The Eight, the top dog spot is definitely between them.

'Yes,' Libby smiles. 'Jonny says we're pioneering the concept of the disposable Land Rover. Like plastic razors.'

The joke doesn't go down as well as she'd hoped. There's a definite atmosphere between the other three, or at least Jenno and Tasha, who both seem preoccupied and glum. She wonders if there have been fisticuffs over something.

The rest of them are in their Eskimo clothes. But Jenno is wearing a dark-blue military-style greatcoat (navy army, ha!). Libby's pretty certain it's Versace. Utterly impractical in this kind of mud, which Beauty and Sprout are already kicking up at their mistress in impatience to be off. You can tell a lot about people from the way they name their dogs. Beauty must be the most obvious thing to call a black Lab and Sprout is just bloody silly. Sure, it was cute that toddler Jamie (an oft-told story) thought Max had said the puppy was a 'Jack Brussell', but, to passersby on a walk, it must sound as if Jenno is some batty biddy ordering the grass to grow faster.

While the dogs sniff each others' bums – Tasha's Clooney trying to mount Jenno's Beauty as usual, even though both have had the ops – the girls discuss the pleasures of a bright, crisp winter's day.

'Isn't it lovely when it's like this?' Libby asks.

'The light! Like a Turner!' says Tasha, like someone on that programme where they arse on about the arts.

Having considered but rejected the idea of saying 'Fred Turner? Our plumber?', imagining the sneer from Tasha, Libby slips the rope lead around Colonel's neck and they set off across the Rutherfords' back fields. Four girls, each leading a Labrador and a scruffy snuffler, they make a neat pattern. Too symmetrical, in fact, for Libby, who regrets the fact that Jenno has exactly copied her in dogs, as she has in cars and kitchens and so much else. At least Tash has a spaniel to go with her Lab, while Emily's other dog is their new Labradoodle. A posh mongrel, in the end, but at least it's a darn sight more original than a Jack.

'How's Hector settling in?' she asks Em, as the cross-breed flops around on the slippery ground, like a novice skier.

'Oh, keeping everyone amused. He's like Mr Bean with four legs and a tail.'

Hector is a recent replacement for the Rutherfords' terrier, Fancy, who chased a tempting scent out of the garden and was a hairy omelette on the village road when they found him. Nobody ever knew who the driver was, although Libby has always suspected Max, the speeds he drives.

'Yes. They're funny little things, aren't they?' she agrees. 'But, then, I guess they were probably bred as a joke.'

'Oh. Oh, not really,' says Em, which is as close as she gets to putting you down. She always looks younger on winter walks, with her rat-grey hair hidden in a woolly hat. 'They started in Australia when they were looking for a guide-dog for people with allergies.'

'Didn't the Obamas have to have a hypoallergenic pet?' asks know-all Tasha, cutting in on their conversation. 'Because of one of the girls? A Portuguese water dog?'

'I think so,' says Em. 'Well, they could have had a Labra-doodle instead.'

'Mmm. Can't quite imagine Hector in the White House,' Libby jokes. 'He'd probably wee all over David Cameron's shoes or something. Although who wouldn't, frankly?'

A nice line; she'll use it when she's Tweeting again.

'Girls, girls!' shouts Jenno, who's over by the hedge, where Sprout is crouching to do his duty. 'We agreed we're not going to discuss 'Dave' and his bloody HS2 again until we're sure of the route.'

But Libby tries to imagine what this green sweep of Buck-inghamshire will look like after the carving of the tunnels and cuttings for the new high-speed service to Birmingham. One of the proposed paths for the tracks would make the trains visible and audible from their hills. She must ask J how his pa is getting on with lobbying the government against it, although the silly fool can't have much influence now that he's been caught with his hand in the till.

Libby is struggling to adjust to being a Conservative who hates a Tory (well, half-Tory, which is the problem) government. Cameron hasn't brought back hunting and now he's ravaging the English countryside to make the trains run quicker. How does he sleep at nights? And, anyway, as Jonny says, if you absolutely had to go to fucking Brum, you'd want the train to get there as slowly as possible, wouldn't you?

'Is Jonny okay?' Jenno suddenly asks, back in line now that Sprout is done.

'In what way?' Libby replies. 'Oh, that horlicks with the shop-girl?'

'Oh, no, I . . .'

But she knows that they have talked about it before she arrived, discussing whether to bring it up.

'These things don't last,' she says. 'It will be an actress getting out of a car without her knicks by tomorrow.'

Saint Emily to the rescue, inevitably: 'I think what Jen meant was this thing with his dad? He was in the Radio 4 headlines this morning.'

'Oh, yes, that. I think he's just got his paperwork in a muddle. It will all be sorted. Actually, bit of a novelty for me. I've got Jonny in bed this afternoon.' Seeing the double meaning, she laughs. 'Not in *that* way. No, he came home feeling tired and off his oats.'

Just a teensey bit concerned that Jonny might be going crackers because of his daddy, she's hoping that Emily will take an interest and offer to do a house-call. But Em carries on as if she hasn't heard.

'Clooney!' Tasha shouts, as the spaniel smells sheep in a neighbouring field and hurtles off there. 'Clooney! How dare you? Come back here now.'

346

Clooney, glancing backwards at the treat he's been denied, reluctantly runs back and takes out his aggression by yapping at Emily's Buster.

'Clooney! Leave Buster alone! He's an old man.'

A name chosen because of his bulk and muscularity even as a puppy, Buster now sounds sarcastic when shouted at the lumbering, arthritic animal who stays as slow and close to Emily as if he were still on the lead. His geriatric irritation with the younger dogs yapping at his backside feels poignantly human.

'What is he? Twelve?' Libby checks. 'Eighty-four in doggy years.'

'Same age as Max's mother,' says Jenno. 'Though better company. And, God forgive me, toilet-trained.'

Tasha makes her question-mark face, like a child doing homework. 'I wonder when that started? Multiplying dogs by seven, I mean.'

'I've always assumed—' begins Emily, then has to interrupt herself to shout: 'Hector, Hector, keep up!' The Labradoodle slaloms towards them, stumbling in plough furrows flecked with unmelted ice. 'I've always assumed,' she resumes, 'that it was someone stuck with explaining a pet's death to a child. Ten or Twelve seemed terribly young to a young person, so they found a way of making it seem ancient in human terms?'

But Jenno changes the subject or, perhaps, doesn't. 'Emily? Would it be possible to have cancer without people noticing?'

'Laugh a minute with you, isn't it?' Libby twits her, retching at the stench from the little one, who has been rolling in fox dung, a canine habit inexplicable to her. 'Mummy doesn't want you near her, Scruff.'

Emily stops and puts a hand on Jenno's arm. 'Are you worried about something?' Generally it's Tasha who has the cancer scares.

'What? Oh, no. It's a weird one. Just my sister works with someone who was apparently having treatment for ages without anyone at work or even in their family knowing. I was surprised.'

'Well, that's what happens on *The Big C*,' says Tash, who seems to spend most of her time watching television.

'You know, what would interest me,' Emily says, 'is not just how they stopped their family knowing but why. Do we know that?'

'Oh.' Jenno looks terribly confused; sometimes Libby suspects she isn't very bright. 'Oh, I'm not sure. Not wanting to worry them? Or pride?'

'Mmm. Stupidly, it is still taboo to some people. As to whether you *could* hide it, loss of weight and hair are the main indicators. So I suppose, if someone was only having radiation or had a mild reaction to chemo, it's possible. Some blood cancers, I suppose, can be visually almost asymptomatic.'

'Right. But, er, what also surprised me is – Sprout, Buster doesn't want you doing that! – is that, I mean, have you ever treated a cancer patient who didn't tell their wife? Or husband? It's a bit odd, isn't it?'

'Oh, Jen, you know me. I couldn't tell you if I had or hadn't.'

Two optical illusions are produced by the weather. The trees look filled with blossom, a trick of heavy frost which, as the late sun warms the branches, falls to the ground like snow. And the light remains unexpectedly bright. Even in February, so often the month when the cold really bites, there's a sense of the days lengthening. Libby sometimes tries to imagine the joy of the first people on earth when they realized first that night had an end and then that winter did.

There's a loud bleep from Jenno's pocket and Sprout stops dead, his ears pinned back. The Dunsters used a dog-taser to train him and he thinks he's being zapped. Libby can't believe that Scruff would make that mistake.

Jenno gropes for her phone, pulls off a mitten with her teeth and and stabs at the screen.

'Oh!' she groans.

'What's up, hon?' Libby asks her.

'Maxie just texted to say he'll be late tonight. Another

fucking meeting.' It's the first time she can remember Jenno dropping the f-bomb. 'He's going to kill himself, at this rate.'

A stream borders the bottom field. The Labs, except for the arthritic Buster, the very definition of hang-dog, bound in, followed by the Jack Russells and the spaniel. Hector looks up worriedly at Emily, his frown exactly that of a person wondering what to do.

Something definitely happened earlier. Mrs Lonsdale and Dr Rutherford are usually the tightest two of the four of them but today Tash seems to be trying not to catch Em's eye. There's much less talking than normal, as the girls watch their charges with fond smiles, much as they used to do when the kids were toddlers. Although it has never been discussed among the women, Jonny has teased her that each of them added the yapper to the Lab when they no longer had a baby to care for. She hated him for saying it but cannot deny the observation.

'They have such happy lives, don't they, on the whole?' Libby says. 'I mean, obviously, I've seen the documentaries about rescue dogs. But if they're owned by people like us.'

The simple happiness of dogs always warms her. Look at Scruff now; running around, his bark so like a laugh that he could be Plum or Lucas on Holkham Beach when they were sprogs. Simon Lonsdale insists that owners project human thoughts and feelings on to animals and she would agree when it comes to cats, who are clearly sly creatures trading the occasional stroke for food and shelter until they find somewhere better. Dogs, though, quite clearly have pseudo-human sentiments and even expressions.

'Beauty's incredibly intuitive,' offers Jenno. 'When Max's dad died, she just sat beside him with her paw on his leg. She knew he was sad.'

Tash gives her pig-snort laugh. 'Yeah. Ella did that when Simon got the call about his dad. But then we realized it was teatime.'

Libby can't let Tash get away with this. 'No. They really

know stuff. There was a documentary about dogs who spotted when their owners had cancer . . .'

'Really? Was there?' Jenno interrupts, actually sounding interested for once.

'Yes. They kept pawing and sniffing at the place where the tumour turned out to be.'

Tasha does her Gloucester Old Spot impression again. 'Well, in that case, everyone in our family must have malignant bums.'

The dogs suddenly go haywire, hurtling round in circles, knowing (put that in your pipe, Simon Lonsdale) that they are back in the top field and so the walk is almost over. The Four begin the round-up of The Eight. Buster, knackered and panting, is already at Emily's feet, but the Labradoodle tries to run away from her, until his legs give way again and he goes splat like a cowpat. Beauty and Ella bound over at shouts from Jenno and Emily, but Spout has to be dragged out of a rabbit-hole by his short and curlies and Tasha has to use her Mummy-very-angry voice to get Clooney out of the hedge.

Colonel and Scruff, though, both rush over at her whistle. Libby tries not to look smug. If Jonny's legal career ever goes tits up, she can always get work as a dog-whisperer.

*

The depot manager has a gut that sticks out like a pillow and a voice that sounds as if he's been gargling battery acid.

'All right, Oxford?' he croaks.

Jason has been called that ever since he told the blokes in the drivers' room what he had been doing for the previous three years.

'Yeah, cool,' he tells Len. 'Roads were like *Dancing on Ice* this morning. But I nailed them all.'

'My man,' Len replies, aiming a fist bump, which Jason half-heartedly matches without contact. 'Here's your drops for tomorrow.'

The manager hands over the manifest, which lists Saturday's

addresses in order of distance from London, the postcodes printed in bold for easy entry in the satnav.

Jason flicks through the flimsy pages, trying to suss out the shape of the day. He's got two Express Delivery jobs, guaranteed before 9 a.m., in Middlebury, which means he'll need to be in the van by 6.30 a.m. latest. After that, he has dozens of repeat clients in a circular route round the M40 corridor. At least a twelve-hour day, even without spazzy traffic. Posh Brits seem to be mainlining overpriced caffeine at the moment.

'Go well, mate,' crackles Len.

'Yeah. Cheers.'

The drill after this is that he packs the van with the boxes for tomorrow, programmes in the postcodes, then hands in the keys at the security hut, ready to be picked up again in the freezing dawn from this corrugated iron prefab on an industrial estate in Perivale.

Heading to the loading bays, he hears banter from the staffroom and looks round the door. Two of the full-timers – Nik and Savo, gaunt, chain-smoking Slavs, as most of the long-time drivers seem to be – are sprawled in the fraying armchairs. They're drinking teabag tea from massive mugs, even though a free CappuccinGo machine is on the table beside the lockers.

'Oggs-furd!' exclaims Nik, when he sees Jason. 'You watch the football last night?'

'What? Man U?'

'Yeah. This retard Bosnian say the second goal on-side. You tell him, Oggs-furd.'

Jason missed the second half – shagged out by the early starts, he's generally in bed by 9 p.m. – but has learned enough of the rules of working life to answer: 'Yards off. The ref must have a holiday home in Old Trafford.'

'See? Eat shit. The professor he tells you,' Nik taunts Savo, then asks Jason: 'You fuck any customers today?'

Nik and Savo claim to have lain a trail of jizz through Middle England.

'No. Oddly enough, once again, they only seemed to want coffee.'

'Hah!' Savo joins in. 'You too shy, boy. You take my words. They say coffee, they mean *cock*.'

The door opens with a thwack, which soon proves to have been caused by Len's belly. At the sight of the depot boss, the two Slavs, like teenagers caught wanking in their bedrooms, hold under the chairs the fags they are meant to smoke outside the entrance.

But Len pretends not to notice and addresses Jason: 'Oxford, you got your sheet? There's a cancellation for tomorrow.'

The manager takes the document and, putting on the glasses he wears on a chain round his neck, flattens the clipboard against the wall and draws a line through one of the orders.

'Payment declined,' Len rumbles. 'So the drop is off. We're getting them every day at the moment. Pain in the arse.'

Well, at least it will make the day shorter. Although, when he's given back the manifest, Jason realizes that it won't. The lost job is one of his two in Middlebury. Tasha, the feisty blonde Welsh one.

'Mrs Lonsdale!' he says. 'Christ! Not much hope for the rest of us. They all look deffo loaded round there.'

'Oh, poor Oggs-furd,' says Savo. 'Is she your CILF?'

'His what?' Len asks.

'Client I'd like to—' Nik begins, but Len, one of those old-type guys who calls people for swearing, cuts him off like a landlord at closing time: 'No homes to go to, lads? And it looks like the chair is on fire. You smoke outside, okay?'

Jason tries to imagine how he will manage if this is the only job he ever gets.

*

Sadkins catches him in the corridor after double English. Doesn't often come for you himself. When he does, it pretty much means you've cut-and-pasted an essay or someone has died.

'Forrester?' he says. 'I think you've got a free now, is that right?'

'Er, yeah, *yes*, Headmaster.'

'Would you be able to pop along to my office now?'

'Er, yeah, *yes*, I guess.'

Mummy's insistence on *yes* always kicks in with authority figures.

'I should say at once: you're not in any trouble.'

Which is bad. Sadkins mad at you ('disappointed') is in the plan and means you've done something bad; Sadkins looking at you like he's got a tube of lube in his study means that something bad has happened to you. He tries to imagine what the beak will say when they're seated either side of the log fire. *Forrester, I'm afraid your mother is* . . . Going in for some tests? In hospital? *Dead?*

At the end of the English corridor, Sadkins palms his passcard to let them into the Administration Block.

'I hear excellent reports of your kicking in the Stowe match, Forrester. Duties, alas, kept me away.'

'Yes, sir. I was really feeling it that day.'

Sadkins shoots the camp flutter of his eyelids that he gives to any pupil who doesn't actually speak in Shakespearean verse. 'And I imagine the ball felt it as well!'

'Yeah, *yes*, sir.'

With a rush of relief, it strikes him that it will be Granny D who has died: shaking like she was on freeze-frame when they saw her after Christmas. Result! No offence to her.

'And Miss Moody tells me that you're shaping up as an excellent Rosencrantz. Or is it the other one?'

'Rosencrantz, sir.'

'What? No, I just couldn't resist it. Terribly clever chap, Stoppard. He's been high on my hit list for a Common Room Talk for some time. But the best are also the busiest, regrettably. You know, with *R and G are Dead*, I've always thought it would be interesting to keep a record of which way the coins actually fall during that scene where they keep coming down tails.'

Awks. Should he? Yeah. 'Heads, sir.'

'What?'

'They come down heads. In the opening scene. And, actually, yes, once in a rehearsal, they did all actually fall like that. I mean, like, for real. I did think, like, what are the odds?'

'Indeed. Although as I may have said on previous occasions, Forrester, I don't like *like*.'

Sadkins scans them through to the beak's study. 'The fire's nicely lit. Do you want to take a seat?'

The head picks up a file from his desk and sits opposite. The folder says Forrester but also his other name – *aka as* – like a crim. Which means this may be something peak. If Granny D is RIP, then why the file? Liking the hip-hop rhythm of the line, he repeats it.

'The issue of what to call you, more than with most students – is *Tom* okay?'

'Sure.'

'Well, I am if you are. Tom, your father has been in contact with me . . .'

Fuck. Call the feds. My fucking *what*? 'You know what, sir. I don't really have much to . . .'

Sadkins waves the file, like he's fanning away a crafty fart.

'Absolutely. Sure, as you young people might say. Tom, a school often has to deal – and increasingly – with – as one might say – divided parental responsibilities. The school does not take sides. Both of your parents – your birth parents – are registered as your legal guardians. The school does not – cannot – show favouritism in these cases. When your father contacted me today, asking me to see you urgently, I had to listen. Having heard what he had to say and I can assure you that I'm no push-over for anyone . . .' – Yeah? Long as he keeps paying the fees, you'd be his bitch – ' . . . it is my judgment, Tom, that it would be in your best interests to talk to him.'

'Does my mum know?'

'Ah. No. And, in these circumstances, would not. *Berzzzzzz-zzzhhhhhhhhhhh.*'

354

He hears the next chunk as white noise. Something about the church? WTF? Church and *state*? Whatever.

'And, if I do, I, what, like, ring him?'

'If that string of monosyllables means what I think it does, then no.'

When Sadkins stands, he suddenly understands where the beak is going, where this is going. Sadkins crosses to the door, not the one they came through, but the one behind the desk, the one they all assume contains the sado-gym.

Speaking through the door: 'Ah. I think we're perhaps ready for you now.'

The Sperm Donor standing there.

'I think I'll, ah, leave you two alone in here,' says Sadkins. Going into the rack room. 'I'll be in here when you've decided what you've decided.'

'Thank you, Dr Atkins,' says the SD.

The door closes. Fed-case face but fighting to smile, like when Grandpa D died.

'Max,' he says. 'Don't think I don't know how hard this is for you. Believe me I wouldn't have come if it were not a matter of life and death.'

*

Nina's brow is much cooler to the touch. The Tamiflu is hopefully beginning to kick in. But it is clear that she has recently been feverish: the 20-tog duvet, a winter insistence for their always ice-blooded daughter, has been shuffled off. Monifa gently snuggles it back around her, a nightly privilege when your children are young, too soon rescinded until restored by illness.

Nina wriggles and seems about to wake. Stroking her daughter's hair until the breathing deepens and evens again, Monifa gets up as inconspicuously as she can. It seems years since she last did this cat-burglar pad to the door, easing it shut without a click. A *Top Gear* rerun booms from Bobby's room. One of her absolute rules as a parent was that the children would never have a television in their bedrooms, but laptops made a fool of her.

She always loves the feel of Friday nights, the four of them back home, with no dawn alarm call the next morning, although Nina's running and Bobby's soccer ('Muum, please, we call it football here') are threatening to make weekends like weekdays now.

The desire of the rich white English to lodge their children in an expensive educational hotel has always been inexplicable to her. The fight with Nicky over boarding was the biggest of their marriage – most couples argue over money and they, thank God, have never had that problem – but, even though she won it, there are games, plays or clubs most school days now and she often has to let them nightly board. How long before they want to stay with friends on Friday nights and she will scarcely see them at all?

The Archers, another peculiar English institution to which she was introduced by marriage, drifts up the stairs from the kitchen, along with the rare thrill of a cooking smell she hasn't made. Nicky, amazingly for once back by five, is chopping herbs, with that ostentatious concentration men bring to domestic tasks, as if they were performing microsurgery. A silver heat-sealed bag lies on the work surface. Fish, then. Nicky will never tell her what he's cooking. He says that she gets bossy and interferes.

He looks up as she comes in.

'How's Noonie?'

'Careful. Don't cut yourself.'

'Yes. I'm not an imbecile.'

'Sorry. Sorry. I won't say anything. The fever's coming down.'

'Good.'

'I think we should pay for everyone to have the jabs next year. I can't stand this whole doom-watch thing on the news.'

'Mmm?' A sudden flurry of quick cutting, like on *Masterchef*. 'It's about understanding risk. If you read the papers, almost everyone who's died has underlying health problems.'

'Yes. And Nina has allergies.'

'Honey, after 7/7, you wanted me to start driving into London. Even though they'd blown up tubes and buses, which I never use. And, as I told you, I was statistically far more likely to die on the roads.'

She love–hates him, as usual, for his rationality. He sips white wine from one of the huge tulip glasses which she worries encourage them to drink more. His, half-full, stands beside an empty one, which he holds up with a questioning look: one of their marital mimes, like when one of them rubs a foot against the other's in bed on a Saturday morning. Tomorrow.

'Please,' she tells Nicky, with more enthusiasm than she feels. It is her minor secret that she doesn't much like the taste of wine but perseveres because sharing a bottle between two (four or even six between eight, at weekends) is almost a Eucharistic ritual among the people they know. For her husband, opening a bottle is a sign that work is over for the day or week.

With his surgical flourish, Nicky pulls their sharpest knife from the multiply stabbed wooden block. Monifa flinches but tries not to show it. Recently, for reasons she doesn't under-stand, she has become convulsively squeamish about knives and guns in films and plays, as sensitive to violence as when she was pregnant with Nina and Bobby. No. No, definitely not. Nicky has always been as careful with his condoms as a diabetic with insulin. Alone among her chums, she has never had a time when she feared she might be pregnant and didn't want to be.

She looks away as he slices the silver pouch. The tang of brine, but not of fish, so he has bought well, but if she compli-ments him he will think it patronizing. He brushes the fillets with olive oil, then, with impressive care, rolls them in the mixture of herbs and rough-grated bread crumbs. Once, before they had children, they did it in the kitchen when he was cooking, leaning up against the wall, the smell of garlic on his fingers as he touched her. As you get older, it becomes an unknowable stranger who did such things.

'Do you think they must get a lot of shoplifting?'

A sip of wine, vinegary to her tongue, her prayers for a palate unanswered.

'Who?'

'The supermarket. With these honesty zappers they have now? It's not like the self-service checkouts in some of them, when the Stephen Hawking voice barks at you *"Please Place Item In Bagging Area"* if you're even a little bit slow. Because the bagging area is weighted and they think you've palmed something into your coat. But with self-scan, you could . . .'

But he is interrupted by a cacophony of dogs, Monty and Biscuit barking in baritone-and-soprano harmony, up on their back legs pawing at the window, as they always do when they hear an unfamiliar vehicle.

'Stop it, you stupid dogs!' she scolds them in the growly tones she always hopes might make her seem an equal to their ears.

Growing up in London at a time when a family like hers could expect the doorbell to result in an empty step or even dog shit through the letterbox, Monifa has never lost her fear of unexpected callers after dark, although they are blessedly rare in the countryside. Once, a poor old lady with dementia was standing on their step with a Christmas parcel, a peril of living in The Old Post Office.

She thinks *I wonder who that can be*, but doesn't say it, having reached an age where she is more and more conscious of rotating a few stock phrases, like a language student. She hopes Nicky might go but he is laying the fish in the sizzling pan with the precision of a jeweller fixing gems.

She manages to slam the kitchen door against the hollering dogs trying to follow her into the hall. There is a spy-hole in the front door and she is spooked enough to use it. If she were white, she would be wary of a black face but, in her position, is never quite sure who in England she is supposed to fear. And, through a one-eyed squint without her glasses, the visitor is a smudged Picasso anyway, but looks respectable enough. Probably a petition against HS2. Or something about Neighbourhood Watch.

She slides back the chain.

The face is vaguely familiar, in the way that you sometimes pass in the street someone you think you might have seen on TV, but the retrieve key of her memory clicks furiously without throwing up a name.

'Oh, hi?' she says.

'Is Nicky in?' he asks in a tone which strikes her as abrupt.

*

Still nothing. Does life come down to the hope and fear of blood? Praying there won't be any in your bum, praying there might be some in your vulva. Tasha tentatively touches herself, but is too unfamiliar with her mucus (a rare contraceptive method approved by the old men who run her church, now almost certainly her former church) to be sure what she's looking for.

They have their own bathrooms. (How long before it is separate bedrooms as well, like proper posh people?) But hers is a Girls' one, shared with Polly, so she checks that the Predictor box, at the back of the medicine cabinet, is still wrapped as tightly as a Christmas present in its supermarket bag. She rearranges the chaos of packets – throat lozenges, squitters pills, holiday-leftover painkillers with French and Spanish instructions, bottles of Calpol, some of them with use-by dates in the previous century – to form a wall in front of the pregnancy test. She positions a box of thumb-prick tests, from the time Simon self-diagnosed diabetes, as the last bulwark.

Looking at the barrier, she tries to talk herself into dismantling it. She knows that she would be better off knowing, one way or the other. But it is the reassuring possibility of two outcomes that makes her delay again. Never professionally psycho-analysed (the family doctrine of getting on with it), she is a good enough self-shrink to know that years of closing her mind to things (marriage, money, now _____ and _____) has made avoidance a habit. But self-shrinks are better at diagnosis than prescription.

These big old houses are cold, however you heat them. In her walk-in wardrobe, buried under enough shoes to supply a high-heeled army, she finds the thick slipper boots from that time in Zermatt.

She pauses on the landing. The children's bedrooms are all quiet, although this may be explained by earphones rather than sleep. In the hall, there is no noise either from Simon's study. Online, presumably.

The DVR is freeze-framed in a segment from *SuperScrimpers*. A family of four has been challenged to live on £50 a week. Tash releases the scene, picks up her notepad and pen from the arm of the sofa, feeling like a TV critic. Clooney, glad to have her back, bounces into her lap, knocking the coffee table and splashing wine on to the folded-open *Radio Times*.

These big glasses many shops sell now, a doctor said on the radio the other day, *can contain a third of a bottle. That way, it can be quite easy to get through a bottle in a night.*

The mum in the programme is cutting discount vouchers out of the papers. Which ones have them? She can't remember seeing any in the *Telegraph*.

Tasha fulfils the radio doctor's prophecy, although the Sav Blank (a half-price bargain offer) tastes no stronger than water. She wonders if she should try gin.

*

Designed to make drivers feel like pilots, the liquid figures on the dash tell him that it is minus 8 outside the house but, although another number in the display reveals that he is doing sixty-eight, the wheels hold the road as if it is dry and July. In line with its ritual punishment of those who have the audacity to live in the choice parts of the county, the council has not gritted the lanes to the three villages but the insult is irrelevant to the Beamer.

Max is not used to having someone else in the car on the

drive home, although his passenger remains entirely silent, plugged into music from his iPhone.

The compacted snow on the gravel, now stiffened by the night chill, might have been a banana skin for a vehicle with fewer safety features, but he brakes and parks at the edge of the courtyard without any screech or side-slide.

Leonard Cohen is playing on the system, thirty-seven seconds from the end of 'Dance Me To The End Of Love'. He needs to hear the song through.

Noticing that the car has stopped, his son unhooks one earphone and says: 'We're here.'

'Can I just get to the end of this song?'

'You still listening to this old guy? He's, like, alive?'

'Seems to be. We saw him in Birmingham not so long ago.'

If Max were a blubber, certain lines - the children asking to be born, the curtains that kisses have outworn - would set him off, no question. When the song – sad, but defiant – stops, he clicks open the door-locks. The frost makes a snowflake effect on the car windows. In the strong glow of the security lights, the house wobbles to his gaze, like a hologram. Does he really remember the time he first saw it, or is the memory a sort of movie adaptation of Jenno's frequent anecdote about how she had loved it at first sight?

Outside the car, the freeze stings his cheeks and the smooth leather soles of his business shoes skitter on the ice. He relishes the tiny triumph of not falling. His son's trainers skid and he reaches out a hand to steady him, which is shrugged off. But that's fine. Dunsters don't need help from anyone.

Coughing as the ice-cube suck of the air hits his lungs, he stamps flat-footedly across the frictionless ground, moving through the harsh illumination of the safety lamps. His eyes adjust to the softer, orange phosphorescence of the kitchen and TV-room lights, spilling from behind the blinds. He imagines a man, trudging lost through the frosty landscape, seeing these friendly rectangles of warmth and light and knowing that they represent sanctuary.

His eyes are already smarting from the wintry kick but now they mist over. The cold, not crying. And yet he suddenly experiences his love for his family as a physical sensation as intense as an orgasm. The most sacred duty of the human race is to raise and protect the next generation.

They are his. They are at risk. But he will, he must, defend them. They are safe here in the home that he has made.

*

After just a couple of school productions, Jenno concluded that she could never become someone other than herself, in the way that those with acting talent – like Jenny Topham, who was in her year at Wellington – were obviously able to do even then. But when she's telling off the dogs, her vocal transformation – a baritone hiss – surprises her.

'Sprout, don't be so ridiculous! You know it's only Master!'

In a bomb-blast of barking, the little dog is trying to climb the radiator, heedless of the heat, to claw at the kitchen windowsill. Now there's a counterpoint of howling.

'Beauty, don't you start!' The low notes grating her throat. 'He comes home every day!'

The Labrador, the well-behaved one, slouches back to her basket by the Aga.

'Please, Mummy!' Jamie pleads, resuming their interrupted conversation.

'But, sweetheart, I don't see why you need another one? Your bedroom's already like the Sandhurst Armoury.'

'The what? *Mum*. It's the newest. Automatic, double-barrelled. Lucas Crossan has got one already.'

It irritates Jenno that Jamie, at eleven, already knows to push the Libby button.

'Okay, cupcake. We'll see what Daddy says.'

'Cool.'

She hugs Jamie, who tries to wriggle away. Sprout abandons his post at the window and hunkers at their feet, yapping up angrily until they break their embrace. The fierce jealousy of the dogs when she touches the children bemuses her. But perhaps animals capable of showing affection must also inevitably possess envy.

'Mummy! He really doesn't need it!' scolds her daughter, who long ago appointed herself Deputy – and, increasingly, executive – Mummy to Jamie. Even on Friday evening, Rosie has a stack of books cracked open on the kitchen table, like a Dickensian clerk. Due to take Eng Lang, Maths and the first three modules of all three sciences in July, she is already adding revision to her weekend homework with a diligence in which Jenno recognizes her teenage self.

Sprout is yelping at the window again. She's beginning to wonder why Maxie hasn't actually appeared – lining up in her mind the two shocks of her day to raise with him – when she hears the door and his feet in the hall. The kitchen door swings open. A third shock. The dogs' cacophony is vindicated; they had sensed a stranger. Standing slightly behind her husband, looking down and to the side, like a presidential bodyguard nervous of cameras, is a teenager, even taller than Max by at least an inch, who she assumes to be, from the startling familiarity of both his height and eyes, the stepson she has never been allowed to meet.

'Darling!' she says, aiming to kiss Maxie's mouth, as usual, but, although Rosie, just as typically, looks away rather than witness this embarassing geriatric physicality, her husband turns his head and so she meets his cheek.

Pressed against the stone floor in pounce positions, Beauty and Sprout are warning off the stranger.

'Stop it, you two!' Maxie tells them and, irritatingly, they fall silent at his command. He says nothing about the giant behind him. But if even the basics of genetics feature in the first three modules of Biology, then Rosie must have guessed the connection. On her face is the twisted quizzicality of a reaction shot in a TV comedy. Jamie looks fretfully at Jenno.

Though a limited actress, Jenno is an expert social improviser. 'Wow! I don't think our kitchen is high enough for *two* such tall guys!' she says. 'You must be Max. The *other* Max.'

'Uh, I'm really Tom?' the teetering teenager says, with that wretched upward inflection the young all have, his head still down.

Jenno eye-semaphores surprise at her husband, but his expression signals back that she should let it go for now.

'I'm Jenno.' She nods at her children. 'Rosie, Jamie.'

'I needed to talk to him about something at school,' Maxie explains. 'Wondered if we could run to a bed for the night?'

Hostess is a role Jenno knows how to play. 'Yes, of course. Do you have . . . ?' She sees a sports bag at the boy's feet. 'Squids, can you show, uh, *Tom* up to Bindy's room?' She aims for her most nonchalant smile. 'I don't know if this is good news or bad news but Bindy won't be in there. Silly, but it's named after an au pair we had a couple of years back.'

A perfect cue to raise the matter of the live-in they have now, but there is a more urgent question to mention first and both subjects must wait until they are alone.

'It's this way,' says Rosie, almost whispering, her blushing unease so great that Jenno almost offers herself as guide instead. But. But.

She is terrified the boy will smash his head on the doorframe but he has the gumption to duck and, awkward as Emily's Labradoodle, follows the children out into the hall and up the stairs.

'For God's sake, Maxie, what the . . . ?'

'I know, I know. I can explain.'

'Not just this. I've had a bit of a day.'

'Oh?' His face clouds, as it does during their worst rows. 'Is everything okay?'

'That's the question. Not here, though.' The children will never hear them arguing. 'The study. *Now.*'

'Oh, lord. You sound like my old beak.'

The grin, the charm, as normal; abnormally, she doesn't laugh. As Jenno leads the way across the hall, her son and daughter are already leading their sudden half-brother down the stairs.

'Sweetheart,' she says to Rosie. 'I just have to go through some really boring tax stuff with Daddy. Do you want to show Tom to the games room and see if he needs a drink of anything? And could you check on the stew for me? If it's bubbling properly, move it to the bottom oven.'

'Will tea be ready soon? I'm starving.'

'Ten minutes,' she says, a holding time with no relation to actual chronology.

'Jamie, set the table,' Rosie instructs her brother.

In the study, with the door shut, Jenno is surprised that her husband pulls her to him and puts his mouth to hers with an intensity she has rarely known with clothes on.

'I do love you so much. You do know that?'

Relief fills her mind and desire her body but fear and purpose overwhelm them. She wrenches away her lips like a ripped sticking plaster.

'No. No. I need to know what the *fuck* is going on.'

'Sshhh. Language, sweetie.'

'How can you fucking stand there and . . . ?'

'I can explain about Max . . .'

'He says he's called *Tom*.'

'I'll explain that as well. I had a phone call from the school . . .'

This throws her. 'Oh. He rang *you*? Today?'

'Who? Yes. Dr Atkins told me that . . .'

Atkins? 'Who?'

'Max's beak.'

Making the boy sound like a bird. 'Oh. Right.'

'He told me that—'

'No. I have to go first. I went to see Dr Welling this morning.'

Wives develop a detective's instinct for deceit. Maxie's big politician's grin switches on but, before it, there is just a second of something else.

'Oh, dear. Why? Is Jammy in the slammer again?'

'What? No, the kids are fine. Credit to their parents, et cetera.'

Max's whole thing is holding it together – she never saw him cry even when his father died – so it must be a trick of the light that his eyes look misty. He swipes a hand across them, violently, like someone pulling off their face.

'You know how it is when you're fighting something off?' he says sniffily. 'Half the office is swooning with this yellow-peril thing. Shows how right I was to get us jabbed.'

Reduced immune system. 'Maxie, are you okay at the moment?'

'I just told you. I . . .' A tiny bump, again, before the smoothness. 'What did old Welling have to say for himself?'

But Detective Jenno has read enough Dalgleish and Rebus to know the risk of the interrogator being tricked into disclosing information.

'He seemed to have had quite a few conversations with you. What had you told him?'

'Jen, I've not been well.'

Cancer. Thank God! The first human being ever to think this, surely.

'Oh my God. Welling says you've got . . .'

'Yep. What Daddy had.'

Leukaemia? No. 'Lymphoma?'

'Mmm. Non-Hobson's? *Hodgkin's.* The quacks are frightfully keen on getting one to say the words these days. I can't imagine it makes much difference.'

'What Bill Adamson had as—'

'What? I hadn't made that connection. Oh, yes, him as well.'

Without being conscious of any thought before it, she is holding him, sobbing.

'Oh, Maxie.'

'Come on, come on. Haven't got to the non-shitty bit yet.

I'm fine. Well, remission. Saw Big Chief White-Coat in Harley Street this morning. Passing-out parade. Flying colours. Six month check-ups. But crack open the Chateau Margaux, basically.'

But. But. But. 'But, Max, you lied to me.'

'Ah. Now. No. *No* . . . Not telling isn't lying.'

'Yes, it fucking is.'

She jabs him in the ribs, then worries about hurting him. Injections, operations, chemotherapy.

'But I saw you naked every day. Most days. Why aren't there . . . I don't know . . . *scars?*'

'What? With this one, zapping and tablets does it, pretty much. Out-patient. I do confess there were days when I claimed to be whacked out from financial planning meetings when I wasn't.'

She hugs him tighter.

'*Why* didn't you tell me, Max?'

'Daddy didn't tell Mummy till he absolutely had to. I'm not particularly proud of it but Dunster men . . .' – a term of his, making Jenno think vaguely of cartoon characters – '. . . we get our heads down and get on with it. Dr Kildare promised me he could knock it out so I took him at his word. Posie's and Jammy's frightened faces at the breakfast table, you asking Emily to bet on my chances while walking the dogs – no, thank you very much.'

But. But. But. 'But, if the treatment was so easy, why can't we pay the school fees?'

It is a frequent groan among their group that her husband always comes back at you so quickly, has an answer for everything, in a way that Simon Lonsdale, on the third bottle, has attributed to the school Max went to. The others have sometimes accused him of inventing statistics and government commissions to win a point. So the silence and its length are unexpected and unnerving.

'Okay,' he says eventually. 'I lied.'

Conversation is a tennis game and there are moments when

the guile and surprises of your opponent are so great that you stall on the court; when, as the television commentators say, *she has no answers*. In her mind, there is a flash from a classroom long ago, the brighter girls delighting in the paradox of the speaker who says that everything he says will be a lie.

'Jesus fuck, Max, this is pretty fucking hardcore.'

He famously dislikes women swearing, except in bed, and flinches.

'Jen. I . . .'

'So you haven't got . . .' She can't say the word. 'You're not ill?'

'What? No, all that is pukka. What I did – I'm not proud of this is . . . Look, even for a business as, uh, robust as Dunster's, this isn't, you know, the date you'd set your time machine to land in. Suppliers paying late, zero interest on cash at bank, orders inevitably down on peak years. And the wretched Steve Pearson obviously did some module at Wolverhampton Poly on maximizing the reserves: what Daddy called the Rainy-Day Fund. So the sensible thing to do is to delay some outgoings. I freely admit that I went and played the Big C card on the beak. So, shoot me. But it doesn't make me Sir Adrian King-Jones . . .'

The night silence is always intense – never many cars on the road after dark – but, in the stillness of the room, the knocks resound like rifle shots. Jenno goes over and opens the door.

'Stop arguing, you two!' scolds Rosie, in her teenage-adult voice.

'We're not arguing, sweetheart. Just trying to sort out something difficult about Granny D.'

On another day, such a lie would have seemed normal, kind. But now she feels a flash of stomach cramp at the facility of her invention.

'The stew's, like, totally *sperrssshhhhhhh* . . .' Rosie does a Pompeii impersonation.

'Is it in the bottom oven?'

'Yeah.'

'It will be fine.'

'I'm not exaggerating, Mummy, but there's people eating chair legs in there.'

'We'll be in in a minute.'

'This Tom guy. Is he, like, one of Daddy's godchildren?'

'Daddy will explain at supper.'

'What, he's, like, a *lovechild*?' Her tone implies a long fence of exclamation marks.

'Posie, hop it!' Max tells her in the commanding way, a spin-off from his dog voice, that always slightly frightens them.

Jenno waits for her daughter's footsteps to recede down the hall but Rosie is so light on her feet that the clue is useless.

As a precaution, she resumes with something she would be happy to be overheard: 'Whatever else, we have nice children.'

'Steady on, old girl. *Whatever else*. Sort of thing people say at the doors of the divorce courts.'

'You lied to me, Max. You lied to me about one of the most important things that will ever happen to you.'

'Jen, Jen, Jen. Only from the best of possible motives. Life doesn't work without lies. Does my bum look big in this? I admit that "does my tumour . . . ? " isn't quite—'

'It's not fucking funny, Max. You didn't tell me you had . . . *cancer*. You didn't tell me we couldn't pay the school fees . . .'

'Not couldn't. Didn't.'

'Same fucking difference!'

'No. It matters. Like tax avoidance and tax evasion . . .'

'Been doing that as well, have you?'

'Hey. Hey. Jen-Pen, I understand why you're so angry . . .'

'Max, every time I've spoken to someone today, there's been some kind of *landmine*. Alice suddenly announced this morning that you've given her the night off!'

'Oh, yes, that. It seemed fine. She's a good worker. It's Jonny's thing. He wants their Abby out of the house tomorrow night. Not quite sure why. Maybe he and Libs are getting out the handcuffs. Begged me to let our girl go as well. It's one night, honey.'

'Yeah. Whatever. That's the least of it now.'

He tries to hold her hands. She steps back. 'You didn't tell me you had cancer. You didn't tell me you were going to turn up here with your son. What else aren't you telling me? Why the fuck is Max or Tom or whatever he calls himself here?'

Max has sat down on the arm of the sofa he keeps in the study for watching his sport. He looks drained and sounds breathy; effects, she assumes, of his illness.

'Getting the all-clear this morning, it's like, you know, one has ducked a bullet. One would want to avoid the dreaded cliché about it putting everything in perspective but that is what happens. Life actually, you know, begins to seem too short to have a son who scarcely even speaks to one. The whole Tom thing . . . these kids, I mean, they change their names these days to DV8 or whatever but, in his case, getting rid of *my* name . . . One doesn't have to be Sigmund Freud. I drove straight to Berkshire and told him what had happened. Sweet-talked the beak into a weekend release. One just wanted, you know, everyone to be together.'

'And *one* never thought *one* had to talk to *one's* wife about it . . .'

Jenno needs to sit down as well, but beside him on the sofa feels too close.

'Yes. Of course. But, to be honest, I was so amazed when he agreed to get into the car that I just put my foot down and drove here. It was a bit like escorting a prisoner. I've seen enough of those movies not even to stop at a petrol station to ring you up.'

He always has an answer. 'Max, I want us to pay the school fees tonight.'

'Absolutely. In fact, I saw the bank when I was in town this morning. Steve P has been a bit too over-eager with his rainy-day fund and we actually need to reduce our reserves.'

'Okay. Tell me when you've moved the money. I'll ring Welling in the morning and explain what's happened.'

'It's fine, sweet. I'll do it. Sensible businesses pay as late as they can.'

'I have to call him. Simple manners. Christ! He actually suggested I should talk to the hardship committee. Chairman Libby. Can you imagine?'

The smile she has always loved him for. 'Ha! Another bullet ducked, then.'

It is as typical for Jamie not to knock as for Rosie to have done so. 'Muuum! When's supper?'

He has pushed the door with such sporty boy's force that it swings back and bangs him on the shoulder. Practicing for manhood, he tries not to show that it hurt.

'We're coming, sweet. Have you set the table?'

'Yeah.' A resigned sigh. An American sitcom kid. 'Bossy-boots made me.'

'Good. And you've set for five?'

'I forgot. But she did it. Dad, Tom's pretty cool. I beat him at *Fifa.*'

Max nods. Jamie stomps off, conveniently signalling the limits of earshot.

'Poor kids. Finding out in the same meal that their dad's had cancer and they've got a half-brother.'

'Ah, now. Steady on. We have to talk about, uh, Tom.' He pauses slightly at the phrase's echo. 'But can we keep the other under our hat at the moment? It will only worry them. And now I've beaten it, there's not really any need. I've asked the big lad not to tell them.'

Jenno imagines the table with an extra place and face. A pang of sadness.

'I'd always thought there'd be three kids. But not like . . .'

Max stands up from his perch on the sofa. She is surprised by the most blinding of his smiles. 'You never know. We might have a trio of our own soon.'

The thought strikes her that he is holding out a child as a bribe to win her forgiveness. But, if so, then he has chosen the inducement she can't refuse. She allows Max to pull her towards him and is startled to feel him hard against her.

She says, in a voice that sounds like someone else: 'Max Dunster, would you be planning on having your wicked way with me tonight?'

'A gentleman never reveals his intentions.'

It feels like normality but surely can't be. She pulls away from him and walks towards the rich smells from the kitchen.

*

He is desperate to open up *Tax Returns 1992–2001* but refuses to do so until he hears Tasha creak the stairs. There's almost no risk these days of her coming in to say goodnight but it's vital to have standards and stick to them. When he finally hears the haunted-house sounds from the hall, 11:18 is glowing from the phone on his desk and in the corner of the flatscreen.

Simon double-clicks the file and nudges the cursor towards *1994–95 Returns and Receipts*. He scrolls down through the pages of figures from that period when he felt rich – the five-figure sums in columns for Holidays and Cars – until the tumbling numbers give way to pictures. They are stored in the order he downloaded them.

He descends through the levels and levels of spread legs and strumming fingers, a play button hovering above the bullseye like the blocking blob on an adult channel. Down and down he goes until the images begin to seem gynaecologically and/or physically impossible.

There's a blanket at his feet, in case Tash or one of the kids suddenly comes down for some reason and he has to cover up. The most recent addition to his files is a clip of one who looks as if she's trying to turn herself inside out: porn-name Candy, Zeppelin tits, shaved slit.

The panic of the parachutist who pulls the rip cord and nothing happens. The body is primed to demand higher doses of the drugs it desires. He closes *1994–95 Returns and Receipts*.

She might still be awake, reading. He can't go to bed. His

phone shows three missed calls: Tom Rutherford, Emily Rutherford, Max Dunster. He doesn't want to know what they wanted.

Simon fires up Safari. In the finder line he types *Fucking*, then flicks the cursor in front of the word and stretches his request: *Live Fucking*.

He reduces the volume to mute so he can hear any sound in the house.

*

Libby is downstairs in the kitchen, which makes what they are doing incredibly risky. But Harry undresses, slowly, taunting him with her Georgina, like a stripper, and comes towards the bed. It is sleep he needs, with an aching, physical craving, but Harry whips her t-shirt over her head and lowers herself down. He can hear Libby coming up the stairs but Harry is smiling down and . . . on the stack of law books beside his student bed, the alarm clock shrieks.

'Darling?' Libby's voice is saying.

Jonny wakes up. His wife is half across him, holding the ringing iPhone that she must have grabbed from his bedside table.

'Oh, Christ, er . . .'

He gropes the phone from her. Gummy-eyed, without his lenses, he has to hold it almost to his nose to see the vibrating name: *Victor*.

His mouth feels sludgy. Normally a light sleeper, he retains a sense of having dreamed deeply and weirdly, although the details are receding. Emily's happy pills.

'Crossan,' he forces himself to say.

'How are you feeling, sir?'

'Oh, you know. I was sleeping it off.'

'Yeah. I'm sorry. Just Hannah Dunn is very keen to know if you might be on your feet tomorrow morning.'

'Ah. I fear I may be off Games for another day.' His mind beginning to sharpen. 'And it's Saturday, isn't it?'

'All day, yes. It's a Sunday paper that's got the story, sir.

Anonymized emergency-injunction hearing. The weekend judge. Blair, I believe.'

'Jonny Crossan, you are going nowhere until Monday at the earliest,' Libby mumbles sleepily, her voice muffled by the duvet she has snuggled under to hide from the bedside light.

'I really think I ought to shrug this bug off properly, Victor.'

'Uh-huh. Miss Dunn has instructed me to say that the client has especially asked for you. Money no object to securing your services.'

He has a stabbing feeling that it's going to be Pa, in which case he can easily refuse, citing, satisfyingly, professional ethics. But Victor would know that.

'Oh, who is it?'

The scratching of paper in the background. 'One Maxwell James Dunster, sir.'

The name fails to register at first, like when old Bloggs the politician suddenly appears in the newspapers as Lord Bloggs of Pontefract.

'Look. I . . . Yes, I . . .'

Libby's elbow in his ribs: 'You're going nowhere.'

'Look, Victor. I don't want to say yes and then let them down. They should get someone else.'

'Right-oh, sir. I'll expect to see you Monday unless I hear otherwise.'

Five coffees knocked down like vodka shots could not have left him more alert than he feels now. He sits up.

'Turn the light off,' drawls Libby yawningly.

'Fuck. Fuck. Fuck. Fuck. Fuck,' Jonny says.

'Really? Oh, you are feeling better.'

'No. I . . .'

11.48: far too late to telephone. But modern social manners offer an alternative. He finds the M section in Contacts and texts: *You okay, old boy.* He is about to press send but stops and adds a question mark.

*

Jenno wakes up to find herself alone in bed. *Urrgggh*. The only disadvantage of unprotected sex – apart from the obvious one, for those who view that as a problem – is being woken afterwards by the cold, damp patch against the back or hip.

The time shines out in bright red from the clock: 11:56. She shivers and fumbles on the floor beside the bed, where she drops her nightie when they make love in winter. Max prefers them to be fully naked, resenting her years of insistence that they stay under the duvet in case the children come in.

Even slipping one hand outside the covers starts her shivering and she switches on the blanket for a quick grill before braving the bathroom. Eventually, she experimentally swings out a leg and stands. The lukewarm trickle down her thigh, an unsettling premonition of incontinence. A minor inconvenience, though; tonight she held him inside her at the end to make sure. Perhaps, as she has read in articles on infertility, she should lie on her back for a while with a pillow under her buttocks. Too late. She catches the splash on her legs and waddle-walks the few short steps across the carpet, grateful for the luxuries of en suite.

Oh my God. A figure in dark coat and black ski cap.

Jenno swallows down a scream when she realizes who it is.

'Oh, Lord. Did I make you jump?' Max asks. 'I tried not to wake you.'

'Why are you dressed?'

'The dogs were going completely bonkers. I'm worried Beauty has shat the bedding again.'

Snuggling up to his coat because it looks so warm, Jenno listens. 'I can't hear anything now.'

'I'd better have a look. Last time she did a Bobby Sands in the kennel, they were yapping all night.'

'You're a hero.' She hugs him. 'Nice evening, Mr Dunster.'

'Rather smooth, wasn't it?'

The children had treated Tom, who seems nice enough if understandably a little wary, as an interesting novelty. Max, in bed, before and after sex, had insisted that he had kept his illness from her for the best of motives and admitted that he had been a bloody fool about the school money. He had transferred the whole year's fees for both children that evening.

She will not admit to forgiving him yet but, as he kisses her and leaves, there is an unfamiliar sadness in his manner, which she attributes to his knowledge of having hurt her.

Running hot water over a flannel, she uses it to clean away the gunk. She needs to wee and, on a sudden impulse, hunts at the back of the cabinet – they have His and Hers – for the box with the blue and pink writing. She knows that it is too soon for tonight's to have stuck, but there was one earlier in the month, when she told him they were safe.

From the loo seat, she can reach the cord for the strip heater high on the wall. She pees on the predictor and rests it on the tiles around the sink. Waiting for it to steep, she massages her arms to keep warm.

Through the window, she hears Max splutter as the night air kicks his lungs. The sound could only be him. It's odd how recognizable such noises are. When she hears a cough in the night, she always knows at once if it is Jamie or Rosie or, when they are staying, Mummy or Daddy or Granny D, as if chests have accents.

The dogs are barking now, but happily, surprised by their master's arrival at such an odd point in whatever sense of time they have. When she has ever had to go to them in the night, Beauty and Sprout have treated it as a game, chasing in and out of the torchlight.

The noise from the dogs stops: first Beauty, then Sprout. It's unfair that Max can control them so easily. Jenno reaches for the results of her test.

*

Aged four, being picked up after playgroup once, Rosie launched herself without warning from the kerb, like a runner at the gun, having seen Daddy's Porsche parked by the village sign. Talking to one of the girls (Tasha? Libby?), Max, in that slo-mo people always talk about, sensed an unpunctual mother speeding round the green and stepped across in front of his daughter, who bounced into the barrier of his knees as he felt the slipstream of the Jeep at his back. He maybe did the pick-up twice, three times, in all Posie's playschool days (when both Jenno and the Antipodean were busy), so why was he there that time?

He is certain that he has saved his children's lives several times. Henry, on the way to that Chelsea match, stepping into the King's Road, Max pulling him back by his hood (thank God, for once, for thug fashion) as the police vehicles screamed past. And it was him who spotted the rash on baby Max that turned out to be borderline meningitis. He remembers pressing a glass against his first son's skin, as the adverts tell you. Doing work and making money have kept him away from them more than he wanted, but he has always been there when they needed him, especially when they were in danger.

Max stands on his frozen land. Sprout is straining at the lead, desperate to chase some tempting scent, but is no match for the strength of his master's arm. Beauty, obedient as ever at his feet, is alert, ears back and flat. As soon as she saw the gun, she thought they were going shooting.

He looks back at the house, his home. All the windows are dark, apart from the kitchen and Bindy's room. What a smashing lad his elder son has turned out to be, not at all damaged by what happened. Leaving Hilary was the best thing he ever did. Max VII, although he may not fully appreciate it yet, has been the beneficiary of the happiness Max has with Jenno. One can only feel sorrow for those who have never known such perfect love.

Light splashes his eyes like acid, the way it must be for an actor, stepping out on to the stage. Pulled closer to the house by Sprout, he has triggered one of the anti-intrusion lamps. Beauty barks gruffly once and looks up at him for instructions, her muzzle completely grey now, like his beard when he stops shaving on holidays. He remembers when they had to put Basil to sleep, the dog looking up trustingly at them as they cradled him on the floor of the vets while the knock-out drops took hold.

The wind is lifting, but he feels no cold. Wedging the broken gun under his arm, he checks for the lump of the torch in the left-hand pocket of his coat, then takes from the right a tennis ball and throws it towards the dip of the hill. Sprout almost dislocates Max's shoulder in his eagerness to chase. Bending down, he releases the lead and the little dog streaks across the field in a furry blur of perfect happiness.

Both hands now free, Max cracks the gun barrels straight. Beauty, hungry for the hunt, thwacks her tail against his leg.

'Good girl,' he says, reaching for her collar.

Even with her super-shaggy winter coat, Shadow must be just so *brrrr-brrrr-brrrr* out in the field, poor baby. Phoebe is meant to be riding her in a cross-country tomorrow but will be totes astonished if the ground isn't too frozen. She slipped and nearly killed herself tonight, trying to get Shadow and Pepperoni into their shelter. TBH, she isn't sure if she should be riding, anyway, with her back so spaz from bashing into that man-girl from Stowe in lacrosse. But the complete bummer of having a mum who's a doctor is that, even if your head is literally hanging off on a thread, she just says: 'Keeping moving is the best thing for it, Phoebe.'

She updates her status: *Sleeplez, boarrrrrring.* Henry is at a sleepover, Felix at a party. Just her and the warders. At least there was no bed-creaking tonight. Grocerino.

Listening to The Killers, 'When You Were Young', on her phone, which flashes with a msg. Rosie Dunster.

– *Hey feebs u awake 2 xxxx*
– *Yeh bro u oyo or josh c with u lol xxxx*
– *imd!!! hey found out got new bruv tonight!!!!!! xxxx*
– *omg!!! she having babeee ??????????*

*– Ewwwww!!!!!!! no my dadz from b4 but 18 fit !!!!!!!!!
xxxx*
   – omg!!! *comes round now* lol xxxx
   – wait someone at door
   – ha good jokes xxxx
   – no reelly coming in
   – Rosie omg is new bruv !!!!!!!!!!!!!!!!!!!!!!!
   – No. DAD!!! Dunno what I dun. laters feebs

*

If his rents hadn't split he'd probably live in a fuck-off palace like this. Safe. What they call Bindy's Room is actually more like a flat, with its own front fucking door and stuff. Most of the bedroom wall is a fucking TV screen. He's watching *Take It Like A Fan*. And, according to the kids, these are just spare servants' quarters now. The nanny they have at the moment has a place of her own in a converted barn across the courtyard. The SD must be really fucking loaded.

Mum phoned tonight and had an epi when she found out he was here but he told her it was cool. Secretly, Tom sees it as a business deal. When he was younger, when he was Max, he thought the SD actually ran fucking Toys R Us. Every time he saw him, he came away with shitloads of stuff. No way he isn't going to go home from here with a phone upgrade minimum and probably a stack of notes ('There you go, old chap, thanks for coming!'). And fair play to the guy. He thought he was dying and now he isn't. But, when he told Mum that, she just said that he was always a hypo something.

The countryside's pretty fucking scary, though. Three or four times, from outside, he's heard what he could have fucking sworn were gunshots. Is that bird-scarers or something? Poachers?

And, now, he could swear there's someone at the door, the main door, not the bedroom one. Jesus Christ, there definitely is. It's like *The* fucking *Orphanage* or something. Footsteps across the carpet outside. There's someone in the other room. The bedroom door is opening.

*

Jamie, at eight or so, beside their bed, his pale face coming and going in the flickers of the torch he kept by his own bed because a night-light wasn't enough comfort. Rosie, unable to sleep through thunderstorms, snuggling between them. He has always protected them. The duty of a man is to keep his family safe.

Max goes up the stairs in a soft hop-swerve, like a childhood game. He knows exactly where the loose boards are, from years of creeping to bed without waking Jammy or Posie. Both the children were light sleepers. As soon as Jenno would allow it, they moved them to the bedrooms on the far side of the landing, because a falling feather could wake them. Adolescents now, though. Sleep for England. They have to be shaken into consciousness on school mornings or for sports at weekends.

He nudges the door open with the pillow he's brought from the spare room. The hinges squeal slightly but his son – his younger son – doesn't stir. There's enough spill from the moon and the security lights outside for Max to make his way across the floor without crunching those bloody splurge-guns on the floor. He positions the pillow. Nothing can hurt you now. Safe.

*

A slight sound wakes her again. Mothers lose the ability to sleep through. The tinkle of coins in a coat pocket. Impatient with shopping, Max always uses notes and ends up with his pockets weighed down like stones.

'Maxie?' Jenno asks.

A tender whisper: 'Yes. Go back to sleep. I didn't mean to wake you.'

He sits on the side of the bed, touches her head. His hand still cold from the frosty air.

'What was up with the dogs?'

'Hadn't settled. You know what they're like. They're fine now.'

His voice is snuffly. How low will the temperatures go tonight?

'You're an angel for doing that. Get into bed I'll warm you up.'

'Yeah.'

She coughs, something catching her throat. A stinging smell. Bonfire night. Gunpowder. He must have put on that awful coat. 'Poo-ey. Is that your shooting jacket?'

'Go back to sleep.'

'Love you,' she says sleepily.

'I love you,' he replies. She's surprised he speaks so loudly; he might wake the children.

He reaches across her.

*

Gloves, hat, scarf. The ritual of dressing, like a soldier. The ice on the path is as thick as a rink. Twice, he nearly falls and has to save himself. In the back of the shopping Beetle, a jumble of mud-encrusted football and rugby boots, riding hats, wellies and padded jackets. He gouges out a channel for the padded bag. Even though the dashboard thermometer registers minus 15, the car starts at the first turn of the key. German engineering, whatever you say about them. On the bottom road, the word SLOW on the other side of the white lines, read blurred in reverse. He ignores an inner instinct to slow down. He does not care about himself. What matters is that his family is safe.

*

The stab in the guts. Instinctively, she puts her fingers to herself down there and feels the blood. The relief sweeps over her as a wave of faintness. Despite all the times she has told herself that she might not be pregnant (that it might be stress), she has never really believed it. *Thank you, God*, she prays, apparently a believer again.

381

Road-drill snores from Simon, who came to bed so late again that he is sleeping like the dead.

In her bathroom, Tasha opens the cupboard and scuffs around for the box she bought the other day. The memory of that expedition triggers another twinge in her midriff, which has nothing to do with the time of the month. Pulling out the tampon packet jumbles the contents and exposes, at the back, the edge of the pregnancy-test kit, which she will not now need. Will never need. She is convinced that she has had her last sex, which will be her penance.

Turning out the bathroom light, Tasha is aware that the courtyard outside is brighter than it should be, even with the security lamps Tom put in.

Her view is blurred through the iced window but she can see a black car, parked with its lights on full beam. *Please God let it not be the police.*

ELEVEN

AN ACT OF LOVE

Deaths have always brought flowers, but now there is a new form of mourning. Within hours of the news of their deaths spreading, each of the four victims has a Facebook tribute page: *Rest in Piece Rosie D*, *Jamie Dunster Never Forguten*, *Jenno (Timms) Dunster (1973–2012)*, *Tom Forrester – Miss Ya Big Man*.

As Lorenzo is guided by the bossy electronic voice to Dunster Manor HQ, Kate scans the remembrances on her tablet. Her murder team now routinely trawls for online references to deaths and forwards selections to the lead investigators: pages set up by or for a victim can provide a biography in fragments.

The digital echo is unlikely to be significant in killings that will never come to trial, so Kate is mainly seeking clues of people to talk to in building up the file for the coroner. A posting from *feebs* is interesting in this respect: *omg omg i can't beleeve it. Reelize i was talking to u when it happened. RIP, Dunce, weel always luv u xxxxxxxxxxxxxxx*. Kate flags this one to be tracked.

Because of the mystery over the elder boy, the Tom Forrester tributes are potentially the most interesting. *Oggywilks*, from internal evidence a fellow sixth-former, writes: *u always said u didn't trust the fucker so y now. We miss you soooooo much, mate xxxxxxx* And *camillaheatherwick*, apparently another class-mate, adds: *Oh, your poor mum. She brought you up without him and now he's done this to you. I treasure every moment we shared and will love you forever. Sleep in peace, my darling xxxxxxxx.*

The girlfriend, presumably, or a former one. Kate remembers the tragic glamour attaching to girls at school who had lost a boyfriend to a car-crash or leukaemia, although, as these pseudo-widows curiously tended to be newcomers in the sixth form, her investigative mind now retrospectively doubts their stories. But these posts confirm her assumption, from the height and what could be seen of his face, about who the elder boy is. So much for her relief that, in this investigation, there would be no phone call to a grieving mother.

Aware that the car is scarcely moving, she looks up. Lorenzo, who knows to leave her to surf, says: 'Saturdays, guv.'

Kate looks out. They are backed up at a roundabout clogged with a line of people-carriers queuing for the supermarket exit. In the inside lanes, cars with football scarves flapping from the windows are heading to the motorways. Whenever Kate thinks about her own death – hopefully peaceful and decades away – this is the ungraspable part: life going on without you. She returns to the screen on her knee.

An agnostic in a country of emptying churches, she is always struck by the Christian fundamentalism of these memorials. *Hope heaven is cool* and *say hi to heath ledger for me* and, self-centredly, *pray for us in our mocks* and, heart-lurchingly, *see u up there soon.* Is this suicidal or a teenager's vague grasp of time? And, dismayingly, even young deaths leave regrets and things unsaid: *Rosie, altho i no i hurt u when we split, i will always love you 4ever joshlonsdale xxxxxxxxx.* And: *Jamie, when i called u fat was just jokes mate ok say hi to the big G mate.* And: *Jenno, I feel so guilty I didn't stop it. I realize I didn't know Max at all Tasha xxxxxxx.*

She flags that one as well; guilt is always a trigger-word. The former school swot and current pushy mother in Kate's make-up instinctively wields a mental felt-pen at the misspellings and almost complete absence of grammar and warms to any poster – almost invariably a friend of the parents, teacher or godparent

– who suggests familiarity with dictionaries or punctuation. Soon, though, her snobbery is overcome by the honest spontaneity of the responses. Why should these immediate feelings be considered inferior to the rote but socially correct expressions – *sorry for your loss, in time your memories will* – which have traditionally been the manners of bereavement.

There is a visual revolution in the tributes as well. By long custom, those who died young were memorialized in formal portraits: stiff required smiles above stiffer blazers, branded sweatshirts, uncomfortably high ties, white clouds of Holy Communion dress. But now the sudden dead stare out at the living in images captured in the midst of life: laughing, goofing, hugging. This means that the subjects are invariably shown to posterity pissed, but at least they are remembered looking happy, loved, alive, in a way beyond the reach of a school photographer pleading *cheese*.

The same names recur on several of the sites, posting comments minutes apart. Almost consecutively, just after noon, a *libbycrossan* has left an identical message for each of the Dunsters: *Our hearts are broken and we wonder if there is something we could have done or said. What drives a person to this? We search desperately for answers but none come. Our thoughts and prayers and love forever lol xxxxxxxx.*

On the *Jamie Dunster Never Forguten* page, this contribution is followed by a post from *smithy7*, who seems to be a classmate of the murdered teenager: *What's fucking funny about it dumb cunt. Fuck off you fucking pervert.* Even though long used to the verbal violence of online – from the global cyber-sleuths questioning her delay in solving cases that seem easy to them – Kate is startled by such language on an obituary site, which feels to her like cursing in church.

A few lines below, though, *plumcrossan* has responded: *hey, smithy7, fuck off, dude. Just my mum. Old folk think lol means lots of love. My mum godmother to both. We all crying all the time.* The quick reply: *omg. Soz. Thought u was fucking greef 2-rist.*

A term Kate's own teenagers explained to her during an earlier investigation. And the angry mistake of *smithy7* is understandable, given some of the messages left on the sites dedicated to the dead children. Before the end of the first *Tom Forrester* page, someone has written: *one less public schoolboy, thatz a result then*, a sentiment liked and recommended by many others, perhaps among them those who have later joined the thread to add comments such as *rot in hell posh twat* and: *now u no how the fox feels, toff boy. Ha ha ha rich cunts, everbody burns the same in hell.*

Although this is an uncertain new area of the law, these remarks are potentially hate-crimes, so Kate highlights them as well. Scrolling down, she finds a note from the squad's online goblins apologizing for the next material but predicting that she might want to see it. From comments at a recent conference, she guesses that it will be a page praising the killer. *Max Dunster, SuperDad* includes a long tail of fathers assuming that the quadruple murderer was driven to his actions by his wife or bureaucracy or both. The posts include: *fucked someone else did she? serve the fucking cheating cunt bitch right* and *only way a guy can be with his kidz now. When will the courts stop favouring mothers?* Supposedly a window on the world, the news is frequently a mirror in which people see only themselves.

The satnav announces their arrival at the business park. Kate looks out to see shaved lawns, sun-glittering windows and ranks of dazzle-polished cars. The hack pack are ahead of them, transmitter vans parked along and on the verges, restrained by crime tape and yellow-jackets.

'Anything useful in the troll trawl?' Lorenzo asks.

'The usual tears and jeers. Couple of people we should see. Sofa Sherlocks have solved it, though. Apparently his wife drove him to it.'

Lorenzo doesn't respond, using as an excuse his duties in winding down the window and badging them through. The press pen is a long way back but, from a general cacophony of questions, one booming inquiry cuts through: '*How many more bodies are there here?*'

Although the surrounding buildings are modern steel-and-glass, the main building, Dunster Manor, is a mock-Tudor construction, presumably in line with the corporate branding. The main door is blocked by constables. A gaggle of men and women of various ages in winter coats stand around in two empty disabled parking bays next to the entrance. Their familiar looks of stunned fascination mark them as employees. Most are filming on mobiles; some of the women working one-handed as they hold to their noses a rolled tissue. Slightly away from the pack, a huge guy in shorts and a blue tracksuit top is jogging on the spot, with training weights in his swinging hands.

Sally Burden comes out of the black-and-white timbered porch. 'Guv. You want to see the scene first?' Kate nods. 'Sure. The doc's just certifying him.'

'Who found him?'

'First response. With the warehouse manager. He went to source, as they say, the first order of the day but found the alarms and so on were off.'

The warehouse is a long, low building of white-painted brick, also with a Tudor roof. They walk past a morgue van and nod at the guarding PCs. Sally stops at the mobile crime-scene vehicle.

'Pyjamas, I'm afraid,' she says.

'Absolutely, Sal,' Kate agrees. 'The fact that there won't be a trial – I don't want anyone getting sloppy. We're not going to have a brief shrieking about contaminated evidence but, in cases like this, people are even more desperate to know what happened.'

'Sure.'

'Sally, anyone here we should speak to?' Lorenzo asks.

'The gorilla with his knees out is his personal trainer. Had a session booked this morning, which he didn't cancel. Don't know if that goes to state of mind?'

'Who ran the money side?' Kate asks, flinching, as she pulls on an overshoe, from a gym blister on her heel. Multiple crime scenes make her feel like an actress, in and out of costume.

'Steve someone, financial director,' Sally says. 'You'd think E had shot him, state he's in.'

'Is he? We should see him.'

Sheathed, they go in. High metal shelves are stacked with shrink-wrapped squares and rectangles. But as Sally leads them down a long central aisle, there's a weird sense of time reversing: stickers on the edge of shelves are marked with receding dates – 2011, 2010, 2009 – like a flashback sequence in a movie. A harvesting scene on the front of one box seems familiar and she remembers seeing it on the wall of the kitchen at the house.

'Christ,' says Lorenzo. 'Talk about sell-by dates.'

Outside, an ambulance siren is shrieking closer and seems to stop not far outside. Odd: has another victim – surviving – been found somewhere? She touches her phone, awaiting a summons.

Towards the end of the corridor of time-expired diaries and calendars, voices and noises can be heard. Turning left at 2003, they find a standard violent death-scene: SOCOs dusting surfaces, a photographer packing up his case. Dr Rafi is tapping at a BlackBerry.

'Ah, DCI Duncan,' he says. 'You've got your full set now. Even Marion Summerly' – a Home Office pathologist with the rep of being a defence poodle – 'would have to rule it was suicide.'

'Pretty sure it's the same gun as the four at the house, guv,' a SOCO (Ainsworth?) says. He heaves a sealed evidence bag towards her. 'And you should see this.'

Encased in decontaminating plastic is a pocket diary – a mental replay of her grandparents' arthritic fingers laboriously struggling with wrapping paper – for this year, broken-backed to stay open at the pages for this week. The days are all blank, except for Saturday where, written in looping but tidy ink – real ink, she thinks – are the words: Maxwell Dunster (1955–2012).

Emotion threatens her and she makes her voice brisk. 'Is that it? No note?'

'Not obviously. We haven't done his moby yet.'

'Okay.'

The doctor is repacking his bag. 'I've had plenty patients – we all have – who took their own lives. But never . . . do we have any idea why yet?'

'We're starting to ask around.'

They change back. Kate finds herself doing a rolling stroll, luxuriating in looseness. Even business suits feel like beach clothes after the constraints of protective dress. Walking back to the car, Kate waves over her crime-scene manager and says: 'Sal, I'd like to talk to the finance guy.'

'You'll have to wait, then. You heard the bells?'

'Yes.'

'That was him.'

'Christ. Shooting?'

'It's not America, Kate. No. Chest pain, sweating. Though the paras were in first gear. So I reckon you'll get to speak to him when he's had a lie down and cup of tea.'

Sex or money. *Money.*

At the car, a question from the loudest yeller in the press pack reaches them: '*Why did no one realize the danger?*' The blame game – long ago supplanting football as the national sport – has begun.

*

The sign at the village limits brags that Eastbury has three times won prizes in the Britain in Bloom awards. The lawns are sharply barbered around well-tended beds, and creepers and roses climb the honey-stoned walls of the rows of cottages they pass before the satnav announces as their destination a long, two-storey house with a blocked-up letter box to the side of the main entrance.

As Kate and Lorenzo approach, the door of The Old Post

Office opens and a broad-shouldered, winter-tanned man in well-maintained middle age steps out into the trellised porch.

'Mr Nicholas Mortimer?' Kate checks, flipping her warrant card.

'Nicky, please. I keep expecting hordes of reporters. I daresay we won't be spared that ghastly ordeal?'

The slow, deep, confident voice of someone used to holding court. Kate senses Lorenzo's class radar engaging and tries to neutralize her own.

'You should be fine for a while,' Lorenzo tells him. 'Relatives and colleagues will be door-stepped first. And you don't fall into . . . ?'

'Oh, no. Train acquaintances, really. Which is why I was so surprised last night.'

Feet are stamped, hands shaken, names exchanged. Nicky Mortimer shepherds them under low, beamed ceilings into a kitchen Kate would kill for, built around a central granite worktop. A black maid is doing something complicated with pastry. The lives of these people.

'Monifa, my wife,' Mortimer identifies her.

Kate tries not to show that she has been humiliatingly out-liberaled. 'Oh, hello.'

'Those poor, poor children. And his wife.' Mrs Mortimer has visibly been crying. 'If even half of what they're saying on television is true . . .'

'Then that would be a very high percentage,' Kate says.

Mortimer waves at a coffee machine even fancier than the one at the crime-scene. 'Hot drinks must be an occupational hazard for you chaps. But . . .'

'I think we're good, thanks.'

'There's a fire lit in the living room. I thought . . .'

On the walls in the hall hangs modern art: canvases divided into three bright stripes of colour, like the national-flags round in a quiz. Two mixed-race children increase in height and teeth in a series of framed photographs. Fancy studio shoots: goofing around on a wooden floor in matching sweatshirts.

'Your wife seems quite upset,' Kate says, as the witness motions them to a sofa. 'People sniff at the idea of counselling. But we do have all that if . . .'

'That's kind. But Mon's a tough cookie. Needed to be. I think it's just the sense of being slightly in the crossfire. *Metaphorically.* That he was here. Inevitably, you think . . .'

'Yes, of course. Mr Mortimer, a "train acquaintance", you said. Can you just fill us in on how you knew Maxwell Dunster?'

'*Maxwell?* I suppose he was. Well, yes, trains, as you say I said. Until recently, I'd pretty much driven but, for whatever reason, the M1 and the M40 are vying to be the new M25. A lot of the chaps in these commuter villages get the 6.38 from Milton Keynes. Puts you in London for a seven start on a good day. So we'd be on it, although he only went to London for meetings, I think. Dunster – *Max* – was part of a little gang. Actually called themselves The Eight, God only knows what this is like for them. I was just on the bench really. Specialist financial kicker, I suppose. We went to the theatre with them once.'

'Had he been to the house before last night?'

'Oh, good Lord, no. The play, as I say. And we went to a Christmas party they were at. But we wouldn't have been on *dinner*-party terms.'

'So he turned up completely without warning?' Lorenzo asks.

'Oh, yes, absolutely, in that sense. We'd overlapped on the train yesterday morning and he was fishing for a drink some time, but I didn't think that was anything more than cigar-waving. Some people call it something less polite than that. The drill is: aren't we all big businessmen together? It was only last night that I came to the conclusion that he'd targeted me, sort of stalked me.'

Because the assumed killer is dead, there is not the sense of urgency that drives most murder investigations. The only pressure is to construct an explanation for the coroner, friends and relatives and the millions of cyber-tecs even now bouncing dubious solutions around the world.

'Was he threatening?'

'Oh, no. Certainly not at first. When he came in – Mon answered the door, I was cooking – he was all charm. Hugh Grant and David Cameron rolled into one. All chuckle and flutter. You'd think he'd come round to borrow a cup of sugar rather than several million . . .'

Always money or sex. 'From you personally?'

'What? Good Lord, no. You've obviously been reading the *Guardian*. No. From RSG.' He reads her quizzical expression. 'The lot I'm with. Venture capitalists, essentially.'

'So Dunster had big financial problems?' Lorenzo asks.

'Well, this is . . . though he's dead now, so I suppose . . . The point is that he made me agree to confidentiality – I mean, actually physically sign something – before he'd tell me the situation last night. I can well imagine what you're thinking: a banker wrestling with ethics. But doctors talk afterwards, don't they, DCI Duncan?'

'Generally, yes. Details that are relevant to the case.'

'Okay. Well, I strongly suspect this is. He told me that he'd been to see the bank in London yesterday morning. They'd called in a loan. It was secured against the company and the house. In fact, he tried to enchant me past some of the paperwork, but I suspect this wasn't the only borrowing against those assets. It was just that the clock had run down on this one. He was looking for three-mill-five or so, to pay down that line but, you know, in these cases, it's like you've a boat full of holes and a single cork.'

Kate is dizzied by the figures casually mentioned. 'And you could have given him that money on your own?'

'Steady on! Good Lord, no. I could have put in some phone calls and made recommendations, looked at a restructuring. Although I say so myself, I wasn't a stupid person for him to come to see. But how much do you know about Dunster Manor?'

'We've just been there. One of my grannies had one of their calendars and an appointments diary every year . . .'

'Well, your *granny*. Yes. Exactly . . .'

'Not just her. My adolescent passions and ambitions were recorded in one of their three-year diaries with a lock.'

'Which wouldn't be that long ago.' While denigrating the tactics of upper-class charm, he is also deploying them on her. 'But the same narrative applies. One of the worst things that can happen in business is cyclical demand that you didn't realize was cyclical. Take Kodak, right? Household-name, blue-chip outfit. Didn't do much wrong, in fact, except that someone else had worked out a way of putting your telephone in your pocket and, the next thing you knew, it was taking pictures as well. Which wasn't great for the old telephone companies either. Or – which was the problem here – if your business depends on helping people to plan their days or their months. Similarly, I wouldn't encourage my kids to go into selling CDs and DVDs on the high street either. For a lot of businesses, the digital handset has turned out to be . . . I was going to say a gun. But . . .'

'So you couldn't help him?' Lorenzo asks.

'Not on the numbers he was showing me. And it's generally sensible to assume people are holding back the worst. Look, the sort of stuff I do, we're the oncologists of the economy. By the time some cases get to us, there's often nothing we can do. Dunster's was terminal. Making calendars and diaries is like, I don't know, bowler hats. There are people who still want them but you're fighting history all the time. And, with Letts around, they were never quite the market leader. Maybe if they'd tried to get into handhelds earlier – or even apps – it might have come out better. But I suspect that he – *Max* – was living in the past. There was no evidence that he'd tried to cut expenditure or staff at all. He was borrowing money not to modernize or diversify but to try to carry on as if it was still the 1980s. Of course, arguably there's a whole raft of countries that have done much the same. And let me say that I never imagined for one moment that it would come to this . . .'

'You couldn't have,' Kate reassures him. 'Was he angry when you refused?'

'Yes. Violently so. Obviously not in a literal sense. But that's why Mon's in such a state. That sense that the barrel was spun and we somehow got the empty chamber.'

'I understand that,' Kate says. 'Although, from what I know about this pathology, it's family members who are in the greatest danger.'

'Really? People are tweeting that one of the children he killed was someone he wasn't related to.'

'Are they? I couldn't comment on that.'

*

Even with an entire family dead, there are next of kin to be informed: Max Dunster's mother, Jennifer Dunster's parents, Tom Forrester's mother. Horrific conversations Kate delegates with only minimal guilt. The press conference at which she will name the victims is provisionally set for 1700. A local GP has officially identified the four Dunsters, though in the capacity of friend rather than medic. They cannot find out who Max Dunster's doctor was – often a problem with the wealthy dead – and so Kate has asked for Dr Rutherford to be driven from the morgue to the murder room in the hope that she can address the killer's state of mind.

The doctor is a tall, elegant woman with feather-cut grey hair. Her eyes are red-rimmed and squinting and Kate guesses that she has taken out her contact lenses because of weeping. It is the first time in an investigation that she has seen a doctor – or someone she knows to be a doctor – crying. But if one of her own friends were murdered, then Kate assumes that her professional veneer would also melt.

'Dr Rutherford,' Kate says, offering her hand.

'Emily, for this, I think,' the doctor says, sitting down.

'We're enormously grateful to anyone who has to go through this ordeal for us.'

'Yes. I foolishly thought that the number of dead I've seen

would . . . but no . . .' A rolled hankie, ready in the hand, dabs the eyes. 'I couldn't help them with the elder boy. I mean, he's Max's other son obviously but . . .'

'Did you – their friends – know about Tom?'

'Well, the *Tom* thing – my kids have told me from the Internet. As far as we knew, all the men in that family were called Max. It was sort of known he had a child from the first marriage. But it was understood there was bad blood, they weren't in contact. I didn't think . . . Jenno had ever even met him. From the ages of the kids now, you realize he must have left his first wife when, uh, Tom was very young. So they might have been cagey about that. Though I'm not judging anyone. But how the hell was he even in the house? Some sort of King Herod thing? Get them all under the same roof and . . .'

'You'd guess it was something like that. I'm talking to our psych guy later. You'll understand some of the questions I have to ask you. Were you aware of any health or mental issues with Max?'

'You know I wasn't his doctor? He had a doctor – well, *doctors* – in London. Obviously, I'm sick with myself for not having spotted anything . . .'

'Don't go there. There's a famous story on our side of the detective who, after a three-year murder investigation, got a call to say his own next-door neighbour had been arrested. We can't be on duty all the time.'

'That's a kind thing to say. Of course, something we're up against is that the streets are full of brilliant actors. Look, in the endless, endless reruns in my head, I keep remembering Jenno yesterday – we were all walking our dogs – asking me about a friend who'd been keeping from their family the fact that they had cancer. And patients rarely have friends, if you see what I mean.'

Taking witness statements is an echo-chamber in which an unexpected word occasionally resounds. *Cancer?* Kate makes a note, as she asks: 'Were you aware of the Dunsters having money worries?'

'What? No. The rest of us worried about keeping up with them. Tom – my husband – always called Max the last of the big spenders.'

'Although, as you say, people can be great actors?'

'Yes. Oh, God. You think he was just fooling us all?'

Kate smiles. 'As I'm sure you must have said to patients: we ask the questions. I have to ask this one as well: did the Dunsters seem to you to have a happy marriage?'

Dr Rutherford thins her lips and lifts her hands. 'Look, my mother always said: marriages and melons – you can never tell from the outside. It was a second marriage and you statistically assume they're more likely to be happy. And Max probably wasn't going to run off with a younger woman – as some men do – because he'd already got one. But, after this, you look at it and think: we didn't know anything.'

*

Some English place-names are poetic but, in this part of the county, they are compass-dull. Northbury is a ragged circle of stone houses around a village green. The Pearsons live in The Old Bakehouse. There must be jokes, Kate supposes, about accountants and bread.

Steve Pearson has the bleached but relieved look of people recently released from hospital. Flecks of grey in the dark brown of his neatly trimmed beard and hair suggest a man turning forty. His wife – whose name Kate has already forgotten – sits attentively beside him on the sofa like a solicitor or nurse.

'You're sure you're up to this right now?' Kate asks him.

'Oh, sure. It turned out to be muscle spasms. Just tension. I say just. Tension's no picnic.' A lilt of Irish in the voice. 'There are a lot of people there terrified about their jobs . . .' Mrs Pearson nods her head. 'We need to move as quickly as we can.'

'How long have you been Financial Director at Dunster Manor?'

'Four – coming up to five – months.'

'And, coming in, what was your assessment of the company's position?'

'Phoooo.' A blow with cheeks puffed out and the hint of a whistle. 'A mess, to be honest with you. My predecessor – Bill Adamson – had sadly, uh, passed away and hadn't been in the office, poor bloke, for quite a while, understandably. So the books were in a bit of a state. We only just avoided a late-filing fine for last year's accounts.'

'What was the corporate structure?' asks Lorenzo, fast-track smart-arse.

'Oh, old-fashioned pyramid. With Max at the top. Most of what went on wasn't best practice, which is always a risk with family companies. There was one outside director . . .' Kate makes a question face. 'Oh, Jonny Crossan, one of Max's mates, who's a hotshot lawyer, allegedly. Otherwise, the board was his mum and his wife. But it was really all Max: MD the MD, as he liked to say. He had single signature on a lot of things, which gets auditors hyperventilating these days. The set-up wouldn't have lasted a minute in a listed company, but it wasn't listed. Some of the stuff I discovered . . .'

'Go on.'

'Well, he finally agreed, after carrying on like a giant toddler for a while, to cancel this big Christmas bash they always had. But, for some reason, the catering bill came in anyway and Max had paid it from one of the solo accounts.'

'Who was the caterer?'

'Oh, I . . . I'll need to go online . . . I'll get it for you before you go.'

'Did you challenge him on that?' asks Lorenzo.

'I tried. He put most things down to confusion caused by Adamson's absences. The last few days, I'd been after him to answer some questions but he'd been going to London a lot more.' Kate nods at him to continue. 'Medicals, he said. Insurance. Although, as far as I could see, his Key Man was in place. Of course, now you think he was up in London with the begging bowl.'

Health, again. There were cases where the mortally ill decided to take everyone with them. But Dunster had told Nicky Mortimer that he had been to see the bank. And came back with terminal results. Different lies to different people, it seemed. 'What did you need to talk to him about?'

'Phooo.' Another puff. 'What didn't I? It's the time of year for it. Even in normal times, things get a bit eggy in February . . .'

'Oh, really. Why?' Kate asks.

'Oh, shortest month, so it's almost automatically worse for sales. And people have spent less in January as well, paying off the Ex-Muss excess. And depending on how your quarters fall – Dunster's Q3 is December, Jan, Feb – this time of year is squeaky-bum time, as the man said . . .'

'So you confronted Max Dunster?'

'I tried. For a start, I kept getting into him about the stock they – *we* – were carrying. You've been in the warehouse presumably?'

'Yes. When you'd think that diaries and calendars are by definition perishable. Why did they keep them all?'

'Mainly, I guess, because he wouldn't – couldn't – admit how ludicrously optimistic their product runs were. They were still supplying demand that hadn't existed since the nineties. But, also, there is, in theory, a tiny market in providing period props for film and TV. If they'd made a *Life on Mars* set in 2008 or 2009, we'd have been laughing. And Max was convinced there was an export portal for us in landmark birthdays. You know, someone who's, say, eighteen or seventy gets a calendar or diary from the year of their birthday, but printed with significant events. To be honest, it wasn't the worst idea in the world – newspapers run a version of it – but he never actually got round to actioning it. And he was never going to task anyone else with it. Partly, I think, because he never really admitted how bad things were. It's only in the last couple of days – I got some papers from Bill Adamson's widow – I've realized that the cash flow was all wind and piss. I now strongly suspect they were listing the unsold stock as assets and it looks like there was significant confusion of funds. There was money coming in from private accounts – but none of it tallied against sales or creditors – which means he was effectively subsidizing the company from somewhere. It's the pension fund that's the cupboard under the stairs in these cases. Yesterday, I took a big gulp and looked.'

Robert Maxwell on the news when Kate was at uni. 'And it had been, uh, plundered?'

'You'd need one of these forensic accountants to be sure.'

'Luckily, Steve's pension moved with him.' The wife speaks for the first time. 'They were paying into it. But . . .'

'I'm not thinking about myself,' Pearson says, an edge in his otherwise gentle voice. He pointedly moves his body to face Kate more directly. 'Look, the fund is way down south even of where you'd expect in this economy. And outgoings are up like rockets on bonfire night when Bill Adamson is the only DIS payment this fiscal . . .'

'DIS?'

'Death in Service. And three of our pensioners had recently come out of the scheme.'

An actuarial euphemism for death out of service, presumably. 'You discovered this yesterday. Did you speak to Max Dunster about it?'

'I tried. He wasn't picking up. In the end, I even gave a message to the ape in the tracksuit.'

Lorenzo grabs the key question. 'And – in the voice-messages – did you tell him what you wanted to talk to him about?'

'No, I don't think so.'

Dunster, though, would have felt the breath on his neck. 'We understand – from other sources – that a bank had called in a big loan yesterday?'

'Phoo. Which one?'

'Did you know about that?'

'No. But, as I say, Max ran the place out of his head and his briefcase. I'd been trying to timetable a meeting about the debts . . .' The deaths—? *Oh.* 'But we call – called – him Max-avity in the office.'

'Okay, then, Mr Pearson, we'll leave you in peace.'

'Cheers. I'll get you the name of that caterer.'

Sex or money. Money.

*

She suppresses a double take as Aberdeen comes into the office with replica rugby shirt, jeans and Nikes showing under his swinging-open overcoat. The psychos don't wear suits except at inquests but she's used to him in button-down shirts and chinos in his office on the campus. Even on a murder investigation, there's a sense of dress-down on a Saturday, of people with meals and families left behind. Kate must phone home soon.

'Got you off the terraces, did I?'

'What? Oh, 5 p.m. kick-off. Thanks to the Great God television. So you're lucky.'

'Yes, we're all grateful to be working this case.'

He's carrying two coffees – flat whites – and hands one to her. 'I gambled you hadn't just got one. And – if you had – you'd take another.'

Amid the darkness of the work they do, tiny human kindnesses blaze like flashlights.

'Oh, Jim. You psychos really know how people tick.'

'Yeah, yeah, Duncan.'

And, with Aberdeen, something else, as there sometimes is with some people, a rumble underneath, of what might have been between them if they had met differently: another risk of studying inhumanity for a living.

Their mouths duck simultaneously into cups wearing brown cardboard wrist-bands, drink, lift and lick the foam from their lips. Kate is behind her desk, Aberdeen using an edge of it as a sort of shooting stick, ignoring the chair, another gesture towards weekend working.

'So,' he says. 'Putting Intranet and Internet together: Maxwell Dunster, calendar magnate, prince of diaries, rounds up his wife, three kids from two marriages, two dogs and shoots them with a sporting gun?'

'There were horses as well, but he left them. Would we . . . ?'

'They shoot horses, don't they? Certainly, in other cases, they have. Perhaps he didn't regard them as family in the same way. Outside pets. Or they were simply bigger than him. These people aren't *mad*, you know. Office joke. Okay. State of mind, state of life – what do we have?'

'It looks as if he'd run out of money. He'd been seeing banks. But also seeing doctors, so there was possibly that as well.'

'Sure, sure.'

Whatever you say to Aberdeen, he has a way of implying he already knew it. He takes another sip and comes up with a latte Zapata. She mimes a wiping of her upper lip. He looks puzzled, realizes, cleans himself up with a finger.

'Jim, every instinct we have as parents is to protect them, save them . . .'

'Huh. Are yours teenagers yet?'

'You know what I'm saying. How does someone reach the point where . . . ?'

'Sure. I mean, it's not common. Although recognized enough for there to be a literature. Actually, what you say about protecting is the key to it. Yeah, you make that face. But the people who do this are essentially narcissists. The world, in the vernacular, revolves around them. Old-fashioned caveman provider types, often, as well: spectacular providers in some cases . . .'

'This guy seems to have been once.'

Kate enjoys another kick of coffee. She's searching for a paper tissue when Aberdeen reaches across and wipes her foamy moustache away. Jesus, the cheek.

'Sure, sure. The classic trigger point is when the lifestyle they've provided collapses – bankruptcy, typically, or a partner's adultery – and he – or she – simply cannot face up to the trans-formation. Although it *is* more often a man. There's a smaller group of cases of mothers who have killed their children . . .'

'That woman in the States who drove them into a lake?'

'Sure. It might be considered revealing that the word *taboo* is used in those cases – more than when men do it. And the women seem statistically less likely to target the children's father as well. Which perhaps plays to a testosterone–oestrogen stereotype. But, actually, in both examples, we seem to be dealing with a perversion of the nurture instinct. The parent believes that he or she is making the child safe – beyond harm – by this action. Of course – objectively – it can be seen as the most arrogant of calculations. Once you have decided that you can't go on, how will they possibly carry on without you? How could they possibly want to? So a sort of super-suicide.'

'And these people are seeking what? Obliteration, or being together forever in some kind of heaven?'

'Now, that *is* a good question.' Patronizing twat. 'In the books, a significant number of these, uh, family multiple killers, for want of a better term, have been strong religious believers. But then a majority of the occurrences have been in the United States, so the sample may be statistically warped. And, allowing for the fact that – we're speaking here between friends, Kate, okay? I don't want a tribunal – the Bible can be used to justify almost anything, but there is, isn't there, the story in which God asks Abraham to kill his son Isaac? I do think it's important to understand that killings of this kind are not motivated by hatred, as other murders often are. In the warped view of the perpetrator, the killing of a partner becomes an act of sparing, of love, even.'

'*Love?* I didn't expect easy answers, but that's a whole set of questions. I just keep wishing we could get inside his head at—'

'At the moment when . . . ?' he cuts across her. 'It's natural to think that, yeah. But the point I'm making is that even if we found some kind of moral black-box recorder, we wouldn't be in the mind of a murderer. Not on his terms. And you can strip his hard disk but I'd be astonished if there's a file called *Why I Killed Them*. He – which is the point – won't have thought of it as killing them . . .'

Kate swills the last bitter, cold trickle around the bottom of the cup and drinks it.

'That's useful, Jim. I'll, um, let you get back to your family.'

'Ha! Yeah, if you spot five empty seats in the family stand, you'll know what's happened. Miracle we stay so well-adjusted.'

She takes his empty cup and chucks both in the bin together, then scrolls through her notes looking for the name of the caterer.

TWELVE

THE LAWS OF REMORSE

Polly, Josh and Henry bleep repeatedly as they receive messages from friends and reply to them with dizzying dexterity, a species evolving to speak through machines. Tasha's usual rule is no phones during meals but she would forgive her children anything today simply for being alive and, anyway, this isn't lunch or supper. Tasha feels even more vindicated in having held the line against boarding school (keep your children with you while you've got them) and convinces herself that Jenno would feel the same now.

They're eating a Victoria sponge Polly insisted on baking (some belief in the recuperative effects of cooking, handed down through the female line?) after they had sat for maybe two hours at the kitchen table, telling each other they couldn't believe what had happened.

It was Emily who told them, just after eleven, although there had already been a call from Libby, saying that Rosie Dunster hadn't turned up at the stables and Tilly wondered if Tasha might know anything. All she could think of to say was that there was this flu going around. But Surinder Rafi, when he got the call from the police, rang Em straight away because he knew she was one of The Eight.

At that stage, everyone assumed a burglary gone wrong – Emily said Tom was in a complete funk because he'd just done a security review at the house – except for Jonny Crossan, who was convinced it was a revenge execution of the wealthy by the

poor. 'England is the new South Africa. You'll see,' he proph-
esied. Then Tom remember Jenno's concern, at what they were
already calling The Last Dinner, about the bloke at the bureau.
Was he called Danny? Tom rang the cops with the name.

When Emily rang again to report, via Dr Rafi, who the
presumed killer was, Tasha was so shocked that her mouth
filled instantly with sick, which she sourly swallowed back
down, hoping that her retching sounds would be heard as
weeping. Emily herself was sobbing so much that Tasha had to
ask her to repeat the details three times, although, even when
she took them in, she couldn't comprehend them.

'Mum, can I have another slice?' asks Henry and, although
she and Simon talked about his weight in the days when they
had conversations, Tasha says, 'Of course.'

'Henry Lonsdale,' says Polly in her other-mummy voice.
'Enough deaths today without another one from morbid
obesity.'

This would usually earn a rebuke, but discipline seems petty
today and so Tasha lets it go and also ignores it when her
younger son thumps his sister with the *Nigella's Winter Collection* which was open on the table when Emily first rang.

Josh is not part of the conversations. He has made a pillow
on the table with his arms and buried his face flat against them,
shoulders shaking. Tasha has rested her arm lightly around him
and it is a measure of his distress that he has shown none of the
usual 15-year-old revulsion at being touched. Poor, poor boy:
the first (she thinks) girl he slept with, he dumps her and then
she gets murdered. The priests and nuns who taught Tasha
would be smirking at this parable for chastity.

With the children having sports in the mornings and going
to more and more parties in the evenings and the rotating social
calendar of The Eight, it's odd for all five Lonsdales to be
around the kitchen table on a Saturday (she still tries to insist
on proper Sunday lunch together) but any sense of what is
normal has been lost and will be gone for a long time now. Sky
News is on the kitchen flatscreen with the sound down but the

405

ribbon across the bottom keeps confirming the numbers of dead over a picture of people going in and out of Max's house, wearing white suits and masks like in those movies where a virus is wiping out the world. Simon is flicking between news sites on his iPad. Every twenty minutes or so, he smokes a cigarette, which is completely forbidden in the kitchen, but she feels she has to let him off, like when his father died.

Tasha adjusts her legs because the warm but scratchy weight of Ella's paws on her knee has become uncomfortable. The Labrador has refused to leave her alone since she put the phone down. And Clooney is curled in Polly's lap, dark eyes seeking reassurance through the cross-hairs of his eyebrows.

'The dogs know,' she says to Polly.

'They know we're eating cake,' Simon snorts, without looking up.

Conversation with her husband, as so often these days, is routed through the children like those operator-placed phone-calls to relatives overseas she can remember from childhood.

'Mummy,' Polly asks, 'will they all be buried together?'

'Good question,' Simon answers. 'In cases like this, there's a lot of discussion about whether the killer has to have a separate funeral. I mean, it is different from if they all died in a car crash or . . .'

'Jenno's parents, Max's poor mother, I suppose, will have to thrash it out,' Tasha says.

'Dad,' asks Henry. 'Did you know about this Tom dude?'

'No. Not really,' Tasha replies, keen to prove herself the superior pundit on the Dunsters. She is just thinking that she can't put off much longer going to the loo (she hasn't been this excited by having periods since she was about thirteen) when the cordless rings on the kitchen table. She eventually finds it under the folded-over *Guardian*, the cryptic crossword half filled-in by Simon before Emily called.

'Hello?' Tasha answers. Polly and Henry exchange grins. They mock her for putting on a special phone voice.

'Is that Mrs Natasha Lonsdale?' asks a young, male, slightly geezerish voice.

'Yes.'

'I'm Detective Sergeant Robert Lorenzo. Would it be convenient to come to see you this afternoon?'

For the second time in the day, her heart hammers as if she's put her hand into an electric socket. From the puzzled look Polly gives her, she assumes the blood has rushed from her face.

'But I thought the shop said it would go no further this time.'

Now Simon looks up and squints quizzically.

'I'm sorry, Mrs Lonsdale? I'm not with you. Me and the lead investigating officer on this case just wanted to, er, come to see you in, er, building up a picture of the Dunsters?'

Fuck. An elementary criminal mistake: false confession. 'Oh, er, yes.'

'We believe you and your husband were part of their circle? And your children may have known, er, Jamie and Rosie.'

'Absolutely, yes. We're here now if you want to . . .'

Coming off the phone, she announces that the police will be here in about twenty minutes. Josh lifts his head. His face is red from crying and pressure-marks from his arms.

'Mum, will I have to tell them about . . . about . . . Rosie?'

'Oh, sweetheart, I wouldn't think so. I can't imagine that had anything to do with it.'

Although the thought has stalked her more than once that the deaths of Jenno and Rosie may have been some kind of honour killings. That Max felt the women had somehow let him down sexually. But, in that case, would he not have killed Josh? And. And. She is distracted by the loud growl of Simon's voice: 'Why the fuck are the police coming here?'

'Dad said a bad word!' chirrups Henry.

'Shut up!' Simon shouts at him. Then to Tasha: 'What do they want?'

'Putting together a picture, apparently . . .'

'But, I mean, it's case closed, isn't it?'

'Jeez, you'd think *he'd* killed them,' Polly says.

'And you shut up as well!' Simon roars. Polly and Henry, recent enemies, are united in a heaving heap of tears.

'Congratulations,' Tasha tells her husband, startled at the rasp in her voice. 'Got the jackpot. All three of them are crying now.'

Simon stands up so suddenly that his chair skids and totters and she has to reach to steady it. There is an instant in which she genuinely fears that he might hit her. He stamps out into the hall.

'Going to get your gun to shoot us, are you?' screeches Polly, the perfect teenage melodramatist.

'Pol!' Tasha scolds her, but is struggling not to laugh. They hear Simon's toddler-stomping footsteps and then the study door slamming shut.

The three children are sitting in line at the table in a sort of group hug, which Tasha joins from behind. 'Everyone okay? All this has put us all a bit on edge.' She rubs each of their heads in turn consolingly, then disengages herself. 'I've just got to go to the loo.'

'Ew! TMI!' Henry complains.

Tasha crosses the hall with withheld steps, like a burglar. But the click of the door gives her away.

'Fucking knock!'

Simon is sitting in front of the flatscreen but with two laptops also open on the desk, like a keyboardist at a gig.

'I'm your wife,' she says, at first sounding pathetic to herself but then enjoying the ringing simplicity of the declaration, the sense of being on the high moral ground, although her right to reside there could be questioned.

'What are you doing?' she asks, but the images on the three screens make her question redundant. Simon looks like someone editing a porn film. Deleting one. Them.

'Oh, Christ. Is this what you do in here?'

He doesn't look at her, just keeps staring ahead, tapping buttons on each of the keyboards in turn.

408

Blocks vanish from the screen, each showing a freeze-framed scene. She blurs her vision in that way you can, as if you've taken off a pair of glasses, even if you don't wear them. She's aware of shades of flesh, with bronze predominating, and of hair, more often hairlessness, but is surprised to feel cheered by what she is seeing. Definitely not a paedophile, then.

'It's not as bad as it looks. Pretty much all Category One,' he says, without turning around.

Good. But. 'But, Christ, Simon, how do you even know how many categories there *are*?'

His silence tells her that she has won a point. With stupid lateness, she understands what he is doing. 'The police, Simon – they haven't come for you.'

'Cops these days are a sort of Dixons in reverse. They always take your laptop off you. They'll want emails, won't they? They always do. Max mailed me last night, just saying *sorry* . . .'

Did he? Fuck. 'Did he? Sorry for what?'

'What?' He is nearly screaming now. The children are bound to hear. 'For the fact he was about to shoot his fucking family, I suppose.'

It is the longest conversation they have had in months. 'I know. But why apologise to you?'

'We were his mates, I suppose, weren't we? And things had never been quite right since The Last Dinner. I imagine Tom and Jonny got them too.'

So the apology was non-specific. What happened in Marrakesh has died with Max.

Sordid squares – a blow-job that looks like someone swallowing a plank – continue to disappear from the screens.

'We'll talk about this later,' Tash says.

'Will we?'

She is walking towards the door. 'Natasha . . .' He has always reserved the full version of her name for moments of extreme love and extreme hatred. 'What you said on the phone about the shop letting it go? Have you been shoplifting again?'

They are like political candidates, revealing knowledge of private weaknesses to bring the other down.

'Again?' she asks, immediately seeing and regretting that she has fallen through the trap.

'One of the boys told me – Max, I think, actually, probably – that the girls were saying you might be abusing the honesty system at your shop . . .'

So they had known what was happening on that first day. How much else does he know?

'Oh, please. Village gossip. I've had a couple of daffy moments with the scanner thing.' The insult comes to her quickly, but she seriously considers not using it. 'You've always been the one who was hot on technology.'

His finger stalls on the delete key, then lifts. He finally turns round.

'Fuck off and go and cook some stolen food!'

*

It's so totally gross, seeing M and D making out like that. She's sitting on his frigging knee for Chrissakes. Awks. At least when it's the bed creaking, it's not, like, in her face. Phoebe hasn't seen Mummy crying since Grandpa died.

M had to go and identify the bodies and though Phoebe has seen it pretty often on TV – the trolley from the fridge, the lifted sheet – she can't imagine what it's like when someone you actually knew is lying on the slab.

Felix and Henry actually volunteered to take Buster and Hector for a walk, which is probably because boys are so hopeless at emotion, although Hec is still totally spaz at walking. Labradoodles look like they were stitched together from other dogs like in a horror film. So it's just the three of them round the kitchen table. Phoebe is downloading her messages on to a memory stick because M says the feds will want to see what Dunce was saying just before before before . . . it happened and she's hoping she can get away with not actually handing over her iPhone.

'It's my fault,' M is saying.

'Don't be so bloody silly, darling, of course it isn't!' D says. He isn't crying but he was in the army and so totally must have killed people himself, although he gets stressy when Felix and Henry ask him about it.

'I should have seen it coming.'

'Look, darling, it's not like there was a *lump* or anything to spot. And he wasn't even your patient.'

'No. There are always signs, clues. Although, actually, in this case, the point is that there weren't.' What does that even mean? 'I spotted Jonny but . . .'

M suddenly stops crying, like she's been slapped, or when Phoebe and her wing-women threw that tooth-mug of wine in Bethan Doogan's face when she was being annoying on the Florence trip.

'Jonny?' asks D, at the same time Phoebe is saying: 'Mr Crossan?'

'Bloody hell,' says D. 'What's up with Jonny, then?'

M gets off D's knee and he reaches out to her but she pushes him away.

'I'm such a fucking useless doctor!' she says, going to the stairs.

Phoebe has never heard M swear before, except when driving.

M hits her head on the low ceiling beam ('Fuck!'), even though it's got that yellow-and-black tape on it and the tall people in the family have known to duck for years.

Phoebe is surprised to see D wiping his eyes with the backs of his hands. She has never seen him cry, not even at Aunty Susan's funeral.

'We originally put that tape up because of Max,' he sniffs. 'One day, the long lank brained himself on it.'

*

There's no siren on the police car – too late for that to be any use – but Ella and Clooney are as good as one. The dogs have

411

been locked in the kennel, just in case they smell police dog on the detectives' legs and start humping them. It's a good thing, Simon thinks, that a culprit has already been identified. He and Natasha are both acting so suspiciously that they'd be straight down the nick for questioning.

Introductions, jokey apologies for the howling hounds, offers and refusals of coffee and tea. They arrange themselves around the kitchen table. Although the Lonsdales have sat in the same places at the table for the decade since they consigned Henry's highchair to the cellar, Natasha, to Simon's surprise, quickly sits next to him in Polly's usual slot and moves so close that he thinks she's going to hold his hand, like married couples do in television interviews. Henry happily accepts an invitation to go to the games room but Polly and Josh ask if they can stay and the main cop says it's fine, that they are just talking informally to people who knew the Dunsters.

DCI Duncan – early forties, with gingery hair cut short – is one of those women with a body so slight that it resembles a child's. Simon thinks of all the surveys showing that the business caste most likely to be fast-tracked are tall men. So this midget lady cop must be professionally exceptional. The sidekick, Lorenzo, is mixed-race, with one of those upside-down male faces in which the skull is smoothly shaven but the cheeks and chin stubbled. He looks at his boss with the deputy's unavoidable combination of deference and resentment.

'Don't misunderstand this question,' the tiny policewoman says. 'This is one of those freak occurrences that nothing could have stopped. But – looking back from where we are now – are you struck by anything the Dunsters did or said?'

While the others make a show of effortful reflection, Simon nips in: 'Max sent me an email late last night. I only opened it this morning. Saying simply: *sorry*.'

His peripheral vision picks up a significant glance between the two detectives but not, he is relieved to see, from Natasha to himself.

'Okay,' the lady cop says. 'We might need to take a look at

that. It won't, I promise, involve taking away your laptop for months on end . . .'

As Simon's hand moves to his jeans, there is just the tiniest of flinches (firearms training?) before they see the folded sheet of paper and relax. 'I printed it out for you.'

'Cool,' says the sidekick, taking it. Simon dares not look to his right.

'These questions we're asking everyone . . .' The soft, apologetic tone of the senior cop, he has to remember, is a trick to make people spill. 'Were you aware of the Dunsters having any marital problems?'

Max was legitimately fucking a much younger woman: what did he have to complain about? Natasha is already answering, like a musician coming in ahead of the beat: 'Absolutely not. They seemed devoted to each other. I think the rest of us were sometimes even a bit envious of them.'

'Speak for yourself, darling.'

He ought to be in movies. Josh and Polly look as if they are going to vomit but the four adults all laugh. He notices that DCI Duncan isn't wearing rings. Divorced or a professional restriction, like footballers not wearing jewellery on the pitch? A risk of knuckle-dustering suspects?

'Let's get the other one out of the way,' she says. 'Any suggestion of money troubles?'

'To quote my wife,' Simon says. 'I think the rest of us were sometimes a bit envious of them . . .'

'Phones, games, trainers,' says Polly. 'They always had them first.'

'Yeah, Simon picks up. 'In a way I feel vindicated.'

'In what way?' the younger cop jumps in. If you were covering up a murder, he would be the one you had to watch.

'I work in business and Dunster's didn't make sense as a proposition, and yet Max was spending money like . . .' Water is a cliché and all the other metaphors he thinks of seem to involve the demand for pornography. 'But I'm still amazed, frankly, to discover the level of trouble they were in . . .'

413

'Were they?' asks the snappy assistant.

'According to what's online,' Simon says, knowing he's lost a point.

'Ah, the gospel of our times.' The sense of an edge beneath the DCI's gentleness.

'Mrs Lonsdale, did you provide catering for the Dunster Manor party this Christmas gone?'

What the? Simon answers for her: 'No. It was cancelled. I suppose – now – we should have seen that as a sign?'

Tasha actually does grab his hand – the damp unfamiliarity of her touch – and he has to struggle not to shrug her away.

'Max said,' she explains, 'with things how they were, *are*, it would be bad form to be pushing the boat out . . .'

The junior sleuth leans forward eagerly: 'Ah. Okay. Just . . . the accounts show that the money seems to have been paid to you anyway. An invoice was sent and paid . . .'

Simon lets out a gasp, which he tries to pass off as a sniff, as Tasha's nails rake his palm.

'Er, yes,' she says, not looking at either her family or the interrogators. 'There was a bit of a mix-up over that. I was, uh, expecting . . .' She digs her nails deeper into her husband's hand. '. . . er, expecting to do the party as usual, so I sent the invoice early. Small businesses get a bit neurotic, especially at the moment, I suppose, with . . . and I just noticed the other day that it had, seemed to have been paid in. I was going to mention it to . . .'

A caveman flash of suspicion that there was something between his wife and Max. But he dismisses it. Why would he want Natasha, with Jenno's tight young body on tap at home?

'Do you have any idea why it might have been paid?' the top cop asks her.

Simon, ignorant of the windfall but already concerned about the possibility of having to return it, says: 'Well, we know now it was a company in chaos.'

But Tasha cuts in with: 'Guilt.'

What? 'In what way?' asks the deputy detective.

'Look, I was a bit of a princess with him when he cancelled the bash. I think even before . . . Max just couldn't bear to disappoint people. I think he settled the bill out of sympathy . . .'

'Another example of pretending to be Rockefeller,' Simon offers, consumed with the question of where the money went; the battered family finances have certainly never seen the benefit of it.

'Will I have to pay it back?' blurts Tasha.

A flicker of a grin from the top cop. 'That will be a matter for the administrators. I don't see this being relevant to the report we send to the coroner. Unless . . . something else we need to clear up. Would Maxwell Dunster have had any reason to threaten anyone here?'

Bowled a doosra, and he didn't begin to pick it. Simon throws a genuine look of confusion around the table, which the others return.

'Okay,' DCI Duncan continues. 'It's just that sightings and sat-tracking show that the suspect drove up here last night between the house and the factory. Did anyone see him or have contact with him?'

So this is how interrogation works. There has been no suggestion in anything the detectives said before this that they have this smoking gun. His wife is gripping the edge of the table with both hands, as if she's just superglued two pieces of wood.

'I had to go to the loo in the night and I did notice headlights down the hill . . .'

'About what time, Mrs Lonsdale?'

'Oh, one-ish.'

'Did you see what sort of car?'

'A VW, I think. Beetle maybe.'

'Which wouldn't narrow it down much round here,' Simon interjects, resenting the attention on Natasha. 'Cars and dogs – people tend to have a mix of big and little ones.'

But the cops ignore him and the woman asks his wife: 'And did you do anything?'

'No. You do sometimes get a lost car. Satnav is a bit patchy in the valleys. Once, years ago, when we first moved in, we drove down and it was . . . I'm not sure how to put this . . . a couple . . . who shouldn't have been together . . .'

'Really? You never told us,' blurts Polly.

'If it was Maxwell Dunster,' the young one asks. 'Can you think of any reason he would have driven here?'

Can he have blamed his payment to Natasha for his downfall?

'No. Really not at all,' Natasha quickly says.

But Simon knows. Max came here to kill him: as revenge for the last dinner-party and the years of class warfare between them. He is working on the wording of his confession when Josh, says, with sniffling adolescent diffidence: 'Yeah. That would be me?'

*

In his mind, he thinks of them now as The Six but doubts that the term will ever be spoken aloud. The day is as strange as the number. Because of the rhythm of the social week and the early starts of the London commuters, Tom can never remember them having a dinner party on a Monday before. The term used for this meal by Libby – now unquestionably, in the absence of Jenno, the queen of their hive – is 'Leftovers Supper'. Tom, reading the email, at first wondered if that was a dark joke, but quickly realized it wouldn't be.

The food is a Lincolnshire Poacher and courgette quiche with salad. A bowl of blueberries and a dish of cream, both covered in cling-film, rest on the dresser. Two bottles of a 2002 Mersault stand opened in silver coolers on the table, although at first everyone except Tasha declines wine. They mumble something about tiredness and driving but Tom guesses that they, like him, feel a primitive instinct that pleasure is inappropriate after what has happened.

Only six places have been set – two of the usual chairs have been placed neatly in the corners of the room – which is a sensitivity that surprises him from Libby, although her precaution has not made the unused portion of the table any less haunting.

'I'm run off my feet,' sighs Libby, as she and Emily – who have shared serving duties – sit down. 'We've had to give Abby a sort of compassionate leave. Jonny said we're not contractually obliged but . . . we've given her and the Dunsters' girl the Norfolk cottage for a few days. And we've had our one's parents on the phone from Wagga-Wagga or wherever, asking how much danger she was in.'

'Which was none, frankly,' Jonny says through a mouthful of chewed food. 'Because he'd got her out of the way . . .'

'Ah, yeah,' interrupts Tasha, reaching for a refill of wine. 'That was one of the bits I didn't get.'

At each end of the table, between the bottle and the serving dishes, lies a copy of the *Daily Mail*, like the ironed copy of *The Times* in newspaper cartoons of breakfasting aristocrats. These editions, though, are folded not to the front but to a two-page article in the middle: WHAT LED A MAN TO KILL HIS 'PERFECT FAMILY'?

Coming home on the train, too distracted by the aftermath to read or work, Tom saw, apparently floating in the window he was staring through, an image of the Dunsters, smiling in a family group. Failing to blink away what he assumed to be a trick of his traumatized mind, he realized it was a reflection from the newspaper being read by the commuter opposite. The newsagent at Milton Keynes Central was sold out of *Mail*s, but he found one at a petrol station on the 422. He brought it to supper, correctly suspecting that Libby and Jonny wouldn't have seen it, but found that Tasha had already given them a copy.

Without her reading glasses, Tasha holds the paper as close as a philatelist examining a stamp. 'This is it. *Others connected with the family had a lucky escape. Alice Bunn, nineteen, from Dunedin in New Zealand, had been working for the couple as a live-in nanny for six months, but escaped the massacre because, on the fateful evening, she was the beneficiary of*

417

theatre tickets in London, given by the Dunsters' close friend and neighbour, Jonathan Crossan, QC, one of the country's highest-paid barristers . . .'

Tasha stops reading. Jonny waves his fork like a conductor's baton. 'It's okay, I'm a big boy, as Mrs Crossan will confirm, if asked. You can out read the rest. *Viral Internet dickhead and son of disgraced Tory peer blah blah blah . . .'*

Even in comparison with the rest of their battered gang, Jonny looks tired and twitchy. Tom has tried to persuade Emily to reveal what she is treating him for but, mortified by her indiscretion, she has returned to maddening reticence. Some sort of nervous breakdown, he assumes.

As Tasha folds the paper, Tom sees the photograph again: Max, Jenno, Rosie and Jamie in Barbados the Christmas before last. Felix and Phoebe say they will have got it through Rosie's Facebook page. Papers favour holiday snaps for such pieces, presumably because the happiness underlines the tragedy. Tom/Max is shown separately in a rugby picture from the school site.

'So why *did* you send the down-unders to the theatre?' Simon asks.

Libby stabs a fork in the air. 'Guys, guys, lower your eyebrows. It's nothing at all like what you might think . . .'

'He . . . he asked me,' Jonny begins. They keep finding it hard to say *Max*, as if disgrace is literally the loss of a name. 'The day before the . . . the *deaths*, I think it was, he asked me if I could arrange to get the help out of the house on Friday night.

'Gosh,' says Emily. 'And what did you think?'

Libby's dirtiest cackle. 'Well, what do you reckon? Jonny, being Jonny, assumed the Dunsters were planning something involving handcuffs and melted chocolate and didn't want to risk the kangaroo girl walking in on them.'

'She desperately wanted another baby,' says Emily quietly, then quickly: 'I know that as a friend, not a doctor.'

'Of course, now I feel a complete bloody pillock.' Jonny

pours himself some wine and, when Simon silently lifts a glass in his direction, fills that as well. 'But, at the time, I thought I was doing a mate a favour.'

Having been fooled so completely by one friend, Tom now finds himself acutely tuned to the moods and attitudes of the others, and Simon's glance at Jonny raises an apprehension that soon proves justified: 'Just like the favour you did your mate by waving through the annual accounts of a company that was almost certainly trading insolvently?'

'Below the belt, old boy,' complains Jonny.

'Is wrecking dinner parties going to be your job now, Si?' Libby says.

Jonny raises a hand from the table. 'It's okay, darling. I'm sure other people are thinking it. Look, Max fooled the board. But I was a non-exec. It was maybe point nought one of my year. It wasn't my *work* or anything. Sure, he fooled me financially but he bamboozled all of us in different ways . . .'

'Did he?' asks Tasha.

'I'd never done the sums,' says Libby. 'Rosie and that Tom were virtually the same age. He must have left the first wife with a kid . . .'

'I know. It was sort of never talked about.' Emily cuts in. 'But we mustn't judge him.'

'There's a long chalk between adultery and mass murder,' slurs Tasha, who leans over the newspaper, still holding it near to her face. '*Sources close to the investigation say that a positive pregnancy-testing kit was found in a bathroom at the house. However, autopsy results are not yet known.*'

'Poor Jenno,' says Libby.

'Let's hope it was her,' says Simon. 'We're terrified it's Rosie.'

'Are we?' Tasha needles him. 'Actually, our Josh had a lucky escape.'

'Josh?' ask Libby and Emily at almost the same time.

Tasha turns to top up her glass from the nearest bottle, but discovers that it contains only a dribble. With as neutral an expression as he can manage, Tom passes her the Mersuault from his end of the table.

'Yes, seriously. No, really, my God . . .' As soon as the glass is full, Tasha half-empties it again. 'The police came to see us . . .'

'What? Little and Large?' asks Libby.

'Mmmm. Apparently . . . *Max* drove over to our place after he'd . . .'

Gossip in the village, online and in the papers has covered almost every possibility – from Max having a gay affair with Jonny's dad to Dunster Manor being a front for Libyan gunrunning – but Tom has never heard this: 'No way!'

'Yes, absolutely. Josh is convinced that, er, Max had come to honour-kill him for deflowering Rosie. We've told him he's being silly but there is a terminal . . .' – terminal? No, *terrible*, she must have said – 'plausibility to it . . .'

'Bollocks,' says Simon.

'Guys, guys,' warns Libby, obviously remembering the final meal.

'I'm utterly convinced he'd come for me,' Simon continues. 'I'd have been number one on his hit list. He saw me as an uppity little northern Jew.'

'Rubbish.' Jonny has just come back into the room with two more chilled bottles. 'I doubt he even knew you *were* a four-by-two . . .'

'A *what*?'

'Anyway, you're not really one.' Tasha has removed the new bottle from the shiny silo before Jonny has even slid it to the bottom. 'Only when you want to take a fence . . .'

What? *Offence.*

'You'd be the one that knows if he's a Jew, Tash,' says Jonny.

'Guys, guys.' Peacemaker Libby again.

Emily's pacifying instincts are also triggered: 'From the little I know about these cases – and obviously he wasn't my patient – nobody who wasn't a Dunster would have been at risk.'

'The wiring, whatever it is, seems to be closed circuit,' Tom tries to help her.

'But you never know, do you?' says Simon, who, Tom hopes, might be going out for a smoke soon. Emily's left shoulder rises slightly: always her tell for tension. He knows how irritated she is by the trend towards treating any comment – even professional knowledge – as opinion.

Libby offers seconds of quiche and Tom is tempted but again feels the impulse to fast. Their hostess sets the fruit and cream in the middle of the table with six bowls. 'There's no cheese course: weekday supper and no au pair. Help yourself to the berries.'

Tom wonders if he is the only one thinking that Max would have lunged forward, serving himself first. Sometimes he took such a large portion that he had to give some back when the final plate was being filled.

'Come on, tuck in,' says Libby. 'We might as well take advantage. Am I a bad person for noticing that grief and shock seem to be better than the Dukan for burning the calories? I wouldn't be surprised if I've dropped a dress size by the funeral. Which we reminds me: are we going in what we've got or going shopping?'

'Gosh. I really hadn't thought about that,' says Emily. Tasha is stretching across the table, like a snooker player with a tricky pot, to reach the bottle of wine at the other end.

'Black, I imagine,' Libby carries on. 'It's hard to imagine anyone, in these circumstances, doing all that flapdoodle about wearing yellow and orange and making it a celebration of their lives.'

'We don't have a date yet, I assume?' Tom asks, looking towards Libby, with her Parish Council hat on.

'No,' she replies. 'Micro-Cop says the inquest will be opened and adjourned and the bodies released. But that's when the fun and games really start. The first wife wants the elder son buried separately. The Dowager Dunster wants a single funeral for all four, but Jenno's parents are, uh, dead set against that. And you can see where they're coming from . . .'

'We went through all that with the 7/7 families,' says Jonny. 'Are we going to need another bottle, Tash? Should the terrorists be listed on the memorial with the victims?'

'Absolutely bloody not,' says Libby. 'It'd be like having Hitler on the Cenotaph.'

Tom wonders whether to take her on, but does: 'Steady on, Libs. That's a bit harsh on Max.'

'I wasn't talking about Max. Anyway, the Red Rev's line inevitably is that they remain a family, whatever. She's probably got that from some lesbo Anglican app.'

'No. I think she's right,' says Emily. 'All we can do is think that he didn't know what he was doing.'

'He couldn't admit failure,' Tom adds. 'Max without money was a contradiction in terms – like de-alcoholized wine . . .'

Tasha further tests the other variety. Libby nods. 'You know what? I can actually almost, sort of, you know, *understand* it? I mean, the rationale.'

'The whatty what?' Tasha struggles to enunciate. Tom hopes that Simon is driving, although he must have sunk the best part of a bottle himself.

'What I'm saying is, I can sort of see what he was thinking?'

Jonny does one of his double eye-pops. 'Crikey! I'm going to double lock the gun cupboard!'

'No. No, I'm serious,' his wife continues. 'I don't mean I'd ever . . . but . . . sometimes when I'm lying awake in the middle of the night . . .'

'Nudge me in the ribs, then, darling. Better things we could be doing.'

'Jonny, SHUT UP!' In its unexpectedness, the shout is like a . . . like a . . . the remaining Six will now hesitate for ever to use the metaphor of gunshots. 'For God's sake, just shut up and let me say this . . .'

'Okay. Okay. Keep your hair extensions on, sweetheart. Is it a Ladies' Day?'

'Oh, for God's sake! What I'm trying to say is that, sometimes, I actually work out the dates. I think, well, suppose all the children live to their eighties . . .'

'Ooh, don't,' says Tasha. 'You might spook them.'

Libby ignores the interruption. 'Or ninety, given the way medicine is going. So sometimes I work it out. That means Lucas would . . . Lucas would be *gone* . . . by 2093 or so. And then the whole of our little family of six would be finished and – I know this sounds stupid – but I wouldn't have to worry about them any more. And they couldn't be upset by having lost me, us. When we fly on planes without the kids – Marrakesh, whatever – I sometimes actually imagine my mother or my sister driving to the school and saying: *Mummy and Daddy . . .* and I can see their little faces and . . .' Libby is crying but they are so used to this since the deaths that, as Tom reaches out to stroke her arm, Emily is handing her a tissue – a grief team. 'Thank you. What I'm trying to say is that, once you love someone, you dread them being hurt, and I suppose that what we have to try to think is that, in some mad way, obviously *mad* way, Max was trying to put everyone beyond being hurt . . .'

'By shooting them?' snarls Simon Lonsdale. 'Yeah, that'd work.'

'Simon,' Tasha warns him. 'Stop it.'

*

The photographers keep their distance, on the village green, as if nervous of being accused of intrusion, so the flashes are behind and distant, like a speed camera, rather than those electrical storms engulfing celebrities, which epileptics are advised not to watch on television.

Nicky had anticipated the presence of the press but is thrown by the sight of the cars: the long line of black vehicles outside the church, like a traffic jam of hearses. At the age of fifty-three, this is, he calculates, his ninth funeral. He has no idea if this is above or below the average experience of death for his age and type.

Three grandparents (he never knew his father's father), Dad, two business mentors who died after long retirements, a colleague of his own age who collapsed at a conference and a school friend of Bobby's who committed suicide after rumours of bullying that were never proved. So there should be nothing shocking in the glimpse of polished wood through long, low windows. But the scene repeated four times in a row is appalling, like a repatriation from Afghanistan or Iraq.

The Mortimers are late because Nina, off school sick, kicked up about being left alone, an unusual insecurity surely caused by the massacre. There have been assemblies and lessons at school, designed to reassure students but perhaps encouraging them to brood.

As they enter the church, Nicky stumbles on a groove smoothed into the stone by eight centuries of the feet of those traditionally called 'believers' but who, like him, must often have been drawn here by ritual, obligation or desperation to find sense. As he trips, Monifa grabs his arm to steady him and then does not let go.

Most of the pews are already full, two on either side of the aisle towards the back packed with the grey–blue of Westbury Park blazers. A tubby, ruddy-faced chap he thinks he's seen on the London train is handing out prayer books and service sheets. There's a gap in the very last pew beside an old lady with a question-mark stoop and a heavy black hat that makes him think of long-dead aunts. As Nicky lets Mon go in front of him, the organ starts up a Bach death march.

*

The Old Rectory, for this morning, has been returned to the vicar. As she vests in the dining room, Sue thinks of her predecessors in this living, who saw such luxury as their due. Whatever waves may have been caused by her sermon at the Christmas service, the Rawlinsons have been complete angels. Toby is at the back of the church handing out sheets, while Ali is programming the digital organ from the loft, as the usual keyboardist is chief mourner. And because – unusually – there is no funeral party leaving from the house of the deceased, the core mourners are gathering here.

Fiddlesticks! She'll need to wee again before they go over; it was a mistake to drink the strong coffee Ali Rawlinson offered her from that whizzy machine, but it is a hazard of her occupation that hospitality cannot easily be refused without offence. Sue feels more nervous than before her ordination or the first people she hatched, matched and despatched as a curate. Surgeons, she imagines, must sometimes face cases they feel to be beyond their experience and expertise, and this quadruple funeral is her equivalent. After two unproductive evenings attempting to write a homily, she has come to the conclusion that all she can offer is sympathetic incredulity. She is not sure if this is useless or the only use she has here.

The loo is the old-fashioned sort with an overhead cistern and chain, which she has to yank three times before the bowl is fit to leave. Walking across the hall, she finds herself thinking of those leaders of apocalyptic cults who announce that the world will end at midnight on the 27th of the month. This is her morning of the 28th. She feels doubted and challenged. Bill Adamson's was the worst funeral until this one, but the congregation accepted cancer as something that happened. Today the eyes and whys will drill into her.

No sound is coming from the drawing room and she wonders for a moment if the mourners have all followed her own precaution and are doing final ablutions. But, when she goes in, she finds several people sitting, although silently and in two distinct groups. An elderly, elegant woman she takes to be Lady Dunster is having her hat adjusted by a willowy forty-something who must be her daughter. Sue does the double take that happens at so many funerals, when the deceased somehow seems to be present as a guest through a trick of family resemblances.

'Reverend, I'm Max's brother Dan,' he confirms her guess, standing and offering a pumping handshake. Lady Dunster frailly wafts a hand which Sue gently squeezes. The daughter flashes a quick, strained smile.

The black-clad couple on the other side of the room stand but move no closer.

'Jennifer's parents,' says a bald, bespectacled man, his arm around the shoulders of a woman who is visibly trembling.

Sue is reminded of an entry on her to-do list: 'Ah, yes. It's a tiny, tiny thing but would you prefer me to say Jennifer? On the service sheet . . .'

'We always said Jennifer.' The mother speaks so softly that Sue has to lean closer to be sure of hearing. '"Jenno" came from school. You see, her best friend was another Jenny.'

This memory triggers a severe bout of shaking, which the husband tries to buttress. Sue turns so that she can address the two sides of the room. The worst funerals – those that allow no consolation of a long life gently ended – always feel to her like being in a black-and-white movie, the convention of dark clothing exaggerating the paleness of faces drained by shock and insomnia. For show, she checks her watch, although she has taken her cue from the grandfather clock in the corner.

'If everyone is ready, I think perhaps we should go over,' she says.

'All right, Mummy?' asks the daughter.

'Let's get it over with,' says Lady Dunster.

Normally, the pall-bearers wait in the porch, but this procession is so long that the line stretches down the path and on to the pavement. The cameras click-click-click like cicadas as Sue leads the chief mourners: Lady Dunster, supported by her children, followed by Jennifer's parents.

She stops behind the last coffin and splits open the BCP at the ribbon that marks the Order for the Burial of the Dead. A biting wind riffles the pages and she is glad of the fleece between her cassock and surplice. The families are wearing winter overcoats but it is Sue's belief that a priest should look like a priest.

In the pause before she begins the prayers, she properly registers for the first time the italic preamble which has seemed irrelevant at the few other burials she has carried out under the old rite: *Here is to be noted, that the Office ensuing is not to be used for any that die unbaptized, or excommunicate, or have laid violent hands upon themselves.* In blander phrasing, this problem was raised in a phone call with the bishop, but they agreed that it was superseded by the modern model of an inclusive ministry.

She breathes in deeply, then begins the prayers over the dead, projecting her voice as loudly as she can. 'We brought nothing into this world, and it is certain we can carry nothing out . . .'

*

Through my fault, through my fault, through my most grievous fault. The words come to her from services long ago. Are they even used now? But this is the prayer that loops through Emily's head. Although Tom, to whom she confided her guilt, told her not to be so bloody silly, she has no doubt that she is responsible for what happened.

'Earth to earth and dust to dust',
Calmly now the words we say . . .

The physical effort of singing – hard enough, for the non-musical, even at weddings – makes her worry about vomiting. She feels very slightly better than she expected, having, against all her discipline on self-prescription, popped a zopiclone with her nibbled toast. Looking around the church – seeing Jonny and Becca Adamson, the poor woman still more distraught as forensic accountants inspect the Dunster pension scheme – she wonders what percentage of the congregation is on chemical assistance.

In her own case, the pill does nothing to reduce the jolt of the four coffins. The human mind – its astonishing resilience the major lesson of her decades as a doctor – becomes just about accustomed over time to the single varnished oblong in the nave, but the horror of this occasion is emphasized by the crowding on the altar.

With insufficient room in the usual place between the front two pews, the caskets have been placed on the other side of the communion rail, fanned out to allow a route to the pulpit for the priest and readers. From the extra-long coffin which must be Max's and the shorter one presumably used for Rosie, it's possible to guess that the children have been placed between their parents in a parody of a family group. According to Libby, Jamie D is wearing his county Under-13 rugby shirt.

Father, in thy gracious keeping
Leave we now thy servant sleeping . . .

Even the hymns assume a single body. She wonders if she should sing the nouns as plurals, then hates her stupid, swotty mind for even thinking it. And music at funerals, unless left to a choir, seems to her a mistake, the loudest singers almost by definition the least affected. But Max, it turns out, had left, along with a will that has been rendered largely useless by his murder of his heirs and the bankruptcy of Dunsters, a note of the songs he wanted sung over his body and the first of these was 'Now the Labourer's Task is O'er', the traditional choice of the hard-working, so therefore very Max and, though arguably inappropriate in these circumstances, *Hymns Ancient and Modern Revised* can hardly be expected to have included tunes suitable for a family shooting.

An almost constant, hollow coughing comes from the school group, with the rhythm of a slow hand-clap. Nerves or boredom, she hopes, rather than another rush of cases of suspected SARS for tomorrow's surgery. Between the expectoration is the sound of relentless sobbing: the symptom she most frequently encounters and for which there is no good cure.

The singing finished, the Reverend Sue stands in the gap left by the opened altar gate. Emily suddenly wonders if clergy are given proper lessons in handling distressful outcomes, in the way that began patchily with doctors of her generation and is now a proper part of medical courses.

'For all of you,' the vicar says, 'this will be one of the hardest days of your lives. And – for those closest to Jennifer, Rosie, Jamie and Max – the hardest you will ever have known . . .'

Although she has always defended their priest against the Anglo-Catholic sexist bigotry of the others, Emily has never been quite sure that Sue had it. But, as one professional to another, she is impressed by this beginning: *you* rather than *I* and the careful reversal of the traditional Christmas card order to set Max apart from the other three. After considerable debate – led by Libby and the vicar – there is no photograph on the front of the Order of Service because a happy holiday portrait seems inappropriate.

'When I meet non-believers,' Sue continues, 'which is sort of an occupational hazard . . .' – oh, no, don't try a joke, although Libby and Max's brother summon up a chuckle – 'they sometimes say: how do you *know*? how can you be so *sure*? And I say: I don't know, I'm not sure, I have faith, which is about not knowing the answers but hoping for an answer. And I don't think we can expect to know today why what happened happened, and there is nothing wrong in coming here in confusion and bewilderment and even anger – hoping for an answer – but concentrating on what we do know: that – whatever happened in those final moments – there was love between these people . . .'

Emily wants to cheer. Although this sort of lukewarm view is arguably why the C-of-E has far fewer recruits than Catholicism or Islam, this seems to her more sensible than the picture at Bill Adamson's funeral of him radically upgrading the software in Paradise PLC.

'And now let us read together Psalm 90: *Lord, thou hast been our refuge: from one generation to another. Before the mountains were brought forth . . .*'

Emily reads the words in a low mumble, but another phrase – on a chiding loop – runs underneath them. *Through my fault, through my fault, through my most grievous fault.* The first SHO she worked under warned her against the delusion that her intervention could have prevented death – and she carries only a handful of patient deaths on her conscience – but she is privately convinced that she caused these five deaths or at least failed to stop them. Cognitive-distortion disorders can present as maximalization or as minimalization: thinking that things are worse than they are or deluding yourself that they are better. She spotted the maximalist – Jonny – but missed the minimalist: Max.

*

A slight tightening on the right side – leg, arm and neck, as if his foot is being gently twisted – is the only discomfort he feels. There is a warming buzz in the blood, like the moment when the antibiotics kick in during an infection, which must be the happy pills doing their work.

'Thank you to Emily for that very thoughtful reading from St Paul,' says the Red Rev. 'You know, I don't think we should underestimate the guts needed to participate in an occasion of this sort.'

And, to be perfectly honest, the liberal lezza has surprised him over this. Never until this week has it occurred to him to think of her as a professional with objectives and skills, but she has been kind and decisive and, though obviously she and Libs both wanted to be the nibs, has given a sense of being in control, which, frankly, someone had to be.

'And I don't think it would be a sin of pride,' she goes on, 'for all of us in this church – and especially the two families – to allow ourselves the tiniest pat on the back for the courage we have shown in coming together in this way. Certain columnists and bloggers have criticized our decision to organize the funeral in this way, and it wasn't an easy choice, but I'm utterly convinced it was the right one and that you will be glad of it in years to come.'

He's on in a minute. It will be fine. He's got up on his hind legs against some of the maddest fuckers in the justice system – briefs and beaks – and won. This should be a breeze. He spoke it aloud ten times in the bathroom – where everything really does sound better, why can't courtrooms be tiled and tiny? – like his closing speech in the Packer libel trial.

He has not been listening to what the divine dyke has been saying, but now she looks directly at him and smiles.

'There – that's it! That was my homily. My husband often complains that my sermons go on a bit, but short and sweet was what you needed from me today. We're now going to hear about the Dunsters from someone who really knew them. Jonny Crossan would like to deliver a tribute.'

Libby squeezes his hand. He stands. Well done, legs, bloody textbook performance, staunch as oak. From the other side of the aisle, Emily gives a nod of encouragement, acknowledging their secret. Her reading of the lesson was bang-on calm and clear, but then docs are trained in this stuff. The biblical bit was *O grave, where is thy victory?*, which wouldn't have been his choice, frankly, as it looks like a pretty decisive 4–0 from where he's standing. 5–0, if you include Max's big lad, who's being buried next week in Surrey. The mother was invited to this one as well but said no, which feels like the right call.

Passing through the gap between the coffins, he instinctively breathes in, like when you steer a car down a double-parked street. But number-one nightmare at a funeral is knocking over the box, just as number-one fantasy is the deceased sitting up and saying it's all been a jape, which he's certainly imagined Maxie doing today.

In the pulpit, he stands as softly as he can, imagining the tension rippling through his body and leaving through his feet, as the CBT chap told him to, using the seconds of adjusting his reading specs to fill his lungs. When he unfolds the paper, the print is as solid and black as the Stevie Wonder letters at the bottom of an optician's chart.

'I am here today,' he begins, 'to talk about four people we knew and – although this word is difficult for an Englishman of my background and generation to say – *loved*. But I must also talk about a fifth person who none of us knew and who we find it impossible to love.'

He's seduced enough juries to know the tricks of getting attention and he can feel the surprise from the pews. They assume, as they're meant to, that he's going to launch some sort of mad attack on the other victim.

'That fifth person is the Max who – for reasons we can never hope to know or understand – did what he did.' He feels the relaxation surge through the church. 'I cannot talk about him today because he was not someone who we knew. Some newspapers have said – and who are we to disagree? – that Max was trying to be something he wasn't. "A Tragedy of Pretence" was one headline. I would argue – though – that he suddenly found himself no longer able to be what he was, what he had become. It is a subtle difference but – I think – an important one.'

As happens in court, with an opener or closer he's properly rehearsed, it's as if a tape has clicked on and he's listening to the speech being delivered. It was between Tom and him to do the eulogy, and he would have been thrilled if Rutherford had insisted, but understands that, as the Bard put it, the election fell on him.

'And so I will talk only about the four people we knew and – yes – loved.' He is soaring. Gettysburg or what? 'We called Max His Highness – for reasons obvious to anyone who ever saw him, but also because there was something undeniably commanding about him . . .'

*

This effortless confidence in a certain kind of Englishman both irritates her – the sense that they have bought or been given a ticket guaranteed to win the lottery – but also attracts her: Nicky has a bit of it, although Monifa is conscious of him suppressing it with her and especially with the Nigerian side of the family, like Tony Blair going cockney as elections approached, although her husband is the opposite: when he answers the phone to a colleague from work, his accent goes up a notch.

But the ginger barrister, it has to be admitted, is doing the business. There's not much about the wife – 'Jenno, an unusual name for an unusual woman,' he is saying now – and you get the sense that he wasn't really sure who the children were – using a Facebook quote from a schoolmate about each of them – but the four-in-one eulogy is thankfully a little-explored form, and he has found a way to do it.

He now turns and address the longest coffin directly: 'Max the Sixth – your Highness – we thought of you as strong. We thought that you had everything: confidence, wealth, a lovely family. The latter you certainly had, and we will mourn and miss Jenno, Rosie and Jamie until the end of our own days, when we too come to this beautiful church for the final time. Just as those who knew Max's other son - as we never did - will miss him. But – as it turns out – you had less wealth than you pretended and perhaps more confidence than was merited. If only, my friend,' on that word, his voice goes throaty for the first time, 'you had understood that the real strength is to be able to admit weakness. If you had come to us, if you had knocked on our door, we would have helped you.'

Monifa wonders if this is a deliberate reference to the play they saw together. Leaving the pulpit, the barrister stands and bows formally to the four dead.

'Thank you, Jonny,' says the woman priest. 'For that splendid tribute and for expressing so eloquently the conflicting emotions we feel today.'

They flick through their books to the last number on the board: 'The Day Thou Gavest, Lord, is Ended'. The hymn is sung patchily, with a few voices dominating: the quavery falsetto of the old lady beside them, the Terfelesque baritone of Dr Welling from Westbury Park but, above all, the Broadway-musical bawl of Jenny Topham, an actress always on stage, in the first row behind the families, wearing a hat like a black flying saucer.

As o'er each continent and island, the dawn leads on another day . . .

As the third verse begins, the coffins are borne out on the

shoulders of men who, unthinkably to most civilians, do this most days of their life. The largest casket is the only one without flowers. Is this a deliberate differentiation or was the killer's mother simply too distressed to think of it? She assumes that the wife's parents will have done the other three.

Monifa recoils at the impossibility of the procession taking so long, a strip of wood visible in the corner of her eye for what feels like minutes. The adults dip their heads – except for the doctor's husband and the little detective, who stand chin-up, soldier-straight – but several of the WP students in the pews in front sneak a glance. She remembers the comfortable young years when death seemed an unimaginable curiosity and is glad that Bobby opted out of this.

As on an aeroplane, the worshippers leave in order of rows from the front, so they are among the last to come out into the churchyard. She is gripping Nicky's hand tightly. Funerals – and especially this one – leave you wanting to hug your children and make love to your husband.

The hearses are already pulling away. Monifa's neighbour at the service told her that this generation of dead Dunsters, unlike so many ancestors, will not be buried here. Max's mother apparently agreed to cremation because of warnings that her son's grave might be desecrated, although the villager also muttered that the other big families might have been reluctant to allocate four more graves in the sparse remaining earth.

Flashes explode from the pack of photographers, at the church gate now, as Jenny Topham, head demurely bowed, moves towards her limousine. How can you know if an actress's grief is real? A small, wiry guy Monifa thinks she might remember from the Christmas party is already smoking beside the porch, which seems a bit much. A man with shoulders so massive that his coat looks about to burst comes up and says, 'This may not be the place for this' – he sounds South African – 'but if either of you needs a personal trainer . . .' He's holding out a business card.

'Do we look as if we need one?' Monifa asks.

'What? No. You look as if you use one but you could use an even better one.'

Obviously a clever business answer, often used. Nicky wriggles his hand free to take a card and moves towards the barrister, who is standing with the Rutherfords and a blonde woman – eyes raw red with crying – who she doesn't at first recognize. But the fitness coach has got there first and is saying: 'Mate, you absolutely nailed Max in what you said. Although I can't agree with you about it being strong to admit weakness.'

'We'll agree to differ on that, old chap,' says the barrister, expertly using the handshake to steer the South African towards a group of people on his right.

'Nicky Mortimer,' her husband introduces himself, in his phone voice.

'Yes, I know. The train, Morocco at a distance, the theatre,' the ginger barrister replies.

'Jonny, isn't it?' Nicky says. 'I have to congratulate you. I thought there were no words, but you found some.'

'That's kind. But I *am* a defence counsel.'

'You're too hard on yourself. It was perfect.'

Jonny, useless with compliments, like all English men of this sort, is looking at the ground. The feisty blonde one who was pissed at Christmas lunges towards Nicky.

'Why didn't you just *give* him the fucking money?' she spits, loud enough that most of those standing on the gravestoned slope turn.

'I'm sorry?' he says.

'But you're not, are you? None of you bankers are – like Sir Adrian Fucking-Jones . . .'

'Tasha, everyone's upset,' says Dr Rutherford, and the smoking man throws down his cigarette and hurries over and says: 'Honey, what's going on?' Nicky tells her: 'I'm not entirely sure what you're talking about . . .'

'In the paper' – she speaks so emphatically that there's a spray of spit – 'it said that he came to see you on the night before asking for a loan . . .'

'Yes. That's right. But . . .'

'And, if you'd just given it to him, they'd still be here . . .'

Monifa links her arm through Nicky's in solidarity as he says, more diplomatically than she would have: 'Well, that's perhaps an over-simplification . . . but, you know, and especially given what's come out now, I think Dunsters was beyond saving. There comes a point when throwing good money after bad . . .'

'Yeah,' this Tasha interrupts, 'so what's good money? The millions you pay each other in bonuses?'

The barrister's wife steps between them, like a rugby referee, and speaks straight into the woman's face: 'Natasha, stop this now! This is not how people like us behave!'

*

The bright-red time in the night: 01:46. Barely two hours sleep, then. Her tongue has the texture of a wire pan-scourer. She feels hopefully for a plastic water bottle on top of her books, but she has forgotten to bring one up again. All that wine at the wake at the Crossans and then three cups of Jason the coffee guy's best Capoeira while watching four episodes from *The Good Wife* season-2 box-set. She'll have to get a slug of water from a tooth-mug, can wee at the same time. Simon isn't snoring, so he's probably awake, although it's hard to know as he's curled as close to the far edge of the bed as he can get. She used to get up quietly in the night, but such courtesies are long gone now.

As Tasha gets back into bed, the mattress gives the haunted-house creak which she thinks may be one of the reasons they stopped having sex: the awkwardness of the children hearing them.

The wisps of the dream she was having stay in her mind: one of those crazy mash-ups of the real, the maybe and the never: she and Jenno in a school production of *Sweeney Todd* with Jenny Topham. Tasha doesn't know her lines. Jenny and Jenno tell her that they haven't had time to learn theirs either but, when they get on stage, they are word-perfect, while Tash stares out at the audience with brain-freeze until she wakes up with a thundering pulse. Yeah, yeah, Sigmund, it means low self-esteem: we won't be needing you. She never got to see who was singing Sweeney, but knows it would be Max.

Tasha rolls into her sleep position and dutifully shuts her eyes but knows that oblivion is hopeless.

'Are you awake?' she says.

There is no reply and she thinks that if they stay together it will have to be separate bedrooms. They have two spares and Polly goes to university in September.

Four people who she knew are ashes. During the service, she tried to pray for them – pray to them – in the way that came so easily in childhood. But, now, she was calling out in a cave, echoing and empty. She understands why the churches resisted cremation for so long – holding out the promise of bodily resurrection – because a person burned and in an urn has more obviously gone. She rehearses the reasons that once made her believe that death is not the end – that the complexity of the world and of humanity could not have come from nothing, that the tenacity of the human need to believe in something suggests that something must be there – but four human beings she knew until a week ago have vanished and she cannot imagine or connect with them.

What she could visualize all too easily, though, during that bleak and unreal half-hour in St John the Redeemer, was another coffin on the altar – hers. And alone, with her bewildered children in the pews. Although she has allowed Josh to think otherwise – and despises herself for doing so – she is sure that Max had come to kill her that night, the final stage in erasing his relationships before he wiped out himself. At first she convinced herself that she was saved by the lack of intensity in their connection, the first time in her life that she has been relieved that a man who slept with her didn't love her. If he had felt anything for her, she'd be dead. But now she believes that her salvation was more pragmatic and that Max was dissuaded by the green lights flickering in the eaves. Although a multiple killer, he was spared the hardest part of the task for an outsider – entry without detection – and may have floundered at the thought of getting into a house that wasn't his. Her life was saved by Tom Rutherford's security system, although she has only been able to thank him for sparing Josh.

The grief and secrecy she carries have felt like a physical pressure inside – a tumour, abscess or malignant foetus – and now it bursts, leaving her body in a surge of tears. She begins to tremble violently, no more able to control the shaking than the feral howling that comes out of her mouth like an exorcism.

'Bloody hell, what's this all about?'

Simon's voice is as surprising as a stranger's in the room. Tasha heaves and breathes until she is able to speak: 'So you are awake?'

'I am now.'

One of the oldest exchanges in marriage. But his tone lacks the usual edge. The bed groans as he rolls over towards her and then she feels his hand on her shoulder, for the first time in bed in, what, two years? He strokes her back, like he does with Clooney. She panics that he's going to say *there, there,* but he doesn't.

'It's a bad business, of course it is,' says Simon, in the low voice, a talking whisper, that she associates with bedrooms and confessionals. 'But I suppose I'm surprised you seem to have got it worse than anyone. I always thought you could – take-or-leave isn't what I mean – Max and Jen . . .'

So this is what it's like to be a spy when the contact in the cafe spots a gap in the cover story.

'I just keep thinking it could have been you,' she lies.

'What? Shooting you all and the dogs? Cheers, mate.'

He always sounds more northern when he's speaking quietly.

'No, no.' She can talk without her throat hurting now. 'I mean, if you were dead and I was . . .'

'*Really?*'

The pleased, keen note he holds on this word startles her, like a key on a piano suddenly unsticking after years of disuse. It strikes her that compliments always work, regardless of the source or sincerity. People permanently need reassurance.

'Yes,' she says. 'Or obviously if he *had* come for Josh . . .'

'Well, that's nice, Tash. I've been thinking you might want to shoot me recently . . .'

'Self-defence. You'd have shot me first.'

'No. No way . . .'

'So it's all *my* fault?'

'I'm not saying that."

'You were *horrible* to me, Simon, after the funeral, at the Crossans. The others didn't know where to look when you snatched the bottle out of my hand . . .'

'Well, you are putting it away a bit at the moment, darling.'

'Pot and kettle in conversation shock. And *I* don't smoke.'

'No, okay. But – look, ask Emily, if you don't believe me – women are smaller – smaller livers and so on – it affects them more . . .'

'At least it doesn't make *them* impotent.'

'I'm not impotent.'

She realizes that they are going to have the conversation, or at least some of it, and perhaps it was inevitable after the deaths, which were the consequence of pretending.

At first she thinks Simon is yawning, which would be a way out, but it's a sigh. 'I suppose we're going to talk, are we?' he says.

'I don't know.'

'Well . . . it hasn't been good, has it?'

'And whose fault is that?'

'No one's talking about fault.'

'Huh.' She wishes he would stop sighing. 'Give it a minute and they will be.'

Tasha thinks of Jenny Topham: how does it become normal for actors to do what is so unnatural to the rest of us? Altering the voice, adopting a different personality?

'Hey,' she says, trying to sound like the wife in a marriage movie. 'Should we have another go at that?'

'Yeah. If you'll stop attacking me . . .'

'I'm *not*—' She manages to stop herself. 'So how do we do this?' she asks in her new Jennifer Anniston voice.

'Do what?'

Christ. 'I don't know . . . you know, talk about it?'

The silence is so lengthy that she wonders if they will abandon the effort and feign sleep.

'Well,' he says, 'you're the one that spends half your time reading fucking agony aunts. What does Zena say?'

Zelda. You've asked for this, sweetheart. 'She says that most of the problems between couples are caused by money and sex.'

'Hagh!,' the exclamation sounds like, as if he's trodden on a nail. 'Well, and we don't have either.'

The pressure of night mumbling is too much for them now and they are talking normally and sometimes louder. She worries about Henry, whose room is closest, and tries to whisper again: 'I don't think that's quite true, is it? I mean we've got less than we had but we're still doing nicely compared to most people . . .' Simon laughs harshly and she clarifies: 'I mean, the money side of things . . .'

'Yeah. So is that why you became a shoplifter?'

'I'm not a . . . anyway, I'm not taking lectures from a porn addict . . .'

'I'm not a . . . okay, who are we going to do first?'

Another enormous pause. 'Okay, me as usual. Simon, how do you think I feel about you sitting there . . . sitting there . . .'

Masturbating sounds too formal, *wanking* too casual.

'Look,' he says. 'If the restaurant's shut, you see what the corner-shop's got . . .'

On first examination, the comparison is vaguely flattering. She tries to extend the image. 'Setting off the alarm, bringing the police . . .'

'No, no. Look, I've told you. It wasn't babies, it wasn't Alsatians. It was grown-ups doing pretty normal stuff . . .'

'Oh, that's all right then.'

'Look, if you took a poll, most blokes do . . .'

'Oh, *do* they? Did Max?'

'What? I . . . I've no idea. And, if he did, it has no connection with why . . . oh, great. We've been through all men are rapists – now it's all men want to shoot their families . . .'

'Oh, for fuck's—' She wants to pummel him with her fists, as she used to during rows, but men are so quick to shout battered husband now. 'Do you know how it makes me feel that you had to . . . ?'

'But we'd stopped . . .' – she can almost hear the alternative verbs churning in his mind – ' . . . sleeping together.'

'And why was that?'

'I . . . I . . . they say most people who've been married a long time . . . they don't . . .'

'Who says?'

'I don't know. The colour supplements run a piece at least once a year. The dark secret of the middle-classes. Actually, I talked to Tom about it . . .'

'Did you? About us, *me*?'

'Only generally. After tennis. I think it's pretty common. After a certain point, it becomes like fucking your sister . . .'

'Oh. Thank *you*. I think I'm a lot more attractive than your sister.'

'Jesus, Tash, give logic a try sometimes. That isn't what—'

'And, I mean, Jonny and Libby, they practically have to be prised apart . . .'

'Yeah. Sometimes the people who talk about it aren't doing it . . .'

'And sometimes the people who aren't talking about it aren't either . . .'

'Has there been anyone else?' he asks.

'*No!*' she lies. 'You?'

'No,' he probably lies.

'So why did you stop wanting it?'

'It takes two not to tango.'

'I always left it up to you.'

'*Yeah*. Except when you wanted to get pregnant. I felt like a stud stallion.'

Don't flatter yourself, she is about to say, but manages to find the pre-delete key. 'That's not true . . .' she says instead, intending to bring up the rejection in Marrakesh, but halted by other dangerous memories of that trip.

Although they are not touching, he is close enough for her to feel his warmth.

'Okay,' he says, his inflection less hostile than she has come to expect. 'That's sex done. Money?'

'Well, as I say, that's not great. But we're okay.'

His snorts are more annoying than his sighs. 'Seriously, Tash, we're not. Okay, why have you started stealing food, then?'

'I haven't . . .'

'How much do you owe on the credit cards?'

She is relieved it is dark and he can't see her face, but can do nothing about the gulp she gives at being discovered, which she tries to disguise as a sniff.

'Look, we can both hack into each other's files,' he says and he is right. It never occurred to her that she was not the only secret agent in the house.

'What credit cards?' she says.

'Even Jonny couldn't make that defence stick. The ones you've been taking out every few months, transferring balances, paying off the minimum. How much do you owe now? I got it to at least 30k before I had to break off to ring NHS Direct about my heart attack . . . I suppose the money from Max for the ghost Xmas drinks vanished into that pit, did it? And that's how you paid for the Morocco flights . . . ?'

Her husband is a better interrogator than the police were. The only answer she can give is a swallowed, 'Yes.'

'Lucky he was so generous. I did wonder if he was fucking you, but I don't think you're very interested in sex in the end.'

She basks in the luck that Simon decided to answer that

question himself. She rapidly calculates if there is a response she can risk giving, and eventually says: 'That's not very nice.'

'I know the answer will be that I wouldn't have listened – but why didn't you tell me?'

'I was always just about to . . . but then you started banging on about how poor we were . . .'

'*Banging on?* Natasha . . .'

'I'm talking shorthand. And then there was the pay cut. So I couldn't ask you to pay it off.' She puts on the cartoon voice – she imagines the character as a Jack Russell puppy suffering from shyness and a lisp – which she has used since their early days for difficult or embarrassing requests. 'I suppose I'm asking now.'

He makes a sound like a martial-arts expert splitting a marble pillar with his fist. The force of his reaction is so great that she is hit by spit and has to wipe it away on the duvet.

'Wake up and smell the coffee, darling!'

'What? I always think that expression is—'

'I'm talking shorthand. Natasha, I couldn't pay off your . . . great big plastic *hole* if I wanted to. If we were a company, we'd be trading while insolvent . . .'

As Zelda often says about affairs, Tasha has always known but chosen not to know. But, while searching for the best rates for zero-interest credit-card transfers, she has also read other sections of the finance pages. 'We've got the house . . .'

'What? Oh, I don't think we're going to lose the house yet . . .'

Their voices are getting louder. She expects the anguished, tousled face of Henry at the door. 'No, I mean – I know the interest rates are . . . but should we talk to someone about remortgaging?'

Another split pillar; another saliva shower. 'Honey . . .' Weird that the first endearments of love are later only used in anger. 'It's already remortgaged *three* times!'

She has a physical, dizzying sense of their home becoming

unstable, an earthquake or landslide, the huge old stones crumbling and being sucked into the mud.

'For fuck's sake, Simon. Why didn't you . . . ?'

'*Tell you?* Because, like everyone else round here, we were playing doll's houses – doll's *palaces*, more like . . . it would have spoiled the illusion. My father, may he rest wherever, was so fucking right – he always told me never mix with people a lot richer than you are. Because they sure as hell won't meet you halfway by pretending to be *poorer* . . .'

Tash feels a fleeting pleasure that her first thought is not for herself. 'Will Josh and Henry have to leave WP?'

'I don't know. I sit in that study – yeah, go on, laugh – doing the sums over and over. At least we won't have Pol there next year. But she'll have to pay her way at uni. Thank God for student loans! Of course, what's so hilarious about this is that it turns out that Max was doing the same. We were keeping up with the Joneses but Jones was broke!'

Though not the one she would have chosen, it is the longest conversation they have had in years, and the silence makes her want to fill it.

'What are we going to do now?' she says.

'In what way?'

Surely not an innuendo? She realizes that she is going to speak the word that has been on their lips for years. 'Are you going to ask for a divorce?'

'Do you want one?'

Life as a game show: the amplified ticking of the studio clock. Natasha, are you going to say A or B?

'Do you?'

'Dividing our assets? Yeah, that'd make sense. I've got a better idea. Pass me that clay-pigeon gun.'

She has a feeling like she used to have when she believed in blasphemy. 'Simon Lonsdale, that is sick!'

She punches him, he resists and the struggle somehow becomes a cuddle. She is jolted by the unfamiliar pressure of his erection probing her down there.

'Oi, what's that doing there?'

'It's a famous thing – funerals make people want to . . . *make love* . . .'

'Do they?'

He ducks to kiss a nipple: a vague memory of the sequence of their lovemaking.

'No,' she says. 'Not yet . . . not today . . .' She tries to push his head away from her stupidly responding boob. 'We will . . . but . . . I promise you we will when . . .'

The shudder of resentment and rejection runs along his body. He makes to turn away. She does not want her children to come from a broken home.

'I'm still bleeding a bit,' she lies.

'I don't care.'

'Oh, all right, then. Yes.'

She reaches down and finds the slimy missile and places it against her, fighting the desire to flinch from the ticklish dry sting which is all that time and tiredness and grief have left of her desire.

'Eighteen months!' he says, trying to push into her, a sexual statistician as men are. He could always remember every room and hotel they'd ever done it in. She tries not to think of the time with Max.

THIRTEEN

A CROWDED ENGLISH COUNTRY CHURCHYARD

Sleeping on his right side, he faces the bedside table and, during the long winter of insomnia, became used to staring down the creeping numbers on the clock, like watching a slow run-chase on the scoreboard at Lord's. But 05:43 is the first thing he sees today, as his eyes open, easily, ungummily. He pushes down the teat, so that his wife can sleep on. Although his inner timer has woken him ahead of the alarm, he knows that he has slept, and feels, if not entirely refreshed, at least rested.

Jonny no longer wakes up with a solid Walter. He isn't sure if this is due to age or what the doctor gave him. Squinting in the bathroom mirror – not wanting to know how much his hair has thinned – he is pleased to see that the pouches under his eyes look less punched. Fumbling at the back of the medicine cupboard, behind the bottle of senna stuff from when he was bunged up after Kenya, he finds the happy pills and swills one down with night-chilled tap water from Lucas's Bart Simpson tooth mug. He manages a quite productive Smedgewick.

The ceiling lights in the dressing room feel unusually bright and he nudges the dimmer switch. He hovers between ties – the beak he's up before this morning is a club bore, so MCC or Garrick might impress, if he bumps into him in civvies before start of play – until he sees one still hanging in its shiny cellophane prophylactic: a navy-blue Oxford dot – Minetti, he

446

thinks – that Tilly gave him for Christmas. It's hanging next to the black one, just back dry-cleaned of the food stains from Max's funeral. As the CBT chap told him, he instructs the omen to go away. Cogno, as Jonny calls it, mainly consists of ticking yourself off like a toddler, but it seems to work.

He stands in front of the full-length mirror. Even in the subdued illumination, the darker silky strip looks good against the light-blue Royal Oxford button-down. There are chip-on-shoulder chaps like Nicky Mortimer who make a thing of wearing M&S or probably damn Aldi if they sell shirts, but once you've felt T&A against your tits, nothing else will do.

Although he tiptoes into the bedroom to get his wallet and watch, Libby snorts and shifts. Bending down to kiss her, he has a sudden image of Max in the bedroom at the end. Libs told him some details from the inquest over dinner, and the papers will be full of it today.

'Goodbye, old girl,' he says, kissing the top of her head. She makes a drowsy *mwah-mwah* noise in response.

It has been a bad night for wildlife, the A422 smeared with roadkill, in such jagged patterns, from cat's eyes to kerb, that he wonders if a bored driver in the small hours has actually targeted the animals. One is a double-hit, a crow crushed into the residue of the badger it was stripping.

A flash explodes at the edge of his vision. Fuck and bugger-ation. At nine points already, he will have to persuade Libs to do *suttee* for him and take the three for the team. Jonny feels the fear building in his chest like poison heading for his heart. Counting deep, slow breaths, he summons up the inner head-master as the panic quack has taught him: *settle, Crossan, settle, you're getting your boxers in a twist about nothing again.* The counsellor (hideous word) always encourages him to call him-self Jonny in these mental pep-talks, but the surname feels more natural. And, as the road curves towards the junction, and he squints against the rising sun, it strikes him that this might have been the explanation for the flash he saw. *Think positively, Crossan, it was just the light of day.*

447

There's a garage on the station approach road; since the day he shouted at the shopgirl, he daren't buy his papers on the concourse. He manages to purchase an *FT* and a *Times* without refreshment being pressed on him, and the Brenda, thank God, doesn't seem to recognize him. The fuel gauge on the Bentley is low – he really wanted to drive it today, despite the risk of being striped in the multi-storey – and he should top up now but decides it can wait until tonight. Despite the breathing exercises and self-bollockings, he still feels slightly lightheaded.

First good omen: his favourite parking space – 8 – is free, although, even at this time, the multi-storey is filled up with cars, waiting all day like faithful, frozen dogs until they are reanimated by their owners. Second good omen: the 6.38, pulling into the platform, perfectly aligns the door of First Class Carriage B with the spot where Jonny is standing at the front of the line. Mixed omen one: he has one side of a table four-seat to himself, opposite a gargantuan Mancunian (presumably) who's asleep with his mouth hanging dribblingly open. An empty plate is on the table in front of him, streaked with grease and skid-marks of brown sauce.

The days of the gang seem to be over and not just because Max is gone. Lonsdale and Nicky Mortimer generally go in later now and apparently the inquest stressed out Emily, so Rutherford has taken the week off to hold a scented hankie to her forehead.

'A very good morning to passengers who joined us at Milton Keynes,' says the Northern Dalek on the annoy-tannoy. 'The onboard shop is open in Carriage G for hot and cold drinks and light snacks. A complimentary food-and-drinks trolley will be coming through First Class now. And if I could just ask again passengers in Standard please not to walk through the First Class compartments. It's not only inconvenient for our customers in that section but may interfere with train staff carrying out their duties.'

Jonny silently applauds the company's rigorous enforcement of class apartheid. Other travellers celebrate more openly; a raucous cheer rises from the table on the other side of the aisle. A quartet of young shavers who look barely in their twenties, in open-necked shirts and sweaters (IT, he guesses), begin a football-style chant: 'We are First, we are First, we are First!'

He gives them a smile of privileged complicity, then squares *The Times* on the table and braces himself to look for the story he is dreading. Flick-reading, he reaches page seven.

MASSACRE BUSINESSMAN
'COULD NOT FACE REALITY'

The owner of a luxury gift company murdered his wife and three children before taking his own life because he was unable to accept the loss of his multi-millionaire lifestyle, an inquest ruled yesterday.

Maxwell Dunster, 56, owner of a family luxury-goods business, had been threatened with a winding-up order by HM Revenue and Customs, and, on the eve of the killings, was seeking an injunction to prevent publication by a newspaper of this fact . . .

Jonny's career has trained him to isolate swiftly the important sections of a document and he swoops on names and phrases.

DCI Kate Duncan told Buckinghamshire Coroner's Court that investigations had revealed that Dunster, on the day before the killings, had attended a meeting in London with a bank, at which he had been told that a loan agreement to Dunster Manor Ltd could not be further extended.

He speeds past details he already knows – 'made a visit to the home of banker Nicholas . . .' – until his progress, like that of any hypochondriac, is halted by the word he most fears seeing in print: cancer. He finds the start of that paragraph:

In a written submission, Dr Thomas Welling, head teacher of Westbury Park, a private school attended by the two younger murdered children, said that Dunster had delayed payment of fees for two terms because his earnings were reduced while undergoing treatment for cancer. But the coroner, Mrs Geraldine Booth-Webb, disclosed that an autopsy and available medical records had revealed no evidence of any such condition. Dr Emily Rutherford, a GP who was a close family friend, said that, although Dunster had shown no outward sign of any psychological disturbance, she now believed that he was suffering from a delusional . . .

He already knows the next revelation from Libby and tries to skim past, but the tragic fact snags him:

DCI Duncan told the court that a post-mortem examination had revealed that Jennifer Dunster was pregnant.

Although it is nowhere close to a panic attack, an apprehension begins to grip Jonny. Coroners – far more than judges – are the moralists of the legal system, prone to delivering their verdicts wrapped up in a sermon about the way the world is going. He forces himself to look at the last paragraphs.

Returning four verdicts of unlawful killing in respect of Mr Dunster's victims, Mrs Booth-Webb ruled that he had killed them and then himself while the balance of his mind was disturbed.

'In this tragic case, we are dealing with a man who could not face the reality that the enviable lifestyle he had built was, in all probability, soon to be lost to him. He perhaps felt a sense of shame and failure, which seems to have been misplaced, as the evidence of Dr Rutherford and others is that his family and friends would have rallied round to help him through this crisis. It is neither my place nor my intention to apportion blame in this matter . . .'

Jonny has sat through enough judges' summings-up to know that someone is about to be blamed.

'. . . but I believe that strong questions must be asked about why the board of Dunster Manor Ltd apparently failed to challenge or to correct the increasingly fantastical balance sheets of the company, which have led, among other things, to hundreds of present and past employees facing the loss of their pensions. In my view, particular criticism must rest on non-executive directors who were not members of the family.'

Jonny's internal urging to stay calm is threatening not to work. He is happy that the coroner has not named the guilty man. The paper, however, is less helpful:

The longest-serving non-executive director of the company was Jonathan Crossan, QC, 48, a close friend of the Dunsters. He is the son of the former Conservative Education Minister Lord Crossan of Westbury, 78, who is scheduled to stand trial in October on charges of fraud relating to his parliamentary expenses. He denies the charges.

October. So, thank God for the contempt laws, there will be four months of grace before his father can humiliate him again. At least they didn't mention . . .

He closes his eyes and regulates his breaths. *Don't blame yourself, Crossan, you couldn't have stopped this, everyone sensible knows that non-execs are just a rubber stamp.*

Once, when Pa was being monstered by newspaper columnists over a supposed gaffe on the *Today* programme about mixed-sex hospital wards, he told an anecdote at Sunday lunch. A great Cambridge mathematician publishes an equation and is informed by a colleague that it contains a terrible mistake. He tells the college porter to cancel the hansom cab that is taking him to the railway station for a trip to London. Asked why, he replies that everyone will now be laughing at him on the platform and the train. The story consoles the publicly humiliated with the thought that most of the world won't know or notice their shame.

Jonny feels the poison reversing its course through his blood. But then his Neanderthal alert system for predators suddenly makes him aware of being watched. He lowers the paper. The gor-blimey foursome at the other table are gawping at him, the smirks on their rat-like faces revealing bad teeth.

'Ere, mate,' says one of them. 'Aren't you the YouTube bloke?'

'You are, arntcha? Ginger Whinger?' another checks.

Jonny concentrates on the front page of the *Financial Times* as if the meaning of life is revealed there. From behind his paper shield, he hears a northern accent attempting a bad parody of poshness: 'I say, don't you know, I'm one of Britain's leading dickheads!'

Shifting the barrier slightly, he is able to see that all four lads have their cameras angled at him: a parody of paparazzi.

The tannoy coughs. 'Watford Junction is the next stop, in a few moments. If you are leaving us here, we wish you a pleasant onward journey, and please be sure to take all your possessions with you.'

Jonny stands. Hello, Harry Carey.

*

Her old supermarket is just visible from the car park of the new one, as a warning or a temptation. Although Tasha has never met anyone she knows here, she still comes early, just in case.

Built – in opposition to petitions from the smarter residential and commercial addresses – on the site of a bankrupt shoe factory, the shop looks more like a warehouse than a store. A low, white-painted building, with a single line of windows under the roof-line, it most resembles a gigantic public lavatory.

This functionality continues inside. Items are displayed in cut-down packing boxes on basic aluminium shelves. The first time, Tasha was reminded of when they went to Poland for a weekend once and then of being in an episode of *Life on Mars*, the prices so low that they seem like a joke. Items for less than a pound fill almost an entire aisle: many of the products are the rubbery sweets and reconstituted soups you'd expect at that price, but others are startling bargains: packets of Parma ham, bottles of olive oil. There are shelves of wines for £1.99. Simon says they must be cleverly playing the EU import game. Breakfast cereals have the right names and cartoon characters on the cartons, but the nutritional information is in foreign languages. The boxes of tampons look like Lillets but are a brand she's never heard of; the energy drink resembles Red Bull but is called Red Thunder.

The trolleys demand a coin deposit – a system she hasn't used for years, except on holiday in France and Italy – and there are no honesty scanners here. Tasha, though, enters every purchase in a calculator app on her phone, frequently checking the total against the budget written at the top of her shopping list. Unlike at her old shop, there are no handy little clipboards attached to the wire trolley. Bulldog-clipped to her scrap of paper are the discount vouchers she has cut out of the newspapers or the leaflets of bargain offers that are pushed through doors. She always previously ignored these but now hoards them in a sandwich box sarcastically labelled BOGOF.

She stacks the trolley with the bare essentials – European breakfast cereals, bread rolls, cheese, margarine, baked beans, milk, rice, tomato puree – before adding a few unexpected luxuries: Spanish ham, Italian olives. Coupons for the cereal and cheese take her under-budget, a curiously triumphal feeling.

Her phone – she switched to a bog-standard Nokia after managing to get out of the iPhone contract – bleeps. Simon texting:

Stuck at Buzzard. Bloody trains X

Trapping the shopping list between two foreign cornflakes packets, she rests the phone on the trolley handle and taps:

Poor U. Anyone u no on train X

Since coming here, Tasha has completely had to rethink her attitude as a consumer. Customers in this shop operate much as they must have done in the old Eastern Europe, buying not what you want but what they've got. Displays are dictated by current supply: foot spas, quilts, camping chairs and tables, rucksacks, oven gloves and stepladders suddenly turning up among the food.

A reply pings in from Simon: *Just Nicky X.*

The message at first confuses a brain used to only revolutionary leaders having X as a surname, until she realizes who Simon means and that he is being specially affectionate.

A hugely pregnant woman with two brats in tow barges past her without asking, clashing trolleys. If her catering work ever picks up again – and it seems almost bad taste to be running a business after what happened – Tasha is not sure that she would have the nerve to buy ingredients here, but it's okay for the basics. Inevitably there's an occasional pang at breaking the pledge she made when pregnant with Polly to breed completely organic offspring – the stuff they sell here must be packed with additives and e-numbers – but you can't expect restaurant food in prison, and there has to be an element of punishment and suffering in their new life; sometimes she thinks her trolley should be filled with nothing but bread and water.

She wonders if, like some recession Hester Prynne, she should wear a smock printed with a letter B. Although, as Simon keeps stressing, they are not technically bankrupt. Perhaps P, then, for Poor. Tasha tries to suppress a blush at the realization that she also qualifies to wear A on her dress. Although, for most of most days, she forgets what happened in Marrakesh. That was long ago in another country and, besides, the man is dead.

Turning into the final aisle, she joins a queue of Soviet dimensions. Physically ticking off the items on the list, she mentally makes an inventory of the items she still needs but either can't or won't buy here: wine (they haven't yet gambled their long-coddled palates on this plonk) and condoms (the resurrection of their sex-life, though generally a relief, is expensive).

The lines are long and slow, clogged by the number of shoppers – wizened young mothers wreathed in the stench of cigarettes, boulder-bellied blokes in replica football shirts – who agonizingly count out the coins for their single purchases. Stacked next to the tills is a cliff of painkillers, topped with a sign limiting purchase to two packets. They live in a world in which even supermarkets are on suicide watch. She clicks out another message:

Ask if N and Mon are up for the Woody Allen on Saturday X

Is this being happily married? She has found surprisingly effective that long-ago advice to keep telling herself that she loves him. Tasha still often has the feeling of being in a creaking revival of a play she starred in as a younger woman, but they are mainly civil with each other again and shagging on Saturday nights. Her inner feminist still intermittently wants to know if the pornography is over, but he has never tried to do anything in bed they didn't do before, which she has convinced herself would be the issue. The biggest shock has been that Simon now seems more religious than her, even speaking of being confirmed. She blames the deaths, which, among their group, seem to have made believers question their faith but agnostics seek one.

Tasha opens her purse to have the debit card ready; another benefit of this shop to her retail rehab is that no credit is extended. Lightened of most of the slices of plastic she used to carry around, her purse feels flimsy, as if she's been the victim of a robbery. Removing her chip-and-pin reveals underneath her Gold User swipe-card for the spa. Having cancelled it, she should cut it up and replace it with the pass for the council leisure centre.

A wheezer-geezer at the front of the line is eventually persuaded by polite staff and swearing shoppers to abandon his attempt to count out in coppers the cost of a packet of fags. The queue shifts and Tasha edges her trolley another few inches forward.

Yes, P, she decides, is her designated letter from the alphabet of shame, and, as a sort of Catholic, understands what it spells. Penitent.

*

Emily read somewhere that bomb-disposal experts who survive a blast will rarely return to work, even if their injuries heal sufficiently. Once their instincts have been disproved, they are useless.

Faced with the potential death-trap of Becca Adamson – her 7.30 – she understands how this could happen. Tom keeps telling her that she cannot logically regard Max as her mistake, but she is more touched by his attempts to convince her than convinced by them. She considers each of her patients as a potential explosion. She got to Jonny in time, but who knows what else is potentially buried in her list? (At their next consultation, she must encourage Jonny to confide in his wife. It is clear from meetings of The Six – more often Four these days, with the Lonsdales frequently absent – that Libby doesn't know about his illness.)

Outwardly the confident, competent rural family GP, she says: 'Becca, what can I do for you?'

'That stronger stuff you gave me, Doctor, it doesn't seem to be making any difference. Is there anything else?'

'Becca, we've talked about this before. If the pills aren't working, it's probably because there are no pills for this; not because I've given you the wrong one. Is it the sleeping . . . ?'

'Yes. No. No, not really. The nights aren't great but I'm probably worse when I'm awake now. I spilled tea everywhere last night . . . I suddenly started shaking so much . . .'

Emily's next question isn't a guess, because she is so familiar with the condition herself. 'Had you watched the local news?'

'What? Yes. I suppose so. I have it on in the kitchen. I don't really . . .'

'Becca, we've talked – and your grief counsellor will have done, too – about the trigger dates: birthdays, anniversaries, things you used to do with Bill. We didn't think you'd have to deal with an inquest but now, in a way, you do . . . with all the stuff about pensions and Dunster's and so on, it's bound to be unsettling.'

'I just feel incredibly angry with Bill . . .'

'That's very normal . . .'

'Oh, no. Not for, er, leaving us, Doctor. I'm over that, as much as I ever will be. I just keep thinking that he was in charge of the money at the company and so he should have damn well spotted what was going on. It's as if he's, in a way, responsible for everything that happened . . .'

Snap. 'No, Becca. It shows what a caring person you are that you think that. But this wasn't Bill's fault. It wasn't anyone's . . .'

This line of argument seems no more to have reassured Becca than it has Emily, who suddenly hears a warning fizz from the wires of the time bomb in front of her. 'Becca, believe me, if I thought there was a better drug worth trying, I'd prescribe it now. But it doesn't mean I'm fobbing you off. There are other types of counselling, therapies we can try . . .'

'I imagine there are, Doctor. But what's the point of any of it? I'm at the bottom of a pit and no one's going to pull me out . . .'

The fizzing and clicking builds in volume, trembling the wires. 'Becca, you wouldn't do anything silly, would you?'

The patient's flushed, defeated face is rapidly defiant. 'What? Top myself, you mean? My sister-in-law's already given me that talk. No, I've got two children who depend on me now. And, don't worry, I'd never ever do what that selfish beggar Dunster did. To myself, I mean. I can't even imagine the other. When I say no one's going to get me out of the pit, I just mean I'll have to crawl my own way out.'

Emily is tempted to stand and applaud. Among all the measurements at her disposal – assessing blood and puff – there is no reliable test of courage, but it is the most impressive life force. Becca Adamson is the best patient a doctor – or at least a bad doctor – can have: one who doesn't need Emily's help. She might have failed to spot a risk, but she can still identify the safe ones.

*

457

The delay has been so long that complimentary tea and coffee are being served in Standard Class, though in paper cups rather than china. It must be half an hour since the train's engines were switched off – never a good sign – leaving the feeling of being on a boat becalmed at sea. And it is at least that long since an announcement acknowledging only an 'incident', sparking lengthy and repetitive conversations among passengers about whether this signified another 9/11 or a tactful train manager using a euphemism for suicide.

Nicky is hankering after being back in First – the table fours in Standard are more cramped and prone to ranty Glaswegians working their way through a tower of Special Brew – but he knows that Simon is economizing and it would have been twattish to leave him on the platform and strut to the front of the train.

The newspapers are scattered between them, folded open to the reports of the inquest. A slick of spilled coffee is melting Max's face. The photograph shows him grinning in bright sunlight on a turreted roof.

'Looks awfully like Marrakesh, doesn't it?' says Nicky.

'Yeah. Tasha thinks they grabbed it from her Facebook page. They've cropped the rest of us out.'

As he speaks, Simon is checking texts. 'Oh, the guvnor wants to know if you two are up for a film at the weekend?'

'Mon's Keeper of the Diary. You know how it is. I'll check.'

Nicky suspects they will be busy both nights. Employing Simon – on a three-month contract in Public Affairs, the best he could get him in this down-sizing climate – was done from a general guilt about being alive and in work after the Dunster stuff. Hearing that Simon had been sacked by Samsons was like being told that another colleague is having chemo: the questions of 'who next?' and 'why not me?'

Desperate to appease the gods with good behaviour, he has even forgiven Tasha, a bit of a loose cannon, but a laugh, for her outburst at the funeral, which merely spoke aloud allegations he had silently rehearsed against himself. But he is effectively Simon's boss – or at least far above him in the RSG hierarchy – and so socializing is awkward. With his packed lunches, advance-purchase rail tickets, talk of family holidays out of season in the UK and obsession with buy-one-get-one-free offers, Simon looms over Nicky like an economic memento mori. Paranoid about seeming 'out of touch' – the current problem of the government, according to polls – Nicky, when they had the Lonsdales round for a kitchen supper, went out and bought supermarket wine cheaper than the cheapest bottles in his cellar.

Electronic catarrh from the tannoy and then actual throat-clearing from the train manager.

'Thank you again for your patience this morning, ladies and gentlemen. I've just heard from Euston Control Room that we're, in all probability, going to be here quite some time.'

The collective sigh that rises in the silent carriage has the sound and force of a breeze.

'The line is closed at the moment and will be for the fore-seeable future, I'm afraid, because of a passenger under a train at Watford Junction.'

'Poor soul,' says Nicky, making another offering to the gods of the unforeseeable future. Then, in another libation of kindness: 'I'll text HQ that we're both going to miss the register.'

'Cheers,' Simon replies. 'Good job Jonny Crossan isn't here. He always gives jumpers both—'

The associations of the image stop him.

*

A day off during the week should be a treat, but Tom always feels uneasy among the retired and the unemployed, both tribes he dreads ever joining.

Outside the newsagent on Westbury High Street, there's a billboard for the local paper: DUNSTER MURDERS VERDICT. A celebrity here, Max is given his name. The national papers, assuming the details long dissolved in the deluge of news, use general allusions: TYCOON KILLED FAMILY FROM SHAME.

Putting the two boxes on the back seat of the Disco, Tom notices daffodils and tulips outside the greengrocer and thinks of buying some for Em. He definitely needs to come up with something to buck her up; she came back from the inquest yesterday as if *she* had been found guilty. But he's parked on double-yellows and the wardens are positively North Korean during shopping hours.

Switching on Jeremy Vine, he gets that little twitch of pleasure that comes from finding a favourite song playing. Held on a red at the Buckingham Way crossroads, he taps out on the steering wheel with one finger the sombre, hypnotic rhythm of 'Exit Music (For a Film)'.

'Radiohead. Great track,' says JV. 'Coming up in the next half hour – what drives an apparently loving husband to kill his wife and family? We'll be talking to a psychologist about that awful case you've probably seen in today's papers. But now the latest news . . .'

Allegations of cruelty in Britain's care-homes for the elderly. Opposition to the new high-speed rail link through rural central England. The bombing in Morocco is third. (Emily, looking up from the *Guardian* at breakfast, had told him of the explosion, attributed to AQ, at the three-tier cafe in Marrakesh where they drank mint tea. 'We were lucky,' she said, with a visible shiver. Tom knows that this is wrong statistically – how many days and how many visitors are there in almost five months? – and specifically: their party that day included someone who, in a quiet English middle-class way, proved as psychopathically destructive as any suicide bomber. But he didn't argue with her. He feels lucky to have a wife and family he has no desire to kill – and, in fact, would die for – and who show no sign of violent thoughts towards him.)

Replaying their conversation, he has missed the last part of the news bulletin and tunes back in for the travel news. It must be a reflection on the state of the transport infrastructure that they always employ for this purpose the sort of voices you'd want to hear in a hospice.

'Still no trains south on the West Coast line into Euston at the moment because of an incident at Watford Junction,' the journey nurse is saying. 'And I'm afraid British Transport Police tell me that it will take a wee while longer to clear the scene.'

Tom imagines himself on a stalled train from the north, the First Class compartment boiling with unspent testosterone. Staying home to nursemaid Emily through the inquest has proved to be a smart move.

'Thanks, Sally,' JV says. 'Next, we'll be discussing a crime that seems to go against nature. Before that, The Killers – 'For Reasons Unknown' . . .'

That pleasant sense that you are somehow subliminally influencing the playlist. It's the *Live at the Albert Hall* version. Somewhere in that howling crowd are Emily and him. Realizing that he is soon to hear a discussion about Max, Tom uses the wheel switch to retune to 5, where he discovers that his old friend and neighbour is the subject of a phone-in. 'That bloke wants shooting for what he done,' a high-pitched Midlands voice is saying. Wondering if this morning's topic can really be 'Have *you* ever felt like shooting your family?', Tom retunes to 2, where the Killers are in the middle of 'For Reasons Unknown.'

He wonders if the name of band and track were chosen deliberately as a sort of theme-tune for Max, although he suspects that the music is scheduled by computer these days.

But Tom will never hear what is said about the incomprehensible events that happened nearby because he has arrived at the church, for the first time since the funeral.

*

Bloody Jonny has gone AWOL again. She's texted him twice about stopping on the way back to get some Comte or Epoisses or similar for when the Rutherfords and the new couple come round tonight, but he has not replied.

461

*J, Have you taken on board about cheese? Something soft
and French but not the obvious L xx*

Cheese, on board, not bad. She watches the screen, hoping
for the instant ping-back that still amazes her about texting. She
can't really concentrate on the rest of her list until she knows
Jonny's on top of the shopping.

A migraine is tightening around her brow like a bandanna.
Hardship Committee days are always stressful and this morning's especially so, with Josh and Henry Lonsdale on the list.
Libby declared a personal interest, then pushed the grants
through in her bolshiest manner. Jack Bracken warned against
being too sentimental in a recession with so many victims,
and Fi Irving-Law questioned whether Henry Lonsdale would
qualify academically for any other kind of scholarship, but
Libby was ready to resign if defied.

She will betray nothing when she sees Tasha, although
they're increasingly unlikely to meet, as Mrs L has stopped
coming to the spa and has been seen wheeling a trolley from the
new discount supermarket. Libby went in once, in the opening
week, from curiosity, and it looked just like any other shop until
you realized they stock only one brand of probably Ukranian
champagne and barely two types of pasta.

Feeling tired – which isn't like her, although it's been a bit
of an epic day, Hardship Committee coinciding with an early
brainstorm on the parish's plans for the Diamond Jubilee –
Libby slips the phone back in her cardigan pocket and stretches
to reach the flowers in the window alcove above the last pew
on the right. The stems are soggy brown with a vinegary stink,
so she chucks them in the bin-bag with the others, holding the
dripping stalks away from her clothes.

That's the last one done. She has always loved the church at
Easter, with daffodils in every cranny, as if the jagged stones
were fertile earth, the bursts of flowers linking back to pagan
festivals of spring.

Two of the bunches are fresh enough to be kept. With one

in each hand, she goes out into the churchyard and, in the garden of remembrance, lays a bouquet on the flagstone below the grey slate plaques bearing the dates and names of Max, Jenno, Rosie and Jamie. She is carrying the other daffodils to Penny Pennington's grave, still marked only with a temporary wooden crucifix, when the gate creaks and she looks up to see Tom, carrying a cardboard box up the path.

'Hiya,' she calls.

'Afternoon, Chairman. I'm just bringing the pamphlets.'

'The whatties? Oh, yes. The vicar's going to give out for the next few Sundays that they'll be on sale at the back after service.'

She kneels and lays the flowers on the still-uneven grass above the most recent burial.

'Old Mrs Pennington?' Tom asks.

'Yes. Sweet old dear. But I hope for the sake of the departed there aren't book-clubs in the afterlife. Funnily enough, you're meeting her successors tonight?'

'What? You mean the next to die?'

'Huh?' Why do men have to turn everything into a joke? 'No, silly. The couple who've bought the Old Schoolhouse. We've invited them to supper with you two.'

'Oh, right. What do we know about them?'

'He's a tax accountant. Jonny's already keen to pick his brains. He's convinced he's still paying too much. She's a "cultural engineer", whatever that means. Talking of selling paintings in the outside schoolroom Penny P never used. Two kids. They're younger than us, but I thought it was worth giving them a try.'

'Okay. Don't suppose Simon and Tasha are coming?'

'Fraid not, Tom. We don't quite seem to be in the Lonsdales' class these days.'

Libby turns her downward glance into a sweep of the hills around the village and the four Grenville manor houses. Even now, after so many years, she feels a pride and longing for their own house. In the bright spring light, the shutters at the windows of the Dunsters' are clearly visible. According to Jonny, the latest gossip is that the address was collateral for at least two loans to the company and so cannot be sold until the financial tangles are unravelled.

She checks her phone again. Wretched man.

'Tom? I don't suppose you've heard from my husband recently?'

'No. I don't know that we'd talk much during the week. Unless there's rugby or something. Anything I should say if he does get in touch?'

'Bring some high-end French cheeses. But not the cliché ones. No Brie.'

'Trains are up the spout this morning, apparently. Sometimes, when everyone's calling offices and homes at once, you get network busy.'

'Oh, really? He went in early. I'm going back into the church to do the dead flowers. Should I take those for you? I can put them in the vestry with a note for Sue.'

'Well, if it's not an awful bore.'

Tom hands her the brown cardboard box. The printers have stuck a sample copy of the cover on top: *A History of Middlebury by Thomas Rutherford*. Tom has used his own photograph of St John the Redeemer in light not unlike today's. With Max out of the equation, Jonny funded the book, so Libby has read a proof: it's surprisingly lively and made her even prouder of her house.

'Okay, then,' says Tom. 'We'll see you tonight. Eightish as usual? What are the new couple called?'

'Good question. I'll text you.'

'Cheer up Em, if you can. She's convinced herself she's a bad doctor.'

Libby sends another message to her wretched husband, then stands, giving him a chance to reply, enjoying the glow of the sun on her face, which surely, even with English weather, must mark the end of this deadly winter. She follows Tom's Land

Rover as it glints towards the hills, and wishes peace to this village and its people, living and dead.

She turns and carries the box towards the church. After much discussion among The Six, the pamphlets make no mention of the deaths.

ACKNOWLEDGEMENTS

This novel is a work of the imagination, directly based on no actual case. It takes place during a version of the winter 2011–12, which in most ways resembles the calendar one, although some events – such as a flu pandemic and a production of Edward Albee's *A Delicate Balance* – have been shifted for story-telling reasons.

Various people have provided technical or professional detail and I am grateful for their imagination and patience. Sarah and Anna Lawson helped me with dogs and clothes, and Ben Lawson with football-simulation games. Dr Arif Supple, Charlotte Supple and William Lawson advised me on medicine; Andrew and Helen Lorenz on business; Colin Sharp on business and clay-pigeon shooting and Joanne Sharp on kitchens and dogs.

Catherine Fehler guided me through aspects of the law and Eoin O'Callaghan, Julie Myerson, Robyn Read, Tanya Hudson and Helen Ullman were helpful with various narrative or factual questions. Paul Baggaley, Kris Doyle and Will Atkins from Picador were beadily attentive to plot and prose.

MARK LAWSON
February 2013